THE CENTURION'S SON

Adam Lofthouse

For Archie
Never stop dreaming

Table of Contents

PROLOGUE

August AD 166 – Syria

His vision was blurred, sweat streaked down his face from damp, lank hair. His mouth was so dry it felt like he had eaten the burning sand that tortured his feet. But still he marched. All around him pox-covered soldiers fell out of line, blood poured from open sores that covered their bodies, thick and black, it streamed out of their noses, eyes, mouths and ears as they fell, never to rise again. But still he marched.

Must get home, was all he could think. *My wife, children, I must protect them from this plague.* These thoughts kept him alive as he trudged through the endless sea of sand. Five years he had been out here fighting, five years protecting Rome from the Parthians. Five years of standing in the shield wall, hunched behind his shield as an endless storm of arrows rained down above him. Five years of hurling his *pilum* at the heavy cavalry that charged towards him. Five years. And he had survived it all. Just when the war was won, just when he thought he was going home, the plague had struck. Hundreds of men had perished in the first week, thousands by the first month. More men died in that month than throughout the entire war. But still he marched.

His thoughts drifted back to the forts they had abandoned in their haste to get home, the horrors he had witnessed along the way.

It had begun in earnest three years previous. A three-hundred-mile march through treacherous mountains had brought them to Armenia. Legate Statius Priscus had planned it to perfection. The advantage of surprise, the easy pickings from the rich agricultural region around the nation's capital, they had even taken Artaxata itself, deposing the crooked king, Pacarus, and elevating senator Sohaemus to the throne.

Such was the devastation caused by the Roman siege, they were forced to build the new king a new capital – it was named Kainopolis, and built thirty miles closer to the Roman frontier. Armenia was Roman, and the Romans intended it to stay that way.

But that was only to be the start of the fun. The next year they marched down the great Euphrates, crossing it on a bridge of boats. A battle on a scale never before seen in those lands erupted. They said the Parthian dead numbered seventy thousand by the time the sun set.

After that it was easy. Ctesiphon fell in a day, and then it was Seleucia, the jewel of the silk roads. They opened their gates without waiting to taste Roman iron; they were force-fed it anyway. Over forty thousand prisoners were shipped back west, a tidy sum for every legionary's retirement pot.

But that day marked the beginning of the troubles. Some said it was the sacking of the Temple of Apollo, others that it was the curse of some revengeful Parthian soothsayer. Others simply blamed the poor hygiene of the defiled women; whatever the cause, Seleucia was the last success the legions enjoyed.

First came the stomach cramps, then the vomiting; it was unstoppable, like a lone twig trying to stop the great river's current. Then came the sweating; it poured down the sick, like rain off a roof. Next was the exhaustion, not helped by the desert's heat. And lastly were the boils, the great green lumps brimming with a vile-smelling pus.

He no longer wore his legionary's helmet, or the leather protector he'd worn underneath. He knew not where he had left his segmented armour, discarded along with his shield, javelin and sword. He had forgotten where he was when he discarded his pack, so he no longer had any utensils to cook with, a cloak to sleep in, or the small bull his son had given him to help Mithras watch over him. *Mithras,* he offered up a prayer, *get me home to my family and I will sacrifice to you the greatest bull you have ever seen.* He looked up into the scorching sun, devastated to see it was not yet past midday. Instinctively he grabbed for his water skin, but he knew before he had even picked it up it was empty. He looked down onto his shit-stained tunic, the only one he had left, and thought back to when his wife had said how handsome he was when he first put the pure white garment on. It was only then he noticed the dark red stains creeping through it from his body, only then did he see the bulges that covered his arms and legs. Angry-looking swollen lumps, brimming with a vile-smelling green pus.

I will make it, he vowed. *I will beat this.* He looked ahead, ignoring the dizziness in his head, the screaming agony in his legs that came with every step. Sand – all he could see was the dazzling reflection of the sun beating down on an endless carpet of sand.

Through the heat waves in the distance, he could make out something shimmering blue. *The sky over the horizon,* he chided himself, *don't get too excited.* But others had seen it too, men who hadn't spoken a word to each other for days started shouting, waving arms and whooping. The pace picked up as more men began to see what it was. *The sea!* His eyes welled up in relief as he realised what he was seeing. *I made it, thank you, Mithras, thank you!*

Looking down on the ground, he almost wept for joy at the pockets of green spaced out in the sand. *It really is the sea. I've made it.* He could see the ships' sails now, the walls of a Roman fortress in front of them. He didn't recognise it, but it didn't matter. It was Roman; it was by the sea; he was going home.

He sped up, matching the pace of his brother soldiers, some who had broken into a run. There was no semblance of rank now, just a clutch of desolate soldiers desperate to survive. His breath became shallow as he ran; he slowed; *I'll be there soon enough,* he assured himself. His thoughts drifting to his beautiful wife, surely the goddess Venus herself reborn, his son, how big would he be now? Almost a man! Big enough to stand with Mars. Already his sword play had been good, how quick would his wrists be now? *Quicker than mine, I'd bet!*

And his darling daughter, the apple of his eye, a depiction of Minerva if there ever was one. They would soon be reunited, no more fighting for him, just the honest life of a retired soldier, maybe get some land, do some farming, teach his son how to plough a field, ensure his daughter's marriage to a good man, and best of all, cuddle up to his wife every night. Yes, that's the life for him. He'd done his twenty-six years, faced down every foe the empire had put in front of him; it was time to go home.

A smile crept across his face; his dried, cracked lips split as it did, but he didn't care. His nightmare was over, soon, he would be home, and everything would be okay. He dreamed of the green grass of northern Gaul as he collapsed onto the sand, black, metallic blood pouring

10

from his mouth and ears. He grasped a small plant, a lonely weed of green sprouting out from the scorching yellow carpet; he thought it smelt of home. *Great Jupiter, Juno, look over my family, let them be safe.* That was the last thought of Legionary Marcus Valerius Decanus, First Century, Third Cohort, Second Legion.

Chapter One

February AD 167 – The Amber Road, Germania

A lazy mist ascended the banks of the river Danube. Its fast, unforgiving, iron-grey waters were obscured in the white cloud. Only the sound of swirling currents gave away its presence, even when standing only yards away. Bird song fluttered overhead; they called to each other as they made their way back home after seeking warmer climates in the south, the bitter winter months in the distant frozen north becoming uninhabitable for delicate wings and fledging feathers. Gazing that way, away from the river; a cobbled Roman road gave way to a path made purely of mud. Uneven and half-covered in frost in the chilly spring morning, it marked the end of Roman territory. It marked the start of the bad lands. The lands that no man travelled alone. The lands no woman should travel at all: Germania. Filled with wild and bearded, chainmail-covered and iron-bearing warriors, it was a land feared by all Romans.

The unconquerable country, an unmanageable people. Even Rome's divide and conquer had not prevailed here. Her invincible legions, the mincing machine that had defeated every foe they had met, had faced their own mortality here. A land that bred men for one thing only.

War.

Shadows of Ash and Yew, climbing towards the gods, a vision of black on grey.

Albinus shuddered as he continued to gaze into the north. Not his first time across the river, but it never ceased to dry his mouth and loosen his bowels. He pulled his cloak tighter around his twig-thin frame, again wishing he had brought a thicker tunic. He imagined the horrors that lay in wait along that muddy road. The tribes of whispered tales told around fires at night. The stories his father used to tell him when he was caught getting up to no good. The ones where he gave him to their priests, and they would sacrifice him to their thunder god Donar, open his bowels on a table made of stone while they howled into the night air. Or give him to the Allfather Wotan, the one-eyed, all-seeing god. Caged inside a weighted wicker basket, and thrown into the nearest marsh, left to choke on liquid mud. Worse still was the one where he was thrust into a pit. Left one on one with a giant warrior, born with ash spear in one hand and longsword in the other. Snarling teeth and wolf like power, a man of iron come to wreak havoc and destruction.

The mood was hushed, anxious in their camp. No one liked to be this side of the river, let alone overnight. But that is where they were. Thirty men in total. Twenty-eight veterans of the Fourteenth legion, accompanied by a reluctant Albinus and an eager Fullo. They had slept in eight-man tents, just like the old soldiers would have done in their army days, when they lived as a *contubernium,* eight men who lived and breathed every day of their lives together.

A small ditch had been dug around their tents, and eight men were constantly on watch. *Always have a watch when in enemy territory.* His father had said. *Nothing worse than getting caught with your breeches round your ankles.* Albinus knew nothing of war, and had no interest in discovering more. What was the point? He listened to endless tales from his father and his friends, talking of their heroics and bravery in battle. Boasting of who had killed the most men, who had been the first to wet his blade in some battle or other. Albinus didn't think it was brave, or heroic. He thought it was stupid. Pointless. His father made him train with sword and shield every day. Leading with his left and thrusting with his right. An endless cycle of back-breaking labour. And what did he have to show for it? An array of cuts and bruises that the quicker and stronger Fullo had left upon him. Albinus couldn't even recall the last time he had landed a blow on his friend. Pointless. But his father insisted. Insisted that one day soon Albinus would be enrolling into the Legio XIV Gemina Martia Victrix – the Fourteenth twinned legion, martial and victorious. To fight for Rome as he and his father before him had.

He cast a glance at his friend Fullo, manning the north-facing ditch with him. Hard to believe the two were the same age. Although shorter than he, Fullo was solid. Every inch of his torso was honed with muscle, thick arms and wrists made hefting shield and sword effortless. Short thick legs that rooted to the ground like the life vines of a giant tree, he would hold his own in any shield wall. A mop of unmanageable bright blond hair sat atop his head. Dark eyes that matched his humour, a wide and flat nose broken too many times in what had to be hundreds of childhood fights, and a thick-lipped mouth that was rarely not smiling, Fullo was the opposite to his friend. No matter how many times Albinus gazed upon his lifelong companion, it was his forehead that always caught his attention. Livid white scars ran along the tops of his eyes, where not a few months ago great balls of pus had erupted from his head.

His torso was covered in them too, Albinus knew. Many nights he had spent in his friend's room, stacking up the fire and mopping his brow, praying to the gods that Fullo would pull through. He was his closest companion, especially now, since his mother had lost her battle with the dreaded disease.

It had not even been half a year since the plague had swept from the east quicker than a Parthian arrow. More than a thousand, thousand people had lost their lives, or so he had heard. Not a day went by without Albinus thinking of her, picturing her beautiful face, eyes brighter than a gleaming coat of mail; a smile so dazzling it could have lifted the mist that shrouded him. A laugh that could have illuminated the dullest of days. She had been the bridge between him and his father. The one that brought them back together after they had fallen foul of each other. Since that fateful winter's day, the distance between father and son had grown so wide you could have fitted a legion in it.

His father had fallen within himself, gone back to being a centurion rather than a father. Albinus had become another soldier to train, rather than a son to nurture. Maybe it wasn't his fault, Fullo would say to him. He's just trying to cope the same as you. As much as he could agree with his friend and see his point of view, it didn't make living with the man any easier. They shared no stories, no private jokes. They had no adventures together, and he had never asked, just what it was Albinus wanted to do with his life. He just assumed his son would be a soldier. Just like his father.

Albinus had tried to tell him so many times. It would get to the tip of his tongue. Then his courage would fail him. His courage always failed him. Deep down he knew. He knew the reason he detested soldiering; the stories of bravery and courage told round fires, was because he could never be in one. He could never stand in the shieldwall, toe to toe with a raging barbarian, spear trying to find a gap in his armour. He would have stained his breeches and ran for cover long before it got to that. *I am a coward*, he thought, lost in his own world as he continued to stare into the shadow-filled haze.

'Can you see that?' Fullo's sudden words snapped Albinus out of his trance. 'There, straight ahead, looks like people on the move.'

Albinus squinted into the distance. *Jupiter curse this blasted fog.* 'I can't see a thing, brother. Should we raise the alarm?' he said in a voice full of fear and uncertainty. He looked across to his friend, trying to avoid those scars, the ones that brought back the visions of his mother. *How could you survive and she not?* Shameful thoughts. He was eager for Fullo to be the one to make the decision, not wanting to risk the wrath of his father. Fullo was still recovering his full strength, no one would begrudge him if he sounded the horn without need.

Coward. Let your friend take the blame.

'Yes! I definitely see movement. Listen. Can you hear? Sounds like a horse pulling a cart,' said Fullo, voice tremoring with excitement. *We couldn't be more different.* Both turned their heads so their left ears pointed north. Albinus could hear it now; the hoof beats of a horse, iron hobnailed shoes plodding along on the frost-bitten mud road. A low rumble of a cart's wheels being dragged along behind.

16

Turning his head back round he could make out the shadows of approaching people. Giants they looked, lumbering their way inexorably towards them. Albinus reached behind him and picked up the *cornu*, a giant horned trumpet made of bronze; with a crossbar running across the middle to ensure it withstood the rigour of a rough life on the march. He blew two sharp notes, the agreed signal that there were potential enemies in sight. Within moments he was surrounded by men and metal.

Silus pushed his way to the front. Huge, barrel-like torso and giant legs making him the biggest person in the group by some distance. Squinting through the mist he stood as still as a rock until he had a clearer picture of who approached. 'It's them,' was all he said.

Turning to Albinus, he put a hand the size of a bear's paw on his shoulder. 'Good spot, son. Well done.'

Albinus flushed with pride at the rare praise from his father. 'Actually, sir, it was Fullo who spotted them first.' Fullo rolled his eyes at his friend's inability to just smile and take the praise. Had to be honest, did Albinus, even if it thrust the limelight from him to someone else.

'Then well done to both of you,' the former centurion said. 'You're both going to be fine soldiers soon.' With that he jumped across the small ditch the group had made, not wanting to let the approaching party get too close to the camp. 'Vitulus, Bucco, with me. Albinus, Fullo, you too. It's time you had some experience dealing with these northern wolves.' An evil smile came with a challenge in his eyes, he turned back and started walking north.

Two men parted from the wall of metal that waited to greet the incoming barbarians.

One short and slim, a matt of grey hair sitting atop his head, a scarred face, dark eyes. 'Stay close to me, son.' He

17

patted Fullo on the back as they made their way forwards. 'And you lot, be ready!' A cry of 'yes, sir' greeted his order as he moved away from his brother soldiers.

'And you stay close to me, Albinus. Your father will do the talking, you stay at the back.' Not that Albinus needed telling that. With a reluctant glance back at the menacing wall of iron, limewood and bared teeth, he followed the others into the mist. Reassured by the presence of his father, his trusted second Vitulus, father of Fullo, and Bucco, a terrifying beast of a man. The only one there nearly of a size to Silus, his pox-marked and scarred face loosened most men's bowels. Many of the stories told round the evening fires were of Bucco and how he could decimate an enemy shield wall. How his sword arm would be blood-red after the fray. He was a man with a hunger for killing. A need for it.

They stopped thirty paces from the makeshift camp. Filing out to block the mud-ridden road, ensuring the approaching people went no further. When they came within ten paces, Silus ordered them to halt.

'Who goes there?' he bellowed. His voice was gravel, a menacing tone that could not be ignored.

'See you ain't lost your manners! Good to see you too, Silus. Been a while.'

A single man emerged from the mist. Tall and well built, if not a little overweight. Long dark, unkempt hair streaked down the sides of his face; his left eye missing, or at least injured. A lank, once white rag tied round his head to cover it up. His nose was small and pinched, hook like at the end. A thinning wispy beard covered the bottom of his face, thin snarling lips round a small mouth that appeared to contain no teeth. He wore full chainmail and a fine pelt running down to his knees, a thick gold torc round his

18

neck and gold and silver arm rings decorated both arms. He looked like a man who could fight, a hardened raider. A huge sword hung from his waist, so long he had to push down on the hilt to raise the sheathed blade, else it would drag on the ground. The hilt was all black, a wolf head carved onto the pommel.

'Alaric, been a long time. I see your looks haven't improved.' Silus arched an amused eyebrow as he addressed the German. Albinus marvelled at how unimpressed or frightened his father seemed; he could feel his own guts churning.

'You're one to talk. You 'ad 'air last time I set eyes on you.' His voice was quiet, but aggressive.

'Yes! And if I remember correctly, you still had two eyes to see me with! Well. At least before the blades clashed.' Silus turned his head and shared an intimidating laugh with Vitulus and Bucco. Albinus shot a confused look to Fullo, who shrugged his shoulders and rested his hand on his sword, shoulders and chest puffed out to look as big as he could.

'Shut up, you Roman dog! That was a lucky blow, on another day I would 'ave gutted you like a pig.' Alaric thrust an accusing finger in the air between the two men.

'I would have thought you would have learnt by now, snakes shouldn't play with eagles.' Albinus could not help himself look at the *gladius* that hung on his father's left side.

A beautiful blade, forged in the Hispanic mountains, where all the best swords came from.

The iron had swirling patterns running from hilt to point, reminiscent of the current in running water. An ivory hilt, and an exquisite eagles head carved onto the pommel. As much as Albinus hated weapons and war, even he could appreciate the sheer beauty of the thing.

Alaric looked past the five Romans to the others lined up behind them, a wall of red as the shields blocked the way to the river. Glancing back at his own men, he looked as though he was deciding whether it was worth starting a fight. Albinus felt his guts move faster. *Courage.* 'Enough of this who 'as the biggest cock bollocks. I'm 'ere to trade; you brought the goods?'

'I have, as promised. One cart of the finest falernian I could get my hands on, one cart of Roman-made vases, cutlery and plates. And one cart of rugs and tapestries, plus a few extra to boot. Now, it stays behind me until I see my amber,' said Silus, no room for negotiation in his tone.

Amber. *All this for amber.* A long way they had marched west along the banks of the river. A day's march had taken them past Carnuntum, home of the Fourteenth where most of these men had spent the majority of their lives. A further ten days marching, in rain and sleet as winter gave way to spring, had brought them here. The amber road. They were half a day's march from Vindobona, a city nearly as big as Carnuntum, and home to Caesar's famous Tenth legion. All for amber. It came from the frozen north. Washed up on the shores of the ice-ridden sea, where it was picked by the local tribes, and sold and stole repeatedly until it ended up in the hands of a man like Alaric. Who would then trade it for whatever he could get his hands on with Rome.

It wasn't strictly within Rome's laws, what Silus and his friends were doing. No tax was being paid on the goods coming into the empire, no border legion inspecting the goods as they passed the *limes* and went into imperial territory. It was a risk his father was taking, Albinus knew.

But being farmers amidst a famine was no way to get food on the table. The world had changed with the plague, and it wasn't just the disease itself that had affected the millions of people who lived under Rome's rule.

A plague brought sickness, and sick men can't work. Neither can dead men. The grain ships from Egypt that fed the masses in Rome had slowed, the great green provinces of Gaul, Germania, Pannonia and others shadowing the Rhine and Danube had been hit with a high death rate. Winter should be spent preparing the land. Digging trenches to stop the rain form puddles on the precious soil. And then digging deeper trenches when the first ones flooded. Slaves would be sent out early in the murky mornings to rake away the morning dew that threatened to freeze, weeds would be pulled, cattle allowed to graze and fertilise the bare fields. But instead of doing these things, Silus and many other farmers across the great empire had spent the winter burning their dead.

It had left the empire with one burning question. How do you feed hundreds of thousands of people whose lives depend on the food you supply them? No emperor had managed to solve the issue, no lightning ideas had formed in the senate. So it was down to men like Silus, a retired centurion, running a small farming settlement with his retired soldiers, to come up with solutions. And the solution they had arisen to was to beg borrow and steal as many goods as they could to get hold of a cart of amber.

One thing could be guaranteed. No matter how many plebs in Rome starved to death in the Aventine, no matter how many farmers froze to death in their empty barns in the provinces, the rich and mighty in Rome would want amber. Rich merchants would cover themselves in it, eager to impress their colleagues and customers with the goods they had on offer. Senators would gift it to wives and mistresses, paying an extortionate amount for jewellers to mould and craft it onto necklaces and broaches.

And so, the plan had been made. Silus had used his contacts in the Fourteenth to find a merchant who would be able to supply him with a cartload of amber, and in return he had been able to cut others into the deal and get hold of the supplies that were in demand by a country full of barbarians becoming more Roman by the year.

And that had led him to what appeared to be an old 'acquaintance.' Alaric turned and hailed his men in his harsh Germanic tongue, and heartbeats later two carts rolled out the mist flanked by warriors hefting ash spears. The first appeared to be the one they came for, six wooden crates sat on the back, iron locks jingling over the bumps in the road. The second had a cage on the back, a boy and a girl, looking to be of Albinus' age, crammed in the back.

'Who are they?' Bucco stepped forward, *pilum* outstretched as he gestured at the cowering couple.

'None o' your business, Roman. They ain't for you. This one's yours, crack 'em open and 'ave a look if ya want, but let's get this done quick, there's a foul stink round here.' Alaric fixed the Romans with a vulgar expression, his thoughts quite clear.

Silus stepped towards the crates, turned the lock and heaved it open. He let out a small whistle as he inspected the goods inside. Albinus, however, was drawn to the cage. He could see them clearer now he was closer; they looked similar, siblings he guessed. The boy was wounded, he lay bent over with both hands clasping his left side, he was deathly pale and his lips were blue.

'Hello?' Albinus said, but he didn't know why. Anyone caged up coming from the north of Germania was hardly going to speak Latin.

'Help us!' squealed the girl, who looked more shocked than Albinus did. 'Please help. My brother, he's hurt. He won't last long without medical aid.'

Stunned, Albinus gaped at the girl locked in the cage. A hundred questions touched the tip of his tongue, but he was too baffled and couldn't manage to unlock them from his thought box.

'Stay away, I said. They ain't nothing to do with you.' Alaric marched towards him, two of his bruisers flanking him, hands on swords as they approached the twig-thin junior. Albinus thought of challenging the barbarian. *Courage.* He backed off sheepishly instead. He wanted to question why this rogue had what appeared to be two Roman citizens locked up in a cage. Why was he leaving the poor young man untreated? The girl had bloodstains on her dress. Specifically, around her groin and thighs. It was clear she had been raped, probably numerous times. Albinus wanted nothing more than to draw his sword and ram it through this one-eyed monster. But he didn't, of course; spine-tingling terror gripped him as Alaric and his two giant men got closer. *Courage. Who am I kidding?* A hopeful look towards his father achieved nothing. The former centurion was still buried in the chest of amber, eyes alight with glee and greed.

'Oi! What's goin' on 'ere?' Bucco had heard the girl speak, and Albinus rejoiced to see he was equally outraged at the treatment and condition the two seemed to be in.

'I said it ain't got nothing to do with you lot! These are my property. I caught 'em. On our side of the river. So back off!' Swords were drawn as the three men made a mini wall in front of the cage, more Germani appearing from the mist to clamber either side, their wall growing more formidable by the heartbeat.

'Sir, you seen this? They're Roman.' Bucco's sword remained in his scabbard, but his *pilum* was still in his hand, the glint in his eyes said he was ready to use it.

Silus glanced up from the amber-filled chest, appearing as if to wake from a daze. Albinus watched him take in the situation with a glance. Vitulus, Bucco and Fullo stood with white knuckled fists wrapped round *pila* shafts. Albinus had backed off, and caught the disappointed look in his father's eyes as they met his own.

'Bucco. Stand down. We're not here to start a fight, we're here to trade. Two young wanderers that got themselves captured in Germania is no concern of ours. Now lower your weapons.' As always, his tone left no room for argument. However, Bucco's moral compass could not let this lie.

'But they're Roman, sir. If we don't stand up for them, who will? You remember that time we were on the border with Dacia? Fighting the Iazyges. You remember what you did then?'

Albinus hoped his father would respond to the jibe; he'd heard the story of what his father had done. Silus had just been promoted, first spear centurion, first cohort. The most senior centurion in the whole legion. And he nearly got his entire cohort killed, all because of one captured slave. A Roman, and he wouldn't let her go. Wouldn't walk away and leave her to her fate, despite being ordered to. A lot of men died because he refused to back down. A lot of men. It had hardened his heart, walking the battlefield at day's end, seeing the corpses from both sides. Fathers, sons, brothers, all sent across the river Styx because he refused to back down and listen to his superiors.

Silus cast a firm gaze at the two captives locked in the cage. *Come on, father, please.* Albinus watched as his father studied the two in the cage. The wound on the boy's side, his pale and gaunt complexion. The bloodstains on the girl's dress, the way she folded over when she stood, as if the pain in her groin was too much to bare. Albinus grimaced as he saw his father come to a decision.

'I said, Bucco, we aren't here for any slaves. That day in Dacia, a lot of good men died because I was stupid enough to stick my nose in where it wasn't wanted. Now for the last time. Stand. Down.' That iron voice, enough to make any legionary quiver in their hobnailed boots.

'C'mon, Bucco, let's leave it, eh.' Vitulus reached an arm up and patted his comrade on the shoulder, trying to usher him away from the barbarian wall of metal and teeth.

'Please help!' wailed the girl. 'We weren't caught here. We were in Gaul. In Elcebus. They stormed into our room and took us in the night. We hadn't done anything wrong! Please! Our father was a legionary too.'

Bucco foamed at the mouth, desperate to charge into the shields of the northmen and rip them limb from limb. Vitulus and Fullo struggled to hold him back; even Albinus found his sword out of the scabbard and his feet taking him towards the others.

'HALT!' A Battleground voice honed though the years of leading men. Silus' voice even stopped the Germani, who had readied their great spears and hunched down behind their round shields.

'When I give an order, YOU OBEY! Is that understood?' Vitulus, Fullo and Albinus immediately lowered their weapons and stepped back, muttering

25

apologies and looking suitably sheepish. Bucco, teeth still gritted, breathing like a wounded bull, finally lowered his *pila* and turned to face his superior. Albinus felt his heart begin to slow, hadn't realised it had been beating so fast.

'Yes, sir!' Bucco rasped a salute and stood at full attention.

'Good. Alaric, I believe our business is done. Wait here, I will have your carts sent over to you and then we can all be on our way.' Silus turned, beckoned on the horse that pulled the amber filled cart.

'Well, you ain't going nowhere 'til I've inspected my goods. I ain't some mug you can cheat with a load of shit wine and poorly made vases!' Alaric stepped out from within the wall of German shields. Hands on hips and a swagger in his step.

'On second thoughts, Alaric. I will have that other eye.' In one smooth motion Silus turned on the balls of his feet and rasped his sword from its scabbard, the blade hissing as it was set free, a viper sensing its prey was near.

Alaric flushed a rosy red. Albinus nearly laughed aloud; for all Alaric's bravado, he didn't fancy testing his iron against the old eagle. 'All right, calm down. I'm sure the goods are fine. I'll wait 'ere while you get your lads to fetch 'em over.'

'Good decision, Alaric. I hope for your sake, this is the last time we ever meet.' Silus turned and walked away without a backwards glance, cartload of amber in tow. Albinus walked slowly backwards, sword still drawn, his gaze fixed on the girl. *Coward, do something!* But he just kept pacing back, unable to look away. 'Please help! You can't leave us!' her voice was desperate now, more a squeal then a shout. *I'm sorry. Sorry I'm not stronger.* How often had he thought that?

26

Chapter Two

February, AD 167 – The Amber Road, Pannonia

The mood was passive as the group travelled south through Pannonia, making their way towards Italy, and Aquileia, where they were hoping to trade their amber for gold.

Bucco still seethed at the leaving of the two Romans in the hands of the barbarians.

Silus had tried to reconcile with him, but the veteran front ranker was having none of it.

'They were Roman,' was all he would keep saying. 'It weren't right to leave them there like that.' Silus had backed off after a while and taken to leading the column from the front. Vitulus, more understanding than Bucco, marched in step with his former centurion. Just as they had in over thirty years of waging war under the beloved eagle of the Fourteenth.

Afternoon was slowly giving way to evening as they made their way along a narrow-cobbled road. Lush green valleys swept away on all sides as far as the eye could see. Farmers tentatively walked their fields, checking the damage the winter had done. *I worry at the state of our own.* Silus stopped to talk to some, asking if they were going to begin planting soon, sharing stories about what he thought would grow well this year.

Albinus loved it when his father was a farmer and not a soldier. As much as he knew Silus revelled in his memories of the fame he carved with sword and spear, he held a great passion for the land he owned. Their settlement wasn't the biggest or most elaborate veteran's settlement you had seen. But it was home. Fifty or so small wooden houses, all one storey, with handsome thatched roofs that kept out the winter hail.

There were no elaborate buildings, no great temples to Mars and Jupiter, but a small shrine to Mithras, the chosen god of most men of war, situated under the granary, which was raised on stilts to protect the precious grain from rodents and the weather. The steps going underground made the hair on Albinus' neck stand up; the chill breeze as he descended gave him shivers. The pitch blackness of the place made him feel vulnerable and alone. To him, Mithras was just another part of being a soldier that Albinus had no interest in joining. After all, Mithras favoured the brave.

He used to enjoy going to the small shrine in the centre of their settlement, where the women would go to pray to Vesta, the goddess of hearth and home, and change the candle that was always kept shining bright. Although he hadn't been since his mother had been taken from him.

The south of the settlement was a sea of fields. The men and boys would spend most of their year out there ploughing and toiling and reaping. This again Albinus loved. He rejoiced every spring when the crops started growing. And the fields would turn from an ocean of brown lifeless mud to a green sea of life and hope. He exulted to see a summer's breeze rip through the tall green plants and could watch for hours as they danced and swayed in the sun.

And then lush green fields would turn a yellow so bright it was as though Jupiter himself had descended from the heavens to paint them with a giant brush. His favourite thing of all though, was the great aqueduct. Built by the engineers of the Fourteenth, at his father's request, the great stone arches rose high above the settlement, spanning from the river in the north to the fields in the south, and ending in a giant water mill. The water would give life to the fertile soil and power the mill that was used to turn the harvested grain into flour.

Collecting the harvest was tough but rewarding work, knowing that you had helped to grow this life source and that it would sustain you and your own through the dark winter months was the greatest feeling a man could feel. Or so he thought. Albinus could be a farmer his whole life. Fullo, he knew, sought the glory of the blood fray, revelled in the sword song of death and wanted nothing more than to carve himself a bloody path to immortality. But Albinus could picture himself an old man, sitting on the deck of his small wooden home as a glorious summer's day drew to a close, a good wine in his cup, children playing on the grass and beautiful fire-haired wife in his arms.

'You're thinking about her again.' An amused expression was on the plague-scarred face of his friend, 'I can always tell when you're thinking about her.'

'Who?' said Albinus, trying to sound distant and aloof. *Got to stop daydreaming in front of him.* He grimaced as he felt his cheeks started to burn.

'My bloody sister, that's who!' a firm nudge in the ribs accompanied the jibe.

'I was not! And anyway, Licina isn't actually your sister.' *Licina. Beautiful, fire-haired, emerald-eyed Licina.* She had lost both her parents to the plague, it had happened early, before the first leaves had turned gold and the wind gathered an extra bite. Her wits had died with her

30

parents, or so the gossiping old ale wives whispered. But to Albinus, she was perfect. Blazing red hair that flowed and swirled in the breeze, deep green eyes that dazzled in the sunlight and sparkled in the moonlight. A long slim nose above a small taut mouth, so unused to smiling. Small firm breasts and long sweeping legs that looked as though they would never end. Albinus knew every detail intimately, dreamed of those details every night.

If there was one ray of sunshine in his life, it was her.

She had been taken in by Vitulus and his wife Turda, who had done their best to try and bring her back to her old self. But it appeared to many as though their efforts had been in vain. Fullo said she fancied him, teased him about it all the time. But Albinus had never mustered the courage to act upon it. *She is still grieving, so am I. Who am I kidding, I'm just too scared. Coward.*

Fullo studied his friend as his blush continued to blossom. Short and scruffy sand-coloured hair, ice blue eyes that were the only physical link to his colossus of a father. A short, stout buttonlike nose that had all the old soldiers' wives broody in a heartbeat in his younger years. High defined cheek bones, so like his mother, and a soft, feminine jawline, making him an easy target for youthful banter. At least when Silus wasn't around to hear.

You're not as bad as you make out, my friend.

'Yeah, but she kind of is my sister. And I want to make sure she marries a real man. Not some twig-thin pasty little farmer who's scared of a little sword play,' said Fullo, throwing his friend a cheeky wink. *Not exactly gonna tell him how great he is, am I!* He laughed as Albinus studied his gangly legs and sinewy arms.

'Well, being a soldier doesn't exactly make you a *real man* does it. Just makes you more likely to end up a dead man. And what use are they to anyone?' He fixed Fullo with a scowl as they continued their march south. Fullo took a heartbeat to decide if he was in the mood to continue an age-old argument between the pair; he decided he was.

'Doesn't make you a real man? Course it does! I can't wait to join up! By the time we get back home I'll be of age to enlist. Imagine how proud my father will be to march with me to Carnuntum and watch as I sign up for the Fourteenth. He'll be welling up, you know. And wait 'til I get leave, and I come home to tell him of my adventures, my heroism in battle! No barbarian will be able to kill me. I survived the plague!' Fullo's arms were in the air as he skipped along the road, his mind lost in his own dream world where he was some kind of hero, being awarded a *corona aurea* for his valour in battle.

'Yes, you did survive,' said Albinus, eyes downcast. *Ahh balls, Marcia. Must stop dragging up her memory. I can tell my scars cause him pain, in some ways more than they ever caused me.*

Guilt filled Fullo, the way rushing water filled the great aqueduct. The pain in Albinus' face was clear whenever the plague was mentioned. It may have left scars on Fullo's face, but his friend's scars were the type that couldn't be seen, only felt.

'Sorry, brother. Didn't mean to dig up old hurts. Anyway, when are you going to speak to the old man about this farming life you're planning on leading?' The old man being the common term about the settlement for Silus, not that he was overly fond of it.

'Soon. When we're home maybe. He will be in better spirits once this amber has been sold and there is gold in his purse.' Albinus had lost count of the amount of times he had tried to broach the subject with his father. Every time he would lose his courage at the last second and walk away. 'I just don't know how to bring it up. All he talks about is *when I join the legion* and *what cohort will I end up in*. He's obsessed; it's the only time he ever really talks to me. You know he's got me doing exercises with a shield every morning? Thinks it's going to build my muscle so I'm better prepared for marching and fighting in armour. Ha! Look at me! Am I ever going to be strong enough to do that?!' Albinus gestured to his stick-thin arms and childlike legs.

'I know! You look like a mild breeze would blow you over, let alone holding your own when the shields come to shoving and you got some great big hairy-arsed barbarian trying to bury his spear in your guts!' Fullo buffed himself up to his full height, bull-like shoulders ridging out of his tunic. *You were born to be a soldier,* thought Albinus with a sad smile. *No wonder my father likes you so much.* Albinus never admitted to being jealous of his friend. But secretly it would grind his bones when Silus and Vitulus would huddle around Fullo and sing his praises and marvel at his physic. *Sometimes it's as though Silus would rather have him for a son than me.*

*

Silus pretended not to listen as the two boys continued their conversation behind him.

It shouldn't shock him, hearing his son say those words. But deep down it hurt. He had always known, not that he would admit it to himself. Always known his son was different to him. From the moment he was born, all arms and legs with his rib cage sticking out, it was clear he would never have the soldier's build. And from an early age, it was apparent he hadn't inherited the soldier's

33

mentality. That toughness. Aggression. Too long he had spent dancing round his mother's skirts, when the other boys were out in the fields and the woods playing with stick swords and rolling in the mud.

But Fullo, on the other hand, was a man born to be a soldier. Built like an ox, a strong and outgoing personality, he would be an asset to any unit. *Oh Marcia. You would know what to do. What to say.* He had tried not to let it show, but losing his wife had hit him like Vulcan's hammer striking the anvil.

He had always found it difficult to connect with the boy, especially in his early days when he was still enrolled in the army. Centurions were officially allowed to take wives, unlike the men in the ranks, so Silus hadn't had to sneak out of the fortress to see them, unlike many men he had served with. But his duties kept him busy, so his visits were often short and sporadic. A young Albinus would seem confused and frightened when his hulking great metal-covered frame would appear at the doorway, and Marcia was forever chastising him for bringing his war kit back to their peace-filled house.

He had tried over the years, Mithras knows, he had tried! Gifts of children's armour, small wooden swords and spears had not peaked the child's interest. He seemed more drawn to ploughs and mills and aqueducts. All useful things, of course. Things Silus himself had come to appreciate as he had settled into the life of a retired soldier, toiling land and growing crops. It was good work, rewarding. But nothing like leading men into battle. Nothing like experiencing the heart racing, bladder filling terror and excitement that came when iron met iron and you could feel the bull god Mithras willing you on at your shoulder. Feel the war god Mars powering your every sword stroke.

And there was no better feeling than when the red mist lifted, and you were still standing and your foe was not. Sitting in camp at the end of battle, revelling in victory with your brothers in arms, sharing stories and spoils. That was the life. A man's life. But it seemed his son would not lead the life of a soldier, would never know the joys of battle, would never strive through the tough challenges that faced every soldier.

The army made me a man. Made me who I am today. Without that test, that discipline, what will become of the boy? His mood grew darker as he envisioned an older Albinus.

Stooped and twig-thin from long summer days spent hunched over reaping his harvest. Armed men descending on him, taking what they wanted. Taxing him on crops he had grown himself, beating his children, raping his wife. *He will not be strong enough to defend what he has.* His mood grew as dark as the evening, with the sun setting slowly behind the great Alps in the west.

'He's stronger than you think, you know. You should be proud of the man he is becoming.' Vitulus marched at a respectable distance behind his friend and former centurion.

Even without seeing his face, he always had a knack for knowing what was running through his mind.

Silus glanced back at his former second-in-command. Short and slim in stature, many men had underestimated his strength at their peril. His muscles were toned and sharp, his reactions lightening. His hair may have greyed, age lines may now surround his dark eyes, but Silus knew that his friend would still give any young man a run for their money with a good blade in his hand.

'Is he? I worry about what will become of him when I'm gone. Is he tough enough to survive on his own? We won't be around for ever, and before he knows it he will be on his own at our little settlement, with over fifty *iugera* of land to farm and protect! What will he do when the wolves start raiding from over the river?' Worry lines creased the old centurions face.

'Then he will pay them off as every other farmer does. Fighting the tribes is the eagles' job. And the eagles ain't for everyone. He's a fine young man. Kind. Considerate. He just lacks confidence. And he ain't gonna get that if you keep putting him down all the time.' Silus spun and gave his former optio an icy stare. *Careful, old friend.*

'Giving me parenting lessons now, are you, optio? I would choose your words carefully if I were you. I'll have you on latrines when we get home!' he forced himself to give Vitulus a tight smile. *He's only saying what he thinks, and he's probably right. Don't bite!*

'Well actually, we ain't marching under the old eagle anymore and I'm no longer an optio, and you're no longer the first spear of the Fourteenth! Sometimes it wouldn't hurt for you to remember that'

Primus Pilus of the Fourteenth. But deep down that is who I still am. The primus pilus was the highest rank an enlisting soldier could ever hope to be. First spear centurion. Silus used to command the first cohort of the Fourteenth, and every other centurion in the whole legion would defer to him. The only other post any non-commissioned soldier could dream to reach was that of camp prefect, but you had to have a bit of luck and a nice habit of surviving battles to ever get there. And not many

36

centurions did that; they were required to lead from the front.

It was hard coming out of the army. Hard to get used to the fact that you couldn't just order anyone to do something and expect them to jump straight to it. He had been lucky, he admitted to himself, that some of his cohort had opted to leave around the time he did. And so they had built themselves a comfortable home, and the old soldiers were happy to let their former commander make the decisions and follow his instructions.

They had acquired some slaves to do the bulk of the work around the farm, and they had lived happily for some years, enjoying the peace that came with retirement. And then the plague had struck. Everything had changed in the space of a season. Marcia had died, along with many others, Silus didn't think life would ever be the same again.

And now he was here, trading for amber and dodging the tax man, just to ensure his people would survive the coming winter. 'You're right, I guess. Hard to shrug off the old life, especially when you've been living it so long. So, as you're in an advice-giving mood, what would you do with the boy?'

'Do with him? Nothing! Just enjoy spending time with him, build a bond. He loves the farming, and if you really admit it to yourself, so do you. So, share your knowledge, work with him, teach him new things. He will make a hell of a living from that bit of land one day.'

Vitulus moved alongside his friend, and gazed up into those cold blue eyes. 'You haven't been the same since you lost Marcia, and no one can blame you for that. But you make no effort to engage him, you just drill him and drill him into the ways of a soldier. Which clearly ain't the life he wants.'

'I know. I just wish he thought differently. I mean look at your Fullo! A born soldier if there ever was one. He'll fly up the ranks once his training is done.' Silus looked back to the two boys, their differences in physicality and personality evident in Fullo's confident and brash stride, compared to Albinus' gangly awkward lumber.

'I wouldn't be so sure about that! He should make a good soldier, but he needs discipline. He's too sure of himself. I worry that one day that arrogance will be his downfall.' It was Vitulus' turn to cast a worried expression.

'Ha! You were similar if I remember right. Remember that time when we were over on the Rhine? You waded right into that tribe we were fighting, nearly cut yourself off from the rest of us! You always were too quick for your own good! Me and Bucco had to come charging into the fray and pull you out! Who were we even fighting?' Silus scrunched his eyes shut as he strived to unlock a distant memory.

'The Chauci maybe? Can't even remember myself! Too many battles…Anyway, back to the matter at hand, are you going to take your trusty old second's advice?

Silus nodded slowly as they trudged along at the front of the small column, the amber-laden cart rumbling along at the rear. 'Okay, I'll give it a go. And you're right, I've not got over Marcia, not sure I ever will. But I need to try, whatever he becomes, he is my son, and I love him. I always will. Now come, let's get to Aquileia and get rid of this amber, and gain ourselves some gold!'

'And another thing to be happy about, from the way your lad and Licina have been eyeing each other up recently, it won't be long before we have the first wedding at our little farm!' added Vitulus, beaming from ear to ear.

The two old comrades marched side by side, into the setting sun, and Silus felt a small ray of sunshine touch his heart, the first he had felt in many sunsets.

Chapter Three

May AD 167 – Veterans Colony, east of Carnuntum, Pannonia

Dawn broke over the eastern horizon. A flat, strong sun, projecting its first rays onto barley filled fields and green-grey water. Licina was already awake. Up with the crows as always. She cast her gaze up as the lightening sky revealed the tops of the trees and the dancing birds. She loved the silence of the morning. Before the horses started whinnying and the ox began to snort. Before the hounds started howling and the chickens started clucking. The silence was bliss.

Even the Danube was silent this morning. There was no great current hurling water at its banks. No violent white-topped waves skimmed from the river into the great stone aqueduct. The quiet ruled in the early dawn haze. Sitting atop the riverbank, with an easy descent behind her back to the sleeping farm, Licina felt empowered. When the day got started and the animals roused the people, she knew she would begin to feel lost. Too many voices would drown out her thoughts, and she would ghost her way through another day.

But in the silence of the morning, before the sun marked the start of another summer's day, Licina was truly alive. Her thought box was full; ideas and dreams burst through the cracks as she marvelled at the distant landscape to the north. Germania. The wild lands. *What lays beyond that horizon? What people? What gods?* It had been many years since her father had taken her hunting north of the river. Her mother would hate the mini adventures she and her father shared. But they didn't care. They would share a smile and a wink round the evening fire as her mother berated her father for putting their only child in danger without any due cause. But they paid her no heed. Those days were as special to her as they were to him.

At least she thought they were. She couldn't seem to remember them anymore. She couldn't picture her father's face, though she remembered he had a great mane of blond hair, and a bushy moustache to match it. But the colour of his eyes was lost to her; his smile that used to brighten her day was gone. Her mother used to sing, and she was told that to listen to her voice was like hearing angels descending from the gods. She knew she had listened to that angelic voice, that it would soothe her soul when the night terrors hit her. That even after years of marriage, it would still stop her father in his tracks and leave him enchanted. She just couldn't remember what it sounded like.

She had no memory of her mother's appearance, though gazing at her reflection in the river would give her some clue, if the old wives in the settlement were to be believed, for she looked as though she was her mother reborn. Although her singing voice was far from angelic. *Verrus and Silana.* Their names came easily to her. Not that she had ever called them by either. For what child calls their parents by their given names? They had met in a village, far to the north of Gaul where land met the freezing sea. They had travelled south together, when Verrus had signed up to the legions and been posted to the Fourteenth. In Carnuntum they had lived apart, with Verrus required to stay in the great fortress, Silana had made home with some of the other legionaries' wives, and they all strived to keep their marriages secret from their husbands' superiors. The men of the ranks were not supposed to take wives.

Verrus had made the post of optio, serving as the second-in-command of the third century, first cohort, and it was there that he had met Silus and Vitulus among others. It was an easy decision for the couple to move to the former's farming colony when Verrus' compulsory twenty-six years' service came to an end. It would be a good place to raise their growing daughter, where she would be surrounded by children of a similar age. A good place for the ageing couple to see out their twilight years, finally living together as man and wife after too many years apart.

Five years. That was all the peace they got. Everything had changed just as last year as summer began to give way to autumn. It had hit her mother first. One day she was fine, boiling water and stirring in the grain and honey, brewing the ale her father loved so much. The next she was slow to rise from her bed. By midday she had a horrid fever, and as the sun was setting her father found bright angry-looking red lumps all over her body. Bursting them open didn't seem to help; the vile green pus that smelled rank and was hot to touch, just kept on coming.

She died just days after it started. Her father was inconsolable with grief. Licina remembered that she refused to believe what was happening, and kept asking when her mother was going to wake from her long sleep. She had been angry and confused when her body had been placed on the pyre and consumed by the great fire. *Why are you burning my mother? She's just sleeping! Stop it! Stop it!* Her screams had filled the late summer's air. Of course she knew deep down her mother had gone, but her heart wouldn't let her believe.

She had still been on the field when a misty dawn rose, and her mother's body had been reduced to nothing but ash and dust. Two days later, her father fell ill with the same symptoms. She remembered hearing one lady remark that he had simply lost the will to live. He died quicker than his wife, in his eagerness to be with her again.

Many others died in the following weeks, but Licina didn't seem to notice or care. There were over fifty slaves on the farm before the plague struck; less than twenty survived it. The small crowded barn they shared made it almost impossible to not fall foul of the sickening symptoms.

In the following weeks, it seemed she had forgotten how to smile, or eat, or talk. She fell completely within herself, and disdained any communication with anyone. Shock. That is what they all said. She was suffering from shock, and soon enough she would recover enough to be something like the person she was before.

But they were wrong. She hadn't recovered. Autumn turned into winter, winter to spring, and now in summer's adolescence she still couldn't rouse herself from her waking dream. She struggled to remember anything about the two people she had loved most in this world. They became a blur, ghosts. All the happy memories of her childhood slowly left her one by one. Until she was left as hollow as a burnt-out tree. Hollow and alone. Before long she began to hear whispers, aimed at her. *Her mind is cursed.* They would say. *Minerva has deserted her. Her wits have gone.* It was nonsense, of course. Licina knew her wits were fine.

Her brain functioned the same as everyone else's, she just chose to keep its contents private.

Vitulus and Turda had taken her in, and life had begun to return to some form of normality. Their son Fullo had been stricken down with the disease, but somehow, he had clung to life like a shipwrecked sailor gripping tight at the last bit of floating rigging. She helped Turda as she cleaned out the chickens in the morning, then milked the cows and cut the sheep's wool. She had learnt the art of brewing ale, so favoured by the retired soldiers it was a staple of their daily diet.

But the memories had never returned. Sometimes when she awoke she recalled the odd snapshot of her parents in one of her dreams, but she was never able to hold onto the thought for long. And so she spent her days in a daze. Often gazing over the great river, staring in wonder at this fabled land. *What lays beyond that river? That hill? Those trees?* She dreamt of finding out. Twice she had tried to sally across the ford and run away to start a new life. And twice she had been stopped in her tracks, Silus catching her and begging her to return home.

They were good people, Silus and his soldiers. But living among them every day just reminded her of all she had lost. She longed to reinvent herself. Go to a new land where no one knew of her past and her troubles. A land where she could learn to smile again, to enjoy interacting with new people. Learn about new gods and different ways of life. She wanted to sail, to feel the ice breeze of the distant northern seas as she stood in the prow of a great ship, ranks of sweating men heaving at the oars as they propelled her to new undiscovered worlds.

One day. One day I will leave this place behind with my demons. But that day would not be today. Already she could hear the farm coming alive. The sun was fully up now, the slaves were already making their way out to the fields. From the top of the riverbank she could see their slow and purposeful descent into the barley-filled valley's. *How can they be happy?* she often wanted to ask, but never did.

Sighing, she stood up and wiped the back of her cloak, now wet and muddy from the morning dew, and turned to make her way back down the gentle slope and into the settlement. It was quite beautiful in its simplicity. She recalled Silus speaking to a passer-by about it once. The retired soldiers had spent their entire lives living in simple accommodation. When they were not in their cramped barracks at Carnuntum, they were squeezed into small eight-man tents, with just enough room to erect four bunks. They had no need to build themselves an elaborate home when they had never had one before. The settlement was laid out like a mini legionary fortress – old habits and all that.

Looking down from the river, a backdrop of thick woodland with fields of swaying barley glowed bright yellow in the morning's sun. In the southwest corner, a giant wooden water mill, rotated in creaky splendour as it fed off the water of the giant stone aqueduct that arced its way down the slope and above the thatched roofs of the small houses. The houses themselves were a marvel in simplicity. Cut from the wood of the trees that inhabited the land before they did, they were all identical, sat in neat rows running east to west across the settlement, just as the legionaries' tents would have been set in a traditional marching camp. They were more sleeping quarters than houses, with each only containing three rooms and all one storey high. In most of the houses lived a couple with two

45

children, but in a few there were three or more retired veterans who had never found a good woman to keep them warm at night, and had stuck to the old routine of bunking up together.

A straight cobbled road ran down the centre of the small town. In its centre was a small square, with a shrine to Vesta in the middle. A candle would always be kept lit inside the shrine, so the goddess would provide safety and happiness to the settlement and those who lived in it. Not that it had done much good when the plague struck. In the far south-east corner was the slave barn. Previously terribly cramped but now more spacious as Silus had never replaced those that had perished during the previous months, they lived in moderate comfort and were well treated by the citizens that owned them.

Next to the slave barn was the livestock. A huge barn filled with cattle, ox and sheep. There was a fenced-off outside area for the animals to graze and enjoy the sun on the north side of the barn. These too were more spacious now; the plague hadn't just stopped at people. Due east of the grazing area and north of the slave's barn were the stables. They didn't keep many horses there, as it was the oxen that did most of the heavy work around the farm. But the horses were useful for trips into Carnuntum as they tended to pull carts quicker than the lumbering oxen.

Fullo had once fallen from a horse whilst trying to ride it from the stables, Licina couldn't recall ever seeing him there since. The great granary sat to the north of the stables. Huge wooden stilts buried deep into the ground kept the grain and flour safe from floods and rodents. A small temple had been dug out underneath, with Silus and co. insisting they needed a place to worship their favoured god Mithras. Licina had never been down there, as women were not allowed; you had to be initiated to the bull god to worship at his altar. Although both Albinus and Fullo had been allowed down once, Fullo surfaced with a look of glee in his eye, clearly besotted with getting the opportunity to pray to the 'war god'. Albinus, however, looked positively terrified, and never spoke about his experience in the deep dark.

On the other side of the road, the west side, a chicken coup sat nearest the fields, just along from the great water mill. Licina would be heading there soon, to change the straw-filled floor and rummage for fresh eggs. A row of houses stood in between that and the kitchens. Silus was insistent that the people who settled here would live as if one great family, and so the people of the colony, as they thought themselves, ate three meals a day in each other's company. And it was here that many of the womenfolk would spend their days preparing meals and brewing ale.

And just to the north of that, and immediately south of where she stood, was a small training square. When the men were not helping the slaves to work the fields, you would find them there exercising their muscles and their memories as they drilled with sword, shield and *pila* on a golden sand carpet.

It was, she had to admit, a fantastic achievement by Silus and his friends not just to build this place but to keep it together. Fights or arguments were rare, and resolved immediately when they occurred. No one had been banished in disgrace, and most surprisingly no one had ever brandished their weapon in anger. Which was a marvel in itself as all the men never left their homes without first strapping on their *gladius*. It was a fine place to live, filled with fine people. But Licina just felt alone here, like she didn't belong.

She cast her gaze to the south-west as she wandered aimlessly down the slope, taking in the view and imagining she could see the great Alps in the distance, where Albinus would soon be coming from. *Albinus*. If there was one reason why she was still living in apparent misery in this place, it was him.

Her heavy mind lightened when she was in his company. He was kind, intelligent, funny and smart. He knew just how the great aqueduct was built, and how it flowed water from the river down into the fields. He knew all about the mill, which was used to churn grain into flour. She loved the spark in his ice-blue eyes as he ploughed and reaped the precious barley he strived so hard to help grow. He was the first out into the fields in the morning, even before the slaves, and was often still to be seen working his way up and down the rows of crops as the sun descended in the evening.

He was at his cutest when his nose was scrunched up, and he concentrated on trying to solve some problem or other with the crops, and often he came up with a better solution to that than the veteran soldiers could summon up.

The problem was, she was just so damn nervous when she was around him. She knew he fancied her, Fullo told her all the time. But whenever she was near him, she just ended up blushing like a silly little girl and would flutter as she felt her knees go weak and her cheeks flush a rosy red. She could never think of anything intelligent to say, no way to bring him into conversation. She had lost count of the times that private engagements between the two of them had ended up being awkward silence, with neither of them sure of what to say to the other.

Well, that is going to change when he returns. She had promised herself, since the day she had watched him

48

disappear into the distance, off to trade for amber and help solve the money problem that their empty granary could not. *When he returns, I will spend as much time with him as I can. I will tell him how I feel, and he will tell me he loves me. We will get married; we are both of age now. We shall run this farm when the elders are gone, and welcome Fullo and other veterans when their discharge day comes. This place shall be ours, our farm, our colony, our livelihood. That is, if I don't crack and run away first.*

She wore a satisfied and confident smile as she entered the north side of the settlement and made her way down the central road to the chicken pen. The mixture of smells of baking bread, boiling ale and animal dung wafted up her nostrils. A strange mix, but the smell of home. All thoughts of escape and adventure left her as she strode confidently through the crowded road, with veterans and their wives rising from their beds to congregate at the kitchen to break their fast. She smiled and nodded to the familiar faces as she made her way through the throng.

Licina would wait until the hall was nearly empty, as she always did. No matter how happy and confident she was feeling, she knew that she wouldn't be missed round the benches. The crushing noise of a hall full of people would only drown her swimming spirits.

*

Turda's age lines shadowed in the sun as she smiled to see Licina striding past. It warmed her heart to see the girl with such a smile on her face. *By Juno, she is beautiful. Her mother would weep with joy to see her this morning.* Too long had it been now that Licina had mooched about their home in distant silence. At one point it had seemed that nothing would rouse her from her waking sleep. She detested the old crones that bitched and whispered behind

49

the poor girl's back, exclaiming that she was cursed by Minerva, the goddess of the wise. Turda knew there was nothing wrong with the girl, and that her mind was just as sharp as it had always been.

But the fates were cruel. Her parents passing had been a harsh blow, too harsh for one so young. Her grief seemed to have blanked her memory, and she knew of the pain Licina felt at failing to recall her loved ones' faces, and the great times they had shared. Verrus and Silana. Turda had known them well. Her husband and Verrus had long been close, sharing the bond of rank, they were always comparing kit and swapping stories, mocking their legionaries for poorly kept equipment and blunt blades.

Silana had been a joy to know. When the ladies were holed up in Carnuntum, sharing a small apartment and taking in turns to do the household chores, her voice would always lighten the darkest of days. When the children were restless, and it seemed that nothing would ever get them to settle, her singing would soothe them into the deepest sleep that the next morning the mothers would wonder if they would ever awake from their dreamless slumber.

No child should suffer such pain. Such heartache. Her thoughts turned to her own, Fullo, for the goddess Juno had only granted her one, despite her fervent prayers. When he had fallen foul of the unholy disease, Turda knew she would have given anything in the world to see him heal. Even her life. Her relief and joy at his recovery was masked with guilt as the pyres were built for many other husbands, wives, sons and daughters. It had seemed as though things would never be the same again. But on such a glorious summer's morning, it was hard not to feel optimistic about the future.

Finally, there was barley growing in the fields again. A wondrous sight after the painful autumn of watching the unharvested crops wither and die. It was the same all over the empire, she knew. What grain there was had been taken by the state and used to feed the dwindling legions. Some of whom had been almost completely wiped out by the never-ending wars and the devilish plague.

Vitulus and Silus would be overjoyed to see the yellow crops dancing lazily in the summer's breeze, and the gold they would bring back would help them to resupply with equipment, wine, clothes, slaves and animals. She had been unsure at first, of their plan to raise some funds. But she understood the necessity of taking such a risk, and hoped the rewards would far outweigh it. She gazed to the east, the stone towers of the great fortress of Carnuntum just visible below the deep blue horizon. They would return home that way soon, any day now. She just prayed they were all safe and well.

Fullo would have loved every second of it, she knew. The marching, the weapons, the banter and camaraderie. He longed for the life of a soldier. He would sit wide-eyed as his father and friends regaled about their lives under the eagle. He would be leaving after the next winter, off to Carnuntum to start his new life. The winter could last for ever as far as she was concerned. A lifetime of seeing her husband bruised and battered and with a fresh new scar every time he returned from campaign set the hair on her back of her neck prickling with fear. The thought of her only child meeting a gruesome ending at the hands of some horrible barbarian was more than she could take.

Albinus, on the other hand, would never turn to the soldiering life. No matter how much his father pushed it down the poor boy's throat. She saw how much he

51

detested every second of his training with sword and shield. She worried for him, and his father. *How will they ever learn to get on?* Their relationship had always been strained, but it had worsened since the passing of poor Marcia. The perfect lioness for the lion.

She made her way over to the kitchens for a hearty breakfast before a long day of organising the farmstead's women and overseeing the men and slaves in the fields. She was essentially in charge whilst Silus was away. It would have, of course, fallen to Marcia to oversee things when Silus and Vitulus were away, but since her death the people had begun to turn to her. She enjoyed the role. Spending her mornings in the kitchen, ensuring enough food and ale was being prepared for the day ahead, but not too much, for they didn't have food to waste. Who did these days? Then down to the animals, checking the chickens had been fed and their hay changed, the eggs rounded up and brought up to the kitchens. This she enjoyed as Licina had made this her job, and it meant she got to spend some time alone with the girl, and judge how well she was feeling that day. *Seems happy today.* A satisfying thought, as that would present one less challenge.

Then over to the stables. Avius and Brutus, two retired cavalry auxiliaries, would be there giving love and attention to the small collection of horses they kept. It had been more before the famine, but horses eat a lot of grain and some tough decisions had to be made in the desolate winter months when the grass was submerged in a foot of snow and there was not enough bread to go around.

Then over to see the other livestock, ensure they were healthy and had been fed, before venturing out onto the great barley fields, speaking with the slaves, whom she knew all by name, and basking in the glory of having fresh crops growing on their land once more.

The days went by far too quickly, for someone of her advancing years. But she was the happiest she had ever been. *And I will be happier still when my boys return home.*

The sun had passed its highest point, and she was down by the watermill, speaking with Hanno, a slave who would soon earn his freedom thanks to his hard work and dedication over his years on the farm, when Licina came bounding over the fields towards her.

Oh no, what has she done now? It was never normally good when the girl got this animated, and only usually occurred after a bad night facing her haunting dreams.

'Licina, slow down, my love. What has happened?'

But she didn't slow down. She hurtled her way over the uneven ground, closer now, Turda could make out the look of utter glee in her dazzling green eyes, even below the wild flapping tangle of unkempt hair.

'They're back, Auntie! I can see them on the road! They're back!' she leapt as she reached the woman she had come to call auntie and wrapped her arms around her in a crushing embrace. 'It's them! I was on the hill up by the river, just going to wash some clothes. And when I turned to look, I could see them! Silus was in front, his frame nearly blocked out the sun even at that distance! And Uncle was next to him, and Fullo was strutting behind. And I could see Albinus, all arms and legs with that silly stride of his—'

Turda laughed a laugh of joy and returned the girl's excited embrace. 'Calm down, dear! You'll cause yourself to faint if you keep bounding around in this heat! So it's definitely our boys then?'

53

'Yes! And they have horses, and cattle! They must have sold all their amber! I can't wait to see them!'

Licina twirled and jumped and tripped on her skirts in her joy. Turda could not keep the delight from her heart; she could barely remember seeing Licina so happy and excited.

'Well, we better go home and let everyone know that they have returned. And we should just have time to make ourselves look presentable. You want to be looking your best when Albinus sees you!' Turda winked and she and Hanno shared a knowing look. Licina flushed redder than she already was. She thought about denying it but decided there was no point.

'Could you help me into that blue dress you gave me? Last time I wore that Albinus said I looked very pretty,' she said looking sheepish, her eyes on the ground, toes making circles on the firm dry earth.

'That's a great idea. And I shall put on that red one your uncle got me last time he was in Carnuntum. You're not the only one who wants to make an impression. No harm in reminding the old bugger what he's been missing out on.' Hanno arced his head back and cackled a laugh to the gods as Licina stood not knowing whether to smile or vomit. More laughter from Turda as she saw the horror-struck look on Licina's face. 'Come on, girl, let us go and prepare ourselves for our men.' And with that they were off, Hanno still leaning on the side of the great mill, enjoying the shade and feeding off the happiness of the two women. *Life ain't all bad.*

Chapter Four

May AD 167 – Veterans Colony, east of Carnuntum, Pannonia

They returned to a hero's welcome. Fellow veterans, wives and children had lined the road where it passed the mill and led into the settlement proper. They cheered to see the fresh horses, the cattle and the men themselves as they brushed the dust from their cloaks and walked a little taller.

Turda parted from the crowd and gave her husband and son a loving hug. Vitulus held his wife in his arms and marvelled at the beauty the woman still possessed. Licina shuffled nervously forward, heart racing like a charging stallion, and approached Albinus with a small cup of wine. Albinus tipped some onto the floor, and offered a prayer to Ceres, god of the harvest. Silus rejoiced to see the look of delight on his son's face, both at the sight of Licina and the crops growing tall in the sun-drenched fields. 'It's good to see you, Licina. You look lovely by the way.' The old centurion cackled aloud to hear the mumbled nothings Albinus was struggling to utter.

His laugh died out slowly as a sadness washed over him, shrouding him like a winter fog. Days like this reminded him of what he had lost. No woman came to hug and kiss him, no wife to bring him a cup of wine and welcome him home. *I am alone now.* He would not be jealous of Vitulus or any of the other men who had wives to greet them, for he knew each man deserved it. He turned his gaze towards the fields, and marvelled at the huge life source that swayed in the afternoon sun. *They have done well.* He moved away from the crowds and down to the fields, grabbing a handful of the precious barley and rubbing it through his fingers. *It appears our luck is turning. Fortuna be praised.*

'Welcome home, master! I see you are admiring our work.' Hanno strolled out of the tall crops and offered Silus a small bow. Of Carthaginian descent, his skin was dark and his head was shaved. He found the thick hair that grew there made the long summers in the fields unbearable.

'Hanno! My friend, it is good to see you! What fine work you have been doing since I have been away. You have surpassed yourself!' Silus slapped the slave on the back, enough force in the friendly gesture to nearly take the smaller man off his feet.

'Everyone did their part, master. But we have done well. No one will go hungry this winter. How was your trip? It looks as though it all went to plan?' Hanno appraised the horses and cattle that were being led to their new homes.

'It did indeed. We secured the amber just as spring began to break through. An eventless journey down to Aquileia, filled my purse with rich men's gold and a nice summer's stroll home. Even had time to do some shopping on the way. Very satisfying, all in all.' Silus cast a contented look at the animals as they were herded through the narrow street onto their new home. The horses would help with trips to Carnuntum, and hopefully would begin to breed so he would never have to purchase more. The cattle would be slaughtered at autumn's end, so the people would feast on salted meat all winter long. 'The only thing

I couldn't get hold of was some more help for you, but I'm sure I will be able to get some slaves from Carnuntum before the harvest needs gathering. And what a harvest it will be!'

Hanno smiled at the thought of more bodies to reap the barley. He had been beginning to dread the long hard days that he and the twenty or so other slaves would be facing as the leaves began to fall from the trees. 'A few extra bodies would be welcome indeed, as long as we find some good ones.' He cast his mind back to some of the slaves that had perished in the plague; some were no loss at all.

'Well, my friend, it will be your responsibility to get them up to speed and manage them day to day. That's what freedman do around farms, you know.' Another hefty slap on the back, but Hanno barely felt this one.

'Freedman? Really?' Tears formed in the pits of his eyeballs, tears of utter joy.

'Ha! Oh yes, I'm being serious. Vitulus and I were discussing it before we left in the winter. You are a good man, honest and trustworthy, you deserve a better fate than one the gods have handed you.'

Hanno was speechless. He had dreamt of this moment for many years. He had been five years old when raiders had taken him from his small African village. He could still remember the spear thrust that burst his father's heart. Still picture the scarred ugly face of the man who had taken his mother and raped her in the street. His had been a long journey to this place. His childhood spent in the hull of a ship, fed manky bread and brown water once a day if he was lucky, until he had eventually been bought by a Roman slave trader. The man, Castro, he had been called, had treated him and his fellow slaves well. Fed and groomed him so he looked and felt more human again. He had still been thinner than a twig when Silus had bought him at market in Carnuntum. His mind cast back to the day his life finally took a turn for the better:

'What's your name, boy?' Hanno looked up, startled. Castro didn't keep his slaves in a cage, as many others did in the crowded market. He was sat on small stage, rubbing his legs where the iron chains had been digging on his long walk there.

'Hanno, sir', his Latin was heavy, his tongue still getting to grips with the common tongue in these green-filled lands.

'Know anything about farming, boy?' The man looked fearsome but his voice was gentle, a beautiful woman in a light green cloak on his arm.

'Err...no, sir. We don't have farms where I'm from. The sun is too hot and the ground too firm.' He stood slowly as he felt the blood return to his aching legs.

'Me neither. Shall we go and learn together?' Hope filled Hanno's heart as the brute of a man shot him a cheeky grin.

'Silus! We're meant to be finding slaves who know how to work land! A boy from the African desert is hardly going to help us!' The pretty woman scoffed the man with a playful cuff round the cheeks. The man laughed.

'I know, my dear! But I like the boy; he looks as if he has spirit. You got spirit, Hanno?'

'Err...yes, sir?' he wasn't entirely sure what 'spirit' was, but he would have said anything to get off that platform and out of those chains.

'You see! He'll do us proud, Marcia, you'll see. Albinus! Come here and meet Hanno. He's going to help your old man to grow some crops.' A small boy walked over, even thinner than Hanno was. He shared the same ice-like eyes

as the big man, but that appeared to be their only similar trait. He looked nervous, scared by the masses of people swarming all around him.

'But I thought I was going to help father? And Fullo?' his voice was high, as he scrunched up his small round nose against the overwhelming smell of excrement and decay.

'You will, son! But we shall need more people than just us! We're gonna grow so much food we could end up feeding Rome itself!' Rome. Hanno had heard of Rome, but never seen it. A city so vast it could hold more people than all the villages in Africa, or so they said.

I wonder if it's close, he thought. Albinus turned and regarding the older boy in shackles.

Curious, he put out his hand and touched the skin on Hanno's face.

'His skin is like your friend Libo's,' he remarked, Libo being a soldier in his father's unit, also from Africa.

'Yes! They are from the same part of the world. Maybe Hanno can tell you about it on the way home. Now then, who am I paying for you, Hanno? Ahh yes, I see…excuse me! Excuse me! Yes you…how much for the lad, and don't try and muck me about, I'm in no mood for haggling…'

And just like that he had been released and walked home with his new master, chain free. He had not seen any chains since.

'Wake up, Hanno! You daydream more than Licina sometimes! So, are you gonna accept my offer or just stand there gawking?'

'Of course! I'm just shocked, is all! Thank you, master, you won't regret it. I promise'. The two men shook hands, Hanno recoiled from the iron lock grip of Silus' palm.

59

'Good man! Now then, let's find some wine and celebrate!' And with that he was off, thronging through the masses of cheery people. Hanno stood as still as a statue, not daring to believe what had just happened. After a moment's reflection, he wiped away the happy tears smearing his dark-skinned cheeks, and made off after the man he owed his freedom too. *Life ain't all bad.*

*

Thrust, shield up and forward, thrust. Thrust, shield up and forward, thrust. Thrust, shield up and forward, thrust. *I can't take much more of this,* thought Albinus, desperately tired now. Wine-soaked sweat ran down him in droves, his once light blue tunic now more resembling the murky waters of the Danube, was stuck to him the way horse shit stuck to his father's plough.

They had feasted last night to celebrate the men's' return. It had gone on late into the night. The benches of the farmstead's huge kitchen hall had been filled with rowdy and drunken people. Songs had been sung; the people had danced and ate and drunk until they fell into a drunken slumber where they were awoken by the baying hounds at dawn.

Albinus had joined in, until the wine had made his bowels lurch and the vomit had defiled his mouth and nostrils. He could still taste it now, sucking in mouthfuls of hot summer's air. His twig-thin wrists shook with the strain of the wicker shield in his left hand and a great wooden training sword in the other. The sword was twice as heavy as the standard legionary issue equipment; it was designed to build a soldier's muscle, so he found it easier when presented with the real thing. Albinus studied his opponent over the rim of his shield. He knew Fullo would be suffering the same as he, but his scar-faced friend was showing no sign of tiring. It just caused Albinus more shame. Fullo had just recovered from the plague, his strength still not quite back to where it was last summer. Yet still he was the better of the two, nimbler on his feet, quicker with the lunge. And all that nursing what had to be one hell of a hangover.

Fullo had been the life of the party, dancing on tables and regaling the old soldiers with brags and boasts about how dangerous he was going to be in battle when he came face to face with the northern wolves. *'The plague couldn't kill me, so what chance do the tribes have!'* It had been about that time Albinus had scurried for the door and emptied his stomach in the cool night air. Staggering down the cobbled road in the centre of town, he had made his way to the water mill and slumped down against the doors to the small barn that accompanied the great wheel.

It had been there that Licina had found him. Quite worse for wear herself, she had stayed in the hall longer than she would normally have, trying to stay as close to Albinus as she could and catching his eye at every opportunity. It had not gone unnoticed by Albinus, but even with a skin full of wine inside him, he couldn't muster the courage to approach her.

She had gingerly lowered herself down next to him, rested her head on his drunken shoulders. 'You smell worse than the cows,' was all she could think to say as she gazed up into those eyes, seemingly illuminating the fields around them with their blue glow.

'Ha! Thanks! You're not smelling so fine yourself!' *What a stupid thing to say.* An awkward silence presided over them. An owl's hoot the only sound. 'Actually, you smell like flowers. Pretty ones.' A snide arm appeared on

Licina's shoulder, Albinus finding some courage at last from the bottom of his wine cup.

'Why thank you! And what, please tell me, do pretty flowers smell like?'

'Well…they err…smell like you!' a beaming smile preceded a hiccup then a burp. Albinus lurched and covered his mouth, horrified he was about to vomit again. *Not now!*

Licina laughed and pushed herself away from him. 'That's no way to behave in front of a lady! Did your father not teach you any manners?'

'No! You know, if it doesn't involve a sword or a shield I don't think he's ever really taught me anything.' Licina's smile turned to a frown. She knew full well of the struggles he faced with his formidable father. She sought to move the conversation on.

'Are you glad to be home?'

'Very! Especially when I saw you on our return. You look so beautiful in that dress. I…missed you when I was away.' He held his breath as he awaited her reply. It was stupid, he knew. They both knew that they liked one another, but neither had the courage or confidence to express their feelings.

'I missed you too, you know. Things aren't the same round here when you're away.' She had snuggled back into the fold of his arm, her head so close to his she could smell the foul wine on his breath, taste it in her mouth. See the small soft hairs of a man growing into his first beard sporadically growing on his soft-skinned cheeks and chin.

He moved his head down so it was level with hers. Looking right into those incredible green eyes. 'I thought about you every day.' He could control himself no longer, in one fluid motion, he arced his head forward and wrapped his lips around hers. Arms encircling the back of her head, locking them into the deep and lasting kiss. Horror and fear filled him as he realised for the first time he had never actually kissed a girl before. *What am I meant to do with my tongue? Why is my head bobbing backwards and forwards? Is that normal?* The feel of her tongue entering his mouth was both disconcerting and enthralling. The smell of her skin and the taste of her lips enchanting. After what seemed an age, the two parted and once again stared into each other's eyes.

Licina burst into fits of laughter. Tears brimming her eyes as stomach heaved and she struggled to breath. Albinus was horrified. *Oh gods! What was I doing wrong?* The stricken look on his face made her laugh even more as she read his thoughts. 'You did nothing wrong. I only laugh because I'm happy.' Albinus puffed his cheeks and sighed in relief, and leant back in for another kiss.

They became so infatuated with each other's lips they didn't notice the approaching torches, bobbing along in the darkness in anonymous hands. Sniggering laughs and loud whispers were the first they heard of the intrusion on their privacy. Fullo stood beneath the first torch, wineskin splashing on the floor as he lurched around. Vitulus and Silus were high-fiving in the torchlight behind. Cries of 'about time!' filled the air as more merry onlookers appeared out the darkness.

Albinus and Licina were too happy to care they had been rumbled. They beamed up at the onlooking intruders, before Licina eventually told them to be on their way.

The two of them had stayed there in each other's arms until the sun broke the horizon in the west, basking them in orange in the early dawn's glory.

A thump on his shield brought him crashing back to the present. Licina looked on, nursing her heavy head with Vitulus as they lay under a near olive tree. 'Come on, Albinus! Wake up! Work that hangover off!' Silus of course been the one who had insisted the boys train this morning. 'Best way to get rid of a hangover, boy!' he had said. Vitulus had joked that maybe Albinus had already had enough exercise the night before, a remark that had Fullo howling at the sky and Albinus blushing like a maiden.

Albinus risked a glance over the rim of his shield and looked towards the towering frame of his father. A colossus of a man, a whole head taller than the veterans standing around him. Despite being past his fiftieth year, Silus still sported a lean torso, thick with muscle, age lines around the corner of his eyes and the odd wisp of silver hair on his mostly bald head were the only signs of age. Piercing pale blue eyes were the only physical trait he shared with his son; his nose was long, wide and flat, broken too many times in numerous battles and skirmishes along the empires northern border. His mouth was huge, and unusually for a man his age he still possessed all his teeth. His olive brown skin proof of a long career spent on the march.

Albinus took all this in the split second he allowed himself to glance across to his father, when another thump on his shield snapped him back to his training. He had a height and reach advantage over his friend, but struggled to put it to any use. He grimaced in fear and shock as he staggered back from the blow, his small button nose wrinkled as he shut his eyes tight and hunched behind the standard issue legionary *Scutum* his father had given him to train with. Whack on his shield again, and still Albinus couldn't find his feet.

'Foot work, boy!' screamed Silus. 'How many times do we have to talk about foot work, bend your legs, back straight, left foot forward and BRACE!' This last word was hurled, as Silus bunched his fists and visibly shook with anger.

Albinus reacted to his father's words, and immediately set his feet; left foot forward, ready to ride the next attack. He took the next one on the boss of his shield, a loud clang filled the air as his opponent's sword rebounded off his shield. Albinus looked to grasp the opportunity as Fullo staggered back, and shuffled his feet forward quickly, thrust his shield up and forward, taking his friend full in the face. He followed through with his right arm in a quick thrusting motion aiming to take Fullo down with a jab to the guts, but all he hit was air. Albinus took two steps back and hunched down behind his shield, surveying the ground left and right for signs of Fullo's footsteps.

He was still standing braced behind his shield when a shadow emerged on his left flank. Before he had a heartbeat to react, Fullo's sweeping sword stroke swiped his legs out from underneath him, and the next thing he knew, he was lying on his back coughing up dust looking up into the smirking face of his friend.

'I'll be thinking of you at dawn tomorrow, my friend, when you're down at the river fetching barrels of water, and I'm still rolled up in my cot, dreaming of that redhead that works in The Sword and Sheath.'

The trading party had stopped at Carnuntum on their way home, so Silus could pay off his friends who had helped him raise the goods for the amber. They had spent a couple of hours in one of the old legionaries' favourite haunts: The Sword and Sheath tavern. Here Fullo had become infatuated with a rather pretty redhead working the bar. Not a bright and flame-ridden redhead like Licina, but deep and dark like a man's life blood. Albinus had to admit he had been drawn to her and her mysterious dark eyes too, and the two had partaken in some competition to see who could draw her attention the most.

Fullo began imitating the redhead in a rather provocative position, angering Albinus and kicking him back into life. He kicked out with his left leg, the iron hobbed nails of his sandal thumping into Fullo's right knee, sending him spiralling away in agony. Albinus was on him in a heartbeat, jumping onto his back and using his helmet to hammer Fullo down to the ground.

'Stop!' bellowed Silus, storming into the melee to drag the two warring boys apart.

'What in the name of Mithras do you think you're playing at? You were beaten...again! Now show some respect to your opponent, and shake his hand. You could learn a few things from him, you know.' Silus grabbed Albinus by his ear and hurled him up from the ground. 'Maybe if you didn't let him beat you like an old carpet every day you wouldn't feel so bitter!' Silus spat the last words right in his son's face, and was disappointed to see that the fire his son had shown moments before was all gone, nothing left there but fear. *How do I make you stronger, boy?* he thought as he let him go and turned to see Fullo making hand gestures at Albinus behind his back. 'And you!' he barked as he grabbed Fullo by the wrist and pulled him towards him. 'Show some humility in victory; there's no room for gloating or complacency on the battlefield, your father will tell you that.' Silus pointed to the olive tree where Fullo's father rose to his feet leaving Licina still lounging on the grass, and gave his son a sharp nod before marching briskly towards them.

'He's right, son,' Vitulus said as he neared the warring pair. 'You're a good fighter. But you're arrogant, a show man, maybe more suited to the arena than the legions?' Vitulus arched his eyebrow, a tight smile creeping across his thin, pale lips. 'Maybe tomorrow you will practise with me, and we will see if I can wipe that smirk off your face.'

Fullo gulped, eyes drooping towards his feet, he knew full well his father would best him. At fifteen, he was already taller than his father; and a great deal broader, but he knew full well the old dog would have no trouble putting him on his arse. 'I'm sorry, father,' he mumbled into the dusty dirt, 'guess I still got some growing up to do.' Fullo's cheeks turned a rosy red as he made his admission. He looked up to Albinus and offered his arm in the warriors' embrace. 'Sorry, brother, still friends?' His smile came back as Albinus clasped his arm, and the two boys went to make off towards the river to rid themselves of the sweat and dust that covered their bodies.

'Albinus, wait,' Silus called as his son turned his back on him, 'come walk with me a minute.' Silus gestured towards the south, away from the small crowd of onlooking veterans, and in towards the settlement.

Albinus paused to look back at the olive tree, and nodded at Licina's reassuring smile. He walked two steps behind his father, knowing full well how this conversation was going to go. Albinus watched as Silus greeted everyone they passed. He was still their leader, even though they were no longer obliged to follow him. Everyone still looked to him for guidance and support, and they all still looked upon him in awe, as if he was the living embodiment of Jupiter himself. *I will never be like him,* thought Albinus sadly. *People will never treat me with such respect. They'll never look at me the way they look at him.* These sobering thoughts were still with him when they reached the fields at the end of the settlement.

Silus turned and looked upon his son, his head bowed down and a thoughtful lonely expression on his face. 'Son, look at me.' Albinus looked into his father's eyes, and recoiled from the icy glare. 'You embarrassed yourself *again* today, you embarrassed me!' Albinus staggered back like he had just caught a spear to the heart, felt like it, too. 'How many months have we been training, how many hours have we wasted day after day going through the same old things, and still you don't get it, still you make the same mistakes!' Silus threw his hands up in the air, exasperated with his son's efforts. 'I just don't understand you boy, it's like you don't want to learn; my father, and his father before him and his before him have all served Rome with honour, and I'll be damned if that tradition is going to stop here, understand?!'

'Y...yes father,' Albinus choked back the tears, eyes firmly fixed on his sandals. Once again, he summoned up the courage to tell his father how he really felt.

'I mean, just look at you, still all skin and bone, have you been doing the exercises I've shown you?'

'Yes, every morning,' Albinus muttered. In truth, he had only done it a handful of times.

'Just look at Fullo – now there's a soldier in the making, I remember when he was nothing but a ball of puppy fat, but look at him now, he's already filling out his armour. Yours still fits you like Licina wearing one of your mother's dresses!'

Mother. If only you were here, you would know what to say. Why did it have to be you, why not father? He pursed

68

his lips in guilt at the thought. He knew her loss had affected Silus as much as it had him, but instead of bringing father and son closer together, it just seemed to have widened the chasm between them.

'I…I…will try harder to please you father,' Albinus stuttered.

Silus looked down upon his son, small button nose bunched up, high defined cheek bones sticking out as he winced his eyes closed. He knew immediately that mentioning the boy's mother was a mistake. *Marcia, my love, if only you were here.* 'I just don't know what to do with you, boy. How am I going to make you into a soldier?' Silus' nostrils flared as his fiery gaze pierced down into Albinus' face, almost as if he was looking straight through him. *Might as well be, for all the attention he pays to me,* the soldier's son mused.

'Maybe…maybe you don't have to make me into a soldier.' Albinus' heart raced even as the words tumbled out of his mouth; he felt his cheeks flush red and his palms go sweaty.

Courage. He willed himself to stay strong, to tell his father exactly how he felt.

'Maybe…maybe it's not my path in life. I have been thinking about farming. You will need someone to look after this place when you're gone. It can't be left to Hanno to run the whole farm.' He flinched even before his father's huge bear like paw struck him round the side of his head.

'Not your path?! Have you not been listening to me?! We come from a long line of soldiers, our ancestors fought with Marius, Caesar, Augustus, Vespasian…I could go on and on! But you…you worthless little runt, think it isn't your PATH?! Where's your pride, boy? Your sense of

69

duty, your honour? Your whole life you've been nothing but a disappointment, too much time spent skipping round your mother's skirts when you were a boy, how did I end up with a son like you? Ha! A farmer indeed.' Silus turned away, grimacing at the green grass as regret and guilt for his words instantly washed over him. He looked up to see Licina poking her head around the side of the nearest barn. She must have followed Albinus and Silus as they had walked away together. She seemed to be looking straight through Silus, a pained expression on her face. She suddenly started towards Silus, who reached out towards her as if to comfort her.

'It's okay, Lic—'

'Albinus! Albinus wait! Come back!'

Silus turned to see his son running off towards the woodland that surrounded the south of their veteran's settlement. He was halfway across the fields of barley when he heard Licina's voice; he turned and gave her a longing stare, which quickly turned to fire as it hit his father. He turned and carried on running, disappearing into the gloomy, thick woodland.

*

Licina watched Albinus disappear into the murky shade of the distant woods. Her heart filled with sorrow for him. She had heard what Silus had said. *An embarrassment, how did I end up with a son like you.* Licina turned back to Silus, who was already making his way back into the settlement.

'Why did you say that to him?' she shouted as she ran to catch up with the hulking soldier. 'You've hurt him. Why do you always hurt him?'

Silus turned back to face Licina; he wore his rage like armour. 'What business is it of yours, girl, how I treat my son? You think because you spent one night huddled in his arms you can give me lessons on how to raise him?'

'It's my business because I love him! I love him! And he deserves better. Deserves to be happy. If he doesn't want to be a soldier, then you shouldn't make him. What's wrong with being a farmer? That's all you are these days, *centurion.*'

Silus was shocked, dumbfounded. He didn't think he had ever seen the girl so animated. 'So, what then? He's gonna spend his life a farmer? Get on his knees to Ceres every day and pray for a good harvest? I don't think so, he needs to step up, become a man, he will see that soon.'

'What if he doesn't? Are you just going to disown him? Do you know what I would do to have my father back? To hold him one more time? Don't waste the only chance you have at being a father.' And with that Licina pushed past the ageing soldier and hurried off through the settlement, making for the river. There she sat and stared across the riverbank, as she often did when she was sad.

'I'm assuming that didn't end well?' Startled, Licina turned to see Fullo strolling along the riverbank, naked from the waist up. He had washed after his afternoon of sparring.

'How did you guess?' Her face was thunderous, her eyes promised murder.

'Just a hunch. It never normally goes well when the two of them actually talk to each other. Father said he had spoken to Vitulus about it when we were on the road. Apparently Silus said he was gonna change. Clearly he forgot that this morning. Even a man his size must get hangovers, I guess!' Fullo lowered himself onto the grass next to his little sister.

71

'Albinus needs to learn to stand up for himself. Tell the old man how he really feels.'

'He did, actually, I listened to what they were saying. Albinus said that soldiering wasn't for him, that he wanted to farm. And Silus…Silus said that he was an embarrassment, that he couldn't understand why he'd ended up with a son like him. All the while heaping praise on you…Albinus looked as though he had been stabbed in the heart. 'I tried to go over to him, but he'd run off towards the woods, probably sulking in that silly little fort that the two of you built.'

'An embarrassment? The old man said that?' Licina nodded her head sadly.

'That ain't right, no son should hear that from their father. I've half a mind to go and have a word with the old goat myself, I reckon I could take him on. Not what he was, you know.' Fullo buffed himself up to his full height, flexing his broad shoulders.

'Ha! Now that, big brother, I would like to see!' Licina clasped her right hand round Fullo's arm and laid her head onto his shoulder. Fullo smiled, he liked it when she called him big brother. And he liked it even more when she smiled, which was all too rarely.

'Come on then, little sister, let's wander home. Mother will have some chores waiting for us, I'm sure. And father wants me to help out with the new horses. Gods! I hate the stupid horses, worthless animals!' Fullo's hatred of horses dated back nearly ten years, when a bay he had been learning to ride on had kicked him off into the road, he had lost most of the skin off his back, and still had the scars to show for it.

'Are you sure you're up for that? I know how scared you get when you go near the stables, want me to come and hold your hand?' Licina threw Fullo a cheeky wink as she jumped off and made towards their home.

'Why you cheeky little…'

Chapter Five

May AD 167 – Veterans Colony, east of Carnuntum, Pannonia

Silus woke with a start, startled by the first strong rays of sunshine creeping through the gap in his curtains. He rolled off his bed, feet slipping into his legionary issue sandals. He staggered over to the basin in the corner of his room and plunged his head into the icy cold water. *Don't waste the only chance you have of being a father. Do you know what I would do to have my father back?* Licina's words rang true in his heart. Guilt weighed him down like a wet cloak. *Have I really been that blind? That stupid?*

He had spent the rest of yesterday alone in his room. Working his way through as much wine and ale as he could stomach. It had failed to improve his dampened spirits. Memories of his conversation with Vitulus out on the amber road came flooding back to him. He had promised he was going to change. To become a better father. Well, that was going to start today. Marcia had come to him again in his wine-soaked sleep, speaking to him in those soothing tones. *He is your son, centurion, and whatever he becomes, you will love him.* 'I do my dear, I do, but you're right, Licina was right, I should tell him, in fact, I'll do it now'. Not bothering to change his wine-sodden tunic, he stormed out of his front door and quick marched over to the home of Vitulus, sure that Albinus would have taken refuge with Licina.

A knock on the door followed by a surprisingly anxious wait, he was greeted by his former second-in-command.

'Oh, it's you. I hope you're here to apologise to Licina.' His voice was stern, without the normal respect it usually carried when greeting his former commander.

'Well, actually I was looking for...well, and I wanted to apologise to her as well...and you, of course...it's just that first I need to see...' Vitulus tried to not let his amusement show. In all the years he had known Silus he didn't think he had ever seen him lost for words. Normally so brash, loud and confident. Even when he was in the wrong. He was quietly enjoying seeing the man so chastened.

'Your son isn't here, if that's who you're looking for. Licina is mortified at what she saw yesterday, and Fullo was raging when he found out. Not to mention Turda! I thought you were going to sort this out with him?'

'Yes, I was...I am. Oh brother, I've been a fool, haven't I?' Shoulders sagged and eyes downcast, puffy cheeks and black rimmed eyes, he was in a sorry state.

'Yep. A right dick, if you ask me. Now go and find your son and sort this out. He's your son, for Jupiter's sake. And he's a good lad. You don't deserve him the way you've been treating him.'

'By Mithras, you're right. I must find him. Where would he have gone?' Squishing his eyes shut and rubbing them back to life, he tried to engage his wine-sore brain.

'The fort, of course. Probably just wanted to be alone. Now go, go and sort this out. That's an order, soldier!' Nodding his weary head, Silus turned and made for the woods, south of the fields of barley. Six years previous, he and Vitulus had helped Albinus and Fullo build a mock

75

legionary fort. That summer father and son had been the closest they ever had been. It would be a good place to talk and resolve their differences.

*

Albinus had not slept well. The previous afternoon had passed with fits of tears and hot, angry flushes. He had been shamed and embarrassed by his father before. But yesterday felt different, personal. *How did I end up with a son like you?* The words exploded in his mind. Repeating over and over until he could take no more. Rising from his bed, he stepped out into the morning air.

He had spent the day and night in the small fort; made by himself, Fullo and their fathers. They had been happier days. It was the summer before Albinus lost his mother, before life had changed for ever. He remembered Silus had been thrilled. *When our fort is made, I can practise at being a soldier. Just like you, father.* Those were his words, but spoken in a different time. The fathers had taught the boys how to dig a trench, keeping it straight and the same depth all the way round the base of their chosen land. Then the trees had been cut down, that work being done by the full-grown men. Albinus recalled that the next part had fascinated him. Shaping and shaving the felled trees until they were solid squared off posts, smooth and flat at one end and sharp and pointed at the other.

The sharpened end had been rammed into the trenches they had dug, the lines perfectly straight thanks to the use of the *groma,* four wooden arms on a staff, each ending in a suspended weight.

Albinus was enthused with the ingenuity of it, the ease with which the perfectly straight walls could be quickly constructed. Thick rope had been used to lasso the posts together. When they were all standing, pointing towards

76

the heavens and sturdy as the trunks they had been cut from, the ropes had been removed and great wooden planks nailed in running horizontally along the top and bottom of the newly made walls. The fort wasn't going to fall down any time soon. A great, three-pronged tree stood in the middle. This had been made into a mini barracks. Using the same principle as with the outer walls, but on a smaller scale; they had built themselves a small and cosy sheltered area, complete with a thatched roof and wooden floors.

One of the veterans from the settlement had donated an old bunk bed, and the two boys had slept out there every night until it got so cold their skin went blue and they couldn't control their chattering teeth. Albinus stood on the mini battlement, no more than five feet from the ground. He ran his hand over the rough wooden wall; it had not been given any attention in a long time. He was surprised it hadn't started to rot. But yew was known to be strong and flexible, and surprisingly resistant to the wood rot and termites that caused many an army engineer a lasting headache.

Casting his gaze through the sun-shaded woodland, he took in the beauty of the dense and silent forest of ash and yew. The trees must have been over sixty feet, rooted here for hundreds of years. Their needles glistened with morning dew, adding a magical feel to a place that was special to his heart. Licina, he knew, loved the river, the ferocious but beautiful beast that it was. Although Albinus could appreciate it, nothing could top the feeling of waking to this place. At this time of year, the trees were littered with small brown pine cones; strong enough to turn your ankle if you stumbled on one whilst running through the small and unkempt paths. Which was something he used to do a lot, whilst playing with Fullo and the other children, using the cones as mock sling-shot pellets as they launched them at each other. He remembered being hit full in the face with one, a lad called Cato firing at him at point blank rage. He had cried all afternoon. It had taken all his mother's soothing powers to calm him down, and weeks for the lump on the top of his head subside.

His thoughts returned to Silus, and just what he was going to do. He couldn't face going home. The sympathetic looks from the women and veterans. A reassuring pat on the back from Fullo, a hug from Licina. And then the thunderous face of his father. *I just can't face it. Coward.* He knew he was not in the wrong, that the fault lay purely at Silus' feet for the tension between them. But the thought of confronting him terrified him. He sighed and climbed down from the battlement, a flimsy ladder being the only way up or down. He was just going back into the barracks, to waste another day listening to the demons in his head, when he heard footsteps approaching, crunching on the debris littered path. He knew who it was.

Didn't need to climb back on the battlements to see. Footprints that heavy, that giant stride, could only be one person. *Father.*

*

Silus approached the fort. Crunching through the fallen pine cones and twigs that littered the small forest path. It was cooler here in the shade, a gentle breeze brushed his skin, carrying the faint but pleasant aroma of the dark green pine needles. He could see the fort ahead of him now. The tree stumps that surrounded it, reminding him of the back-breaking labour of cutting them down. The ground was clearer around the fort, evidence of more regular footprints clearing the debris with their steps.

He stopped in front of the small gate and looked up, half hoping and half dreading to see his son's face staring back down at him. He stopped to compose himself, shuddering as he slowly exhaled. The fear, it was spine-tingling. Never in his life had he felt like this. Nearly thirty years of soldiering, of pitting his sword against barbarian spear. Thirty years of rasping his shield boss against his foes, shoving with all his might as he roared in defiance and urged his brothers to break the enemies wall. But not once had it made him feel so afraid, so insecure and insignificant.

He went to call out his son's name but stopped as soon as he opened his mouth. *What should I say?* Again, he wished his beloved was still with him. She would have known the right words. She always did. *Gods, I miss you.* Clearing his throat, he summoned his courage and called out the boy's name. He could feel his thumping heart against his chest as he waited; he fought to slow his breathing to try and stop himself shaking.

It seemed as if he had been waiting an age. He was about to turn away when a high-pitched creak stopped him in his tracks. They had fitted iron hinges to the small gates, and they had not been oiled for a long time. The gate swung slowly open, revealing the lanky frame of the old man's only flesh and blood. There was no fear in Albinus' eyes, just a coldness. A hardness. *By Jupiter. He looks like my father.* Silus had not thought of his own father for many a year, but gazing into those crystal eyes, a thousand long dead memories awoke in his mind.

His father had been a soldier. Never made it up from the ranks, but had marched proudly under his eagle until his death. He had been serving with the sixth legion, and had been killed in the Jewish revolt some forty years previous, when Silus had been a strapping young lad dreaming of following in his father's footsteps. Now he thought about it, he must have been a similar to age to his own son now. *How different we are.*

With a hot flush, Silus realised his daydreaming had prolonged an awkward silence between the pair, with Albinus waiting to hear what his father had come to say.

'Hello, son,' was all he could manage to mumble out. He edged closer to the gates, half expecting them to be shut in his face at any moment.

'Why are you here? Come to abuse me some more?' Albinus had crushed his fears. He was sick of spending his days creeping around this man and hoping to go unnoticed. Tired of spending his life living in fear and shame, never knowing where the next humiliation was going to come from. He would suffer it no more.

'I have come to apologise. For everything.' Silus stepped into the shadow of the gate, so close to his son he could reach out and touch his face. Not that he dared. 'I am going to change. Things are going to be different now. I promise.' The words were weak and awkward on his lips, and didn't sound in the least bit sincere, at least not to his own ears.

'Ha! My whole life has been one big laughing stock to you. Not once have you ever shown any affection towards me. I've always been a distraction, an entertainment. So how is it going to be different?' He stood in the gateway with his hands on his hips, actually wishing he had done more exercise with the shield so he could look more intimidating and not like the men made out of straw and sticks they put out in the fields to deter to the crows from eating their precious crops.

'Because you are my son, and I love you. Because I have realised what a fool I have been. Your whole life I have talked of soldiering, of leading a life the same as mine. It is only now I realise I had not stopped to ask what it is you want.' Tears formed in his eyes, the first he had shed since losing his wife. 'I am here to ask for forgiveness. For an opportunity to start again.'

Albinus wanted to tell him to leave. To walk away and never return. But something in his father's tone made him hold his tongue. This was not his normal father. The man so brash and arrogant and blind to other people's feelings or hurt. This man was different. Humbled. Sincere. Gone was the old commander of men. 'The lion of the Fourteenth' as he had come to be known, although he had never told his son how he came by that name. The man standing in front of him now was the man that Albinus had needed all these years. His father.

'How can we start again? I can't just forget the years of hurt and abuse. It doesn't work like that.' Despite himself he took a step towards the old man. Studied the age lines that crossed his face, and wondered if they had been there the day before. He didn't think so. He had never thought of his father as old before; he found the realisation saddened him.

'I know it won't be easy, or quick. But I do feel as though we can, with time. I just need a chance, Albinus. A chance to be a proper father. I know my behaviour has been shameful since your mother died. I see that now.' His words tailed off. He could think of nothing else to say. His son would either give him a chance, or he wouldn't.

'Shameful?! That doesn't even begin to cover what you are! An *embarrassment*. You called me an embarrassment! In front of half the settlement. How can we ever move on from that? I'd be better off just leaving.' He half turned away, brushed off the tears that threatened to stream down his cheeks.

'I am sorry, son. It was the heat of the moment. I never meant to hurt you.' He visibly sagged as he said the last words. The pain on his son's face hurt like an arrow piercing armour.

And he knew what that felt like. *I have been a fool.*

'I have two terms.' A shaky voice that didn't sound as powerful as Albinus had hoped. But it lightened Silus' heart all the same. His head snapped up with a hopeful look in his moist eyes. 'One. I'm not going to be a soldier, so stop trying to make me one. We both know I'm not cut out for it anyway. Two. I want to marry Licina, if she'll have me.'

Silus was already nodding. If he was being honest, he would have agreed to anything.

The two conditions were of no hardship at all. 'Okay, son. With all my heart, I agree.' The old centurion could hold himself no longer. He took a giant stride forward and swept Albinus up into his arms. The grip so tight the former struggled for breath inside that bear like embrace.

'Father...oh...father.'

'I know, son. I know. It's okay...'

'No.... can't...breathe'

'Oh!' Silus relented his hold and Albinus dropped to the ground like a sack of grain, gasping for breath as he rubbed some life back into his chest. 'Sorry! Didn't mean to hurt you!' Despite himself, a booming laugh echoed from Silus' lips and his head bent up to the gods. Albinus soon joined in and the tension between the two evaporated like puddles of muddy water after a summer shower.

Silus gripped his son's hand and pulled him back to his feet, helping him wipe the mud and leaves off his cloak and tunic. 'So, you want to farm, eh?' Gone was the mocking tone that would have formally gone hand in hand with that question. A serious interest lied behind the voice.

'I do. I love it. I always have. There's something magical about it. Can't really explain it.' Their hands still locked in a firm grip as they looked each other in the eye.

'The barley swaying in the sun. The satisfaction of watching rainwater run down it and into the earth, pushing it further into the sky. I know about the magic, lad. Farming is the teacher of economy, of industry and justice. You know who said that?'

'Cicero. You read that to me when I was little. When we were moving here.' Albinus was stunned. Never had he heard his father speak of farming with such enthusiasm or passion.

'Ha! Your brain is like a sponge. Always was. Yes, you're right. Took a while to persuade your mother to come out here. I think she envisioned us living in a nice house in a city. Carnuntum, or even Aquileia. Jupiter himself only knows how she thought I was going to provide for the two of you. But she came, of course. And she came to see the same beauty of it that we do.' He let go his grip of Albinus' hand and put both hands on his shoulders. 'You still have much to learn when it comes to running a farm. Especially one as big as ours. So I have two terms of my own.' His face grew stern and the iron returned to his voice. Albinus couldn't help but gulp.

'You listen to Hanno. He has grown into a fine young man, and he's a free man now. His knowledge of growing

83

crops is second to none. And he loves that land more than I do. And the second. Your weapons training doesn't stop...no, I know you hate it, but listen. I won't be around for ever, and neither will my old comrades. We live right on the banks of the river, the *limes* of the empire. Right now, we have peace, but we won't always. You must know how to protect yourself, and your wife.'

Albinus nodded distractedly as his thoughts switched to Licina. *Will she marry me?*

Silus read his mind like a book. A slow smile spreading wide across his face, almost running from ear to ear. 'I don't think she's going to resist you. You two have been infatuated with each other for as long as I can remember. And especially since the two of you have...got to know one another a bit more.' An amused eyebrow arced above those blue eyes. Albinus' blush making his father laugh. 'I remember my first time...'

'Oh gods, father, don't...'

'Lucia her name was. Lovely little thing. From Rome. Father was a Praetorian. Ha! He chased me half way down the river when he found out! Course, I met your mother not long after and that was...'

'Shut up, old man! I really don't need to hear this! Jupiter's arse no one needs to hear that! And anyway, we didn't...you know.' Albinus didn't think he had ever felt so awkward in his life. He didn't know where to look, completely unable to meet his father's eye.

'You didn't? Oh, well that's okay. It comes with time. I can give you some pointers if you need...no, maybe not. Anyway, you have a farm to learn to run and a girl to woo to the marriage bed. So it looks as though we are going to be busy for the rest of the year! Come, shall we go home?'

*

Alaric made his way steadily along the mud made road. Not much made him happy these days but the arrival of summer always seemed to raise his spirits. The luscious sight of green fields and the invigorating smell of blossomed flowers, the sun beating down warming his old bones. It was his favourite time of year.

He had been on the road since early winter, and was looking forward to returning home to his wife and two daughters. He marvelled at how they must have grown whilst he had been away. Time moved too quickly, he mused.

He had been busy since his less than friendly exchange with Silus and his friends. He had first made his way east, into the lands of the Iazyges. Here he had been well met by their chief, who had feasted him in his hall and listened to the whispers and messages that the old trader brought with him. After that he had taken the western road along the river. The Quadi, Langobardi, Obii, Cotini, Norisci, Alamanni, Burgundi and the Chatti had all taken him in with equal enthusiasm and glee. Something was afoot in the wild lands north of the river, and Alaric revelled in it.

His next movements had been north along the Rhine, the powerful factions of the Franci and the Saxones being the most formidable people in western Germania. But they were also at peace, with each other and Rome. *Not for long,* the old rogue thought with an evil grin. His last stop had been in the north, and the icy reception that greeted him at the hall of the Harii. The most devout followers of Wotan, they painted their shields and bodies in black and attacked their foe in the dead of night. It was said that the greatest gift you could grant these mad men was an honourable death in battle, where they could die with their sword in hand. And therefore, be granted entry into the

Allfather's great hall, where they would feast and train for the great war between men and gods.

Memories of that night brought shivers running down Alaric's spine. He, who had fought in more raids and battles than he cared to remember. He, who had raped and killed his whole adult life. He was not afraid to admit that those mad men in the north scared the shit out of him. He had sat through one of their sacrifices. A small boy, taken from the home of the Jutes who lived on the shores of the frozen sea. He had been laid out on a table made of stone, deep in a sacred grove in a dense forest of ash and pine. The thick, gruel like potion they had forced down his throat before they started had driven any fight out of him. He lay there in a daze, not awake and not asleep. Dark eyes smiling to the skies as his long chestnut hair sprawled out around his young face. He seemed to be speaking as the priest carved into his chest and revealed his still beating heart. 'Hear us, Donar, lord of thunder. We give you this heart, use it to give strength to our spears. Grant us passage to your father's hall, so we may fight at his side when the day of reckoning comes.' With that the priest had ripped the heart from the body, the boy had still been smiling. Cries of 'Donar' filled the still night air.

Each of the warriors had taken their turn at approaching the innocent child and covering themselves in the still warm blood. More black than red in the weak moonlight, Alaric had witnessed first-hand why the Harii were the most feared tribe in the land.

In the Roman lands, he knew, people thought that human sacrifice was commonplace in 'barbarian Germania'. The truth, as Alaric knew, was that the German people had moved on from the days that Arminius had untied the tribes and slain Varus and his legions deep in the

Teutoburg forest. The people were just tribes back then, small-minded people who were more interested in killing each other than fighting Rome. But times had changed.

The tribes had grown fewer in number as one tribe was consumed by another. Now the remainder were huge, they lived in great fortresses and were infatuated with roman wine and tapestries and ornaments. The women now wore fine dresses and had special paints from the empire to help prevent the signs of age. The men had begun to trim their beards and sport fine tunics and boots; a small wine cup had replaced the great horns of ale.

It sickened Alaric. The tribes had been so busy drinking fine wine and decorating their halls with fine tapestries that they had not seen how weak and pathetic they had become. How utterly dependent on their great enemy they were. Well, things were about to change. One man had not forgotten the old ways. One man was determined to see things restored to the way they were. And Alaric was nearly at his hall.

The timing of this king's plan was not without its needs and desperation. A storm was brewing across the land. First the plague had ravished on the people's flesh, eating away until they were left as hollow as a burnt-out tree. Famine had been quick to follow. In a land of lush green valleys and sweeping fields, there had been too few left on the isolated farms to maintain their crops through the vital autumn season.

No farming meant no food. Nearly as many greybeards and children had perished in the bitter winter months from starvation than had died of the plague itself. The tribes needed coin. There was food to be had, from distant cousins on the wide plains far to the north and east, but that food came at a price. And Rome had stopped paying its promised tribute, a choice she was soon going to regret.

These thoughts consumed Alaric's mind as he trotted his horse out of the woodland path he had been following and his destination came into view. Balomar, king of the Marcomanni had his fortress in a perfect location. Set atop a hill, its tall walls would be an attackers nightmare as they trudged up with their ladders whilst the defenders rained death down upon them. He gave a satisfied growl as he took in the sight, knowing his journey was nearing its end. Craning his neck round to check on his column, he was satisfied with what he saw. His men rode in good order, weapons sheathed and shields slung across their backs, it showed they came in peace. The carts of goods he had traded for the amber had all survived the great journey, minus some treasures he had been forced to give the tribal chieftains for bribes and gestures of goodwill.

The two soon to be slaves were still in their cage. The boy's wound seemed to have worsened, and Alaric was worried he didn't have long left in this world. A nearly dead slave was no gift for a king. The girl, however, was fit and strong. He had bought her a new dress at the last town they were in; gone were the bloodstains that revealed the mistreatment she had suffered at the hands of Alaric and his men. He would need to caution her to silence before she was brought into the king's presence, it would do him no good if Balomar found out how she and her brother had come to be in his care.

He rubbed his sore gums with his tongue, feeling the holes where his teeth used to be before they rotted away. He winced as he caught a sore spot, and once again cursed himself for trying to eat salted pork that morning. Not a good meal for a man with no teeth. No matter how much you sucked it never seemed to soften enough.

He stopped his horse with a harsh yank to the reins as he turned his head back to the front. The horse shook its great head and whinnied in frustration at the harsh feel of leather on its coat. Rearing up on its hind legs it was all Alaric could do just to stay in his saddle. A rider had appeared in the road. Seemingly coming out of thin air. Alaric stared in disbelief and scanned the fields for signs of more. *Where the fuck did he come from?* Halting his small column, he trotted his horse forward to greet the stranger.

His cloak was a fine dark green, and his mount magnificent. An all-black stallion, nearly twice the size of the small bay Alaric himself rode. The man was as still as a rock, even his cloak was unmoving in the summer's breeze. He glimpsed a fine sheet of chainmail beneath that cloak, a sword hanging on his left hand side.

'Can I 'elp you at all?' His tone as always was blunt as a dull blade.

'Is it done?' came the voice almost a whisper, hoarse, but savage.

'Eh? What you 'arping on about?' A small gesture with his right hand and he was flanked by his armed retinue. He hoped at that moment he had paid them well enough to draw swords with him if it came to it.

'Have you delivered the king's message to the tribes?' Again his voice was no more than a whisper, but the light wind carried it loud and clear.

'Yeah, I 'ave. What's it to you?' he was unnerving, this man. His stillness was unsettling the horses. He had an aura about him. A hint of a greying beard under that hood was the only confirmation he was in fact a man at all.

'We are of the same mind, your king and I. Our ambitions are aligned. I am merely ensuring you have kept your side of the bargain.' There was movement under his cloak. His right arm, thought Alaric. *Just changing the grips on his reins, no need to get excited.* But the more he looked, the more the movement seemed strange, inhuman. Whatever is was, whoever this man was, Alaric was certain he had no business speaking with him.

'Well, err…guess I should be getting to the king then?' With that he snapped his reins and set his horse lurching forward. His bodyguard joined him leaving the hooded man no choice but to move off the road.

'I will see you soon, Alaric. Be sure to kiss your daughters when you get home.' The voice carried over the stampeding horses and the rumbling carts. But still it was no more than a low murmur on the summer's squall. Glancing around, it seemed none of his comrades had heard the voice, or if they had they'd done a better job at ignoring it than he. When he looked behind, the man was gone. Vanished into whatever god deserted place he had appeared from.

Despite the heat, a chill ran down Alaric's spine as he made his way into Goridorgis, capital of the lands of the Marcomanni and home to their king Balomar.

Chapter Six

December AD 167 – Veterans Colony, east of Carnuntum, Pannonia

It was well into the night, but the party was just getting started. Saturnalia was a time for rejoicing. For indulgences in good food and fine wine. And thanks to the money they had received from selling their amber, Silus and his friends had plenty of that to go around. He had been named by the people of the colony as the *Saturnalicius princeps*, or king of the Saturnalia. It had been he who had offered the prayers to Saturn whilst the people had lit their wicker candles, symbolic of a people on a quest for knowledge and truth, and held them up towards the home of the gods. He who had sacrificed the suckling piglet, as was the tradition across the empire.

He had worn a fine blue robe: one Marcia had bought for him the first time he had been asked to ordain for the people. He was bareheaded, same as the priests who would have been that day in Rome. Saturnalia was about role reversal and breaking down social barriers, even if only temporary. It was a time that a slave could sit and eat with their master, or even be served by them.

Silus had stood at the head of the congregation, as the sun began its descent in the west. He had spoken the words to Saturn, although he did not know if he spoke the right ones. Same problem every year. He had held the squealing piglet up to the gods, and offered it as sacrifice. The piglet had no idea what was going on, and when Silus put it down on the ground, it sniffed for food. Unfortunately for the piglet and its increasingly worried mother, all it found was the edge of Silus' knife as it sliced across its throat. The thick dark blood warmed Silus' hands as it poured over the frozen ground and sent sizzling air steaming into the sky. Cries of 'Io Saturnalia' greeted the death of the defenceless animal, as the people of the settlement, free and slave alike, hailed great Saturn on his day of worship.

Albinus had watched intently as his father had dispatched the piglet. Silus had told him that from next year it would be him who made the offering to Saturn and spoke the words in front of the people. Licina had buried her head on his chest and shuddered as the poor animal's lifeblood had gushed out of the thin wound running across its neck. But Albinus had marvelled at how seemingly little effort it had taken to bring the knife across its throat. *It seems harder to cut a loaf of bread than take a life.* Although Silus had much experience when it came to taking lives, and Albinus certainly did not.

Once the sacrifice was made, the people of the farmstead made for the kitchen hall for a feast to remember. Albinus did not think he had ever seen so much meat laid out for one sitting. Of the cattle they brought back from their journey to sell the amber, nearly half had been slaughtered to provide them enough food to last the night. The slaves had been given a place of honour in the hall, and sat at the front where Silus himself would normally sit, the table raised on a small dais so that no matter where you were in the hall your eyes would always fall there.

Silus and the newly freed Hanno had been the first to serve the delighted slaves, whose eyes lit up when they saw the mountain of meat, bread, vegetables and fruit that was theirs to consume. More than they would eat in a normal week. Vitulus and Turda had been next to take their turn, ensuring the workers did not run dry of wine or ale. Each free man and woman had then done their own bit of serving; merriment and camaraderie filled the hall as the slaves took their one opportunity to join in the teasing and banter that was flying around.

Albinus sat at the rear of the hall with a contented look upon his face. His bride to be, she had of course agreed, sat snuggled into his arm and the two watched in amusement as Fullo took on and lost an arm wrestle with a grey-bearded veteran. With much cursing and gesturing, Fullo tried to blame his defeat on the slippery surface of the table. So Vitulus, always keen to see his son knocked down a peg or two, set up another table for a rematch.

Sadly for Fullo, the result was the same.

'Yeah, well it's this ale, ain't it! Can't have been brewed properly, got me feeling all funny.' Roars of laughter greeted his latest excuse, and he stormed out the hall with rosy cheeks and eyes like thunder. The betrothed couple shared a knowing look, knowing it could be days before their friend got over his shame at defeat. Albinus was refilling his wine cup when his booze-ridden father slumped down onto the bench to his left.

'You 'avin' a good time, son?' At least it was something like that. Albinus wasn't quite sure Silus was capable of speaking Latin any more.

'Very good, father, you sure you want more wine?' Silus' unsteady hand was splashing good wine all over the table and himself.

'Don't you fucking patronise me, you little shit! I could still 'ave you. Don't you worry about th— ahh bollocks!' A violent hiccup and he had spilt the contents of his cup

93

all over his fine blue cloak. Taking off his felt cap, worn by all that day to show they were all equal under the eyes of Saturn, he tried to mop the wine off his cloak. 'Your mother would 'ave my balls if she saw the state of this,' he said, a sad smile on his drunken face.

'Don't worry, father, I'm sure I can get most of it out in the morning.' Leaning across Albinus, Licina helped to mop up the running wine. Silus smiled at the girl calling him father; it was like she was reborn after the engagement had been announced. It was rare not to see her smiling and chatting with whoever crossed her path, and he had never seen Albinus so happy or confident.

'I'm sooooo proud of you two, you know.' His cheeks were flushed with wine and his voice only just comprehensible, but the praise made Albinus grow a little taller all the same. The rest of summer and the autumn had been the happiest times of his life by far. He and Silus had grown inseparable, spending dawn to dusk out on the fields with Hanno and his slaves. The harvest had been the best they had ever produced, and they had even laid out the foundations for his very own house, right down in the valley by the great mill.

After years of awkward silences and uncomfortable conversations, it seemed that he and his father would never run out of things to chat about, and Albinus had developed an unending amount of respect for the old first spear and what he had achieved in life. It had been his vision to start this farm, and his will had made it a success. He didn't think there was another man alive who could have accomplished what he had. Even the compulsory weapon drills had become more bearable, Silus leaving the drill sergeant in him behind and taking the time to coach and tutor Albinus through every lesson. He had managed to floor Fullo a good number of times now, and Licina doted over his growing biceps and chest.

He beamed back at his father, feeling rather drunk himself. 'Thank you, father. Once the worst of the winter is behind us we should start thinking about a date. We were thinking spring, if that's agreeable with you?' The couple would have been married tomorrow if they had their own way, but were sensible enough to bide their time and 'do it the proper way' as Turda had told them.

'Spring would be perfect! Just as the flowers are blossoming and the trees a shimmering green. Can't wait!' There was a sparkle in Silus' eye as he envisioned that perfect day not too long into the future.

'Blossoming flowers? Shimmering trees? Never thought me old first spear would turn into such a tunic lifter in 'is old age!' Bucco's huge calloused hand crashed down onto Silus' shoulder, nearly sending him sprawling off the bench.

'I dunno, Bucco, he always was a bit too sensitive for my liking. You remember the amount of time he used to spend gazing lovingly at his own reflection? I reckon he could just never find a man that looked like him!' Vitulus' face was filled with mischief, a little nudge into the back of his former superior righting him on the bench.

'That's fucking rich, coming from you! You streaky little piss stain! Lemme tell you something!' A wandering finger circled the table as Silus squinted to try and work out which one of the blurs was his old optio. 'Lemme tell you. When this short arse met Turda, he must've tried on about ten different tunics before he first took her out! And he even wore this great big 'orrible belt, just cos he reckoned it held his little pot belly in!' He roared with laughter at the memory. Bucco matching him as he remembered better days when they were all men in their prime.

'You're right, Silus, I remember! And what was that stuff he put in 'is hair? Stunk like a rotting carcass, but he thought he looked like Caesar reborn!' Everyone joined in with the laughter as fingers were pointed at a humbled Vitulus. Turda moved in quickly to give her husband a comforting hug.

'I'd never seen a man so handsome. And I haven't since.' Her lips locked with his as the old couple proved that Cupid's arrow still bound them together. 'Now husband, maybe we should go home before you get too drunk to…enjoy yourself.' Loud whistles and roars greeted this remark, which Vitulus was quick to hush with some rude hand gestures.

'One thing, Vitulus! Before you go and…enjoy yourself.' Silus could not help but splutter out a laugh; you could leave the army it seemed, but the humour was with you for ever. 'We have not discussed this young lady's dowry.' Gripping Licina in a stifling embrace, he continued: 'And a daughter as beautiful as this should come with a dowry to match.' The whole room it seemed had stopped to listen to their conversation. Albinus and Licina threw each other an awkward look. They had agreed between themselves that they would not ask Vitulus and Turda to provide a dowry, as they were not after all Licina's birth parents.

'It's okay…' started Albinus, but he was quickly cut off.

'Do not be silly, young man.' Vitulus held up his hand to silence the younger man. 'My wife and I have already spoken on this and we will of course provide you both with a handsome amount. It is the least the two of you deserve.' More roars and applause greeted this; it seemed there wasn't a man woman or child in the whole settlement who wasn't delighted to see the young couple so happy.

'Thank you, uncle. We shall not forget your generosity.' He bowed his head towards the man who had raised his love. Who returned the gesture even as his eager wife dragged him off to bed.

*

Albinus sweated in the freezing night air. As the festivities had drawn to a close, he and Licina had crept out of the hall and made their way through the ice-ridden fields and into the fort in the woods. They came here often now, it being the one place they could be alone. The cold wind seemed to freeze the sweat on his naked skin. He rose from the bed, shuddering as the cold bit deep in his bones. He went over to the window and rearranged the fur he had covered it with, hoping to minimise the chill blowing through.

'Come back to bed, my love. It is cold without you.' Licina stirred and turned around under the blankets, moonlight revealing one naked breast as she disturbed the covers.

Albinus couldn't help but feel aroused at the sight, even after what felt like hours of frantic and passionate lovemaking. He wondered if the sight of her naked body would ever cease to excite him. He didn't think so.

Licina laughed to see the attraction growing on his naked body. 'I think I have seen quite enough of that for one night. Any more and you shall have to carry me home. Come back to bed.' Albinus wordlessly crossed the room, slightly embarrassed by her over emphasis of the power of his loins. He snuggled back under the blankets and thought of something to say, but no words came. 'I can't wait to marry you,' was what eventually came out. The only reply was the soft snoring of his future bride as she drifted off into a deep sleep.

Kissing her cheek and running his hands through her fire-bright hair, he marvelled at the power that lovemaking suddenly held over him. He was obsessed with it, could not stop thinking about it. His hand rubbed over a particularly sore bruise Fullo had left on him the day before. So lost in his dreams about Licina's body, her long and flexible legs, the cute little mole just above her pubic hair. He hadn't even seen the sword jab coming. He could tell his father had wanted to berate him then, but credit to the old man, he had bit his tongue. *Even he must have felt this way once.* Thoughts of his mother and father in their younger years immediately washed away any lingering arousal the young man felt.

For some reason unbeknown to him, his thoughts tracked back to that piglet earlier on in the evening, before the drinking had started in earnest. Would he have the courage and the steady hand to strike the blow so mercilessly and firmly? He doubted he would be able to see it through. *Coward. Can't even kill a suckling pig.* It was just one more thing to give him cause to doubt himself for another year. It seemed even when he was happiest, there was always some niggling doubt lingering in his thought box trying to break his spirit.

His thought chain grew darker still as he imagined a life without his father and Vitulus and the other grey beards to help protect the farm. His father's words whispered through his mind. *I won't be around for ever, and neither will my old comrades.* One day, maybe in the near future, it would be up to him to defend the land his father and so many others had worked so hard to build up. He sent a prayer up to Mars, promising the god of war the greatest sacrifice of cattle and sheep ever seen if he would give him the strength to stand and fight if the time ever came. His next prayer was to Juno, whom he thanked for giving them a lasting peace with the northern wolves and their cousins; he just hoped it would continue for many years yet.

*

Licina woke with a shudder and a thumping headache. *Gods! But I do not have the stomach for wine.* She vowed never to touch the stuff again. It was still dark in the small barracks room, and ice cold. Shivering, she shimmied out of Albinus' arms and quickly threw on her dress and cloak. Her mouth was as dry as dead and crispy barley, which had not been watered all summer long. Fumbling into her warm leather boots, a gift from Turda the winter before, she crept outside in search of a water skin. Not finding one, she decided to make her way back into the settlement. *I shall bring back water and bread for breakfast.*

Albinus and I can enjoy a few more hours of privacy. We won't be missed for one morning. She flushed as she pictured the two of them carrying on from where they had left off in the night. She had become completely obsessed with Albinus and his manhood. It really was a gift from the gods, the way he could make her feel, once she had got over the initial pain.

She could still feel the marks on her skin where he had kissed, licked and bitten in his passion. She felt the wetness between her legs begin to spread as the memories whirled through her mind. She could still feel the tingles under her fingernails where they had bitten into his back and his perfectly round behind. *Do people over get bored of doing that? We shall never leave our bed once we are married!* Licking her lips and tasting his there, she smiled the biggest smile as she slowly made her way back through the woodland path, wishing she had a torch.

It was deathly quiet in the heart of the settlement. Even the hounds seemed exhausted from the day's festivities. Creeping through the cobbled road, she stifled a laugh to see Bucco stripped naked and snoring like an ox over a straw-filled cart. Arriving at her home, she crept in, quiet as the smallest mouse, just as a weak winter's sun began its ascent in the east.

*

Alaric stood in the shadows of the trees. Shouts and screams of joy and laughter filled the air from over the river. Cries of 'Io Saturnalia' and 'Io Bacchus' could be heard as the revellers had their fill of wine and ale. *Well, they better enjoy themselves. Won't be no more feasting and fucking after tomorrow.*

The night was dark, which suited him well. The river was at its narrowest here, where it wended towards the north and east. A small rock-filled beach lay between him and the river itself, the north bank providing rougher terrain than the grass-covered bank on the other side of the ford.

A lazy mist was rising from the swirling water. Swirling and dancing its way into a sky filled with heavy cloud that threatened snow. The smell of roasted meat lingered in the freezing night air, causing his stomach to growl in hunger. *There'll be time for a snack before it starts.*

His audience with the king had gone well. Balomar had heaped praise and gold upon him for completing his mission, and he had returned home to his wife and daughters a happy man. He cast an evil gaze at two lovers across the river, who wrongly assumed their lovemaking on the south side of the bank was going unwatched. *They'd better make it a good one.* A sickly smile that didn't spread to his eyes sat on his mouth.

The sound of footsteps roused him from his thoughts. Adalwin, chief bodyguard to king Balomar approached in the gloom. 'The men are all set. I still don't understand why we don't send them across now? Right now, they are just a bunch of old greybeards sleeping off their wine-filled bellies. But in the morning, they will be eagles. Veterans. We will lose men by delaying.' Alaric had known Adalwin for many years. And yet it amazed him still how such a formidable warrior could worry like an old woman.

'Corr, 'ow many times I got to tell you. We want 'em to be awake. We want 'em to know they're dying. Slitting a man's throat in his sleep ain't right. Ain't no way to earn your spear fame.' He hadn't told Adalwin, or Balomar for that matter, how much he longed to see Silus meet his end at the sharp point of a German spear. When Adalwin had suggested the raid take place along the amber road, much further to the west, it had made sense. It was closer to Goridorgis, so the king would know the outcome quicker. Also, there were many farming settlements there that were not protected by any swords, let alone a bunch of tried and tested legionaries.

Alaric had to use all his cunning to change the king's mind. *This place is further from your lands, no one will expect your involvement, my king. You want to remain anonymous in this, let the Quadi take the rap, it will be mostly their men doing the raid anyway.* His arguments had won through in the end. And he would get his revenge. *Silus. You old cunt.* There was no man on this earth Alaric wanted to see dead more than he. The man who had taken his eye, and more importantly, his reputation.

101

Before that day, many moons ago, Alaric had been a warrior to be feared, a leader of men. His was a spear for hire, allied only to the tribe with the deepest pockets. And he and his men were the cause of many a greybeard's nightmares. For well over twenty years they had roamed the land, their land. They slept where they wanted, ate what they wanted and took what they wanted. At his prime he had commanded nearly five hundred men, each battle proven and with the scars to prove it. They had earned their coin by wading into the tribes' petty and many wars. And siding with the king who offered them the most gold and taking the head of the one who did not. Over twenty years and he had not lost a battle. Until one spring night when he had been tricked into a quick march to the fortress of Parienna, out east in the lands of the now extinct Arsietae, with the promise of his weight in gold if he would help them repel the invading Iazyges.

Except when he had arrived, and the sun was setting and his men were saddle sore and hungry, Parienna had been deserted. The gates were open and the streets were clear, there was no sign of struggle, not so much a skirmish. There were no cart or horse tracks leading away in any direction. It was as if the whole tribe had vanished into thin air. Not seeing much choice but to rest his men in the town, which remained stocked of wine and food, he had joined in the revelry as the five hundred ate and drunk their fill.

In his drunken sloppiness, he had not set a perimeter or even a watch. Each man had slept where he fell, and died there. Too late did he realise he had been summoned there on a ruse. Too late did he see the frailties and holes in the forged note that had sent him galloping in gold lust half way across the country. It was only when he woke to the screams and saw the red-cloaked killers marching under their eagle that he filled in the blanks. Found the hidden truth. It was true, he had rallied some of the men. They'd had a pretty good go at forming a shield wall and making a stand. But it had been Silus himself that had struck the decisive blow. A short thrust with his *pila* at point blank range. Alaric's right eye had watched in horror as his left was caught on the head of the dart and was ripped out of the socket, leaving a bloody tangle of muscle and ligament trailing in its wake.

And so the battle had been lost, his men slaughtered to a man. But Silus had left him alive. *You are nothing but an outlaw now. No king will hire a one-eyed swordsman. Your time is over, now run back to whatever shithole you crawled out from.* Some jokes about sleeping with one eye open had followed, but he had tried hard to erase them from his memory. Yet now it was all flooding back to him, as if it had been carried by the great river he stood in front of.

Now finally, after years of hurt and scrounging and stealing and trading for petty things with the cursed Romans, he was going to have his revenge. Adalwin clearing his throat brought him back from his dark and blood-ridden walk down memory lane. 'Why are you so set on this, Alaric? Why do we need to take such a risk? Let us kill them now, while they sleep. The message it delivers will be the same.' He was not short of courage, Alaric knew that. He was just speaking common sense. Of course, it would be easier to raid in the dark whilst their prey lay snoring after a hard day's drinking and feasting. But Alaric would not do to Silus what he had done to him. He wanted that bastard to know that death was coming, to feel the fear he had felt at Parienna. To know that he and all he loved were doomed and that he was helpless to prevent it. But he couldn't tell Adalwin that. The old rogue clicked his tongue as he turned the cog in his tired think wheel, summoning up the right words to hush the other man.

'Because, my ol' friend, we want them to know who did it, don't we? The whole bleedin' reason we marched all the way down here in the middle o' winter is so those fuckers think it was the Quadi who are behind this. We're the only two people here who know o' Balomar's plan and for all our sakes it need to stay that way. You get me?' Folding his arms and leaning up against a tree, he watched as the rutting couple finally climaxed and slumped down onto the frozen ground.

'Well, I suppose you are right there—'

'Course I'm bleedin' right! And when our boys stalk over there come sunrise, whose banners will those sheep fuckers see? Whose colours will be painted on our shields? Not Balomar's, but Areogaesus'. The Quadi, the Langobardi, the Obii. So, who will they come looking for? The Quadi! And who will step in and treat with the Romans on their behalf?'

'My king,' Adalwin's voice was grave, as though he still was not completely sold on what they were about to undertake. He had always preferred the life of an honest warrior. A good blade in his hand and his enemy to his front. The game of deception and trickery he found himself webbed in did not sit easily upon his shoulders. But he knew he would pull through. He would fight through Hel for his king.

'Exactly! Now, go and fetch Euric so we can run through the plan one more time.' Adalwin made his way uncertainly through the uneven ground under the blanket of blank pine. It was not the unsteady footing that made him uncertain, or the lack of a torch, for obvious reasons. It was the fact that old Alaric seemed to be taking command. And no matter what tales he spun, deep down he knew the real reason why they had come to this place. *This will not end well.*

Alaric took a moment to enjoy the silence of the winter night. *A sleeping land. Not for long.* He did not hear the footsteps approaching, but the whispered voice brought back an unwelcome chill down his spine.

'You have done well.'

'What the—? 'ow did you—?'

'A man cannot see that, which he is not searching for.' Silent footsteps as the man came forward. It was as if his feet did not even touch the ground.

'Who are you?' Alaric's hand instinctively gripped the hilt of his great sword, the black pommel a comforting feel as he gathered his fleeting nerves.

'I told you before, on the road to Goridorgis. I am a friend of your king.' He stepped closer, out of the shadows of the trees. The moons weak light revealed the same greying beard Alaric had seen before.

'Yeah, well 'e never mentioned you to me. And 'e ain't my king anyway.' He couldn't help but back away from the man, if that was even what he was. He appeared to be wearing the same fine green cloak he had been wearing that day in the summer. His mail vest glistened underneath, a Roman style *gladius* sat on his right hip. Alaric jumped in surprise as his right foot splashed into the shallows of the great river; he hadn't realised he had backed away so far.

'I am a silent partner in our arrangement. But you will be getting to know me better once it's all done, of that you can be sure.' Once again, Alaric's gaze was drawn to the mysterious man's right arm. The movements were unnatural, circular. *Like a snake.* The hooded man slowly backed away into the pitch-black forest. Alaric was left alone on the beach in the bracing night's air, wondering just who exactly this man was and why the Hel Balomar had been making dealings with him.

Chapter Seven

December AD 167– Veterans Colony, east of Carnuntum, Pannonia

Silus woke as the winter sun's first weak rays fluttered in through the open window. His head pounded like it had stopped the butt of a spear, and his stomach whirled round like the great mill down by the fields. Rising unsteadily to his feet, he stumbled over to a basin of water in the corner of the room and plunged his head under. After a few heartbeats of icy cold relief, he slowly pulled his head out and ran to the window to vomit. *Gods! Have hangovers always been this bad?* He didn't think so. Slumped down beneath the open window, he tried to remember what in Jupiter's name he had got up to the night before. Hazy memories came back of him and a few of the lads stripping a passed-out Bucco naked and throwing him in the back of a cart.

Chuckling to himself, he rose awkwardly to his feet, feeling slightly better for bringing up the contents of his stomach. The day had gone well, if he recalled it all correctly. The slaves had behaved themselves. Although they were 'free' for the day, all knew they weren't really. Silus sent a thankyou prayer to Saturn that none of them had forgotten their station and taken the opportunity to throw some cheap remarks at any of the citizens. He recalled the festival three years prior, when he had been forced to sell his best worker because he had got drunk and abused Vitulus the whole night. It had taken all his great bulk to stop his former optio beating the man black and blue.

Throwing off his dirtied tunic and putting on a new one, he picked up the blue cloak he had been wearing the day before. *Bollocks*. The cloak was sodden with wine, dark red stains blotted over the whole thing. *Marcia would not be pleased!* Throwing it back to the floor and picking up another, one from his old army days, he opened the door to his room and crept out into the small hallway. His son's room was opposite his and he didn't want to wake him. The door was ajar, peering his head through the gap he saw the room was empty. *I know where that dirty little bugger is*. A wide grin spread across his face as he trudged down the small hallway and into the only other room in the small house.

Not much was in here as Silus rarely used his home for anything other than sleeping. Parking his behind on a small wooden chair he picked up a discarded water skin off the floor. *Damn, empty*. He sat in silence for a few moments, and his grin returned as he thought of the fun his son would have been having once the party had drawn to a close.

It seemed like just yesterday that he and Albinus had made a peace in the woods. Time had simply flown by since then. Silus could not remember even a morning passing where he had not revered to be in his son's company. Never before had he appreciated the intelligence of the lad, the practical way his mind worked and his passion and love he so clearly felt for the land that had raised him. Their relationship had blossomed quicker than the flowers in spring, and Silus was immensely proud of the man Albinus was becoming.

And as for Licina. It was as if she had been taken and replaced with a different person. Gone was the young girl full of hate and tears, who would sit and stare at the river so blankly that people whispered she had lost her mind. In her place was a young woman growing into her beauty. Her smile reminded Silus of his wife's. The way the sight of it could snap you out of the darkest of moods. Not that he felt them anymore. Thoughts of his Marcia's smile reminded him of the only sadness that remained in his heart. If she were still here then he would be complete. He liked to picture her, sitting in the sun-drenched fields of Elysium, awaiting his arrival with that smile on her face. *I will be with you again one day, my love.*

Deciding that sitting in a rickety old chair brooding over things he could never change was not the way to start the day – too many of his days had started that way – he rose and opened his front door and breathed in deeply the brisk morning air. Two things sprang to mind: the need for food and the need to pray to Mithras. It had been too long since he had entered the shrine under the granary and spent some time with his favoured god. It would be freezing down there this at time of year, he knew. The steps would be covered in black ice and the air in the gloom cold enough to turn your breath to little icicles which froze to your face as soon as you exhaled.

His home was opposite the small training square where he spent most of the winter days, his being on the first row of homes built all those years ago. His lean torso thick with muscle was evidence of that. He had not allowed himself to run to fat, much like most of the other veterans. The kitchens were closer to where he stood, so he figured he would head there first. Snow drops began to fall, initially sporadically, as he made his way over the sanded ground of the training square. He cursed as looked at his feet to see he was wearing his old army issue sandals, which gave little or no protection from the cold and the wet. *Ahh well, it's not far.*

He stopped as he reached the cobbled road that ran from north to south through the heart of the settlement. His ears pricked at a small sound, from the river in the north. Just a small splash, and then the whinny of a horse. *Strange,* he thought, *who in the name of the gods is up at this hour?* Standing in silence, he waited a full ten heartbeats but heard nothing else.

Just a trick of the mind. Starting back off again heading south down the road, he heard it again. More splashes, more whinnies and snorts. *There are horses on the ford.*

Turning around and marching at double pace up the gentle rise to the riverbank, he slowed and moved into a crouch. *Probably just some of our horses. Not locked in last night.* If everyone was as drunk as he had been, it would seem reasonable to suggest that the evening checks on the livestock had not been carried out.

The approach to the river was covered in mist; he crept up the riverbank like a predator stalking its prey. The combination of the snowfall and mist made it hard to see his outstretched hand, let alone the river. But he was sure there were shapes moving under the carpet of fog, dark shadows extenuated against a backdrop of white. He squinted as the wind buffeted his face. Moving closer, cautious, he listened as the sound of movement grew closer. He squatted down to remain out of sight. *Not just horses.* The outline of men were visible now. Some astride horses and some on foot, they were crossing the ford from

110

the north, eight abreast. *Who in Mithras' name is this? A cavalry detachment coming back from patrol?* Plausible, he thought, the Fourteenth's cavalry had used the ford before, but only because they had to. Their usual route home would have been the bridge at Carnuntum.

He crawled closer, shielding his eyes from the thickening snow; he could hear them now, voices, and a lot of them. It wasn't Latin they were speaking, but the harsh Germanic tongue of the tribes from across the river. *Raiders!* he thought with a start, and a lot of them. He could begin to make them out now, tall and well-built. Could see their beards blowing in the wind under helmets of iron. Spears pointed upwards as they were rested on shoulders, shields held high so as not to drag in the murky waters. A wet shield weighed a man down.

The old soldier jumped up and ran at the double back to the settlement, hangover all but forgotten. 'To arms, to arms. Men of the Fourteenth to me!' He crashed into his own home, panting as he ripped open the chest in his room, no time for armour, just his sword belt complete with his ivory-hilted gladius, carved into an eagle's head, awarded to him on his discharge from the Fourteenth legion. He slammed his helmet onto his head, grabbed his shield and *pilum* and marched out into the morning air.

'To arms, to arms, Fourteenth on me, ON ME'. The last two words were barked, throat muscles well-toned after nearly thirty years barking at legionaries up and down the banks of the Danube. He stopped where grass met cobbles at the north of the place he called home.

Looking to the north, a wall of armour and horses greeted him as they reached the top of the riverbank and descended towards him. The first of his veterans lined up beside him. Bucco, the giant balding old eagle, was one of

111

the first in line. He was still completely naked, but had had the presence of mind to run home and grab his sword and shield.

Silus appraised the soldier who had served him with distinction for more years than he could remember, and couldn't help but bark out a laugh. 'Morning, brother. How'd you sleep?'

Bucco rubbed his eyes to double check the mist-shrouded soldiers in front of him were not a bad dream; he flexed his shoulder and vomited at his feet. 'Fuck me. Hangovers never used to be this bad.'

'Ha! You're right there, brother. Though if it's any relief to you I fear our hangovers may be short-lived.' The Germani had stopped at the top of the small rise. Sixty paces at most from where Silus stood.

'What in Jupiter's name's going on anyway? Who are these goat-fucking turds?' Bucco rubbed his eyes again and shook his head to try and shake the worst of the previous night's exertions.

'I don't know, brother. But it doesn't look as though they have come to join us for breakfast.' Their ranks were swelling as word spread of their impending doom. More and more sore-headed greybeards answered their old first spear's call. Some came fully armoured and some came with nothing more than sword and shield. It mattered not to Silus; just that they came.

One man moved forward in the snow from the ranks of the wolves. He stopped twenty paces from the Roman line and called Silus by name. 'Well then, let's see what's going on, shall we?' Without looking back, he moved toward the lone German warrior. The combination of snow, mist and wind almost blocking him from view of the rest of his comrades.

112

Euric stood at the front of six thousand hardened raiders, and wondered why his king had insisted he take so many. No more than fifty old men with shaky old shields stood in the way of him and an abundance of women and food and livestock to round up and take home. He would make himself a rich man today, he thought, as he squinted through the worsening snow that buffeted into his eyes.

A plan was afoot, although he knew none of it. Behind him stood not just men from the Quadi, but from the Langobardi and the Obii too. If he thought it strange his king should order him to raid a Roman settlement in the depth of winter with a mongrel army so close to the home of the formidable Fourteenth – with whom he had had plenty of experience – none of it good, then it was not his place to question. He was a warrior, a leader of men. He would not let his king down.

He watched as Silus, the former first spear of the Fourteenth, a man that had provoked fear right into the very heart of Germania, prowled out of the Roman ranks. *May the Allfather damn him to Hel. But by Donar, he still casts an impressive sight.* He had been pleased when Alaric had told him they would be raiding this man's home. He had killed his father in single combat, many winters ago, when the former king of the Quadi had overstretched his ambition. Euric had been a pup then, and Silus would have been in his prime. With the might of a full legion behind him. *And now it is me who is in the height of my powers, and you have less than a century to challenge my wall of spears.*

Alaric's instructions from the night before ran through his mind. *Tell him you have come for revenge. Tell him you're here to avenge the death of your father and so*

113

many like him. This man has made too many widows among our people. Killed too many fathers and sons and brothers. Too long we have lived in fear of Rome and their bleedin' eagles. Today is the first step in taking back our freedom. Our destiny.

The old warrior had given a good speech. It had roused Euric and rekindled the fury he kept buried deep inside over his father's death. Though not for the first time he wondered why the old one-eyed rogue wasn't here with him to face Silus himself. He knew of the stories, everyone did. Of how Silus and his legion had tricked the one-time war leader and massacred his men to a man. Only Alaric had been allowed to live. Disgraced and humbled, Rome no longer saw him as a threat to the peace they liked the tribes to keep. If there was to be war between the tribes, they'd much rather it be a war of their making, one they could control.

Instead of disappearing into obscurity, Alaric had taken a new role within the tribes. He was seen by some as the living embodiment of Wotan himself. All knowing and cunning as a fox, the one-eyed man had even taken to wearing a dark cloak and a huge hat. Euric thought Alaric probably enjoyed his new status among the German people, although he would never admit it to others. So he had gone to his king with a plan, though Euric did not know if it was of his own making. Just like he did not know who the mysterious man in the hooded cloak who did not speak was, although his companions looked as though they came from within the empire. All he knew was that his king had agreed, and now here he was, about to face the man that murdered his father.

And now he stood in front of Euric, he could appreciate the work the old man must do every day to keep himself so trim. His legs were still taut with thick muscle, his waist a little thicker than when he had last laid eyes upon him, but it complemented his great arms and shoulders. Age lines surrounded the old centurion's face as he grew closer. A silver lining on his cheeks and chin showed he hadn't had time to shave that morning. He wore only a white tunic and sandals, a red crested helmet and a rectangular shield that still had the striking colours of the Fourteenth embedded on the front. Euric hoped the rest of his men hadn't maintained themselves so well, or this might not be as straightforward as he thought.

The two men stood five paces apart; no words were spoken as eagle and wolf stared each other in the eye. The mist danced around them as they were attacked by the heavy snow, now falling so thick it had begun to cover their feet.

'Good morning, first spear. I trust you enjoyed yourself last night? Sounded like a Hel of a party from where we were.' He kept his voice neutral, relaxed and quiet. He did not want to reveal the build-up of emotions that seeing this man again brought bubbling to the surface.

'Euric of the Quadi. Chief protector of King Areogaesus. Son of Sisbert of the Quadi. Chief protector of King Roderic. The apple doesn't fall far from the tree, it seems. What are you doing on my lands? Your people are at peace with Rome.' His words added ice to the driving snow. He was as still as a rock, as if the elements had no effect on his hulking frame.

Euric was freezing, though he would not show it. His toes screamed in agony; though they were protected by thick leather boots, it seemed that the icy waters of the river had washed their way through leather and stitching. His left hand frozen solid, he wondered if he would be

115

able to grip his shield when the time came. His breath had turned to ice on his thick blond beard, he could feel the particles running up the hair and stinging his skin. 'I have brought some old friends to see you. Although my tribe may be at peace with Rome, not all my cousins are. Behind me are men of the Langobardi and the Obii, who do not feel so *friendly* towards your empire.'

'Why? Why here? Why now?' There was iron in those words. Fury. They cut through the mist like sharpened iron through flesh.

'Why not? I am not the only man in the north who dreams of your death. I have come to take from you what you have taken from so many of my people. I will take your life. I will kill your friends. I will burn your homes and rape your women. You will know fear before the sun has fully risen. You will know pain and suffering. The pain I felt when I watched you cut my father down in front of our walls. The suffering I endured as you spat on his corpse and cut off his head. Hear me, Donar, lord of thunder. Slayer of ice giants. I give this man to you in my father's name!' Head raised to the gods, he howled the last words, sending the packed men behind him into raptures.

'Ha! You speak as though the deed is done already. I am not an easy man to kill, just ask your father. But I do not think you have thought this through. My old legion is half a day's ride from here. I have already sent riders to warn them of your presence. You will not leave here alive. As Mars is my witness you will meet your end today.' He spat on the floor and the ball of phlegm melted a patch of deepening snow at Euric's feet.

'Then let them come. We will deal with them once I have your head. I have nothing else to say to you, old man. I wanted to see your lank old face one last time before I thrust my spear through it. I have done that. Now go back to your men and prepare to meet your gods.' With that he turned away and walked deliberately slowly back to his howling wolves, barely able to hold themselves back any longer. He willed himself not to turn back round. To look one more time into those cold blue eyes. They had still forced an unhealthy amount of fear to surge through his veins. The man was a killer, it mattered not how much he had aged. He would still be a dangerous foe. Re-joining his men, clenching and unclenching his toes to try and rid himself of the glaring pain, he readied himself to avenge his father.

*

Silus walked back down to the growing roman wall of metal and lime wood. He stopped and surveyed them in the mist and the snow and his chest swelled with pride. They were all there, it seemed. Nearly numbering a hundred, they stood in varying degrees of dress and some didn't even have a shield, but they were there. He could hear the shouts and screams, faceless voices of the women and children as they grabbed what belongings they could and made haste to the south.

'Vitulus, to me,' he barked.

'Orders, sir?' The ever loyal optio was at his side in a flash. One of the few to appear in full armour, he looked as impressive as he had in his prime.

'This is it for us, Vitulus, can't see a way out of it, but we must give the women and children as much time as we can.'

'...Yes, sir, I agree. Always thought I'd die in battle. Huh, was only just starting to think I might get to go peacefully.' A sad smile crept into the corners of his mouth.

'I know the feeling brother, a lifetime living in the middle of the iron storm. Jupiter's balls! We even survived the plague. And now it comes to this. Sometimes the gods are cruel, these boys deserve a better end.' Silus spat in disgust, guilt raged in his heart, *I'm sorry, brothers.* 'Are Turda and Fullo out of your home?'

'Not yet. I've told Fullo to get her and Licina out towards the woods straight away. The stubborn old cow was refusing to leave!' Turda had never been one to follow an order given by her husband. In truth, that was one of the reasons he loved her so much.

'Licina? Why is she there? Where's Albinus?' Silus had thought his son and bride to be safely hidden away in the woods. The thought of them both getting caught in the middle of this sent his heart racing in a way his own impending doom could not.

'Albinus is in the fort. Licina had come home to get them breakfast. Don't worry, brother, Fullo will get them to him. They will be safe.' He spoke with such certainty it eased Silus' panicked mind.

'Okay. Thank you, brother. Right then, we have the houses for cover on the right, but the training square on the left leaves us wide open. There's no way we can hold these bastards back with a hundred men. We're going to have to charge them, on my order. We form a wedge and make legs up the hill, with luck, and some help from Mithras, we will bide our families enough time to get away.'

'Yes, sir I understand... just one thing, sir, before we...go... I want to let you know that it's been an honour, sir. To serve under you. Never thought much of myself before I met you, and when you promoted me to optio…well…never been so proud.' A shiny tear sparkled in the corner of Vitulus' eye, quickly swatted away.

'Nearly thirty years I've known you, optio, that's probably the finest speech I've ever heard you give,' choked Silus. A wry smile on his face, covering, he hoped, tears of his own welling behind his eyes. He held out his arm, quickly gripped by Vitulus, as for the last time, the two great friends embraced in the warrior's way. 'Now, optio, get in line, and get these men ready.' Without another word, Silus turned away from his oldest friend, lowered his helmet into place, and ran his fingers across the horsehair plume.

'Bucco, come here,' the old centurion ordered quietly.

'Sir,' Bucco rasped. It seemed one of his brother soldiers had done him the courtesy of fetching him a tunic and some armour to cover his naked self.

'How's the hangover?'

'Better, actually. So, who are these whoresons?' He jabbed through the snow towards the wolf pack, who were busy readying themselves to charge down the slope.

'Remember Sisbert? Of the Quadi?' Bucco nodded. 'It's his son. Come for revenge apparently. He says he has six thousand men. Some Langobardi and Obii with him. Something's going on here. Someone is trying to send Rome a message. I have a job for you, brother, the most important you will ever do. I need you to go to Carnuntum, to the fortress. I need you to speak to Taurus and get the Legion down here as quickly as you can. The lives of the people here may well depend on it.' Silus saw the pain appearing in the eyes of Bucco.

'But sir,' splattered the veteran soldier. 'I can't leave you, and my brothers. Send Avius and Brutus, they are quicker on a horse than me. They were cavalrymen after all! I'd rather stay and fight with you, sir, to the end.' The old warrior's head dropped, shame burning over him as he thought of the prospect of leaving his comrades to die.

'It's your brothers you're doing this for, Bucco. You are remembered well at the Fourteenth, and I trust you implicitly. Without support from the legion, we have no chance. You need feel no shame, my old friend. Just promise me one thing.'

'Yes, sir, anything.' Bucco looked on his grizzled old Centurion as if he was looking onto Mithras himself.

'If we have all departed across the river by the time you return, look out for my son. Albinus will need someone he can turn to for support, and I don't think he will find any comfort in the ranks. Tell him I am sorry. Sorry it took me so long to recognise what a diamond he is. Sorry I wasted so many years.' Silus gave a heavy sigh, old regrets weighing him down more than his heavy shield and helm. 'Tell him I love him. And that he will make me proud whatever he chooses to do with his life.'

Bucco drew himself up to his full height, realising the importance of what he was being asked to do. 'I give you my oath, sir. I will find Albinus, I will guard him with my life for the rest of my days.' He gave his centurion one last salute, before turning south, and setting off at double pace towards the stables. He didn't dare look back.

Silus surveyed the approaching Germani over the rim of his shield. His palm clammy on the familiar, worn handle. *This is it,* he thought, *one final battle, I will be with you soon, my dear. But first, my sword will taste blood one final time.* His veterans were gathered around him. He cast his eyes left and right, and saw the ageing soldiers lined up, no fear in their eyes, just grim determination. Ready, as they always were. A wry smile touched the corner of

Silus' lips. *These wolves thought they were here to get some easy pickings; how wrong they are.*

'Soldiers of Rome!' he bellowed. 'You have lived your lives by the sword. Served your legion, and your empire with honour!' The veterans roared. Vitulus, howled in defiance, drew his sword and rasped it against the worn iron boss of his shield, soon the rest joined in. BANG.

BANG. BANG. The noise was like thunder, raging across the snow-covered sky. 'For over twenty years, we have kept these Wolves pinned down on the other side of the great Danube. And we have all lost friends to the thin kiss of their blades.'

The veterans growled in anger, red hot rage burning in their hearts. BANG. BANG.

BANG. Swords crashed against shields, the noise rose to a pitching crescendo. 'Today brothers, we fight our last fight. But do not despair, for tonight we dine with our fallen heroes. Mithras watches over us, brothers. Let the Bull's rage pour from you today. These Wolves thought they were coming here for an easy raid. They came to kill you. To rape your wives. To take your hard-earned coin. Will you let them trample over you? Will you go quietly into the next life, or will you show them what men of the Fourteenth are made of?' Swords thrust into the air as the veteran legionaries roared in defiance, each determined to sell their lives dearly.

Sixty paces or so separated the two forces. The Germani advanced slowly, each building up the courage to charge a wall of shield boss and sword point. No matter how small the wall, even the cockiest warrior found himself questioning his choices when faced with a snarling warrior tucked safely behind a lime wood board.

121

Fifty paces, and Silus could make out individual faces approaching out of the mist; they were like a hedge row topped with spears. He spotted Euric in the front row of his men. He was a barrel of a man, in the prime of his youth. Long blond hair turned white in the blizzarding snow. He screamed and yelled as he urged his men on. The bloodlust seemingly already upon him. *You're mine,* vowed Silus. Tightening the grip on his shield, the Capricorn emblazoned on the front still as impressive as the day he was issued it.

Thirty paces. 'NOW!' barked Silus. Thanks to years of iron discipline drilled into the veterans, they immediately formed into a wedge, with Silus as its tip. 'Fourteenth legion, move out, double time.' The wedge was moving forwards before Silus had even finished speaking.

The Wolves started to howl, but the Eagles made not a sound. 'Ready javelins.' Men picked their targets as they eased their first *pila* out from behind their shields.

Twenty paces. 'Loose!' A hundred *pila* were thrown with a grunt. At such short distance, all found their mark. It was carnage in the front rank of the raiders. *Pila* crunched through armour, bone and muscle, gore splashed into the misty air and turned the snow red as it drifted ever downward, covering the ranks behind in crimson blood. Horses bolted and threw their riders as they were struck by the incoming hail.

Euric watched as the first wave of javelins arced into the air and were lost in the haze and snow. *There is a reason no one fights in winter.* He had no idea what was going on around him. He had to remove his helmet just so he could hear the man standing next to him, such was the force of the snow-driven wind. He thought of how he was going to give his king a piece of his mind when he returned home.

Surely no revenge or reward was worth this? His hands were blue and gripping his spear and shield had become too much, so he had discarded the heavy oval shield. The pain in his feet had spread past his ankles and every step was agony. His helmetless head was covered in wet and melting snow, freezing water dripping down his sodden hair so he had to squint to keep it from his eyes.

Again, he cursed the old bastard Alaric. Safe and dry on the other side of the river waiting for him to do all the hard work. Still, there couldn't have been more than a hundred men facing him. Soon he would be warming himself on the fire of Silus' burning home. The thought made him smile as he trudged through the snow. He was still smiling when the *pilum* fell out of the sky and burst through his left eye socket, powering through his brain and breaking out the other side. An explosion of hot brain, bone and blood burst from his skull and covered his neighbours. A spark of red and brown in a morning of grey, it was the last thing some of them saw.

'Ready, second *pilum*!' No let up from the eagles. Their blood was up now and they had seen their prey falter. 'Let 'em have it!' At point-blank range the second volley did more damage than the first. Javelins flying straight and true into the faces of their targets, the field was an orgy of blood and guts now.

Silus watched in satisfaction as Euric's head exploded as his *pilum* ripped through his eye. *Say hi to your father from me!* The pure white ground was a murky lake of red and brown now. Dead men littered the ground and the mongrel raiding force had to slow and pick their way over the bodies. Some of the younger ones were throwing their heads to the rear, their nerves shredded under the brutal barrage of lead-weighted *pilum*.

123

'Draw swords!' Five paces now, the wedge running full tilt over the gore-splattered snow, iron hobnailed boots giving them an advantage in grip and balance. 'THE FOURTEENTH!' cried the eagles as they smashed into the front rank of the withering Germani. Shields held high as they ripped a great hole through the centre of their ranks. Silus' sword arm was blood-red already. He smashed his shield into the nearest man, his right arm reached under his shield as he scythed his gladius up into the groin. The man dropped to the floor without a sound.

A spear point appeared out of the blood-tainted mist, Silus threw his head to the right and sent a quick prayer to Fortuna that he had seen it in time. Using his shield to pin the spear past his left shoulder, he stepped inside the shaft and head butted a grey bearded warrior. He swiped his sword along the other man's throat as his head was thrust back. He had stepped out of the wedge now, but he didn't care. Death came for them all that dark and miserable morning; he would take as many with him as he could. Two oval shields appeared at his front, veteran men who knew a killer when they saw one, coming on steadily and not taking any chances.

Buric had stood in so many shieldwalls his brain found it hard to remember one from the other. Though he didn't think he had ever fought in weather this bad. He had stood in the fourth rank – alongside his brother Tivok – and the two had joked that they need not bother drawing their swords as it would all be over before they had walked ten paces. But here they were, standing in what was now the raiders' front rank, and he began to regret leaving the warmth of his fire in the depths of winter.

The man they faced was the one they called Silus, and it appeared he was a man worthy of his deathly reputation.

124

He was covered in gore and the hot crimson steamed off his body. His face and right arm were stained with the lifeblood of his victims, and he screamed in defiance as he saw the two of them approaching at a respectful pace. The brothers shared a glance, reading each other's minds in the split second their eyes met. Buric circled round to the left and Tivok hunched behind his shield and continued to creep towards the giant.

Buric watched as his brother took the first blow straight onto his shield boss. The force of the blow was evident as Tivok – who was among the broadest men in the Obii tribe – was thrown onto his back. The next great blow cut the top of his shield to shreds. Throwing it aside, he roared and thrust his spear into the face of the blood-crazed Roman.

Judging the time was right, Buric leapt towards the back of the old eagle. Thoughts of his son's awestricken face when he would regale him with the tale of the time he killed a first spear centurion in the snow and fog filled his mind. He was only one now, but before long he would be out in the fields with the other young boys learning which way round to hold his first spear. His wife would revel in it when he returned home. Her father had been one of the greatest warriors of his generation, and he'd had to fight him to first blood to earn his daughters hand in marriage. He was already yelling in victory as a short sword plunged into his exposed left side. He felt the blade twist in his guts before it was pulled free. Slumping to his knees, he gazed up into the driving snow and concentrated on keeping hold of his spear. It seemed he would be filling the benches of Wotan's hall that night, rather than planning an exaggerated story of his heroics against a few old eagles on a miserable winter's morning.

Silus dropped his shield and caught the shaft of the hastily cast spear in one fluid motion. *Still got it.* He ripped the spear from the grasp of the terrified raider, spinning it in his hand so the point now faced its owner, he drove it through his face and felt it stick in the frozen ground.

There was no one willing to face him now. A half-circle of shields sat shaking in the cold as each man willed another to step forward and face him. The sounds of battle raged all around him. Grunts and screams and wails in victory and terror. Red-shielded veterans were appearing on either side of him, as the old-timers fought like devils to catch up with their leader.

'Still here, sir?' Vitulus' face was a harrowing vision with thick black blood pasted over his linen-white scars.

'Just getting warmed up, brother. You lot got another charge in you?' They were surrounded now and Silus reasoned there would already be men scurrying off towards the farm in their eagerness to be the first to get their hands on some gold. *Just got to keep as many of the fuckers here for as long as we can.* 'Well, what are we waiting for then? At them!'

With another rousing cry of 'the Fourteenth' the remaining eagles swooped down into the leaderless wolves. Keeping as a unit, they thrust and hacked and stabbed their way through the Germani until their sword arms tired and their shields felt like dead weight in their palms.

Silus felt himself start to tire. His second wind not carrying him forward as much as the first. In the centre of the shrinking wedge, with shield and spear all he could see, he didn't notice the heavily armed cavalry preparing to charge on his left. He couldn't see the panicked German infantry scurrying out the path of the charging horses. He

126

did not hear the order from Vitulus to turn and face the oncoming threat.

The eagles fell in droves. The remaining men quickly found themselves isolated.

Silus' head darted from left to right, seeing not his brothers but German riders charging all around him. One rider was making right for him, a merciless grin on his face as he leant from his saddle, his blood-soaked spear tip ready for another kill. Silus shifted his weight to his left, and raised his shield to block the blow. As he raised his arm, a spear from his blindside ripped into his armpit, tearing bone from limb. The charging horse then tore him from his feet, and sent him spiralling through the air.

This is it, was all he could think as he crashed back down to earth, the air sucked from his lungs on impact. His sword and shield were gone, ripped from his grip the moment the beast tore through him, his left side drenched in hot black blood. *I will not go lying down.* Finding the strength to move, the old centurion clambered to his feet, a spear finding its way into his palm.

A rider approached at an easy canter. The noise of battle had died with the last of the ageing legionaries. Silus gripped his left side and felt the pulse of the lifeblood pouring onto the snow. He breathed in deep, the smell of blood, shit and piss. *The smell of war.* The metallic taste in his mouth and the urging need to vomit, he knew he hadn't long left in this world. *Marcia, my love. I am coming.* A thousand thoughts spun in his weakening mind. Albinus at the forefront of them all. *If only I had come to my senses earlier. We would have had more years together. Get yourself safe, son. Live well. Remember me.*

'Well, well, well. What 'ave we got 'ere.' Of all the voices Silus expected to hear at that moment, he knew immediately that he should have guessed it sooner.

'Alaric. I should have known.' The one-eyed man vaulted from his horse like a man half his age. He strutted towards the dying first spear, revelling to see him brought so low. 'I swore to meself that day. When you took my eye and my pride. One day I would 'ave my revenge on you. I didn't pray to no god, didn't give any great sacrifice. But I swore to me. I wouldn't do it for no god, or no other. But for me! I swore to end you. And 'ere we are.' His toothless grin sent red-hot rage burning through Silus.

'You son of a cur! I should have finished you when I had the chance.' He changed the grip on the long spear in his palm, determined to take this old crook with him.

'Yes. Yes, you should've. But you didn't, and 'ere we are.' He drew his great sword in one fluid motion, the dark iron blade with the black pommel fitted perfectly in his palm.

'Any last words?'

'AAALLLBBBIIINNNUUUSSS!'

The two men struck at the same time, Alaric's blade whirling over his head in a great arc as he sent the edge biting down into Silus' skull. The Roman's spear ripped up from low to high and took the one-eyed German high in the right shoulder. With a loud thud and crack, both men collapsed onto ground that was mush, a mixture of trodden in snow and mud and men's blood and guts. The snow continued to fall on the still men's bodies, the wind carried on blowing and a flat winter's sun was just starting to break the shrouding mist that had covered them all morning.

*

Albinus woke with a start. It was dark still, in the small barracks room. Dark, and freezing. His throat was as dry as the desert. His head pounded like Fullo had whacked him with the butt of his spear, but still he could not help but smile at the memories of the night before.

He stretched his legs and gently rolled over, cautious not to wake Licina from her slumber. But she was not there. He panicked for a moment, sprung up out of the blankets and called her name. He got no reply. *Where is she?* Reason won over his mind in the end. *She always was an early riser.* His stomach rumbled as he nestled back down in the warm bed.

Maybe she's gone to get me breakfast.

It was to wails of terror he next woke. The sun was out now, the pale white light peeking through the open gap where the blanket had slipped off the window. The screams were getting louder. Desperate, terrified voices clearly in flight.

Leaping from his bed, he threw on his tunic and cloak. Couldn't find his belt. No time to spare. Plunging his feet into leather boots, he ran outside and through the open gates into a snow-covered wood. *Beautiful.* Despite the urgent need to discover what was afoot, he took in the sight of pine and yew, needles covered in glistening snow against a backdrop of black trunk. Winter did throw up some great looking scenery.

More screams snapped him out of his trance. People were approaching. He recognised some. Old wives and young children surrounded by hounds appearing out of the dense fog.

'What's going on?' *Where is Licina?*

'Raiders! By the river! The men have stood to face them. But there were so many! We must get away!' The grey-headed old wife spent not another second on Albinus, and ushered the children she had been harrying along into the small fort. Walls were walls, after all.

A whimper left Albinus' mouth. He was ashamed of it immediately. Raiders were attacking his home. Hardened wolves from across the river were stalking his father and tearing their claws into the people he loved. But instead of running and meeting his foe, he stood still, frozen to the spot. And whimpered. *Coward.*

People streamed past him. Many still wore their night clothes, some were fully dressed and seemed to have all their possessions in their hands. One old lady bowled right into him. He recognised her, Martha. She used to sing him to sleep when his parents went out to party with their friends when Silus was off duty. She gave him not a second glance now. Eyes wide in horror as she hitched up her skirts and ran barefoot behind the fort's walls.

Still frozen to the spot, he wondered what he should do. *Licina. Must find Licina.* Surely she would be with the crowds, making her way to safety. Yes, he reasoned. He would find her if he just followed the path out of the woods.

He fought against the oncoming tide of fleeing elderly. He scanned every face, hoping to see her or Fullo or Turda. He had seen none of them by the time he arrived on the fields covered in fog and carpeted in thick snow.

The sounds of battle raged in front of him, though he could see no evidence of it. More people were flooding from the settlement, the black shadows clear in a morning of white and grey. A horse whinnied, off to his right. And then two shadows exploded from the swirling fog.

Albinus felt his heart thud like thunder and his bowels nearly void down his leg as he saw what he thought were two raiders heading at break-neck pace to spear him in his guts. He didn't move, didn't even cry out. Just stood there and winced. *Pathetic.*

The horses reined in right in front of his face, sending snow spraying all over him. 'Mount up, lad. Quick!'

Bucco loomed over him. His eyes red-rimmed and his expression gaunt. 'Quickly, Albinus, let's go.'

He stood there dumbstruck. Gaping like a simpleton. He had expected to be killed. For there to be a shining spear tip flying towards him and tearing apart his rib cage. Instead he looked into the eyes of a man he had known his whole life. A surge of confidence and courage flowed through his veins. It warmed him.

'What's going on? Where's father? Licina?'

'We've been attacked. Thousands of the sheep-fuckers. Your father is doing what he can to hold them back, but he won't last long. I don't know where Licina is, but she's a smart lass, she'll see herself safe. Now come on! You're with me and we're going to get the Fourteenth down here. Teach these whoresons a lesson they won't forget in a hurry!'

The shouts and screams and clang of metal on metal seemed to subside as he vaulted onto the spare horse. Flames appeared in the never-ending grey. The only sign that there were homes there to burn. The screams of the women and children continued, more and more still appearing out the mist with panicked expressions and wide-eyed looks behind them. He gazed into the flames and thought of the rock that was his father. *Surely a man as stubborn as him could not be dead?* No matter what he had thought of him, he had always been there in his life. A formidable man, feared and respected in equal measure by

131

almost everyone he knew. It seemed impossible that he could be killed. *Did I ever tell him that I loved him?*

And Licina. *Where are you? I will return with the legion and see you safe. I promise, my love.*

Albinus cast one last look back towards the blazing inferno that had been his home, the only one he could really remember. Tears streaked down his face as he forced himself to turn away. As he kicked his horse into a gallop after Bucco, he could have sworn he heard his father scream his name. But when he turned back, all he could see was smoke and destruction

Chapter Eight

December AD 167 – Legionary Fortress of Carnuntum, Pannonia

'Taurus, d'you see 'em?'

'Yeah. They look well pissed. Purses still jingling though, shall we 'ave 'em?' Taurus was the youngest of this gang of street kids. This was his first chance to show the older kids what he could do. Furius, the leader of the group, was watching on, and Taurus was keen to prove his worth. Taurus peaked his head around the corner again. Peering into the pitch black alleyway the two legionaries had stumbled down, just about managing to make out the two hulking, stumbling forms of the soldiers making their way to the east gate and out towards the fortress.

'Yeah, I reckon, got to have a fair few denarii on 'em.' Niger slid down the alley behind them. A predator stalking his prey. Taurus made to follow, bare, dirty feet silent on the cobbled floor. They were closing on the two soldiers, and could hear snaps of their wine-soaked conversation.

'D'you see the state of that barman by the end? Ha! You could practically see the shit coming out of his breeches!' The bigger of the two lurched to the left and hit the wall with a crash as he recalled some tale from earlier that night.

'I know!' replied the smaller. 'Thought he could overcharge us for that horse piss?! These pricks need to know not to mess with the Fourteenth, if I ever go there again I'll rip his fuc—'

Niger smashed into the smaller man with a howl, knocking him off his feet and sending him crashing into the side of a small cart the street kids had positioned there earlier that night. This being a common spot for relieving soldiers of their possessions as they stumbled back to their fortress. The smaller soldier gasped in shock as his head bounced off the side of the wooden cart. Dazed, he slumped down onto his back, unable to rise.

Taurus was too slow in getting to the bigger man. Instead of committing to a headlong charge like his mate, he came forward at a slow pace, knife slowly circling in his right hand. 'Don't want any trouble, mister. So just hand over that purse and you can be on your way.' His heart was beating like the clappers, his palms sweaty, knees weak, but his voice was steady.

The soldier drew himself up to his full height, puffing out his huge chest in the process, 'You know what you're doing with that, boy?' His voice was iron, fearless. Taurus gulped, and took a step back. Eyes darting left and right for his partner. But all he could see was the other soldier, still flat out on his back.

'Vitulus, you old dog, still with me?' The huge soldier's eyes never left Taurus as he spoke.

133

'Y...yes, sir. Head hurts like hell. Can't believe that puppy got the drop on me.' The man called Vitulus winced as he rose to his feet. Staggered back against the cart and rubbed the open wound on his head. He turned towards Taurus as he spoke, moonlight revealing his claret-coloured face. 'Where's the other one then? I'm gonna cut his balls off and feed them to his fu—'

'Peace, brother, no one else needs be hurt tonight. What's your name, boy?' The old soldier's eyes still hadn't left Taurus and his knife, who was suddenly transfixed by his icy blue stare.

'Taurus...sir.' Sheepish now. Taurus looked at the floor, embarrassed and scared, the fact that Niger had left him to his fate dawned on him.

'Made quite a habit of robbing my soldiers, haven't you, boy? I never quite believed them myself, which is why me and my optio here decided to wander back this way to see for ourselves. You got a home? Family?' The soldier took one step forwards towards Taurus, his huge frame filling up the moonlit alley.

'I... err...I... it's my first time. Don't have any family, sir.' He wondered why he was calling the man 'sir' even as he did.

'Then where do you live?'

'On the streets, sir. Just sleep anywhere I can find really.'

'Your mother, father, where are they?'

'Dunno, don't remember 'em. Been on the streets my whole life.' Taurus was still looking at his bare feet. Scared now, he knew he had no chance against this giant of a man.

'Would you like a family? A sense of belonging? I may be able to help you with that.' The soldier took a step

134

towards Taurus, arm outstretched. 'Give me the knife, lad, no one needs to get hurt.'

'Sir, you're not seriously think—'

'Quiet, Vitulus.' The smaller soldier muttered to himself as he continued to get himself to his feet. 'Army's no place for a kid like that.'

'My name is Silus, I'm the first spear centurion, first cohort, Fourteenth legion. Why don't you come with us? We can give you a bed, clothes, food. You can help around the fortress, then when you're old enough, you can sign up to the legion. Gotta be better than robbing people for food and sleeping in the streets. What d'you think?' The soldier called Silus took another step towards Taurus, a warm smile fixed on his huge mouth, those icy blue eyes lighting up the dark alley.

Taurus was taken aback, him a soldier? He thought through his options. He had no real friends out on the streets, any he did have were long dead now. No family to go home to, and after this disaster there would be another gang he would have to avoid. Huh, he chuckled to himself, wasn't like Niger had stuck around to help him out. And this man, Silus, was the first spear of the Fourteenth legion. The most senior centurion in the whole legion, a man that would keep his word. Well, Taurus thought, don't have any better ideas.

'Okay, I'll come. Can we go now? Rest of the lads are back that way, rather not bump into 'em.' Taurus cast a wary glance behind him, conscious of Furius, whom he was sure was still watching from the shadows.

'Of course, I can already feel the beginnings of a rather horrific hangover coming on anyway, and Vitulus here is going to need some medical attention after what your mate did to him! Come on, let's go, I'll introduce you to my

135

wife, Marcia, the most beautiful woman in all Pannonia. She'll fix you up with something to eat. She's pregnant, you know, it's gonna be a boy, Juno has answered my prayers, I can feel it...'

First spear centurion Taurus snapped out of his trance. 'Silus...dead...he can't be...tell me everything again, Bucco, from the beginning.'

Tired beyond exhaustion, hungry beyond starvation. Bucco sighed as he prepared to tell his old centurion his story again.

'We were ambushed, sir, wolves from across the river. They came at dawn; whole settlement was asleep. Except the old man, o'course. He called us to arms. Got the whole lot of us together, gave the women and kids a chance to get away. He ordered me to leave them. To come here to you and tell you what happened. Told me to get you over there straight away and deal with 'em. When I left...it was looking pretty bleak for the lads, sir, whole settlement was up in smoke. There were thousands of the bastards, no more than a hundred of us old eagles. No chance they would have made it, sir.' Tears welled in Bucco's eyes as he finished his tale. Shame filled his heart, guilt that he was still alive and his brothers were dead.

Taurus was speechless. Silus had been like a father to him. Ever since that night in Carnuntum, where he and Vitulus had saved him from the streets. Silus had fulfilled his promise, given him a home, a purpose. When he had been big enough, Vitulus had enrolled him into the first century, first cohort of the Fourteenth. Best damn day of his life that. Until, when the two old soldiers had retired, Taurus had been called into the Principia. Named by the legate as the new first spear of the whole bloody legion.

136

That had been a shock! *No other man for the job,* Silus had said.

He suddenly realised he hadn't seen his old mentor since that day. *How many years now? Eight? Nine?* Full of regret like a brimming barrel of ale, weighing him down. *Even when Marcia died, I should have gone.* Taurus was re-awoken from his gloomy thoughts by his optio clearing his throat.

'Sir? Orders, sir? We should march at once.' Abas stood at his centurion's right side. He too had come through the ranks under Silus and Vitulus. But he knew the pain he felt at their loss would be worse for his superior, having witnessed first-hand the close relationship they had shared.

'Abas, get the first cohort ready to march at once. I will go and speak to Felix.' Without another word, Taurus turned and exited his small office, sited on the end of the first cohort's barracks. He stepped out into the freezing winter air, this morning's hangover all but forgotten now. He walked slowly out onto the Via Principalis, the main road running from east to west through the Fourteenth's fortress. He rubbed his huge calloused hands over his tired and unshaven face, and winced as he caught the beginnings of a scab on his split bottom lip. Caused by some argument or another about a rather pretty redhead working the bar in the Sword and Sheath last night. *What was her name again? Probably not the right time.*

He made his way through the traffic on the road and came to a stop in front of the *principia*: the legion's headquarters and where the senior command spent their days. Nodding to the soldiers on guard as he walked through the stone archway entrance, he turned right in the small open top courtyard and made towards Felix's office.

137

He wondered how he was going to break the news to his superior.

Felix was the legion's camp prefect, and deferred only to the legate himself. A career soldier. He had no social standing as such. He'd spent his whole adult life in the army, having signed up at the *campus martius* in Rome when he was fifteen. He hadn't seen Rome since.

The prefect was at his desk when Taurus stepped into the small and cluttered office and offered a quick salute. 'Sir, sorry to barge in, but I thought you would want to hear this straight away.'

Something in Taurus' tone made Felix put the wax tablet he was studying down and rise to his feet. Short in stature, big in girth, the veteran had let himself run to fat. The role of camp prefect being more administrative than physical, he no longer felt the need to try and keep himself in shape. He hadn't even donned his armour in years. A long mane of chestnut brown hair, slowly turning an ash grey topped his head. Dark brown eyes, a short stout nose and a mouth usually quick to smile. Felix was well respected around the Fourteenth. 'First spear, are you okay? You look awful.'

'I've just received some unwelcome news, sir. The veterans' farming settlement, the one Silus set up, was attacked this morning by a raiding force from across the river. Silus rallied the old eagles to make a stand, but from the sound of it they didn't last long. I'm requesting permission to take the legion after them, sir. If they're still on our side of the water, I'll make them pay.' A single tear appeared in the corner of the first spear's eye, the reality of the situation becoming more painful now he had spoken it out loud.

'Silus...dead?' Felix slumped back down into his chair, hands rubbing his face. 'This happened this morning?'

'Yes, sir, Silus sent a runner. Bucco, a former soldier from the first, to break the news. He said that when he left the whole settlement was aflame, women and children were running to the woods for safety, we need to act now if there are to be any survivors.'

Felix looked into the eyes of the first spear, assessing whether the man was in the right frame of mind to lead this attack. Taurus was one of the biggest men in the legion. A huge and finely muscled torso, legs like tree trunks, he could hold off numerous opponents in the shield wall alone. And could hurl a *pilum* further than any man Felix had ever met, even Silus. Long, dark, flowing hair that wouldn't be uncommon with the barbarians across the river, a nose so flat and broken it was almost embedded in his face, and huge broken lips surrounding a mouth missing most of its teeth. Taurus looked every inch the fearsome centurion that his reputation carried. But it was those big circular dark eyes that worried Felix: pain and anger were evident there. *Can you be trusted to make the right decisions in the field today? Will your thirst for revenge cost your boys their lives?*

'I'm worried about your temperament, Taurus, you're angry, upset. I'm not sure you're in the right frame of mind to lead men into battle. You can go with your cohort, but legate Candidus will command the legion. And I will be instructing Maximianus to stay close to you'

'Maximianus? Arrrghh, Mr By-the book, he'll just slow me down, sir.' Taurus threw his arms up into the air, frustrated with his superior's decision.

Maximianus was the Fourteenth's senior tribune, an experienced military commander. He was very cautious and did everything in accordance with his studies on

139

historical military actions. Taurus had a tremendous amount of respect for him, but didn't necessarily like him.

'That's my final decision, centurion, and take the cavalry with you. I'll send a runner to Maximianus and to Tribune Vindex. Now go, go and avenge Silus and his men. I'd better go and inform the legate. Get the legion stood to; I'm sure he will want to move as he soon as he's been briefed.'

Taurus saluted the prefect and made his way out of the small office. Felix sat staring at the space the centurion had just left. *Seems like yesterday it was Silus standing there, talking back, arguing my every point.* With a sigh, Felix rose to his feet, collecting his cloak and vine stick, never been without it since he made centurion, all those years ago. 'That's the problem with getting older, all your friends just seem to die.'

*

Albinus sat slumped on the bottom bunk in one of the first cohort's barrack rooms. It appeared this particular *contubernium* wasn't at full strength, as three of the beds were unoccupied. The other occupants were dead silent, unusually so according to optio Abas.

Footsteps followed by a barking of orders announced the return of Taurus, who marched straight back into his office. Not a glance left or right at the men of his cohort, getting kitted up in their armour in their rooms.

'Abas, Bucco in here.' The two men hurriedly ran into the first spear's office, situated next to the room Albinus had been told to wait in. He could hear mumbled tones as the three men discussed their plans for the march, and some grumblings about an 'uptight arsehole tribune' who it appeared would be joining them.

His ears began to burn as he heard Bucco mention his name. 'Albinus, Silus' son is here? Why didn't you tell me, man!' Taurus burst into the *contubernium*, causing the four soldiers, in various states of undress, to quickly form up and thrust a salute in his direction.

'Rullus, what in Jupiter's name are you doing with that armour? Get some that fits or go on a bloody diet! Longus, wipe that smirk off your face, puppy, if that blade ain't sharp it'll be going up your arse! Calvus, look at the state of those boots, if I see them that filthy again you'll be thrown into some shitty auxiliary unit on reduced pay, where your barbarian arse belongs! Habitus, I know you easterners are quite averse to taking it up the chuff, but if you don't put your fucking breeches on you'll be sitting on my vine stick. And as for you, Libo, you lumbering African bastard, that tunic is no longer white and that cloak is more brown than red, get new ones! Now then...' Taurus turned to the corner of the room, where a stunned Albinus sat gaping at the formidable first spear, *so like my father*.

'You remember me, son?' Taurus' tone became more gentle as he approached the grief-stricken lad.

'Yes. You're Taurus, my father's friend. I remember you visiting us when I was young.' Albinus' pain was plain to see, his voice cracked when he spoke, breath coming in short rasps as he fought back the tears threatening to pour down his face.

'Yes, when you were younger.' *How long had it been? Gods, he only lived a morning's march away.* 'Your father, he took me in when I had nothing. Gave me home, a sense of belonging. I'd have died on the streets of Carnuntum if it wasn't for him. I tried to rob him when I first met him, he ever tell you that?'

141

A shadow of a smile whispered across Albinus' face. 'How did that go?'

'Not well! Vitulus didn't talk to me for nearly a year! My point is, Silus was like a father to me too. I loved him, and your mother. I can't imagine what you must be going through now, but you need to know that whatever you need, I'll be here for you.'

'Aye, and me,' Bucco gave Albinus a nod. 'The Fourteenth look after their own. Speaking of which, are we going to get going, sir?'

'We? You're no longer part of this legion, Bucco, you wanna come with?'

'Yes, sir. And sign me up for three years an' all. Never had a family of me own, those lads were all I had. There's gonna be a war coming after this, I reckon, and I wanna get at those bastards.'

Taurus looked over the old soldier. Still in shape, to his credit. Patchy dark grey hair, surrounding an enormous white livid scar that took up most of the top of his head. Light brown eyes that were pure fire, a ragged, wind-worn face and a mouth with less teeth than his. Yes, Bucco would be a welcome return to the cohort. 'All right, Bucco, you're in. Back in the first century, you can join this *contubernium*, they're all as mad as you are.'

Bucco appraised the five men still standing to attention in the small room. From his experience, the *contubernium* who bunked next to the centurion's office were there because they were the most likely to get into trouble. In fact, that's where Silus had made Bucco and his mess mates bunk. Yes, these lads should do.

'You're gonna have to sort that armour out, though. We ain't used that segmented stuff for years now. When we get back, we'll get you signed up and issued with a proper

142

mail shirt. Anyway Abas, why are the boys still in here? I want them outside the east gate in one hundred heart beats, get to it!'

'Yes, sir! You heard the man, get that bloody kit on and get out now!' Abas stormed down the corridor running in between the men's barracks rooms. 'Out, all of you out! East gate, in formation. NOW!' Abas gave some of the lads a helping hand out the door with the butt of his *pilum*.

Taurus turned back to Albinus as the room emptied. 'I'll take you to our camp prefect, Felix. He can watch over you whilst we're gone. Get you some clean clothes and some food. I promise you, son, we're gonna get these whoresons, and make them pay.'

'I don't want to stay. I want to come with you. I can fight. That was my father they killed, and my friend Fullo was there…and Licina. Please, let me come.'

There was an icy look in Albinus' eyes. *Gods, but those eyes remind me of Silus.*

'Okay, but you're to stay at the rear. I'll get Abas to watch over you. Us centurions lead from the front, so I won't be able to look after you. Now let's get going, before they decide to slip away.'

Chapter Nine

December AD 167 – Veterans Colony, east of Carnuntum, Pannonia

Maximianus surveyed the ground from the riverbank. A sea of corpses littered the snow-drenched grass between the first cohort and what was left of the veterans' farming settlement. Black smoke filled the air and the smell of smouldering timber helped to mask the stench of open guts, blood and piss. Crows circled above, calling loudly to one another, their bellies filled with freshly dead flesh.

He'd always considered himself a student of Minerva. And with a helping hand from Fortuna, it looked as though his plan was coming off. Instead of taking the direct route to the farm, with tribal scouts watching their every step, Maximianus had ordered the first cohort to cross the Danube at Carnuntum and march along the river on the other side.

Crossing at the ford, he'd ordered the small number of cavalry he'd kept with him to go ahead and scout the Germani. It seemed everything was going to plan.

A wry smile touched his thin dry lips. *Nothing like being in the field.* A career soldier, he had been with the army since he'd been old enough to apply for a commission. Refusing advances to move further up the *cursus honorum* – the political ladder for men born to high ranking families – he had taken every commission in the military he could get hold of. Over twenty years he had served now, all over the empire commanding infantry and even once with the navy. His previous position had been commanding cavalry in the Parthian war, where he had earned praise and reward from Emperor Lucius Verus himself. *Not that the fat bastard saw any of the front himself. Ha! A warrior Emperor indeed.*

They had tried to retire him after that. Tried to get him to take a seat in the senate. With the opportunity to be consul and maybe even govern a province one day. But he had refused, instead taking the senior tribune's post with the Fourteenth, Pannonia being the one part of the empire he had spent little time in. Maximianus had no time for Rome. The cloak and dagger world of imperial politics was not for him. He belonged right here, out on the frontier, sword in hand and an enemy in front of him.

Removing his helmet to reveal a short crop of greying hair, he rubbed his hand through his growing facial hair, silently reminding himself to shave when he got back to base.

Roman officers should look the part, as he hopelessly told Taurus day after day.

Piercing hazel, almost silver eyes locked on to the waiting scout. 'Tell me again, soldier,' he ordered.

'The raiders are on the fields, south of the settlement, or what's left of it anyway. You'll have to take the main road through, no more than four wide. Once through, you should be able to get formed up quickly and advance on 'em down the hill. Only way out for 'em is south through the woodland. But it's thick, no real path and with the amount of numbers they have they'll never make it. Or they go east, towards the rest of the cavalry.' A sickly smile spread across the cavalryman's face. 'Rats in a trap, sir.'

'Nice work, soldier. You've done well. They have any scouts looking this way?'

'No, sir, all looking east towards Vindex and his lads, who are doing a pretty decent job of making a show of it, dust cloud must be a mile up. Some of 'em look to be getting ready for another fight. Most are just herding up the prisoners they've taken, roping 'em to horses ready for the ride home.'

'And numbers?'

'Bit more than a legion's worth, I reckon. Quite hard to count when they're swarming all over the bleedin' place.'

'Good, you've earned yourself an extra ration of wine tonight, now get back to your unit.'

The cavalryman's smile spread to his eyes at the sound of wine. He saluted smartly, vaulted back onto his horse and made for the rear of the column.

Maximianus strode along the front of the waiting column, gazing up at the weak winter sun. *Still early afternoon, plenty of time to finish these wolves. Praise the gods it's stopped snowing.* 'Taurus, signal for the other senior centurions and report to me. But quietly, no trumpets.'

What felt like an age later the first spears from every cohort were saluting and standing to attention.

'Right, men. Here's the plan. These cursed wolves are to the south; we must pass through what remains of this place. The road isn't wide enough to march in battle formation, so we stick to the column until we're through. Once we get on to the slope at the other end, we get into formation as quickly as we can. We'll keep it simple. Taurus and the first take the left, second and third in the centre and the fourth on the right. Fifth, sixth and seventh forming the next line and the eighth, ninth and Tenth in

146

reserve.' The huddled centurions all nodded. It was, after all, the most standard battle formation for a legion. 'The idea is that the first and fourth push round the sides and envelop the raiders. The rest then push through the middle and finish them off. Questions?'

'One thing to add, sir. Make sure your boys see the dead eagles strewn across this plain as we pass. Nothing like seeing your dead comrades to fill your heart with rage. This is about revenge, we need men filled with the iron will of Mars today.'

'As much as I agree, Taurus, it's imperative to keep your discipline. If the men go charging in like they're in the Iliad then it could be a disaster. Now, back to your units, we march at once. Keep it quiet 'til we're out the other end of the town; no sense in giving them any warning.' With a curt nod, the dismissed officers ran back to their centuries. Maximianus went in search of the colour party and legate Candidus, knowing Taurus could be trusted to lead the men through the gore-splattered fields and into the smouldering ruins of the farm.

*

Taurus marched at the head of his men. Everywhere he looked there were bodies, horse and men. Clearly, the old timers had put up one hell of a fight. For every Roman soldier, there were at least three dead Germani warriors. He recognised some of the corpses as he passed. He willed himself to keep his discipline in front of his men, and save his anger for the fight that was about to come. *At least the blasted snow has cleared.* The sun was out now and just a small layer of snow lay nestled on the grass. The wind was still bracing, and he shivered as his wet clothes clung to him under his armour. *Who crosses a bloody ford in winter?! Bloody Maximianus and his plans.* He turned to his cohort's standard bearer, Rullus, a real bear of a man, in need of a distraction.

'See you managed to get that chainmail over that lump of lard you call a stomach. At what age precisely do men stop growing taller and start getting rounder? You're a bloody disgrace, not sure you're fit enough to be my standard bearer anymore.' The grin that followed the last comment was enough to reassure Rullus that he wasn't in any real trouble.

'Tell you what's a disgrace, sir. These fine men being sent across the Styx by a bunch of hairy-arsed barbarian scum. You wait 'til we reach 'em. I'll show you I'm still the man to carry this.' He proudly hefted the weighty standard up on his right shoulder.

'You'll bloody well stay behind us when we get there! Nearly lost an arm last time you went marauding through the front line.' Habitus called out from the front rank. The ageing, bearded Syrian bore his left arm to show a viscous scarlet red scar running from his wrist to his bicep.

'Jupiter's hairy balls, are you still 'arping on about that?!' Calvus the Briton pitched in. 'I've seen worse than that in a tavern brawl in Londinium! You easterners are nothing more than a bunch of hairy-arsed tunic lifters.' He spat on the floor in front of the marching easterner to show exactly what he thought of his scarred arm.

'Why you little tattooed up fuc—'

'Shut up, both of you! I'm tired of you two old women having a pop at each other all day! Any more and you can join the corpses here and fatten the crows with what remains of your bodies!' Libo, the giant Numidian, cast a fearsome gaze left and right, making old Habitus shudder and Calvus' tattooed face go as red as his bright red cloak. 'Look around you, and remember why we're here. Most of

148

us served under the old man, and I'll be damned if you two bickering like old women is gonna get in the way of our revenge for his shade.'

A solemn silence settled over the marching ranks, eyes staring at the harrowing sight of the mass dead, breathing in the stifling stench of their entrails.

'Don't worry, Habitus me old mate, when I open my tavern in Syria, you'll be able to regale the local whores with tales all about your courage and valour. They'll be eating out of the palm of your hand!' A collective sigh swept across the front rank, even Taurus rolled his eyes. All of them were fed up of hearing from Longus, about his retirement dream of heading out east 'where the wine is endless and the women are plenty'.

'Out of his bloody purse, more like!' Rullus cackled a laugh as he turned back towards his mess mates.

'Longus, mate, how many times I got to tell you. If my homeland was full of pretty young drunk girls, up for a good ol' shafting from dawn 'til dusk, you really think I'd have wasted thirty years of my life trudging up and down this poxy river, trying not to get shafted by these tattoo-loving, animal skin wearing, inbred fuck faces!'

'Congratulations, Habitus, you've managed to insult me and Calvus in one sentence! And anyway, everyone knows you can only sign up for twenty-six years. Minerva has deserted you in your old age!' Rullus threw a wink back at the smirking soldiers, straightening the bear skin that ordained his helmet, customary kit for standard bearers throughout the legions.

'How many times do I have to tell you! My discharge papers were lost! Poxy clerks couldn't keep a record of the boils on their arse!' Four years now Habitus had been droning on about his lost papers, convinced he had already served his compulsory twenty-six years.

'Silence in the ranks!' Taurus stopped dead in his tracks. Eyes transfixed on a horribly mutilated corpse blocking his way. The neck had been carved down to the spinal cord. There were more gore-filled holes on the front of the torso than on a worm-ridden old hull that had been stabbed by Neptune's trident and sailed through his claret-coloured waters. The left arm was gone completely, but the right still gripped the hilt of a black blood-covered blade, which had sung its last song of a life spent stabbing and hacking and widow-making.

The face was untouched. An oddly peaceful picture amid a newly brewed storm of iron and destruction. 'It's Vitulus.' Taurus sank to his knees next to the old optio of the first cohort.

Vitulus had sold his life dearly. All around him were dead barbarians. Some piled two high, as they had charged into his shield and tried to hack and chop him down. A formidable warrior. He would have killed them quick with lightning thrusts of his short stabbing sword. *But there were just too many in the end.* Taurus reached out and gently shut the eyelids of the man who had helped shape him into the leader he was today. *I swear it by Mars, and Mithras, you will be avenged this day, old friend.*

A stony silence filled the ranks. Even those that had not met the man were aware of his legend. Mars' fury ran through those that did, like un-watered wine after a long day's march on a scorching summer's day.

A white crested helmet burst through the mass of sombre soldiers. 'Taurus, what's the delay?'

150

The centurion's tear-rimmed eyes showed nothing but fire as he turned to Maximianus. 'Found Vitulus,' was all he could mutter through chattering teeth.

Maximianus strolled over to the seething first spear, and got down on one knee to speak to him quietly. 'What was it you said to the other centurions earlier? Let them see what these wolves have done? Well, now they've seen. Let's use this anger, and turn it into a victory for the Fourteenth.'

Taurus absently nodded to the tribune and slowly rose to his feet. 'Can you see what these savages have done to our people? These men were soldiers of Rome, and they deserved a better end! We're going to rip these horse-fuckers limb from limb! We will take their eyes, their arms and their legs. We will rip off their pricks and stuff them in their mouths! They will lie on their backs for all eternity sucking their own cocks, unable to rise and greet their gods! This I swear on the great Jupiter, best and greatest! WILL YOU FIGHT FOR YOUR GODS TODAY?!'

The gathered soldiers roared so loudly the ground shook as though Vulcan had stirred his furnace so hard it was going to erupt onto the dead-covered earth. Maximianus threw his arms into the air. 'Well there goes our sense of surprise! Form up, we march at the double.'

Taurus thundered through the smoked-out remnants of a happy riverside settlement. His eyes gazed neither left or right at the smouldering buildings and burnt-out corpses. He had all the fuel he needed for his fire. The first cohort quickly reached the downward slope on the south of the settlement, where the road led onto a wide valley plain. He knew in the summer these fields would be covered in glorious barley, shimmering and swaying in the breeze. Today they were littered with mail-clad raiders. They snatched at their shields and rushed into a battle line at the sight of a full legion taking the field against them.

The first cohort veered to the left without an order from their centurion, who spat curses and phlegm at the first sighting of the enemy. Habitus drew a small slim bow from behind his back, and threw his shield at Longus. 'Make yourself useful lad, hey Calvus! Usual wager on the body count?'

'You can pluck as many as you like with that pretty little bow. Once the shields meet, I'm gonna cleave me some skulls! And yes, normal wager! I look forward to drinking my winnings tonight.' A crazed smile swept across the Briton's face, as he pulled a razor-sharp single-headed axe from his belt, deadly in a shield wall. Calvus could pull down his opponent's shield and stick a head of iron between their eyes whilst they were still pulling back their swords for the first thrust.

Taurus' ears were filled with the sounds of men readying for war. Centurions barked orders along the ever-growing Roman line, bullying and hitting men with their vine sticks to get the formation right. Metal clanked on metal as the legionaries adjusted their sword belts over their chainmail; he smelt the worn leather of his chinstrap as he checked it was secure. His shield suddenly felt heavy in his left hand, as it always did, his greasy palm sliding on the handle as he used his right to tuck away the straps used to sling it over his back whilst on the march.

His eyes scanned the forming mass of Germani not fifty paces in front of him.

Directly in front of the Roman left flank, a circle of captured women and children tied to carts and horses were shouting in adulation at the familiar colours of the force coming to rescue them, and fighting back at their would-be captors with added vigour and spite.

Trudge. Trudge. Trudge. The old Roman mincing machine continued its steady march towards the wolf pack. Forty paces, and the first *twang* of Habitus' bow claimed its first victim, a white fledged arrow replacing an eye in a nameless helmeted raider.

Thirty paces and the veterans' voices could be heard, telling the younger lads to raise their shields, adjust their grips on their *pila*. 'Ready javelins,' Taurus' command echoed down the lines by centurions and optios.

'Loose!' The sky went dark as nigh on three thousand *pila* arced their way towards the expectant crows and crashed back down into the mass of German raiders. Waves of them fell in a splurge of blood and screams, as the lead-weighted javelins ripped through mail, bone and gristle.

The raiders took a step back, the second time they had faced the storm of *pila* today. Sensing their fear, Taurus ordered the second volley immediately. Men who were clambering over their dead friends suddenly had to throw their shields over their heads; most reacted too late.

Two waves of *pila* had devastated the ranks of the leaderless raiders. Ash-made poles stuck up from the ground like a forest of death, their iron-tipped roots buried deep in the fertile ground of human remains. Ten paces now and the advancing Romans had to pick their way over the man-made mountain of the dead and dying. The raiders kept retreating, predator turned prey, they threw their iron-clad heads left and right, looking for an escape.

But there was none.

Taurus was the first to smash his way into their flimsy wall of wood, flesh and metal. He thrust out with his

153

shield, knocking his opponent flat on his back. Not bothering to stoop and finish him off, he used the hilt of his sword to rob a man to his right of his wits, then throwing his arm back to the left, he relieved a terrified raider of his windpipe and lifeblood.

'Into them! Come on, the first!' The blood lust immersed him from the first. The need to wet his sword on barbarian blood, he longed for it. He did not look back to see if the deep ranks of eagles followed him into the fray. He threw his shield rim first into his next opponent, the sharpened iron underside sliced through skin, tissue, bone and gristle to burst out the other side, another nameless son sent to meet his maker.

*

Maximianus stood in the front rank next to the first spear of the second. The raging sounds of battle filled his ears as his sword claimed its first victim, a vicious thrust with his short sword exploding through a raider's mouth with such force that it sent his helmet flying as the point ripped a hole in the top of his skull.

He hunched back behind his shield and revelled in the surge of energy that coursed through his veins. *As Mars as my witness, there is nothing like the fray!* Legate Candidus had offered him command of the battle. But who wanted to sit astride a horse at the rear while the men got to have all the fun? *This is where I belong.*

The raiders were scared. That had been clear as soon as they had lined up. He looked past his shield and tried to spot the leaders, but they must have already been dead as no one was trying to get the barbarians into line. *Lambs to the slaughter.* The battle was in full swing now and the Fourteenth were making it look easy. Each of the front-line cohorts had followed Taurus' lead and launched their

154

pila together. It had been devastating. Thousands must have died with iron points filling their torsos. Maximianus didn't think he had ever seen a wave of the deadly javelins do so much damage.

He cast a glance to the left where the first cohort had pushed forward well ahead of the second. He had decided not to fight with Taurus as Felix had asked him too. The first spear was a veteran and well tested when the blood started flying. He hoped he didn't make him regret his decision. He backed out of the front line and called for a runner.

'Get over to the first. Find Taurus and tell him he needs to slow his advance and wait for the second to catch up.' The scout saluted and galloped off towards the increasingly isolated first cohort. He grabbed the arm of the nearest legionary. 'Get back to the fifth and tell their first spear to come and bridge any gap that appears between the first and second. Run!' He watched until he was satisfied that the startled legionary was doing as ordered.

'Bloody Taurus! He's going to get us all killed!' Wading through the ranks of pushing legionaries, Maximianus headed to the front line to find some barbarian flesh to take out his frustration on.

*

'You're too far forward, you need to hold your ground and let the second catch up or you're gonna be cut off!'

'Tell me something I don't know! Taurus is lost in the fray. There's no holding him back now. Leave it to me, I'll get the lads back in line.' With a nod to the messenger, Abas turned back to the cohort and studied their right flank. The fourth line of their advance was now level with the front line of the neighbouring century. Sprinting over, he nodded to the optio of the left-side century second, desperately urging his men to push forward as fast as they could.

'What is it with you lads in the second? More used to sticking each other's "swords" in a rather more forgiving place? Maybe you'd rather be left back at home nice and safe where you can keep each other warm with a nice cuddle by the fire? Push, you useless bum-loving curs!'

Tides of abuse met Abas' shout, but the second reacted immediately, desperate in their attempts to prove Abas wrong. He watched on with satisfaction as they caught up with the second rank of the first cohort. Standing back and watching the battle unfold, Abas took in the unforgiving sea of destruction that was a Roman army in full swing.

Across the line, Abas could see the barbarians being pushed further back. The sound of war filled his ears. The steady trudging noise of the Roman advance, the shouts in joy and fear as spear and sword met flesh and guts. The metallic 'clang' of sword on shield as legionaries angled thrusting blows designed to bring their foe to their knees. The gut-wrenching, potent shit-filled air made Abas scowl as he pushed his way through the ranks of his cohort. He stood in the second rank and watched the veterans in front go about their business.

Habitus, bow now strapped on his back, gladius in his right hand, long knife in his left, swivelled and lunged as he cleaved a bloody path through the terrified barbarians. Libo, a full head taller than anyone else on that field, snarled his teeth as he tore a shield from a bearded raider and rammed his sword through his breast bone, gore-splattered point bursting out of the doomed man's back. Calvus, axe in one hand, shield in the other, was counting the corpses as he hacked and chopped his way through the

156

endless sea of metal and men. Longus was ducking and weaving as he came under attack from two brazen wolves. Abas moved to help the man, but as he took a step forward a giant roar fixed him in place. Bucco, old segmented armour ripped and covered in barbarian blood, threw himself at one of Longus' attackers, sending him flying across the field. So covered in claret he looked as though he was born with his veins on the outside, he jumped straight back to his feet and hacked his sword into the neck of his closest foe, his blood thirst clearly not spent yet.

Abas pushed his way up to Rullus, the standard bearer using the standard as a spear as he held his ground whilst the battle raged around him. 'Where in Ares' name is Taurus?' Abas had stayed true to his roots and continued to worship the old Greek gods.

'Up there somewhere, sir! He's lost in his rage. Ain't seen him this worked up in years. They're nearly broken now, sir, I'm sure he'll be all right.'

Abas continued forward, following a corpse stricken path clearly caused by his hurricane commander. He had to raise his shield to parry a blow from his right and then duck under one from his left as he searched for the rage-filled centurion. He brought his sword up to catch an arcing longsword and rammed the top of his shield into the jaw of his attacker.

Frederick recoiled from the strike to his jaw. The metallic taste of claret filled his mouth as he felt two of his teeth snap and fall onto his bitten tongue. He growled in anger and spat blood and teeth at his attacker. He was tired now. So tired. He struggled to remember why he had agreed to join this doomed raid.

His father had fought with Alaric, after he had been expelled from the lands of the Obii. That had been part of

157

the reason why he had joined this mongrel band of dead men.

Alaric himself had come to their home, spoken to their king and then to the men themselves. All knew of him. He had fought many battles over the years. Even one against the Obii, many years ago. But still he was respected by young men and greybeards alike.

He had spoken to them about their future. About what was important to them. Not about the wants or needs of petty kings who curried for favour with Rome and squabbled amongst themselves. No tribute from Rome meant no silver from their chief. No silver meant no home, no hope. Frederick had boiled with rage as the one-eyed old veteran had told them of the riches of Rome, the gold to be had, the grain to be taken. He had roared in anger when Alaric had asked them if they wanted to starve while Roman senators bought amber-laden jewellery for their mistresses and gorged on fresh meat until they were sick. *'Rome thinks us soft, come with me and let's prove them wrong!'*

Frederick roared his agreement with the rest. They would come with fire and sword and they would kill, rape and burn everything in their path. The only way for the tribes now was south. Into the empire to take what was theirs. That was the only path now. The first thing was to teach Rome a lesson. Make sure they were reminded of the power of the wolves. Make them remember why they paid the tribes to stay at home. That is why he was standing in a frozen field far from home in the middle of winter when he could have been laying in front of his hearth and whiling away the dark days with a full cup of ale. To make a statement. To be heard. At least that is what Alaric had said. But Frederick had noticed the old man hadn't crossed the river with the first men. He had hopped across when the vicious old soldiers were finished, and scampered right back quickly enough.

Should have gone back then. Rueful thoughts ran through his mind even as he parried the next thrust from the Roman's short stabbing sword. He hadn't managed to grab himself anything of value. All the women worth taking had been grabbed and their captors were having their fun with them before he could get his hands on any of them. And still the greedy raiders hadn't taken their prizes and made legs back to safety. Leaderless, they had grouped in the valley and hung a few slaves from the top of the mill. Then set it alight once they had finished wagering on who would stain their breaches first.

So lost in his misery and bitterness at the thought of returning home empty handed, he didn't notice the blade that crept underneath the big red shield that was reaching for his face. He met his shield with his attacker's, a loud clang as the iron bosses kissed, and just enough time to wish he had fathered sons before he fell lifeless to the ground, his guts following the sharpened iron out of his stomach.

Then suddenly there were no more wolves. Abas pulled his sword from the dead man's belly and looked for his next victim. He suddenly noticed he had reached the woodland that had been on the other end of the field earlier in the afternoon, and it was only now he noticed the sun was beginning to set over the distant Carnuntum in the east.

'Ahh Abas, glad you could join me!' He turned to look upon the speaker. Taurus was covered from head to toe in blood, guts and mud. His helmet was gone, and his long dark hair was lank and tangled with sweat and other men's insides. His face was so covered with crusted blood it was only the fire in his eyes that identified him as a still living man.

'By the will of Zeus, you okay?'

'Think so. All a bit of a blur, to be honest. One minute we were throwing our *pila*, the next…well, here we are! How are the lads? I'm assuming you kept 'em in check?' Taurus looked down to his hands and realised he couldn't unfold his right from the pommel of his sword.

'Just about. They pushed so far forwards chasing after your crazy arse that we nearly broke off completely from the second.'

'Huh! Bunch of useless cock-suckers. You know, I once walked in on their senior centurion being "unarmoured" by some young slave boy. Guess his men all take after him!' Taurus slumped down to the ground, grimacing as he sat in a brown puddle of snow and blood and shit.

'Right! Go and get them formed up. We'll retake the prisoners and round up any of the survivors. The legate's gonna want to know who organised this raid. Oh, Albinus okay?'

'Yes, sir, I'll get, right…Albinus…shit!'

Chapter Ten

December AD 167 – Veterans Colony, east of Carnuntum, Pannonia

A pale blue sky was turning the colour of the deep blue ocean as the sun set far away in the west. Albinus didn't know how long he had been standing there, staring at the mutilated corpse of the man who had been his father.

Crows squawked all around him, robbing the dead of their redundant flesh. The smell was appalling. Dead flesh, open bowels, piss-stained tunics and dead horse filled the air in his nostrils, not that he noticed.

The sight was something from one of his father's stories. The ones he would tell his old comrades round a fire at night. A story of blood and guts, of sword and spear. Clearly, it had been one hell of a fight. To his front, a long line, two deep, of dead Germani with *pila* pinning them to the ground littered the green carpet floor. Behind them, evidence of a Roman wedge tearing through the raiders' formation. Droves of barbarians must have fallen in the first seconds, in some places the bodies piled three high. Clear evidence of the Roman short sword doing its work, all the bodies had stab wounds to the neck or groin. And then, twenty steps further on, the cavalry must have charged. Hoofprints from the west converged on a mound of pale lifeless eagles, thick ash shafts pointing up to the sky as if they were daring Jupiter himself to save his precious soldiers.

But some of the eagles had fought back. Vitulus had made it through, and carved himself a bloody path across the river Styx. But not as far as his father. He had staggered west. Or maybe been thrown, judging by the horrific wound down his left side. He had not been wearing armour, not that it would have saved him. That though, hadn't killed him. Following the scarlet trail on the damp grass, Silus had made it back to his feet. Though not for long. The blow that had killed him was to the right side of the head, a savage lung-busting swipe from a German longsword. Judging by the size of the wound, Albinus doubted he could have even picked it up, let alone wielded it in battle. Silus had been a true eagle 'til the end though. Another puddle of blood lay where his attacker must have fallen. A crusted blood-tipped spear lay where the man would have lain. He didn't know if the man had survived and escaped, or whether some of his comrades had carried his body from the field.

Despair gripped the bereaved son. In one day, he'd managed to lose his father, best friend and the girl he loved. Not to mention everyone else he had ever known. He knelt by the body, hand gripping his father's, he said his goodbyes. 'I'm so sorry, father. I'm so sorry I didn't grow into the man you wanted me to be. I tried, gods I tried, but I'm just not as brave as you, not as strong. I hope...I hope I made you proud, in my own way. I love you, I truly love you so much...' Tears streamed down his cheek like rushing river water tearing down the great aqueduct.

'I wish we had more time to get to know each other. To be a real family. A team, like Fullo and Vitulus.' He shuddered in despair as he spoke those two names aloud, tearing his eyes from his father to look upon his lifetime friend and second. His ears pricked at a rustle in the grass to his front; wide-eyed he ripped his head back around, expecting to see a still breathing raider come to finish him off.

'He was proud of you. He loved you from your first breath to his last, and don't you ever think anything different.' Bucco looked like the walking dead, even his eyeballs were blood-stained. He knelt the other side of Silus, opposite Albinus.

'His last words to me weren't about his men, though he knew he was leading them to their end. It weren't about the women and children, who he knew he couldn't save. It was about you, lad. "Look out for my son," that's what he said. "Tell him I love him, and that I will be proud of him whatever path he chooses." Those were his last words to me.' Bucco put a giant, blood-black hand on Albinus' shoulder, and gripped him tight.

'And you're more like him than you think,' Taurus appeared behind the tear-rimmed Bucco. 'It don't matter you're not built like an ox like he was. Don't matter that you're not as handy with a sword and spear. It's those eyes, lad, those bright blue deep eyes. That icy stare, the iron behind it. You're your father's son, ain't no doubt about it. I know you'll make him proud.' The crimson-infested centurion knelt next to Bucco. The battle rage gone now, replaced with weariness and sorrow, he raised his right hand and handed a bundle of cloth to Albinus.

The centurion's son took the bundle and opened it up, revealing his father's sword. The blade just over a foot in length, a beautifully detailed, sun-stained yellow ivory handle, leather grip running around the middle. But what caught his eye was the same part that always had, the eagle carved on the handle. Gods only know how many days he had lost staring at that eagle, it used to make his father smile. *'How did you get this sword?'* His father would just smile.

'Why was he awarded this?'

'Huh?' Taurus startled out of his trance by Albinus' sudden question.

'He never told me why it was awarded to him.'

A sad smile tinged the corners of Taurus' mouth. 'Because he was the finest centurion this legions ever had. I'll tell you some stories one day, but not now, maybe once you're out of training.'

'Training?'

'Oh gods, yes! We were talking, me Bucco and my idiot second over there – he motioned to a guilty-looking Abas, standing twenty paces back from the three kneeling grievers. He was still recovering from the rollicking Taurus had given him for losing Albinus.

'We're gonna take you in, same way the old man did for me. Now I know that soldiering might not be your thing, but there's plenty other things you can do. Clerk, hospital attendant, stables, bath house…anyway, point being we ain't gonna leave you here alone, the Fourteenth will always have a home for you.'

'No… I mean yes! No, I mean…I mean I want to be a soldier. I want to fight, there's going to be more battles now right? Rome won't let this go unanswered?'

'I'd imagine so, yes. We got a few prisoners, once we get them talking, we'll find out who arranged this, and we'll get 'em back'

'Then I want to be there. Fighting, with the first. First century, first cohort, that's where I want to be.' *Just like my father.*

Taurus cackled a quick laugh, though his smile never reached his eyes. 'Said I was like your old man, didn't I?'

*

The pyre's flames glowed a bright orange against a backdrop of purple in a sky full of stars, like drowned gold sinking to the seabed, trapped aboard a sunken ship. Hot, angry tears flowed down Fullo's face, like an old steaming pot left out in the rain. He'd tried to fight back when the raiders had downed the veterans. Fighting in the porch of his home, his mother and Licina terrified and wailing inside, he'd stood his ground against the first two that tried to take him. He was sword to sword with a grey-bearded raider when a thump followed by a blinding light floored him. The last thing he had seen was his mother, knife in hand, being swatted like a fly as she tried to defend Licina. An unforgiving spear driven through her heart as she fell. And Licina, whom he had come to love as a sister, beaten and kidnapped, taken back towards the great river.

He had tried to get his mother to leave. But she refused. Wouldn't leave her husband to his end. And he wouldn't leave her. It had been too late by the time he had tried to get Licina clear. The veterans had already fought their last, and the rampant wolves were loose amongst the houses. Snow had blinded him as he frantically dragged Licina back to their home and tried to barricade the door. But it had been too late.

He had awoken to a Roman soldier – a tribune judging from his muscle-framed cuirass – feeling his neck for any signs of a pulse. The afternoon had passed in a hailstorm of grief and despair. Finding his father's body, reunited

165

with a broken Albinus, the pair stood and watched as their father's shades were sent to meet their gods. Fullo offered a prayer to Pluto, the god of death, and asked him to guide his father shade across the river Styx, and keep him safe from Gorgon, demon of the underworld and taker of dead men's souls.

Fullo turned towards Albinus, whose sharp blue eyes illuminated in the flame-bright sky. His hair was matted with dirt and sweat, two lines ran down his cheeks, scarred from floods of sorrow-filled tears. His right hand gripped tight around his father's prized sword, it looked as though the sadness had left him now, nothing but a thirst for revenge showed in those cold eyes. He still wore the faded blue tunic he had been wearing at the feast the night before – gods, that felt an age ago now – it clung to his skinny frame, unbelted and sodden. He no longer wore a cloak, though he must have been freezing. He just stood, still as a wheel-less cart, and stared into the flames.

'What will you do now, brother? Our homes have gone, our families too. What is left here for us in this world?' The hardest part of the day had been telling his friend about his wife-to-be. The pain and anguish on his face when he'd told him she had been captured.

'Revenge, brother, that's what we have left. I'm joining the legion, going to sign up to fight under Taurus. He thinks there will be a war. Rome will not let this go unanswered; already a messenger has been sent to the governor. They say he will gather the tribal chiefs, find who is responsible for this and make an example of them. I will be there when that happens.' His eyes never left the pyre of burning flesh as he spoke, as if he was trying to watch his father's shade cross into Elysium.

166

'Then I will join too, I won't leave you alone. We will have our revenge; this I swear on Jupiter and Mars. We will find who did this, and give them a bloody end.' The two men, for that is what they had become this day, clasped hands and turned back to watch as the huge golden pyre began to collapse. The weight of the burning bodies on the ashes of timber was finally too much. 'And we will find Licina, and get her home. Wherever she may be.'

Chapter Eleven

December AD 167 – North of the Danube, Germania

Licina woke to a pale, dull dawn, white light flooding in through the gaps in the tall pine trees. The tragedy of yesterday hit her like a well-placed arrow the second she opened her eyes. Fullo, fighting like a lion at the doorway to his family home, sword whistling in the blood-drenched air as he raged war against the raiders. Turda, knife in hand, teeth gritted, snarling defiance until the very end, when a barbarian spear point burst her great heart.

The smell of Germanic breath on her neck, harsh ale mixed with roasted meat. The feel of teeth and hands exploring her reluctant body, and the sight of her home being burned to the ground, of women and children locked in barns whilst they were put to the torch.

Just when she thought she was to be raped and burned with the other women, four men had stepped in. Not from the tribes, dark-skinned complexions, trimmed and oiled beards with neatly kept short dark hair, they had fought off her attackers. Tied her to a horse and whisked her back across the river. She had heard Fullo scream her name as she splashed into the Danube. As she was dragged out the other side, onto not a wet, green bank, but a shallow, lifeless, stone-filled beach. She turned back to see fire, smoke and blood-covered German warriors. Everything else was gone.

Albinus. He had been asleep when she left him. *I hope you stayed there, please be alive. Please.* Tears hot on her cheeks, burning her eyes as she silently sobbed into her grass-, blood- and mud-stained dress. With a guilty heart, she realised her tears were not for Vitulus, who died a hero's death with his brothers in arms. Or for Fullo, who emulated his father with his heroics defending herself and the lioness Turda, defiant to the end. *I did nothing.*

Everyone fought, and I did nothing. They were tears of shame.

The pain at losing those she loved she could have handled, recovered from. After all, she had been through that before. But the guilt of knowing she had just stood back, frozen by fear as people died trying to protect her, she could not. And where had it got her? Stranded on the other side of the river, with four strange men, who had shown no evidence of being able to speak Latin. They had ignored her yesterday. All day they had ridden, though she didn't know where. Tied to a horse and left to her grief, she had sobbed and wailed until darkness had fallen. Untying her from her horse and re-using the rope to tie her leg to the nearest tree, she had been left to cry herself to sleep. She had no idea where they were taking her, or why they had even bothered, when everyone else had been put to the sword.

Very slowly, trying not to make any noise, she turned her head to look at her captors through tear-stained eyes. The four men sat around a small fire, chunks of meat on the end of twigs sizzling away as they talked. Taking in her surroundings, Licina tried to work out where she was.

Surrounded by rock, pine, and giant yew trees, they were in some thick woodland, with the sun's first rays still struggling to force their way through the barrier of trunk and needle. They appeared to be at the bottom of a large hill, rare in these parts. Probably one of the ones she could have seen from across the river, as they couldn't have travelled far. One she would have longingly stared at from her comfortable home, wishing someone would steal her away for an adventure, where she could reinvent herself, start again. Well, that wish had come true, but all she wanted was to be back in her home, head on Albinus' shoulder as they kissed and cuddled the day away.

Casting her eyes left and right, she sought some sign of familiarity. Something that would jog a memory, a tree or rock she would recognise. This wasn't her first time across the great river. Her father used to take her hunting. She used to marvel at his ability with a bow or spear, the way he could strike down a fleeing deer at fifty paces. Those tears were back, threatening now, and the breath was knocked from her lungs, as for the first time since his death she could imagine her father's strong, manly features. A short ruff of dirty brown hair, that her mother kept short even though he preferred to wear it longer, in the way of his ancestors. Pale green eyes, so like shallow water sleeping in a summer's sun. That broad, powerful, chiselled nose and matching jaw line. A smiling mouth, big full lips, red like her mother's hair.

Licina sobbed aloud, shocked at the powerful memory of her father. She grabbed a handful of black, frozen soil, crumbling it through her fingers. It was as though she could see him now, stalking through these very trees. Pale eyes a picture of concentration, bowstring pulled back, broad head primed and ready, a small red scar on his right cheek where the iron-tipped arrow had pierced his skin so many times at the moment of release.

170

Closing her eyes tight, she tried to shake the memories. *Not now, not when I need my wits about me most. I must be strong, for Albinus. I must get back.* Unwittingly, her thoughts strayed to her mother. But still she could not picture that beautiful face, just a blur below hair made of fire. *Fire.* Suddenly her thought box thrust her back to the day before. The gut-wrenching stench of flesh set alight, of claret-coloured walls and black plumes of smoke. *I must be strong. I am not weak. I am cursed by no god. I must be strong. For Vitulus, Turda and Fullo. For Albinus.*

Slowly, she raised her head, still not ready for the four men to know she was awake. They all wore the same green cloaks, with a curious brown circular patch carefully sewn onto the back, as if there was something underneath they were trying to hide. The language they spoke was foreign to her ears, Greek maybe? Definitely not from among the tribes then.

She continued to stare, to try and get some understanding of who these men were. They were all in matching armour, which looked impeccably maintained under their green cloaks. Glistening chainmail, polished so it would shine even on the dullest of days.

Beautifully crafted brown belts tied around their torsos, with long curved spathas securely slotted into black leather scabbards. She would have known these men were wealthy even before she had a good look at their horses, which were unlike any she had seen before.

As black as the darkest night sky, they stood a full head taller than she. Dazzling, perfectly kept coats of short hair, shining silver in the dawn's pale light. Muscled torsos, they looked as though they belonged in the Iliad. Charging great Hector and Achilles through the bronze blazed melee, guiding their chariots as they fought their heroic

171

duel under the great golden gate. Five horses. *They were expecting to come back with someone. They were there for a reason.*

Raised, urgent voices snapped her from her trance. One of her captors had seen she was awake, and quickly marched towards her. Armour chinking as he made his way over the uneven ground littered with rocks and branches.

'Good morning. I am glad to see you awake. Would you like some breakfast? We are just humble servants, so do not have much, but there will be plenty for you when we arrive.' The man gave Licina a small bow, hands clasped solemnly together at his front.

'And where is it we are going? Why have you taken me? You could have just left me to my fate like my friends.' Licina was confused by the man's pleasant demeanour. Especially since not one of them had spoken to her the day before. The questions exploded out of her, unstoppable, just like when her father shot an arrow at a fleeing deer.

'We have been instructed by our master to find a suitable gift for the king and take them to him; we have selected you. You are to be a gift from our master to the king.' Another short bow, Licina still trying to place that accent.

'A gift? I am no slave! Who is this king you speak of?'

'Balomar. King of the Marcomanni. His hall is a few days' west of here. I do not know if you are to be a slave, merely a gift. It is up to the great king what he does with you.'

Licina sat in shocked silence. *Balomar? The Marcomanni have long been allies of Rome, something is not right here.* 'Was it Balomar who organised that raid yesterday? Has he turned his back on the empire?'

172

'My lady, it is not for me to say. I am merely a servant, carrying out my master's bidding.'

'And who is that?'

A raised voice, gruff and final in manner from one of the speaker's companions, cut short their conversation. 'I am afraid, my lady, it is time to leave. We are in the lands of the Quadi; they are not many, but unpredictable. We should not tarry here.' With that he turned away and went to ready himself for the day's journey, leaving Licina, emotionally drained and confused, to ponder what in Hades was happening.

*

Four days' riding passed without incident. Licina had been unable to coax any more conversation from any of her saviours, or captors, she had yet to decide what they were. She had been tied back to her horse, and had become so engrossed in her surroundings that she had almost forgotten the horrors that had befallen her sleepy home town, and the all too real memories of her long-forgotten father.

She had expected the terrain to be savage, the ground to be unfarmable, the people to be barbaric. She couldn't have been more wrong. They had exited the woodland onto a vast valley. Small hounds played with children as their parents quietly surveyed the land, checking the damage the winter had done to their fields. Inviting plumes of smoke lazily snaked their way towards the sky from the chimneys of the farmhouses. People stopped their work to raise their heads and say hello as their small party trotted past. Licina didn't speak the harsh Germanic tongue that was common in these parts, but interestingly, it seemed her companions didn't either. Once again, she wondered who these men were and just why she was being taken to the king of the Marcomanni.

The days went by fast as she rode, mostly in silence. She was amazed at the seemingly fertile land, the friendly farmers and the impressive-looking homes. It surprised her how much it saddened her heart to see the mass graves being dug for the dead. *It seems the plague knows no boundaries.* She imagined the food that could be grown on the vast farmland, and wondered how little had actually been produced in the last year. *It would seem as little as at home.* The weather was no worse than she was used to. Freezing during the day and near unbearable at night, she longed for even the ice-ridden barracks in Albinus' small fort, anything to protect her from the blistering wind.

Farm after farm they passed, each seeming bigger than the last. *So much land. No wonder Rome want this country so much. You could feed the whole empire with this many fields to plant.* Again her thoughts went back to Balomar and his tribe. Why did they need to raid? These were his lands they were on now, and they must have been growing twice the crops they needed. So why bother antagonising the empire?

'Why are you taking me to Balomar? The Marcomanni are a long way from my home. Surely, if anyone was going to risk a raid near Carnuntum, it would be Areogaesus, the Quadi are known raiders. My father used to speak often about skirmishes along the *limes* with him and his father.' *Limes* being the Latin phrase for border.

'Because my master has tasked me with taking you to Balomar, that is all I know.' The man, still nameless, did not take his eyes from a group of five or six bearded farmers, who had stopped working and come to stand by the side of the small road on which they were travelling.

174

Itchy fingers fondled axe handles, clearly as handy with them as they were their pitchforks.

The nameless man made eye contact with one of his companions as he spoke. She hadn't seen his face; he kept it concealed under his hood at all times. Hints of a growing grey beard were the only feature she could make out. He kept his right hand concealed, but Licina noticed he constantly looked into his cloak, reaching in with his left hand, as if there was something there he was protecting. He gave a slight nod to the speaker, as if he approved of his answer. *So, he understands. Is he the one in charge here?*

'You're lying, you must be. If you didn't know who ordered the raid, then why were you there with them? Something is afoot here, something much bigger than you or me, and you're too scared to tell me, I can feel it.' Licina eyed the man, whose dark eyes winced as she spat the last words with scorn.

'You will find out soon enough, child. Now be quiet, it would do none of us any good to be heard speaking Latin in these lands; we are in *his* territory now.' Licina assumed *his* was Balomar's, but satisfied that she had at least been able to ruffle the mysterious man's feathers, she settled down to a consented silence.

It turned out she didn't have long to wait to find out. By mid-morning they crossed a small rise to gaze upon a fortified town on the horizon. A huge hall could be seen, sitting atop a steep, well-rounded hilltop. Other buildings could be seen, jumbled and in no order, sloping their way down the hillside to the wooden defences surrounding the town. Huge billows of smoke plumed from the top of the giant hall, which Licina assumed was the home of Balomar.

175

Nervous now, her thoughts turned to what awaited her once they entered the home of the Marcomanni king. *What will he use me for?* And why was she being given to him in the first place? *I'll know soon enough. Must stay strong. Must find a way to get home. I will not fall back into the abyss of my mind. I will survive, for Albinus, I will survive.*

They arrived at the gates. Huge timber beams, twice the height of the godly black horse on which she sat, straddled together between great iron bars, surely bought from somewhere within the empire. Four giant men stood atop the parapet, patrolling their king's defences the way a mother lion patrols the ground around her cubs. They hailed a challenge to the approaching party, long ash-clad, iron-topped spears in their hands, white flashes of teeth through heavy-set beards.

Licina looked up into the great gates. Fierce, wolf like eyes piercing down beneath long manes of hair and dull, unpolished iron helmets. Another challenge, again no response from the four men who had brought her here, miles from her home into the heart of barbarian Germania. 'You don't speak their tongue, do you?' She arched an eyebrow at the only one that had spoken to her. 'Neither do you,' was his quick reply, before kicking his snorting horse forward, head rearing as it responded to its master's touch.

'We are here to see the great King Balomar, I bring a gift from my master.' The man reached within his cloak, pulling out a small brown pouch. Still mounted upon his great horse, he arched his right arm and launched the pouch, a huge throw, arching over the heads of the confused-looking guards.

'You...wait here.' With that he was off, leaving his three mean looking companions to watch the waiting party.

176

Licina studied the settlements defences, formidable looking, this place had been built to last. Huge timber beams rooted into the ground in an otherwise grey and lifeless land. All she had been told of the Germanic people led her to believe that they were nomadic tribes, constantly on the move, ravaging and raping their way through the endless sea of grass from the eastern plains all the way to western coast.

'What do you know about this Balomar? What hold does your master have over him? Clearly, you are not from these lands, I would like to know how your master and this king crossed paths.'

'I have never met the king, and what makes you think my master could have a king as powerful as Balomar in his power?' Not that he would let Licina know, but he enjoyed her questions; it had been too long since he had enjoyed any intelligent company, a shame he hadn't had the opportunity to speak with her more. *There will be occasions in the months ahead, I'm sure,* he thought with a smile. 'And as for where I am from, it is a long way from here. Where the east meets the west, and two great seas become one.'

The gates gave a sudden groan as it started inwards, old iron hinges left to rust in the rain and mist. 'Clearly he has something; the "great king" has kept us waiting no time at all.' Licina kicked her horse into life, tired of knowing nothing, tired of the silence, tired of being atop this great beast all day. She rode into the town at a gallop. *Must stay strong. After all I have endured, I will endure this.*

'Welcome to your new home!' the still nameless man called after her, chuckling into his well-trimmed beard. 'They call it Goridorgis, the fortress of the Marcomanni.'

Must stay strong, I must get back to Albinus.

Chapter Twelve

April AD 168 – Fortress of Goridorgis, Germania

Life had been strange for Licina since she had entered the great Goridorgis, fortress of the Marcomanni. She had been presented to the king, a barbarian war chief if ever there was one. Possibly the tallest man she had ever seen, to look upon his bare torso you'd think you were looking upon the god of war himself. His arms were thicker than the great wooden beams that sprung out of the earth and held up the great thatched ceiling in his mighty hall. His chest and stomach so rippled with muscle it would seem he would require no armour in battle, as surely no blade could pierce something so solid. His legs were wider than a hundred-year-old ash tree, and looked as though they were more durable too, with huge leather-booted feet rooted into the ground. This man would be a mountain in a shieldwall.

His age was hard to determine. His was not an old face, but a wise one, a learned one. It was a face that told a story of war, bloodshed, rape and murder. Deep, dark, menacing blue eyes looked down into your soul when their gaze locked upon you. Those eyes had seen murder, revelled in the blood fray, and wept for lost brothers when it was done. His jawline was expansive, well-built like the rest of him. A long and broad nose, and thick scarred lips, a mouth that possessed all his teeth, rare on the Germanic side of the river, where hygiene was said to be less of a priority.

He had looked upon her for less than five heartbeats, but Licina had felt her legs go weak, bladder fill, her heart start like one of those great black horses when they went off at a gallop. A small gesture with his giant right hand and she assumed she was dismissed, cast aside so the king could study his other prize, the great stallion that had brought her to this distant place.

Only three of the men that had brought her here entered with her. The one that had spoken to her turned to his companion just before he rode through the gate, the man with dark hooded face and the shadow of a greying beard, the one she thought was truly in charge. When the gates had opened he had lowered his head, half turned away from the onlooking guardsmen as though he did not want to be recognised. A muttered conversation had followed, before the younger Latin-speaker had followed her through the great gates and into the fortress.

Licina had no opportunity to question why the older man had not followed them in, or why he didn't want to be recognised. A thousand unanswered questions swirled around her mind, like fish caught in a fisherman's bucket, endlessly circling with nowhere to go.

They had been led into the king's great hall. Up a mud-made road, snaking its way through the appalling smelling town. Tribesmen, women and children lined the excrement-filled street, mostly in silence, lifeless, as they watched the party ride past. Licina took it all in. The poorly maintained, leaking wooden homes. Thatched roofs that hadn't survived the winter, and showed no signs of being repaired. Market stalls selling pelts, tunics and boots, merchants that had travelled through the empire and back struggling to sell their wares to people who had no wealth to buy with.

The men were thin. Armour drooping where once huge torsos had filled it out. Children wearing hole-ridden tunics, women wandering bare foot and in some cases wearing nothing but a rag. Everyone was filthy; it seemed no one had journeyed to a stream for a wash in a very long time. Her suspicions were confirmed then. These people were just as desperate as those living within the *limes* of Rome. She caught the eye of her nameless companion, who read the anguish on her face. 'The plague knows no boundaries – did you think your homeland was the only place affected?'

Her meeting with the king had been brief, and after her terrifying five heartbeats of being examined, she had been led away, unable to hear the muted conversation in muddled Latin between her companion and the formidable king.

Four months or more had passed since then, and she had barely any contact with the king, and assumed her deliverers had left the day they arrived, for she had not seen them since. The days had passed quickly, and she found the life of a slave not to be entirely disagreeable. She had even made two friends, siblings called Aelinia and Julius, twins from distant Gaul. Their father had been a legionary, but had never returned from the Parthian war. Their mother had died trying to fight off bandits from their doorstep. Julius had killed them over her dead body.

They had fled, made their way to the Rhine border, as they had no idea where else to go. Julius, who had always been handy with a sword, had entered into tourneys in the small arenas dotted down the river, his strong shield arm and quick wrists had earned them both a decent living for a

181

while. Until he had come across a fighter better than he. Aelinia had turned to selling her body in the months that had followed, keeping the coins trickling in needed to keep a roof over their heads, food in their bellies and daily doctor visits to drain and wrap her brother's wounds.

He had still been recovering when they had been captured. Taken in the depths of a dark, starless night. A cohort of auxiliaries, who had been manning the fort at Elcebus and lining Aelinia's purse, had marched out and left one spring morning, leaving the two of them coinless and in trouble with the innkeeper. He'd had enough one night and arranged for Alaric, a heartless slave trader, to tie them up and take them into the depths of wild Germania.

Weeks had passed in the captivity of Alaric and his band of crooked men. Julius had had to endure watching his sister get raped and beaten daily, all the while chained up in a cage. His wounded right side, still open and full of pus after catching the edge of a bad blade, ensured him helpless to save his sister. Eventually, after many weeks of travelling through a rain swept and barren winter Germania, they had arrived at Goridorgis. Alaric had offered the two to the king, seemingly in exchange for settling an old debt. The king had accepted, and the two had partaken in a deep and whispered conversation. The siblings hadn't been able to learn much, but some talk of raiding and other tribal kings was mentioned. They had been so desolate and desperate at the time, they were close to forcing the sharp edge of German iron into their own hearts, just to be free from their spiralling life.

That had been over half a year ago, and in that time, they had adapted and recovered.

Aelinia cleaned, cooked and served in the king's mighty hall by day, and kept his bed warm at night. A task she was growing increasingly fond of, she didn't admit it, but Licina saw it in the glow of her cheeks and the flutter in her eyes. Julius had recovered, after being given the proper care, and now worked as a blacksmith's apprentice, although chained to a giant iron ball, in case he got too friendly with a freshly forged sword.

'We've even picked up some of the language, enough to get by; it's not the life we planned to have, but all things considered, I'm grateful to Juno for what we have.' Aelinia finished her tale, sitting round a small hearth fire in the back of Balomar's hall, where the slaves and servants slept and ate in cramped but not uncomfortable cots.

Licina sat in silence, stunned by the tale, amazed that these two seemingly ordinary and innocent people had survived such a horrendous ordeal, and that they had come to accept and even enjoy the wicked hand the gods had dealt them.

'And what of you, Licina, tell us your tale, how did you come to be a slave of the Marcomanni?' Julius leant forward, flamelight flickering in his dark sun-drenched skin. Hazel-coloured eyes, moist and intense as he gazed upon her, lust in his every stare.

'I used to think my fate was the cruellest, that the gods had abandoned me and left me to my misery. When I lost my parents, I fell within myself, people used to whisper that I was cursed by Minerva, that my wits had deserted me. But after listening to what the two of you have been through, it would seem my life hasn't been so bad after all.' Licina began to speak about her life with the retired veterans, how she would help the men work the fields in the morning, sit with Turda in the afternoons, learning how to weave and repair tunics and belts. Her eyes lit up as she spoke of Fullo, and especially Albinus, and how he was the brightest spark in her life. Her head cast down as she spoke of the plans they had made for their wedding. 'We should have been married now. But the day after Saturnalia, we were raided. Probably the same one you heard Alaric speaking of with the king.' Licina noticed the siblings share a look at the mention of Albinus' name, and thought it strange. She decided to leave it and carry on.

Her story got darker as she spoke about the raid. Being taken by four mysterious men, her confusion as to why she was brought here in the first place, and why these mysterious men would bring a gift to a king so far from their home. Tears rolled down her cheeks as she spoke of her despair of not knowing whether Albinus was alive, her guilt at doing nothing whilst all around her people had fought for those they loved.

'But you are not a warrior, Licina. Violence is not within your heart, do not blame yourself for the deaths of those people, what could you have done for them?' Julius' hand reached out to stroke Licina's arm, lingering strokes that were not entirely necessary, and noticed by his sister.

'Do not worry, Licina, what is done is done. You are here now and you are alive, and we will look after you, won't we, brother? As your *friends,*' Aelinia lingered on the last word as she gave her brother a warning look, who responded with a knowing glance and quick sly grin.

'Of course we will. The people that brought you here, what can you tell us about them? We have seen them here often, but never have found out why. The king only speaks to them in private, and never seems to talk about why they are here, even in his most *intimate* moments.' Julius' turn to mock his sister with a knowing look, that quick grin wiped off his face by Aelinia's quicker wrist.

'Nothing really, just that there were four of them, only one of them spoke to me at all. The younger of them, although I do not think he is the one in charge. There was a man, older I think, all I ever saw of his face was the hint of a greying beard. He didn't speak much, and never in Latin when he did, but I knew he could understand. He would growl at the other when my questions got too much, or too close to the mark. The younger man feared him, I could see it in his face. The other two appeared to just be swords for hire, showed no interest in me or my questions, not even sure they understood.' Licina paused, unsure how much she should be sharing with the king's bedwarmer.

'Go on...we won't say a word, we are just as curious as you, and as my brother so candidly put it, I have been trying to find out more myself, but with no success,' Aelinia saw Licina's reluctance clear as the sun's reflection in still water on a summer's day, and sought to erase any doubt from her mind.

'Well, when we got here, the older man, the one who always shielded his face, turned the other way, so the guards only saw his back. It was as though he wanted no one to know he was here. It's just strange, all I was told was that I was to be a gift to Balomar from their master, I never found out who that is. Or why their master, who I'm assuming lives somewhere within the empire, would want to give gifts to a king in Germania. Something is going on, I just don't know what.' Her gaze drifted to the dancing flames, her mind a smoky haze, as if the answer was in there somewhere, she just couldn't find it.

'Well, if Balomar had ordered that raid, he's kept it quiet. The people here are desperate for food and money, so they could definitely do with the rewards a raid would bring. But there hasn't been an influx in food, no slaves and coin coming in, just you.' Julius still had his hand on Licina's shoulder, and was now edging round the fire to be closer to her, sensing how vulnerable she was.

'But what about all the land I saw? Surely there are people here who could replenish the dead on the farms? You could feed the whole empire with the number of farms I passed to get here.'

'If you'd grown up in a city, would you know how to farm? Same here as everywhere else, the people that knew what they were doing died,' said Aelinia. Licina wondered at the look of mild annoyance on her face.

'So, what is Balomar's plan? He must surely have a solution for his people? How secure is his position in the tribe?' Again, Licina wondered at Aelinia's scowl. *Are you growing affectionate to the man who let you in his bed?*

'Well. if he has, he hasn't shared it with me. Now I think it's time we turned in for the night, *Julius?'*

'It's okay I will stay and make sure Lic—'

'I said I think it's time we turned in, *all* of us.'

'Err yeah right, night Licina, see you in the morning.'

Aelinia and Licina shared a knowing smile as the twins went their separate ways, Aelinia to Balomar's bed and Julius to his sleeping quarters behind the blacksmiths, leaving Licina alone in the dark with her thoughts. She tried to push the doubt about Aelinia from her mind, but something didn't seem right. *Why is she so interested in the men who brought me here? What is she hiding?*

The following days passed without any real incident. She woke in the morning, served the king and his hall full of warriors breakfast, snuck some in herself. Cleaned up the mess, helped cook and serve a midday meal to the same

186

people. Cleaned some more. Then did the same for the evening meal. She had learnt the basics of the harsh Germani tongue, with help from Julius who had proven as hard to shake as an itchy rash. The work was hard but not unbearable, and her fellow slaves seemed nice enough. She was, of course, well used to spending her days in silence, with very few people paying any attention to her.

One bright early spring morning, she was up with the bird song, helping to prepare breakfast as usual, when she heard a commotion in the hall. Raised voices, panicked in tone. She didn't understand much, but the word *Romans* she got clearly enough. It seemed an *alae* of cavalry had arrived at the gates, full strength with over a hundred shining swords, their Decurion demanding an audience with the king.

She snuck through the kitchen – located in the rear left of the hall – crept up the stairs that led past the king's bedchamber and peaked round the curtain separating the small hallway from the main chamber. The king was questioning one of his guards. Again, she struggled to understand what was said, mumbled phrases of their strange, coarse language. After what seemed like an age a decision was made, and the guard went running back down the hill to the gate, and the king's whole household guard rallied, slipping on mail and helmets, spear tops polished and blades bare. Balomar wanted to make an impression.

Looking behind her to make sure no one had noticed her earwigging, she settled down behind the thick woollen curtain to listen to the exchange between the king and the Roman officer. *Maybe I will know him,* she mused, and thought of ridiculous ways the Roman could sneak her out of the fortress and back into friendly lands.

In less time than it took to knead a bread dough, the Roman officer was shepherded into the hall. He walked proudly, seemingly unafraid of the barbarian spears pointing at his throat as he strutted to the king's throne, though Licina imagined his guts were churning like a morning after drinking bad ale.

She recognised him, but was unsure of his name. A tribune, judging by the bronze-plated, muscle-sculpted *cuirass*. Iron helmet polished to dazzling perfection, his white plume freshly brushed, he looked every inch the Roman commander.

Throwing back his blood-red cloak, left hand resting on his wooden handled *gladius*, he stopped before the king's elevated throne and raised his head to gaze at him with those hazel eyes.

'King Balomar, my name is Maximianus, senior tribune of the Fourteenth legion. I am here on the orders of Governor Bassus, who has requested you attend a peace treaty in Carnuntum at summer's end.'

Silence in the hall, tension so high you could cut it with even the dullest blade.

'And why, *Tribune*, does your governor wish me to attend? I am already at peace with the empire, I see no reason for me to renew it.' His voice was stern, his authority clear in the silent room.

'As I'm sure you are *aware,* Balomar, there was a raid across the river in the winter, an innocent settlement put to the torch. Over one hundred retired Roman soldiers were killed, women raped, children burnt alive in their own homes. Rome would rather settle this matter peacefully than march up here and return the favour to you and your kin.'

Shocked gasps filled the air. That this Roman would march into their king's hall and speak to him in such a manner. Warriors growled and hefted spears, ready to bury them in the tribune's neck with one word from their king.

Balomar leant forward in his carved wooden throne, fists bunched by his side, all his self-restraint being used to stop himself picking up the giant slab of sharpened iron propped up against his leg, leather-wrapped hilt desperate to feel its master's touch, he could almost hear it calling to him.

'How dare you!' More spat than shouted, spots of spittle hurling through the dust sprinkled air to land on Maximianus' face and armour. 'How dare you come into my hall and speak to me in such a manner! Is this what I get for being a friend of Rome? You are in the Allfather's den now, Roman, and you will show me some respect, less I decide to sacrifice you to the Allfather himself, and take my war host to meet this governor of yours.'

Licina shuddered at the mention of the Germanic gods. Although she had not heard much, she knew enough for her blood to turn to ice at their mention. Wotan was known as the Allfather, the oldest and wisest of all the gods. He wandered the earth, disguised as a one-eyed old man, huge grey beard sticking out from a long dark hood concealing his face. He possessed two ravens, Huginn and Muninn, or 'thought' and 'memory' who spied on the world of men for their master, bringing him every scrap of news they saw and heard to tell of.

The men of the tribes were obsessed with Wotan, and desperate to earn spear fame in his honour. It was said that if you died in battle with your sword in hand, you would earn passage to Valhalla, where there was an endless sea of long-dead heroes, feasting and fighting through all eternity.

They had no temple for their one-eyed god. Instead they worshipped him in secret groves, deep in the forests of ash and yew, where dark-robed priests lived in solitude, breathing in deeply the dizzy fumes from long lit fires, dreaming the fates of those that asked. Battles had been won and lost not in the haze of the shieldwall, where axes chopped shields and spears pierced mail and skin. They had been decided in the mind. Warriors convinced they were Wotan-favoured because of the words of a blinded old priest, would carve a bloody path through the battlefield. Emerge from the spear-din unscathed, and round up defeated warriors, bring them back to their lord's secret grove, and spill their blood in his name. Praise him for granting them spear fame. Plenty of legionaries had gone to meet their gods this way, Licina knew.

Donar was the son of this Wotan, and Fjorgyn, the goddess of earth. Their god of war, invincible in battle, Donar was a giant of a man. Red-haired and bearded, he possessed a great hammer – Mjolliner. Whenever he beat it on the ground, thunder would rumble around the land. He fought an eternal war with the frost giants in the north, across the frozen sea. The Germanic tribes believed these frost giants would overrun their lands if not for the great Donar, their protector.

The hall was still silent, waiting for Maximianus to rise to Balomar's taunt, the way a young buck would rise to a charging wolf, unaware of its impending doom.

'You are unwise to threaten me, king of the Marcomanni. I am here in peace as a messenger for Rome, who would not take kindly to my guts being opened in the name of your phoney god. Now I shall repeat my message and be on my way. You have been invited to attend a peace treaty with Governor Bassus, the supreme military commander of Pannonia. He would like you to attend the fortress of Carnuntum at the end of summer, where terms for a lasting peace will be made. And the people responsible for ordering a raid onto Roman land will be identified and punished. Do you understand the message?' His voice was iron and his stare formidable. Maximianus refused to be cowered by a barbarian king from the north.

'Very well, tribune, I shall attend at the end of summer. I will confer with my brother chiefs. It may be seemly if we go with one speaker. The tribes tend not to agree on much, so all our voices in one room could lengthen the negotiations to no end.' A grim smile touched the lips of the king, not quite reaching his eyes.

'Please show the tribune back to the gate. I will see you soon, Maximianus.' With that the Roman was escorted out of the hall, without a backwards glance to the king. When he was gone Balomar called for a slave to attend him.

Licina, still squatting behind the curtain and enthralled with what she had just heard, waited ten heartbeats before appearing round the curtain, not wanting anyone to know she had listened in to the conversation. She walked to a small table on the right of the king's throne, throwing him a quick glance as she walked past. A strangely satisfied smile twitched the corners of his mouth, raising the corners of his great red moustache almost up to his eyes. She began to pour ale from the wooden jug on the table into the king's favoured horn, when Adalwin, captain of the king's chosen men, approached the throne.

'What is this all about, my king? Why have you agreed to this peace treaty? What need have we of further humiliating ourselves to the Romans?' Confounded by what he had just witnessed, he felt the need to approach his king immediately, even with a host of warriors in hearing distance.

'Do not worry, my friend, all part of a plan. I will tell you when we are on the road. We should leave soon, it is mid-summer already by my reckoning, and I plan to take all my warriors to greet this Roman, and we will be meeting others on the road.' Balomar took the horn out of Licina's hand with glee, gulping down the sour ale with barely a breath in between. 'More, girl,' he commanded as he threw the horn back in her direction.

'But are you not going to speak with the other kings? It may be that one of them would go in your stead, after all, we all know Areogaesus must have been behind this raid. Unless there is something you are not telling us?'

The whole hall had stopped pretending they weren't listening now, including Licina. All eyes were on Balomar, who took a swig from his refilled horn of ale. That same smile still on his face.

'Areogaesus led the raid, yes, or at least sent one of his champions out with a war band. But he was not alone in his planning. Too long we have lived under the yoke of these Romans. Having to give up food, money and warriors every time we fancy a spot of raiding. Is it not in our blood to raid? To invoke fear in our enemies? To feel skin, bone and muscle break under our swords and spears? Wolves, that's what they call us in the empire. Wolves. We're more like puppies these days. Wotan's arse! We barely even fight amongst ourselves anymore! All we do is farm, and now we don't even do that! All the men who knew one end of a pitchfork from the next are buried in the ground they toiled. We need silver, gold! And where is there any gold?' He was on his feet now, voice raised so all could hear.

'Rome! That is where! It had been three years since their last tribute. Three damn years! Do they really think us so weak? Well, I tell you now, brothers, we are strong! We shall march on their lands and reap us a bloody slaughter! We will take their gold, and their cattle, and then their women.' His grin was evil, the malice oozed out of him like steam from a boiling broth. Murmurs of agreement swept through the hall. Warriors shared knowing looks and slapped each other's backs.

'My brothers, we will go south to Carnuntum. We will agree a "peace" with these Romans, and when they least expect it, I, Balomar, king of the Marcomanni will lead the whole of our people, all of the tribes along the river, into war with these Roman scum, who think they are so much better than us! We will crush them on their borders, and then we will continue down into Italy itself! Until we stand at the gates of Rome, and their Emperors beg us for mercy, and shower us with riches.' As one, the warriors of the Marcomanni raised their spears and roared so loud even Donar could have heard them, across the distant frozen plains, hammer in hand as he fought great monsters of ice.

'We have seen them here often...the king only speaks to them in private.'

'Now I think it's time we turned in for the night.'

It all hit her like Donar's hammer, striking a frost giant square in the forehead. Like Minerva had removed the wool from over her eyes, allowing her to see again. The four men, her captors. They had been the ones arranging this, ensuring Balomar would be the one to go to the peace treaty, that they must have known Rome would demand. And they were responsible for the pact between the chiefs, the one responsible for making Balomar their leader. This was all pre-arranged.

And these northmen, the more she thought of it, the more she was convinced Aelinia knew. These mysterious monsters, massing in the north, preparing for invasion into her homeland. The way she had cut their conversation off that night. When she had been asking questions. And Julius? What did he know? Surely, he wouldn't support a barbarian race intent on conquering Roman lands. Suddenly, Licina felt very alone.

Looking from Adalwin to Balomar, and seeing the victorious glint in both their eyes, she knew the champion's public questioning of his king was also all pre-planned. *Adalwin already knew.*

She scanned the room, looking for the woman she had considered a friend. And there she was, half hidden behind a mass of cheering and whooping mailed and bearded raiders, swords and spears shaking in the air as they basked in the elation of the upcoming downfall of the hated legions and their cursed eagles.

Their eyes locked in the midst of the chaos, and in that moment, both knew what the other was thinking. *Courage. Must be strong. For Albinus.*

Chapter Thirteen

August AD 168 – Legionary Fortress of Carnuntum, Pannonia

Albinus stood with Fullo, mouths open in shock and awe as line after line of Germanic warriors marched along the eastern road from the bridge, ash-clad spears held high, iron pot helmets bobbing up and down in the scorching summer sun. Chainmail vests shimmering beneath coats of bear and wolf.

'I'm boiling my arse off in just this tunic; they must be sweating like a caught thief on his way to the chopping block!' Fullo, as always thinking of the simple things, seemed none too bothered by the fact that King Balomar had brought what looked to be his whole army to a peace treaty. Instead he was shocked that they seemed to be wearing more layers than a winter legionary, patrolling a snow-topped fort in the distant northern borders of the empire.

It had been six months or so since the raid that had changed both their lives for ever, and Fullo had adjusted well to the life of a legionary. Much better than Albinus. His hands were now well beyond being blistered; huge open callus wounds ran along the top of both his palms, meaning that for the last three months of training, he had to wrap damp rags around them before he could even grip his weapons. His feet were in ruins, bones bruised, skin blistered and muscles screaming as he had been forced to march across what felt like the entire length of the Danube. His standard issue iron hobnailed sandals rubbed the tops of his feet, with sore patches from the leather straps causing livid red marks that crisscrossed their way up to his ankles, much to the amusement of his new colleagues in their *contubernium*.

His sword belt didn't fit, the quartermaster had told him they 'didn't make 'em for runts like you' so he had to use his knife to puncture extra holes to tighten round his skinny waist. Which wasn't going to get any bigger due to the seemingly tiny and disgusting portions of food he was fed three times a day.

And that was before he got to the armour. Mars curse the blasted armour. His head was too small for his helmet, which again was made to a standard size, and couldn't be altered. So, he could either tighten the straps just enough around his neck, and have the solid iron pot constantly fall in front of his eyes, and his wide and aggravating cheek pieces slap against his face. Or he could tighten the helmet right up, making the strap unvaryingly painful on his chin – so much so it had actually cut through skin and bled him one day – and of course, since he wore it every day, the scab never had time to heal, so he had to relive the unpleasant experience time and time again. At least when he did this, the huge slab of iron that acted as his neck guard didn't dig into his back every time he raised his head, causing the links from the chainmail to rub on his skin through his hopelessly thin and itchy tunic.

The mail itself was incredibly heavy, and he struggled to even raise it above his head to put it on every morning, let alone march and fight in it. The metal links seemed to absorb the sunlight. Meaning they got so hot in the sun it would burn your skin to touch, and by the end of the day, it actually felt as though your skin was melting under the weight of burning metal and simmering leather.

Just wearing and marching in all this kit was bad enough, but when he was given the weapons and pack to go with it, it seemed that his equipment weighed more than he did.

He had not been allowed to keep his father's sword. Taurus had taken it from him when they got back to the fortress after the raid, 'You'll start with the same as everyone else, lad. Your father earned this sword, and when you have, I'll see it returned to you.' So he had been given a standard issue *gladius*. Sixteen inches in length, the blade was narrow, with a short, wicked point at the end. Bucco had dismissed the weapon as soon as it was issued to him, preferring to keep his old-style sword. The same in length, but it started wider and curved in slightly, then back out again, ending in a broader and longer point. 'Do more damage with a wider blade, boy, you wanna be ripping out guts, not leaving pretty little pockets for the crows to nest in.' The sword ended in a heavy wooden pommel, that and the thick handguard giving near perfect balance.

On his left side he would wear his *pugio*, the standard issue military dagger. Much shorter in length, it was a stout backup to the longer *gladius*. And also useful, as Albinus had discovered, for prizing splinters out of his broken hands. The shield, or *scutum*, was as unbearable as he knew it would be. Three solid layers of wood, cut out in a rectangular shape and held together by glue. Added to that, the circular iron boss, with a reinforcing iron plate behind, held on with iron nails. Also, the brass trimming running around the edge, which according to the veterans needed replacing after every fight. It weighed more than a

197

hound and was a nightmare to grip with its horizontal handle, sweat-infested blisters slipping up and down, once making Albinus yelp out loud, much to the amusement of Fullo, Bucco and the others. A leather cover was issued with it, which was fine when marching in the sun, but when the sky turned black and the rain fell in droves, his shield would double in weight, meaning the leather straps used to secure it over his back when he marched dug into his shoulders through his mail.

His other weapons were two *pila*, iron-headed javelins, taller than Albinus, meaning he had to hold them high or their butts dragged on the ground. He had taken to using one to sling his pack round, on the advice of the veterans. Their ash shafts joined to the soft iron head. Designed to bend on impact so as not be re-used by the enemy, with a long iron-made tang, which screwed onto the shaft itself. This meant that the shafts could be used over and over, and many legionaries had taken to inscribing their names or taunts such as 'catch this' or 'heads up' onto the wooden shafts themselves, therefore able to recognise their own after a battle, and see if their missile had hit its target.

This was by far Albinus' favourite weapon. When doing *pilum* practice, he wasn't getting squashed in the middle of a shieldwall, he wasn't having to endlessly stab his sword at a wooden practice post, or double march twenty miles a day through the rough Pannonian countryside. He could just loosen his shoulders and practise his throw, which, although it didn't possess great distance, was becoming pretty accurate. He had even received some rare praise from Abas, who had said 'you could hit a raging bull at twenty paces' with a sly smirk across his face, as though he was telling a joke only he was in on. Albinus took it as praise anyway.

His pack was bearable compared to all this. Each member of the *contubernium* carried something on them to contribute for their life on the march. Albinus carried the pots and utensils needed for cooking. It was suspended from one of his javelins and he threw it over his right shoulder when he marched.

He continued to stare at the endless tide of German warriors marching steadily towards the fortress and their iron-enforced timber gates.

'I wonder where Balomar thinks all his warriors are going to go? There's no way Legate Candidus is going to let them all inside, where would they sleep? Not to mention the fact that Governor Bassus is here as well.' Albinus chewed his bottom lip in worry. *Why bring so many warriors? Especially when you have been given right of safe passage, from the governor and the two emperors themselves?* Marcus Aurelius and Lucius Verus had not travelled north for the negotiations. Aurelius was no military man by all accounts, and Verus had not long returned from the east, where a hard-fought war with their Parthian neighbours had not long been won. *Where that cursed plague came from in the first place.* Flashes of Marcia ran through Albinus' mind. *I still miss you.*

'The last thing Rome wants is another war; I doubt there'll be trouble. You've seen how under-strength the Fourteenth are; I'd imagine all the legions are in the same boat. The plague killed a lot of people, brother, on both sides of the river. Easy to forget it weren't just us that got affected.' Fullo put a reassuring hand on his shorter friend's shoulder, the other subconsciously tracing his forehead for the rough marks that would always mark his skin. Badges of honour he used to call them, only recently had he become wary of people's stares.

It amused him that Albinus always seemed to concern himself with things he could neither affect or control. He knew his friend thought he was making a right mess of becoming a soldier, but in truth he was doing well. He was just completely unable to hide his pain and discomfort, something Fullo was well used to doing.

'Then what price will this king pay for murdering our fathers, our people? For stealing Licina? There must be a war, Fullo, we must get our revenge.' Bleeding hands bunched together in a fist so hard his knuckles whitened. Fullo stared at the blood dripping out of the bottom to form a red puddle on the timber wall. As much as he wanted his revenge the same as Albinus, he was more realistic about things. There was no proof that Balomar had arranged the raid back in the winter; any survivors that were tortured after the battle with the first cohort had all said they were from the Langobardi or the Obii. With both tribes being based closer to the settlements ford than the Marcomanni, and both tribes being considerably smaller, poorer and in need of the food and loot from a mornings raiding, it made more sense to think they had been responsible.

But Rome had demanded peace treaties with up to eleven of the tribes based the other side of the *limes*, and with the Marcomanni being the biggest and most powerful of those tribes, Balomar had been asked by his brother chiefs to come and treaty with the Roman Governor.

They could see him now, coming down the road astride a magnificent looking horse.

Blacker than a blacksmith who'd been hard at work at his forge all day, the horse stood taller than any of Balomar's physically imposing looking bodyguard. The king himself was impressive in appearance. Even from this

200

distance, Albinus could make out a full head of dark red hair, well maintained and flowing down his back under a gold encrusted horned helmet. A full and bushy beard, a strong and imposing nose and a mouth that appeared to have all its teeth. Huge arms laid bare in all their tattooed glory and hands that looked as though they could crack your skull gripping leather reins.

His warriors stopped outside the great east gate and formed an honour guard either side of the walkway as their king marched his shimmering horse through. He scanned the top of the battlements as he approached the gate, and deep dark-blue eyes seemed to lock onto Albinus as he passed underneath.

The young legionary realised he had been holding his breath as the king rode through, a dark, nervous feeling at the pit of his stomach. 'I have a bad feeling about this king, I can't quite place why, though.' Albinus cast a worried look to Fullo, pale blue eyes reminding him of a lost puppy, wandering the streets of Carnuntum in search of its mother.

Fullo sighed and raised his head to the sky. 'Got to have something to worry about, don't you! Look on the bright side, we got no training, no drills whilst this king is here. All we got to worry about is when we're on sentry duty, which ain't tonight and ain't tomorrow. So why don't we pop down the old Sword and Sheath and get ourselves a few jars of the good stuff?' He gave Albinus a cheeky wink. 'You never know, that redhead might be working tonight, you know she fancies me, right? Play my cards right and I'm well in there.' Fullo rubbed his hands together in glee, before puffing himself up to his full height and ruffling his ever-growing mop of hair. Not that he would admit it, but Albinus was convinced he was growing it to cover the scars that ran across the top of his head, above his eyes. The plague may not have taken him, but it had certainly left its mark.

'Well in there? You wouldn't know what hole it went in even if you did have a shot. Which you don't, as last time we were there her eyes never left me.' Albinus' turn to throw a wink of his own. *Although she's not a speck on my Licina.* Sadness engulfed him like a winter storm.

'We'll see about that, my friend! Come on then, let's see what Bucco, Rufus and the others are up too. They're normally game for a few drinks.' Fullo turned away and made to go down the wooden staircase that would take them off the battlements. Albinus paused for one last look over the gates, in time to see the king's retinue make their less glamorous entry into the Fourteenth's home. *Fifty slaves at least,* he thought as they were herded in by the king's bodyguard. He was just turning away when a flash of fiery red hair caught in his peripheral vision. His heart skipped a beat as he thrust his head back around for another look. There one second and gone the next, as though someone had lit a torch, and dropped it deep into the river. *Eyes playing tricks with me,* he thought as he turned away to catch Fullo. *No way it could have been her.*

Albinus turned back and walked down the wooden steps from the battlement. He felt a burning sensation on the back of his head, like he was being watched. He turned back round; a man stood where he had been just heartbeats before. He wore his long hair pulled back into knot behind his head, dark skin, a wisp of a black beard round his chin. His chainmail gleamed in the sunlight, his green cloak willowed in the breeze. *That's the second time I've seen him. He's one of Alexander's people.*

Albinus had sought a prophecy from the old soothsayer. It hadn't been worth the coin he'd paid the man. *The man's a fraud.* He'd been told he would lead a prosperous life, that his demons would be crushed under his hobnailed shoe. *How many men had he said that to over the years?* He'd asked if Licina still lived, and if they would be reunited. Alexander had asked how they had become separated, he had seemed agitated, distracted after that. His answer had been curt and dismissive. *Nothing but a fraud.*

*

Eight of them sat in the tavern that afternoon, sharing jokes and downing wine. Albinus and Fullo sat tucked in the corner, unable to tear their eyes off that redhead, chucking them mischievous grins as she served wine and ale to the rowdy and impatient punters jostling for space at the bar.

Bucco was next to them, his hulking body mass making Albinus and Fullo look like children sitting by his side. He was never far from Albinus' side when they were out and about; it seemed he hadn't taken his vow to Silus lightly, and was determined to protect the younger man at all times, even when out for a drink.

Rullus sat opposite Albinus, felt cap on top of his head. Thanks to his Germanic descent, his family originally from the north of the wild land, where the sun was sparse and the wind carried an icy hale, his fair skin did not cope well in the sun, giving his mess mates great joy in the summer when his skin went redder than a plump tomato picked fresh off the vine.

Habitus was next to him, his dark-skinned complex being in complete contrast to that of his standard bearer. Long, dark hair streaked with grey, a freshly cropped beard a flash of silver on sun darkened skin. His right hand fingering the long livid scar running up his left arm.

Calvus the Briton sat picking his nails with his knife. His bald head lined with sweat, he was still unused to the blistering summers in this part of the world, being more used to the wind and rain of his homeland. It had been fifteen years since he had left; he'd still not told the only friends he had in the world exactly why he had journeyed so far just to join the legions.

Longus, the only Italian in the group, sat at ease as he watched the world roll by. He was the youngest of the *contubernium*, until Albinus and Fullo had enrolled. Short in stature but big in personality, he was always the first to tell a bad joke or strike a conversation about varying nonsense subjects. Silence, it seemed, was his biggest enemy.

Libo on the other hand, liked nothing better than to sit in friendly silence, lost in his own thoughts with a good cup of falernian in his hand. A man born to violence, his moods could become as black as his skin if he didn't get a good fight on a regular occurrence. Normally a trip to the Sword and Sheath tavern provided such an opportunity, although today everyone seemed to be in an annoyingly jovial mood.

The eight men shared their whole lives together. Living in an eight-man bunk, there wasn't much these men didn't know about each other. But they still found something new to tease each other about daily.

'So Rullus, we know you're desperate to make optio and all that, but don't you think styling yourself to look like Taurus is taking it a bit far?' Longus could barely hide his snigger as he spoke, gurgling wine up into his face as he laughed into his jar. Rullus ran a hand through his growing dark red hair, a big bushy beard being a recent addition. He had started to be confused for Taurus around the fortress, the main difference being the size of Rullus' girth.

'Fuck off, puppy! I'm still trying to work out why you're trying to look like a pampered whore! I'm sure one day you're gonna wake up a with a great big pair of tits! A man your age should have a beard, and some muscle! You look like you stopped growing when you turned twelve!' Rullus launched a bread roll across the table at Longus, who took the hit square in the face and watched in horror as it landed in his wine cup.

The others broke into fits of hysterical laughter as a desperate Longus tried to rescue the roll from his precious wine, before it soaked it all up.

'Ain't you ever seen him without his loincloth on, Rullus, I think he's already more of a woman than you think!' More laughter at Habitus' quick remark. Longus gave the bread roll a rueful look before shoving it in his mouth and chewing.

'Don't wanna waste good wine!' he managed to stumble out from his dough full mouth. 'You know, that weren't half bad!' he said as he swallowed the last of it, washing it down with a gulp full of wine. 'I might just serve that when I have a tavern of my own.' Groans filled the air as Longus once again mentioned his retirement plan, an occurrence that happened more than once a day.

'When are you gonna listen to me, you overgrown bit of cheap skirt!' Habitus smashed his hand on the table, thoroughly fed up with his colleague's 'superior knowledge' of the country of his birth. 'There are more taverns in Syria than there is sand in the pissing desert! And they all have the same cheap old whores and the same horse piss they call wine! As I've said a thousand bloody times, if life was so great there I wouldn't have bothered to join the bloody army, would I! Or stayed here so long!'

'Bloody clerks, huh Habitus,' Calvus chuckled to himself, knife still working out a rather stubborn piece of dirt.

'Shut up, you muppet! Ain't you gotta go and get some more ink stitched into your skin?! Proper barbarians, you lot, why you here anyway? Don't see many of your kind earning their corn in the legions. You always say you gonna tell us one day. Why not tell us now?' Habitus opened his arms and raised his palms, as if he was on stage at a theatre, giving the floor to another actor.

'Oh, don't get into all this again. I wanted to fight, so I joined the army, and here I am. End of' The Briton shot the Syrian a warning look, which he completely ignored.

'Yeah, but there are loads of units up on the wall. You could have trudged up there in half a day and signed yourself up. Kept a woman at home, gone back to give her one whenever you got some leave. Instead you jump on the first available ship, and end up in Pannonia neck high in German blood. I don't get it! That's all.'

'You need to learn more about geography if you think you can get to the wall from Londinium in half a day. It would have been quicker for me to walk to the Rhine frontier! And anyway, as I've said a thousand times, my grey-bearded friend, it's none of your fucking business!' In one fluid motion his knife threw across the table, landing blade first with a thump, in the small gap between Habitus' thumb and forefinger, who sat there in shocked silence as the blade hilt quivered in the wooden bench.

'Why you inked up bald barbarian cu—'

'Okay, brothers! Let's have some peace, eh? We got an army of Germani sitting outside the walls, they'd love it if we started gutting ourselves, wouldn't they!' Fullo rose to his feet, arms held out either side to hold back Calvus and Habitus, who would have been tussling on the floor by now if they had it their way.

'Well said,' added Bucco, who hadn't moved an inch to stop the squabbling pair coming to blows.

'Well, look at young Scarface woken from his daze! She gone on break, has she?' Libo sniggered an evil laugh, gesturing to the bar, disappointed a potential bar fight had been stopped.

Fullo went as red as his cloak, and sat back down slowly. Hands creeping reluctantly to his forehead, pulling his hair down so the white patchy scars, made more evident by his sun-stained skin, were hidden from view.

'Leave it out, Libo, that's not fair.' Albinus jumped to the defence of his friend, nose scrunched up in anger as he fixed the African with one of those ice-cold stares. 'It's not his fault he has those scars. You've never had to go through what he went through; he should be proud that he's still here to tell his tale.' His hand rested on Fullo's shoulder as he sat back down, giving him a reassuring smile.

'I do believe, young Albinus, that you're starting to grow some bollocks,' remarked Habitus as he leant back on his stool, right hand fingering the other where the blade had missed just moments before, as if he could feel it piercing his skin. 'It's good to see. When you first joined up I wasn't sure you were gonna make it, but you seem to be shaping up just fine.' He raised his cup to the younger man in salute. 'Your father would be proud of the man you have become. You're gonna be a fine soldier.'

The others round the table added their agreement, then joined in a toast to Albinus and his father.

207

'Thank you...I err...I can't say I agree with you. I feel like I've been struggling with everything! My armour doesn't fit, my shield weighs more than me. I'm a liability when the shieldwall comes to a shoving contest. And with every march we do I come more convinced my feet are going to give up and seizure on me!' He cast his eyes down at the floor, hoping to conceal his shame.

'Nonsense!' buffeted Bucco. 'You're doing fine, lad. You think you're the only one who had troubles in first months in the army? It's tough, ain't it, boys?' Albinus and Fullo shared a glance as they nodded in agreement. Both looking at their palms to study open blisters and bruised fingers and wrists.

'I joined up with your father, lad, and yours too, Fullo. And let me tell you, we struggled like you'd never believe!' Bucco smiled at memories of distant days never forgotten. 'None of us could get our armour on in the mornings. It was that old segmented stuff. Tough leather underneath and huge overlapping plates on top. The straps used to break all the time! Your old man Vitulus was so skinny he couldn't get it to tighten up properly. Ha! You could have fitted another whole person under that armour and still had room to catch a spear through one of the gaps and it would only hit air.'

Albinus and Fullo leaned forward into their grins as Bucco told a rare story about his early days in the legions. 'All that bragging we did around the fires in the evenings, tales of our heroics and bravery! What a load of crap! Let me tell you, there weren't a day that went by when one of us weren't dragging our arses on the floor. Not a day where we thought we'd made a mistake signing up for all this. But you know what? You learn fast, you have to if you wanna stay alive.' Nods from the veterans round the table at this, all lost in thoughts from their own early experiences after signing up under the eagles.

'Your old man made it so easy for me when I joined.' Calvus considered that so-familiar ice-cold stare. *But so different*. 'He made an effort to look out for me, didn't have to, but he did. It was Vitulus who used to make my guts go runny!' Calvus cackled away to himself as he prepared to share his story, but he was interrupted before he could get going.

'Aaah, so here are my favourite front rankers. Or spear fodder as you're more commonly known!' Abas strutted over to the group, sword pommel resting easy in his left hand. 'Thought I'd find you slackers here, having fun?' Abas had this annoying trait of always looking amused, an arched eyebrow and a slight smile always left people wondering if they were speaking to him with a penis sketched across their face.

'Our day off, ain't it?' sneered Libo, who had always felt indifferent towards his superior.

'Well, I'm afraid that's just been cancelled. Talks with Balomar are over, and you are all expected to be on parade first thing tomorrow morning when he leaves. The legate wants to put on a bit of a show. And who better than the first cohort!'

'That was quick, weren't it? He only rocked up this morning. Was hoping for a few days of piece!' Longus tossed his empty wine cup onto the table, his disgust that he would not have the chance to refill it evident.

Tuts and groans greeted the optio's announcement. 'We are to form an honour guard outside the east gate as Balomar makes his way back to that bloody great war band he brought here with him.' More groans as the legionaries pictured themselves standing in the sweltering

209

morning sun in full kit, trying not to move as wine sweated out of their every orifice.

'Now let's get back to barracks and make sure we are ready for the morning.' Abas stood aside as the eight disgruntled men filed out of the tavern and took the eastern road towards the fort.

Albinus shuffled past the bar. He cast one last glance to his left, hoping for a final glance at his favourite barmaid, but instead locked eyes with a man. Slicked back dark hair, emerald eyes burning into him. A menacing grin surrounded by a well-trimmed beard, a dark green cloak around a gleaming mail vest. *Do I know you?* he thought as he walked past the man. *Why are you staring at me?* He had no time to question the man even if he'd wanted too. Rullus shoved into the back of him as he slowed, and pushed him out of the door. *Strange man.*

Chapter Fourteen

August AD 168 – Legionary Fortress of Carnuntum, Pannonia

She arced her hips to match his thrusting body. His breath hot on her neck. Her nails digging into the soft skin on his back. His hands pulling her hair. She felt herself begin to climax. He sensed it too, the thrusting becoming faster and desperate. They finished together, an eruption of fluids and pleasure. He lay atop her, still inside her. Her lips sought out his and they shared a deep and passionate kiss. 'I love you.' A gentle whisper into the curve of her neck. She went to reply, to say the same. But she found she couldn't speak. Couldn't breathe.

She gagged, choked as she desperately tried to gulp in mouthfuls of precious air. She beat at his hands, to no effect. They stood firm, unmoving, like a stubborn old tree that refused to be parted from the fertile earth. Panicking now, she shook her head left and right, rolled her body one way then another as she tried to throw him off. But he was strong, stronger than he looked. Those skinny arms had so much power behind them. High, flat shoulders pressing all his weight onto hers. 'Albinus! Stop!' More a croak than a scream. It was all she could manage.

The world went dark. She felt her heart begin to slow and knew it was the end. She couldn't understand why he was doing this to her. Why would a husband kill his wife?

She mourned for the children she would never bear. The joy at watching them grow into adulthood and discover their place in the world. One more time she summoned the strength to grab his hands with hers. They were alien to her. Soft when they should be rough. Small when they should be big. 'Who are you?' Just another croak. He was getting further away now. His arms weren't moving but his face was rising, the room getting bigger, the ceiling taller. She closed her eyes, a perfect picture of her parents greeted her. Sitting by the river in the sun, sharing a small jar of wine. Laughing in joy as their daughter danced and played in the grass…

A loud thump filled her ears and she opened her eyes to see her attacker slump to the ground. The room was dark. Small, back to the size it should have been. Licina's breath came in huge gasps, she almost choked on the air. Her throat was raw, the pain intense. It felt as though someone had forced a burning torch down her throat and into her chest. She rolled onto her front, her muscles aching through lack of airflow, screaming at her to stop.

Clenching and unclenching her fists and toes, she tried to slow her breathing. The vomit took her by surprise, covering her pillow and getting tangled in her hair. She felt a little better when it was out. Slowly, she rolled back to her back and sat up gently. 'Water,' was all she managed to say. Wordlessly, she was handed a small wooden cup, half filled with water. She drank it deep. Revelled in the coolness that doused the fire in her throat. Lowering the cup, she looked upon the eyes of her saviour.

'Julius?' she croaked, shocked. He met the croak with a sorry smile.

'Licina. Are you okay?' Julius leant over, cradling her head in his arms. 'Gods! I got here just in time!' He held her head in his arms as she began to sob. Hot tears streaking down her face as the shock subsided and the fear crept in.

'What happened?' She looked in confusion at the body laid out on the floor. *Not Albinus. But I knew that.* She had been dreaming, she realised. She often awoke to find herself wet between her thighs, and vague, lingering thoughts of her man in her mind. She leant towards the body, getting a closer look in the night's gloomy light. 'Aelinia?'

'Yes. It is a long story. Maybe now isn't the best time to explain. We must get you away from here, before she tells him what has happened.'

'He?' She knew the answer before he said it. Had already pieced together the fragments of the puzzle.

'Balomar. It seems she has grown closer to the king than even I thought. We must go, he will have his dogs out after us when he finds out.' Without waiting for her to rise, he ran to the open door to her small room and checked all was clear outside. 'Get a cloak, and whatever else you can carry, we're going now.'

Throwing on her summer cloak, thick enough to shade her from the burning sun but thin enough to ensure she didn't roast underneath, she grabbed a half-empty water skin off the floor by the bed. Slipping her feet into her sandals she was at the door in a matter of heartbeats. She paused there, and cast one look back at the prone figure laying on the floor, a small dark puddle leaking out of her long dark hair. *She raped me. She raped me and tried to kill me. But why?*

Those questions would have to wait as when she turned back Julius was already halfway down the corridor, light footed steps as he tried to maintain the night's deathly silence. They were in the fortress, and had been given quarters in the northwest corner – the Tenth cohort had been re-housed outside the walls to the south. Due to her being one of the king's slaves, she had been given her own room close to him, the others were all bunked up in the cramped eight men rooms.

They reached the entrance to the building and once more Julius paused, keeping his head still and his eyes closed, waiting for them to adjust to the changing light. 'Why did she do this?' It was too much for Licina, she had to ask, couldn't hold it in any longer.

'She believes you will betray the king. You were there, in his hall that day when the Romans came. You heard what Balomar said to his warriors. There's going to be a war. No matter what was agreed yesterday, there's going to be blood. Aelinia has turned her back on Rome.' He spat a bitter laugh. The effects of betraying his sister to save Licina, leaving a vile taste on his tongue.

'How could she turn her back on her own people? I don't understand.'

'It was our own people who betrayed us to Alaric and his slavers in the first place. And…and something else happened whilst we were on the road. On the way to Goridorgis…' He paused, undecided as to whether he should continue.

'What? Tell me!'

He let out a sigh. 'On the road to Goridorgis, I was still wounded, pretty bad. Alaric took us north first, and he and his men robbed some people, don't know who. But they took amber, and a lot of it. Then they took us down the amber road, ended up near a place called Vindobona…' He paused again.

214

It all clicked in Licina's mind, took less time than it takes to tie a cloak. She gasped in shock, and horror. 'Albinus?'

'Yes. He was there. There were thirty or so Romans, led by a man called Silus, who, if I remember from what you told us, is Albinus' father?' She nodded, mouth wide open still.

'Albinus spoke to my sister, she begged him for help. But...Silus wasn't having any of it. Even when she told them that we were taken in Gaul, that our father served under the eagles, they didn't lift a finger to save us. That's when she turned, I think. Before she had even met Balomar. All this time she has been warming his bed, saying she's trying to gather information for us, for Rome, I fear she has been doing the opposite.' Tears welled in his eyes. He knew he was doing the right thing, but it didn't make it any easier.

'You met Albinus? And Silus and Fullo and Vitulus? It was you?' she held a hand to her heart, tried to slow its rapid pulsating with deep slow breaths.

'You knew?'

'Albinus told me they found two Romans caged up. A brother and sister, and the brother was hurt. He said he had wanted to help, but his father wouldn't. He said Silus had mentioned something about Dacia, about sticking his nose in where it didn't belong. He got a lot of his men killed that day, apparently.'

There was silence between them. Each momentarily lost in their own dark thoughts.

'I'm so sorry.' Whispered, it was all she could think to say.

A smile returned to Julius' face, a reassuring arm on her shoulder. 'You don't need to be sorry, Licina. Not like you could have done anything about it. Now, back to the present.

You ever been in here before?'

'No. Never in the fortress. Legionaries aren't allowed families, technically.' They shared a knowing smile at that, both being born to serving soldiers and their illegal wives.

'My home is to the east, at least what's left of it. Carnuntum proper is through the west gate, the bridge back to the river also through the east...'

'Well, we can't go east, that's where Balomar's army is camped. I don't quite fancy braving the streets of Carnuntum before dawn, and we may get spotted if we're still there in daylight. So...'

'Back across the river then?' She shuddered at the thought. All she wanted was to go home, to find Albinus and hold him tight. But she knew she had to get out of here first.

'We could cross, go east along the bank and re-cross at the ford, by your settlement?' She could see his mind working.

'Why are you helping me?' She hadn't wanted to ask, but couldn't hold it in any longer.

He opened his mouth to answer, then closed it again quickly, seemed to be struggling for the right words. 'I like you. I know it sounds stupid, but I do. And I know you are in love with someone else, but it doesn't change the way I feel.' He studied his feet as he spoke. The embarrassment showing in the night's gloom as his cheeks flushed red on his pale skin.

'I like you too. But you know my heart belongs to Albinus. I must see if he's alive.'

She gripped his hand. 'And thank you. Whatever your motive, I will be forever in your debt. You saved me.'

216

He flushed a deeper red at her touch. 'No problem. Now then, how in Jupiter's name do you escape from a legionary fortress?'

*

Marcus strolled along his part of the battlement, lost in his own thoughts. He hated the nights. Seemed longer every time he had to work one. He knew he should be alert. The governor was inside the fortress, so was that barbarian king, not to mention the horde of warriors camped outside the east gate. But that was the east, he could see their fires in the distance, hear the roars and laughs of the drunken spearmen as they drank and wrestled their way through the night. He pitied the poor bastards that had to patrol the eastern wall, *no rest for them tonight.*

But he was on the north, and all was quiet here. He looked back into the fortress, the torchlight lighting the way down the main roads revealing no movement. All were asleep. Except him. *By Mars, I hate working nights.* It was boring. Nothing ever happened. Twenty-five years he had served now. The gods only knew how many nights he'd spent patrolling this damn fort. Nothing ever happened. It was better in the daylight. People were in and out of the gate all day. There were carts to check, tolls to take off the grumbling merchants, pretty women to wink at. Nights, nothing. At least it was warm. Winter was the worst. Freezing your balls off all night and trying to keep moving so the frostbite didn't get your toes. He'd seen a few old comrades discharged after their ash black toes had been lopped off, some even lost a whole foot. *Fuck that.*

No way for an old soldier to go. *Rather catch a spear in my belly. Ain't ending up no beggar.* He saw them. When he was given a day's leave and went to empty his purse in the first brothel he came across. Lining the streets of

217

Carnuntum, huddled in groups and pestering everyone that walked past. A soldier's biggest fear, that. No way to earn money, no home to go to. Just stuck out on a street corner until the cold got you. Or someone with quicker wrists and a sharp blade.

He gazed out at the north wall, trying to recall the name of an old comrade who had lost his half his leg to the biting cold. *Jupiter, what was it? How many years had it been?* He rubbed the dull grey stubble that covered his square framed chin. *Seen too many men lost down the years, can't remember one from the next these days.* He turned his mind to happier things, like his upcoming discharge. His time would up this time next year, and he thought of the lavish return his brother would give him when he finally got home. He had been sixteen when he left Rome for the army. His brother had been twenty, and even then, was known to run one of the best fish stalls in the Aventine market. He'd made a killing in the years Marcus had been trying to avoid getting split by a barbarian spear, and the promise in the share of a successful business to help him see out his final years was a welcoming thought.

He smiled to himself in satisfaction. *Ain't ending up no beggar.* A small sound pricked his ears, a soft padded foot getting caught on a loose stone on the road. He swung round with the agility of a man half his age – you don't survive to your last years' service unless you keep yourself in trim. A man stood in the road, looking up at him in deathly silence. It was one of that priest's men. They had arrived with the governor, with the promise they would help smooth the negotiations with the barbarian king. He stood there, unnervingly still. *'The fuck he looking at?* He hated these priests. Five men in total, all wearing the same

218

dark green cloaks. The pattern on the back gave Marcus the creeps, a swirling snake, light brown in colour, but with long flowing light blond hair. It was encircled around a broken goose egg, which it had supposedly just hatched from. The snake was Asclepius reborn, or so the priests said. *A load of bollocks, say I.*

This man had his hood over his head, so his face was swallowed by the night's dark.

At least it wasn't the soothsayer himself, Marcus thought. Alexander was his name – Alexander of Abonoteichos, he called himself. He had discovered the miracle, or so he called it, at precisely the time he said he would. *Funny that.* He was a fraud, or so Marcus thought. He walked round like he owned the place, Marcus had even seen him giving orders to a legionary the other day. *Ha! I'd have told him where to go!* He smiled at the thought of hitting the old fraud, right between his squishy eyes. Just as the smile hit the corners of his mouth, there was a blur of movement to his left, a flash of orange hair. 'What the—' He didn't see the blow that hit him, a solid block of wood sending him slumping to the parapet floor.

*

Licina's heart was beating so fast she could almost see it pumping through her cloak. They had made it to the top of the parapet with relative ease – thanks to a sleeping guard and the soldiers' set routine. Waiting for the two patrolling legionaries to walk past each other without a word, they'd skipped up the steps on light feet and crept along the parapet until they reached the gate. There had been one guard there, stationary, staring back into the fortress at the road. Licina had crept round the back of him to distract him, then when he'd turned to face her, Julius had clubbed the back of his head with lump of wood he'd picked up on the way.

Julius uncoiled the rope he'd acquired on the way, and threw it out over the northern wall, and prayed it was long enough to make it to the boggy ground below. He heard it hit the ground with a soft splash, and sighed in relief. Tying the rope to the top of the wall, he turned to Licina, who was staring in horror into the fortress.

You! She wanted to scream it but she didn't. The nameless man. The one who had taken her from her home and at the mercy of Balomar and his tribe. She could hear her heart in her ears now, felt them go red as the blood was forced through them in waves. He lowered his hood, and even in the dim light she could see him smile. He simply raised his hand and waved, the rest of him didn't move an inch.

'Licina, quick!' The clubbed soldier was already beginning to stir, and Julius did not want to be on this side of the wall when he woke. Five heartbeats he waited for her, stood there panting in fear as he thrust his head left and right to ensure none of the patrolling soldiers appeared too early. Eventually he had enough, grabbed and almost threw her over the wall. She stifled a gasp as she gripped the solid timber and steadied herself.

'Just grab onto the rope, use your feet to push yourself down the wall. It will be over before you know it. Now go! We must hurry.' In a moment of utter panic, Licina realised she hadn't thought through this bit of their plan. Not like scaling down walls was one of her pastimes. A wave of fear engulfed her as she leant back and caught nothing but air. Her head swam and her palms went slack with sweat. They slipped – just an inch – on the rope and her heart nearly fell out her mouth. She sucked in some air, tried to breathe deep and regain some composure. Found it impossible. She looked up, Julius was there, throwing his head in all directions, fear written clearly on his face. 'Go! Go!' So she went.

It was slow-going, the leaning back was the worst. Her head felt like it weighed more than the wooden block that had sent the legionary to sleep. It rocked left, then right, causing her to sway both ways rather than a straight trip down. *Just look straight ahead. Don't look up. Don't look down. Just look at the wall.* She wanted to be sick. Then pass out. Or maybe just the latter. Her palms were ablaze, she could feel the skin ripping, breaking on the rough rope. Could see the dark red stains she was leaving behind, she worried it would make Julius' descent trickier.

She tried to keep her legs straight, a slow but purposeful stride. A breeze rippled the air and it was cool on her sweat-soaked face. She savoured it, imagined opening the water skin strapped to her back and drinking deep the cold, life giving liquid. *Plenty of that below me.* A bad thought to have. The rope lurched, throwing her into the wall, her feet lost their grip on the smooth wood. She crashed into the wall, back first with her head tucked into her shoulders. The pain was intense, the back of her right shoulder taking the worst of the impact.

She screamed with the pain, and felt her grip loosen on the rope. Her arms were on fire, muscles not used to supporting so much weight nearly ready to give up.

She gripped the rope so hard she thought her white knuckles would pop. Glancing up – *so far up* – Julius was on the rope. She risked a glance down and nearly cried in relief as she saw how close the ground was. *Thank you, Juno.* The closeness of the ground re-assured her and boosted her courage. Leaning back out on the rope and finding her feet, the rest of the descent passed quickly.

She lay in the shallows, panting and laughing in the sheer unbridled joy of being alive. She was flat on her stomach, sure she would have vomited if she had not done so earlier. *By Juno, that feels a long time ago now.* The trip down had almost wiped her memory of the events of the night. She sat up and waited for Julius to finish his descent, a lot quicker then hers was. She was gulping greedily from her water skin when he leapt to the ground and made straight for her.

'Get up! We must go. One of the sentries saw me, that's why I had to jump on before you reached the bottom. Will there be sentries on the northern side of the bridge?' He was breathing hard, coated in sweat, his black hair shone in the moonlight with it.

'I guess? There's a fort there, just an outpost really. I'd imagine they keep it manned.' She got an immediate answer to her question. There was a commotion atop the wall, and a beacon fire was lit. It was quickly answered by a fire at the other end of the bridge, the sentries acknowledging the warning from their comrades. She panicked as she imagined being caught, and what fate would have in store for her if she was dragged back to Balomar.

She sensed she wouldn't live long enough to regret her attempted escape.

'Julius, can you swim?' He nodded, as if he was already having the same thought.

'Yes. It's our only chance.' He didn't wait for her to follow. Out they waded, the moonlit waters freezing. Licina shuddered as she forced her shoulders under, legs and arms moving in unison as her muscles remembered the movements her father had taught her as a young girl.

The first floating island they reached gave them a small time to recover their breath. No more than ten steps wide, they hopped into the thick brush and shared the last of the water skin.

'The current will be stronger on the other side,' Julius whispered, lips purple in the moonlight.

'That's encouraging! We best hurry, I can hear more noise from the fortress, I don't fancy facing a line of spears as we go under the bridge.' Licina shivered as she spoke.

'You're right. And the longer we're here, the colder we'll get. Come on, let's get this over with!'

With that he was off, plunging into the dark waters, his head emerging as powerful strokes swept him east. Licina cast a last glance back at the fortress, aware it could be the last time she laid eyes on Roman land for a while. They would be hunted now, and Pannonia was too small to hide in. They would have to go north, deeper into Germania. *For Albinus. Courage.* His picture drove her on. She threw herself back into the river's currents, and focused her mind on keeping pace with Julius.

Chapter Fifteen

August AD 168 – Legionary Fortress of Carnuntum, Pannonia

Alexander stood on the parapet and basked in the early morning sun. He felt at peace, more so than he had in years. It had been a long road, the one he had travelled. But now, at the grand old age of sixty-two, he was on the cusp of achieving his wildest fantasy.

Over twenty years it had been. Years of hard work, of lies and deceit and murder and whispered conversations in the dark. But finally, his time was coming.

He had always known he was destined for greatness. Even as a young man. Plying his trade as an assistant to a travelling soothsayer, he had been able to travel all over Greece. But that hadn't been enough. He had begun to form his plan, the one that would make his name last throughout the ages, even back then. That plan had taken a back step, though, when the old soothsayer himself had caught him thrusting between his daughter's skirts. A prophet, he had called himself. A true follower of Apollonius of Tyana. *Now that man was a fraud.* He had watched him, studied as the old man used his shaking hands to conjure strange concoctions from the various potions and plants he collected as he travelled. Potions he claimed could heal a dying child and bring back an old soldier's failing eyes. Alexander looked down at his own shaking hands, and sighed as he realised how old he had become.

The soothsayer's daughter had given him a daughter of his own, and died a blood-soaked death for the privilege. Another sigh as he remembered what a beauty she had been. He had never loved her, he admitted to himself, but the lust he had felt had been strong enough to mourn her at her death. The soothsayer had been distraught when he heard the news, and had immediately set forth from Athens where he had been tricking the rich and the poor alike out of their hard-earned coin. He had packed his potions and made for Abonoteichos, where Alexander had taken his pregnant daughter. The sleepy little town on the banks of the Dead Sea had been where he entered the world, and it was there he decided to return when the soothsayer had thrown him from his party of wanderers.

Unfortunately for the old con, he never made the long journey north to grieve at the remains of his dead daughter, or to gaze lovingly into the eyes of his beautiful granddaughter, who looked so much like her mother. The journey combined with the stress had been too much for him, or so his followers had said when they carried his body into the town. Not that Alexander cared. Although he had been grateful to receive the bottles and packs filled with the mysterious potions that made things go bang and fizz and had wowed people across the Aegean. With these he could begin to set his plan into action, and make himself rich.

He started off by becoming an oracle of Asclepius, the Greek god of medicine. Women would flock to his shrine – an old statue he had stolen from a long forgotten rural temple – and ask him to help with many a thing, mainly getting pregnant. The old man smiled as he thought back to those days. *Oh, they got pregnant all right.* After some unsavoury incidents with husbands who weren't so convinced it was the divine power of Asclepius who had planted the seed in their woman's bellies, he started to recruit men to his cause.

His recruitment process was simple. He would ask them five questions about the gods, questions only a learned man could answer. If they got them all wrong, they were in.

He didn't need intellects; he had enough of that. He needed muscle, to sell swords. And they flocked to him like wolves to a wounded sheep.

Soon he had a small army, all funded by the queues of people who would stand outside his shrine for days just to seek advice and wisdom from the oracle, and pay a gold drachma for the privilege. He was rich, powerful, but it wasn't enough. He was ridiculed outside of his small hometown, and he was running out of young women desperate for the oracle's conceiving powers. So, he hatched phase two of his mastermind. He told the citizens of Abonoteichos that an incarnation of Asclepius was coming to their town, that he would be born three days hence in the market square of their very own sleepy seaside town.

So, three days later, Alexander entered the market square at noon. Crowds of people had flocked from the nearby towns and farms to see the incarnation – or to mock him when it didn't occur, either way, the important thing to him was they came. He strolled into the centre of the square, eyes downcast, mumbling a low prayer. His men fanned out either side, it was the first time they had all been out in public in their matching green cloaks – the cost of the dye alone had been extortionate, but they looked magnificent.

He had kneeled in prayer at the centre of the square as his men circled him, covering him from the view of the watching masses. Their prayers had raised in volume, and just as they reached a pitching crescendo, a thick green fog appeared from nowhere and covered Alexander completely. Alexander had arisen to his feet as the green mist descended, beholding a large goose egg. 'The god is here!' he had screamed. The people did not join him. 'An egg?' They mumbled to each other in confusion and disappointment. 'Surely no god could hatch from an egg?'

He had shown it to the crowds, even let some of the children touch it in their awe. Then he had taken a small knife, and sliced the egg open. He could still remember the collective intake of breath and loud gasp from the people as it opened. The wide-eyed looks of shock and confusion. A snake. But not just any snake. A snake with hair. Long blond locks that sailed the light breeze, sprouting from atop its head. It glided across the dust ridden floor, arcing its head and sprouting its winged tongue at the gasping peasants. They had come to see a miracle; they had been given one.

From that day on, the only thing to grow quicker than his fame and wealth was the snake itself. Glycon, he had called it, and people were drawn to the new god like bees to honey. He had travelled east first, and wowed the inhabitants of the eastern empire so much that after some years he had been asked to dine with the governor of Asia himself. Publius Mummius Sisenna Rutilianus had been so taken with Alexander and his god, that he married his daughter and declared himself the protector of Glycon. He had also been among the first to suggest that such a learned and holy man should be draped in purple.

Soon the great gold mines in Dacia were producing minted coins depicting the face of Glycon, and everywhere he went people stopped to ask if the god could heal their children or fill their bellies with one. Alexander was always happy to oblige – for a fee. Before he knew it, word had stretched to the ears of Marcus Aurelius himself. He had asked Alexander for a prophecy, one to help revitalise the spirits of the men and women on the Danube frontier, who had suffered badly through plague and famine. He had delivered, and his stock had risen with the Emperor. *Not a bad friend to have. For now.*

And now here he was. Attending a treaty between the governor of Pannonia and one of the most formidable kings north of the river. Balomar had spoken well, he thought. He had arrived in a blaze of iron, hundreds of warriors and slaves at his back. A force meant to intimidate, a hint of what could be expected if his demands were not met.

Governor Bassus had been furious. Firstly, with the men the king had brought with him, and secondly with the attitude of the king in the meeting itself. 'It is I that have summoned you here, not the other way around. You do not get to make demands of Rome.' Alexander had chuckled into the hood of his cloak at this remark, made because Balomar had started the days talks by demanding Rome pay double tribute for the next two years, as they had missed their payments this year and last.

The talks had become more productive after a while, with Balomar agreeing to find and hand over the perpetrator of the raid that had ruined a small retirement settlement to the east. In return, Bassus would petition the

Emperor to ensure the promised coin was delivered to Goridorgis by autumn's end.

Alexander had remained silent throughout, hesitant to throw his weight behind either side. 'I'd have hoped from more support from you,' Bassus had said when they had dined together the previous evening. 'You could at least have brought your snake with you, that may have unnerved that ungodly man a bit.' He had replied that Glycon was a god, not just a snake. And that he hadn't seen the need to bring his mighty lord into a small negotiation with a minor tribal king.

Their dinner had ended in an uncomfortable silence, with Bassus still irritable and Alexander detesting the man more and more by the second. *Maybe my snake would like to eat you?* The idea brought a wicked grin to his face, but he pushed the thought aside. *The man may still prove useful to me.*

He was lost in his thoughts, oblivious to the world around him, when a small cough snapped him back too. 'Sorry, my lord, were you praying?'

'No, Cocconas, just lost in an old man's mind. How are you this morning?' He studied his young apprentice and was slightly disturbed by what he saw. The Thracian, from Constantinople, where east meets the west, was worried. Stress lines circled those dark, almost black eyes. His pitch-black hair was tied back in a short knot, a look often in fashion with the men on the Asian border. His skin was dark, stained darker still by spending the long summer months on horseback both in and out of the empire. His teeth were perfect, something which always annoyed Alexander, who couldn't stop himself rubbing his gums with his tongue, feeling the sore spots where he had some removed before the rot had done further damage. Short in

229

stature, but lean in frame, Cocconas had the sort of body made to don armour, and on this bright summer's morning it dazzled in the sunlight.

'We may have a problem, my lord. I thought it my duty to bring it to your attention.' His tone was cautious; he spoke slowly, unusual for a man from the east.

'Well, spit it out then!' No matter how hard he tried, he could never get his voice above a whisper these days. Too many years spent preaching to big crowds, throwing his head up to the gods and chanting and shouting so loud it would leave his audience in no doubt they were witnessing a true spokesman of the gods in action.

'The girl. The one we took from the raid and gave to Balomar. She escaped last night.' He hung his head, part in shame and part to cover the fear. He knew what was coming. 'Fool! What did I tell you? We should never have taken her in the first place. You put the whole mission in jeopardy when you went hacking your way through the barbarians to get her! It was only Glycon's will that got us out of there in one piece, and even that hadn't been enough to save poor Nicoli.' His voice was rasping; you would have thought it nothing more than a trick of the wind if you hadn't seen his mouth move.

'I know, my lord. I just thought it couldn't hurt to give Balomar an extra incentive to aid us in our plans.' Despite his fear at his master's anger, he hid a smile at the older man's use of 'will of Glycon'. The two men knew only too well the god was as genuine as a gold drachma even a toothless baby could chew through.

'What a load of tosh!' Alexander's whisper was finally finding some gravel. 'You wanted nothing more than to discover the contents of her skirts! And don't you try and deny it.' He stopped his tirade as he thought through their

230

potential problem. 'We don't actually know she knows anything though, do we?'

'No, not for certain. Although I spoke to her much throughout our short time together. Licina is intelligent. I don't imagine it would have been too difficult for her to put together the pieces once inside Goridorgis.'

'Balomar was foolish to bring her back into Roman lands. Almost as foolish as you were to take her out of them in the first place!' He enjoyed watching his young apprentice's face flush at the put down. 'Did she have family? Back at the settlement?'

'Her mother and father were dead, if I remember correctly. But she was betrothed. Albinus was his name. I have already taken the liberty of tracking him down.' He tried to meet his master's eye and fix him a smile, certain he would earn some praise for his work.

'He survived the raid?' Alexander's husky voice back to a whisper, a shadow on the breeze. He gave Cocconas a meaningful look as a patrolling sentry marched slowly past with a nod.

'Yes, my lord.' The younger man was whispering too. 'And more than that, he is here, inside the fortress. Turns out his father, who was killed in the raid, was a retired centurion from this very legion. Silus, his name was. His son, Albinus, now serves here with the first cohort.'

'You have seen him?' A nod sufficient to answer the question. 'How did you find him?'

'I have my ways.' He beamed in delight, it was matched by his master.

'Then I shall ask no more! But the question is, does she know he is here? And where is she going?'

'I do not believe she did, and he certainly didn't. I spent some time watching him yesterday; if he knew she was

231

here, he would not have spent the afternoon drinking in a tavern. Now as for Licina…' he scrunched his face as he thought. *How can I explain she went over the north wall without revealing I watched her go and did nothing to stop her?* 'She would have gone north. She wouldn't have risked running across the whole fortress to get out, so that rules out the south and east, assuming she would have been with Balomar's other household slaves in the northwest corner. She wouldn't have gone west, that gate leads to the short road into Carnuntum, that place is a maze if I ever saw one. North, that's the logical way. Across the river and into Germania. More scope to manoeuvre in whatever direction she desires.' A pause, as he waited for his master's comments on his thoughts.

'And what will she run into if she goes north?'

'Huh? Oh! Where are Balo—'

'Quiet! Do not even whisper the words within these walls.' He stopped to look around; the nearest sentry was fifty paces away and gazing dozily into the distance. 'If she sees *them* and comes back to warn the legion, then everything we have planned is at an end. Understand?' Cocconas gulped.

'Yes, my lord. What should we do?'

'We? Nothing! You? Get a bloody horse and go and find her! If she ruins my plans – twenty years' worth of plans! Just because some pup saw his chance to get his leg over, then you will find yourself ending your days in some crappy gladiatorial arena on the outskirts. Do I make myself clear?' The gravel was back now, his voice sounding almost human.

'Yes, my lord. I'll leave right away.' Cocconas turned and made to scurry away, not wanting to stay and get abused some more.

'Wait a second.' Alexander's right hand waved his apprentice back. 'Set a meet with Balomar, north of the river. I won't be able to join you for obvious reasons. Ask him for a few men, to act as guides and translators for you. You will soon be lost in that vast land if you go alone.'

'I will, my lord. I will fix this, I promise.' With that he was gone, down off the battlement and quickly lost between the rows of buildings.

Fool. He liked Cocconas. He was the most intelligent man he had recruited to his service, and he had hopes the man may succeed him one day. *If I don't bloody well kill him first.* His peace over, he made his way stiffly down the stairs to his rooms to prepare for the day. *Leg is getting stiffer by the day.* Two years his left leg had been slowly swelling. It had now got to the point he couldn't hide the limp, and riding could be agony. *Oh to be young again, just for a day.* He shrugged off his green cloak as he got to his rooms, glanced at the wicker basket in the corner, could see the movement as his snake realised his master had returned. He looked from the snake to his cloak, *if all goes to plan in the coming days, I won't be needing this green cloak much longer.* He still wore the same evil grin as he took the lid off the wicker basket and carefully lifted Glycon out.

'Come, my old friend, our work is nearly at an end.'

*

Albinus stood sweating in the morning sun, his head a whirlwind of emotion. His sleep had been interrupted – everyone's had – by the disturbance in the night. Two people had escaped from the fortress, something the proud legionaries would have thought impossible when they slumped in their cots last night. But it wasn't the below-par performance of the sentries that had Albinus' heart

233

racing like a poor farmer helplessly watching the crows feast on his crops, it was the description of the escapees the struck sentry had given. *A long mane of fire-red hair. That's what she had.* He'd heard it from the man himself. Marcus, his name was. An experienced soldier who would have preferred to be dead than to have to recount to his superiors how a young slave girl and her accomplice had managed to get the drop on him.

Taurus had heard his account of the night before, and awoken Albinus and Fullo from their drunken sleep so they could speak to the man himself. Albinus didn't think he had blinked since.

'Brother, you know it's not her, right?' Fullo was worried. It was only in the last few weeks his friend had regained some of his former humour, and he didn't want to see him dragged back down the same grief-stricken path they had both been treading. He stood next to Albinus, roasting in the sun on the south side of the bridge, waiting for Balomar and his entourage to take their leave back into their own lands. He was trying to decide if the dizziness he was feeling was because of the heat or because he was still drunk. Bit of both probably.

'But it could be, brother. Do you not see? You said yourself she was taken by the barbarians. Is it that hard to imagine she could have ended up as Balomar's slave?' His eyes were wide, no sign of a hangover in the big circles of crystal blue.

'I know you have hope, my friend, and it warms my heart. But don't let yourself get carried away. I'd hate to see you relive the pain we both went through in the winter.' The first weeks had been hard. The sorrow at losing his parents and Licina in the space of one day, plus adjusting to the rigorous life of a legionary, had nearly

234

broken him. But he had put a brave face on it all, for Albinus.

'I won't Fullo, I promise. But this is a lead, a genuine lead. We have to follow it up.' The cog in his head was already turning as he began to work out how he was going to get messages to the traders and merchants he had paid to bring him information regarding his lost love. Practically all his wages had lined their pockets as they had left the fortress, wandering off into the wild lands to sell their wares to the Romanised tribes. He hadn't told Fullo – or anyone for that matter – about his private investigations, he knew he would be ridiculed if they found out.

'How? We're in the army, in case you'd forgotten. Not like we can just leave, is it?'

'Silence in the ranks! They're coming.' Abas stalked along the line of sweating legionaries, the cohort split in two halves either side of the bridge. He stopped in front of the two new recruits. 'The legate had chosen the first as we are *supposed* to be the finest unit in the whole legion. Let's show him he was right, shall we?'

'YES SIR!' The pair threw matching salutes to their optio. Abas turned and nodded at Taurus, who was on the other side with the other half of the cohort.

Balomar's retinue came into view. Legionaries that were leaning on shields and waving their pila in front of their faces as makeshift fans suddenly snapped to attention. Albinus straightened with the men around him. Eyes fixed to the front as he prayed to Jupiter this would be over quickly; he was finding it difficult to breathe in his armour. The horde of barbarian warriors came first. To say they marched over the bridge would be flattering. They lumbered, feeling the effects of the non-stop drinking and revelling all the legionaries had heard in the past day and

235

night. There was no cohesion to their march, they strolled in groups, spears and axes slung over their shoulders as they smirked and laughed at the legionaries, practically melting as they stood to attention.

Albinus longed for a long swig from his water skin. He could see it from the corner of his eye, hanging mockingly on his right hip. The arrival of the king drew his attention from his quenching thirst. He was mounted on the same fine black stallion on which he had arrived. A girl rode next to him. *She wasn't there on his way in.* Her head was heavily bandaged, and she looked dazed. Albinus couldn't help but turn his head slightly to get a better look at her.

Why does she look familiar? Hints of long dark hair peaked out of the bandages. A hooked nose, that wouldn't look out of place on a senator's wife, as she looked down in disgust at the peasants lining the street outside her carriage. A taut mouth, not dissimilar to Licina's. But it was those hazel eyes that locked onto his that kicked his memory tank into gear. *The girl in the cage! On the amber road!* He was stunned. He stood there, gaping and sweating as she rode past on a small brown mare.

He tried desperately to get Fullo's attention, but he knew if he was caught he would be punished. He let his shield fall slack in his left hand, so it toppled slightly to the left and nudged Fullo's *pilum*, which he held in his right. Fullo pulled his *pilum* closer to his body, irritated that his friend was slacking in front of the barbarian king.

Albinus knocked his shield into the *pilum* again, desperately trying to catch Fullo's eye. Fullo went red with frustration, sure they were both going to end up on latrines. He shot Albinus a dark look, and caught his friend's urgent stare and frantic head movements. He was gesturing to the king. Fullo looked, studied the king and saw nothing that captured his attention. 'What is it?' he muttered from the corner of his mouth, eyes never leaving the front.

'Not the king! The girl, next to him.' Albinus did the same, a wary glance to his right to be sure Abas had not heard their muttered conversation. Fullo looked closer, studied the pretty face under the bandages. His heart skipped a beat. *Her!* Those eyes gaping back at him, she was clearly just as shocked to see them as they were to see her. She recovered from her surprise quicker than the legionaries, her gaze quickly turning to poison, it felt like her stare went right to their souls.

And just like that she was gone, carried with the crowds as the king's retinue continued to pass out of the gates. Albinus and Fullo barely noticed the others to pass them.

The heat and hangovers all but forgotten, they stood in shock and waited to be dismissed.

The last of the Marcomanni were soon out through the gates and over the bridge, and the first cohort marched in formation back into the fortress, where Taurus quickly dismissed them.

The men filed past the two shocked recruits, happy to be off duty and quickly taking the opportunity to get out the sun and rid themselves of their armour.

A long moment of silence passed between the two, they hadn't even looked at each other, both lost in their memories.

'You remember her, I assume?' Albinus finally breaking the silence.

'Yes. From the amber road. The trade with Alaric. She was in a cage, with her brother if I remember right. What was her name? You remember?'

237

'Aelinia. I spoke to her, a little. Said she had been taken somewhere in Gaul, can't remember where now. I wonder how she ended up with Balomar?' He scrunched his face as he tried to remember, but it hurt. All that came back was his father's face, that trademark pirouette as he rasped his sword out the scabbard and pointed it at Alaric's face. *He was so strong, fearless. I will never be like that.*

'Alaric must have sold them to him. Makes you wonder if that one-eyed prick had anything to do with the raid. Just to get one up on your old man.' Fullo hawked and spat on the floor, a puff of dust flying up from the water deprived surface.

'I don't know, brother. Listen, I must do something. Not long after we joined up, when we first got paid, I put some coins into a few merchant's pockets, gave them Licina's description and asked them to let me know if they found anything. One of them, a Greek, was heading to Goridorgis. He should be on his way back by now, I'm thinking of heading north and trying to meet him on the road. Will you come?' He blushed as he finished speaking, head cast down to the floor, certain his friend would reprimand him for his actions.

'Ha! So, that's why you never get a round in when we go out for a drink. Well…as much as I think you're an idiot, it's gotta be worth a shot. What about all those hairy-arsed barbarians out there?'

'Can't say I've thought much about that. Guess we should hang back, stay well away from their rear guard. Doubt they will pay us any attention.' Fullo looked unsure, the risks weighing heavy in his mind. 'She's out there, brother. I can feel it, in my heart.'

Fullo studied his friend. Those eyes, ice cold, so like his fathers. His cheekbones were moving, teeth grinding as his mind worked out the potential problems he would face on the road. He thought himself a coward, Fullo knew, but in truth he was anything but. Full of fear, but who wasn't? But he always faced his fears; he proved that with Silus. Practically had the old man begging at his feet, not many people could say they had done that.

'Well, I'm with you. Always. Whatever obstacles we come across we'll face them together. Speaking of obstacles...'

'Taurus?'

'You read my mind! Got a plan?'

'Not really. Thought I'd just be honest. Shall we go find him?'

'Ha! You know we could end up cleaning latrines for the next month? Argh, come on then, I'm right behind you!'

Chapter Sixteen

August AD 168– North of the Danube, Germania

Aelinia sat astride her mare. Her head throbbed. It ached worse than a morning after consuming a skin full of cheap wine, a feat she had done a lot in the days when she had sold her body for money. No one gives themselves to a stinking old auxiliary sober. But there was a greater pain wearing her down. The pain of betrayal.

My brother did this to me. My brother. After all she had done for him. The months spent opening her legs to anyone who would throw her a coin. Finding doctors, healers, anyone who would offer their services to help heal the wounded gladiator.

The time spent stricken in Alaric's stinking cage – the smell of old shit and blood, not easily forgotten. But of course, Julius would have. He had been in and out of consciousness the whole time they had been in there. It wasn't him who had been dragged out as the sun set every evening to be passed around and raped. Not him who had been forced into Balomar's bed and ordered to please him. That at least, had turned out better than she could ever have imagined.

She had been horrified when she first set eyes on the king of the Marcomanni. He was huge, fearsome, and she feared he would treat her as roughly as Alaric and his cronies had.

But nothing could be further from the truth. She had found he wasn't as barbaric as he let on in public, not as terrifying or bloodthirsty as his hearth warriors believed. He was kind, gentle, and very insecure.

Plagued by doubt, he constantly sought reassurance that the path he was treading was the right one. The brash and bold figure he cut when he spoke to his people, turned out to be just another layer of armour to be put on every morning. His people were starving. The plague had weakened them, the famine that followed almost destroyed them. His people queued outside his hall every day, desperate for gifts of food or coin, and the king had none to give them. Aelinia had watched as he grew more desperate by the day, his insecurities made plain as they whispered to each other each night in the darkness.

Without the ability to grow their own food, they were having to buy heavily from the tribes to the west and north. But to do that Balomar needed gold, and Rome had stopped paying their tribute. That had been her window. Her opportunity to plant a seed in the king's mind, to strike back at the cursed empire that had abandoned her and her brother to their fate.

She had started whispering between the sheets at night, probing and guiding until Balomar had come to the conclusion she desired – the fall of Rome.

All they needed now was a plan. Word came through some traders in the east that there was a man who desired the purple. A man so close to the gods he had predicted the reincarnation of a god, and it had happened. All it had taken was one letter, and a few short months later that man himself had arrived at the gates of Goridorgis – Alexander of Abonoteichos.

All night the three of them had sat by the hearth in the king's hall, his whole retinue evicted. They had spoken in whispers, wary glances to the doors to ensure they were not overheard. Eventually a plan had been formed. A plan to shake the foundations of the empire to the core, and with some luck change them for ever.

After months of careful planning, that plan was finally coming together. But now, on the brink of victory, her brother had thrown a mighty obstacle in their path, a great hurdle to overcome. *Licina.*

Her arrival at Goridorgis had changed everything. Julius, who had already been reluctant to listen or partake with her scheming, had grown further apart from her. Choosing to spend his spare time with *her* rather than his own sister, he had fallen completely in love with the homesick redhead. He followed her round like a lost puppy. Helping her in the kitchens in the morning and lighting her fire in the evening. It was disgusting.

Aelinia hadn't liked her from the first. Full of self-pity and utterly deprived of any sort of knowledge of the harsh realities of the world, she had led a sheltered life. Sure, she had lost her parents to the plague, but so what? She'd had people around her to care for her, *more than Julius and I had.* She hadn't needed to sell her body, to watch her brother fight in the arena, suffer rapes and beatings daily. *Well, she's had a taste of that now.* An evil grin spread across her full lips as she recalled thrusting her fingers into her wet cunny the night before. Oh, how she had rejoiced in the sleeping girl's moans and gasps in joy, as she cried her lover's name aloud. She had meant to hurt her, use her, the way she had been used. It had been oddly satisfying watching Licina gasp and moan in pleasure, it had excited her, aroused her, in ways she had never felt before.

As if she hadn't detested the girl enough, her hatred had consumed her when she had heard *that* name fall from her lips. *Albinus.* She had spoken so passionately about her fantastic husband to be. How brilliant and clever he was, how he knew all there was to know about aqueducts and mills and growing crops so straight and true they were like a golden forest in the summer's sun. And his famous father. The formidable Silus. A man even Balomar begrudgingly spoke highly of. A name that sent sparks of terror flying round the lands north of the river. *Well, he didn't seem so formidable to me.* It had been cowardly of him, to leave her and Julius in that cage. *All those men with him, how hard would it have been to free me from that prison?* That had been the moment she turned her back on Rome. A moment that hurt more than being betrayed and captured in the first place.

To hear that name spoken by Licina, to hear her talk of how high and mighty he was, it had been too much. It had taken all her self-restraint not to kill her there and then. But she had bided her time. Had rejoiced in the moment she had seen the look of horror on that too thin and taut face. Their eyes had met. Across the king's great hall. It had been one of the sweetest moments Aelinia could remember having. But then Balomar had insisted on bringing her with him. *Oaf.* Casting him a stern but affectionate look – the one you give to your bouncing puppy when their demands for affection become too much – she laughed at his puzzled expression.

'What?' Balomar looked angry, cheeks flushed and a murderous stare fixed his face.

'This is all your fault. And you know it!' Aelinia rubbed her head, just to make sure she made her point.

'Okay! Okay! It was stupid to bring the girl. I admit it. Happy now?' He gave her a thin-lipped smile, amusement clear in his eyes. Aelinia knew that no matter how angry the king got with her, she could always win him back round.

'No! And neither should you be. They could ruin everything we have planned.'

'They won't, my love. They won't. Cocconas has got word to me, I am to meet him at a bend in the road, not half a mile from here. Between us we will solve our little problem. And anyway, this isn't *entirely* my fault. It was your stupid brother who knocked you round the head and helped her to escape!'

Her horse stumbled on a loose stone in the road, the sudden rocking and swaying sending waves of pain through her skull. Wincing, she fought back the urge to vomit.

'That's true,' she managed to mumble through the throbbing agony.

'Are you okay? Do you need to stop? You could have gone in a litter.' He leant over from his saddle, his touch tender, words soothing. Aelinia caught the hot glances of the nearest warriors, she knew they despised her. Often she heard whispers about the 'king's whore' around Goridorgis. Balomar's warriors wanted their king to secure a bride from amongst the tribes, but they knew he never would while Aelinia was still around.

'No. No! Roman ladies ride in litters. Marcomanni women ride horses.' She gave him a smile, but it was weak.

'Marcomanni? So, you are of the tribes now, eh?' He didn't smile, like she hoped he would. Instead he just

244

looked thoughtful, and shared a look with Adalwin, who rode to the right of his king.

'Am I not? I live with the tribe, with you. I live and eat as you do. I am more Marcomanni than Roman, I think.' His sudden distance concerned her. She had been lightly probing about his marriage plans since the arrival of summer, all too aware that if he succeeded with their plan he would have no end of suitors.

'Maybe. We'll see.' Balomar slowed his horse. The cobbled Roman road had long given way to one made of dusty dirt. The road bending away to the right, now running more north than east. There was a rider at the side of the road, taking shelter under a tree. 'There is Cocconas. Come, Adalwin, let's go see what he has to say. No, my love, you stay here, I will catch you up on the road.' And with that he was off, kicking his horse into a gallop, barking orders as he went. Aelinia was suddenly alone. Head pounding, stomach churning, but whether that was from the head wound or her sudden apprehension, she couldn't tell.

*

Balomar lurched his horse forward, the great black stallion responding to his command. *I must think of a name for you.* They had pulled out to the side of the column, and were riding on the grass towards the waiting Cocconas.

'My king! May we have a word whilst we ride?' The king of the Marcomanni reluctantly slowed his horse, all too aware of what his most trusted companion was going to say. 'It is about Aelinia my king, and your intentions towards her.' Adalwin's tone was cautious, his voice quiet. Balomar let out a small sigh, and braced himself for the inevitable.

245

'Yes, Adalwin?' He didn't turn his head to look at his captain, and tried to keep his voice neutral.

'Some of the lads been saying… been saying you intend to marry her?'

'Really? And what if I did? Would "the lads" object?' Again, his tone was light, as if he had no real care to Adalwin's answer. In truth, it was something he had long been thinking on.

'They aren't happy, my king. They say you should have a bride from the tribes. The daughter of one of the other kings. There are many that would be suitable. Areogaesus, for example—'

'Has a daughter that looks as though she has been hit with Donar's hammer! Several times. Ha! Spit it out man, you're saying I will have a problem if I choose to marry Aelinia?'

'Yes, my king. I am sorry if I have offended you.' He bowed his head. Balomar knew Adalwin would do anything for his king, he would ride to the frozen wastelands in the north and fight the ice giants side by side with the great Donar, if that's what his king desired. But he would not stand by and let him put his kingship on the line for the sake of a pretty bed slave.

'Do not worry, my friend. It is your job to be honest, you are my link between me and the men. My position is not so strong that I do not have to consider their feelings. I will think on what you said, I promise.' He offered his arm, quickly grasped by a relieved Adalwin.

'Now let's go and see what we can do about our runaway, eh?'

*

Cocconas dismounted from his horse. Another fine black stallion, if not a little shorter than the one he had gifted the king. He swigged greedily from his water skin, and wished he had felt confident enough to meet the king without the need for chainmail and a sword. *Not that they will do me much good against this lot.* The mail was causing him all sorts of grief in the scorching sun, and he could feel a bruise blossoming on his right leg where his sword had been slapping against it on the ride out here. *How do the Roman cavalry do it? I must check how they wear their swords next time I see them.*

'Greetings, Cocconas. How are you on this fine morning?' Balomar appeared in high spirits; he vaulted from the giant horse like it was a pony, and barely broke stride as he landed and took a step towards him in one motion. Up close, he seemed to block out the sun all together. *The gods help the man that meets him in the shieldwall.*

'King Balomar, I am well, thank you. And you?' A respectful nod of the head, he only bowed to his lord.

'Good. Except for this itch. This irritating little itch, I am hoping you can help me scratch it?' He made a show of itching his groin, much to the amusement of Adalwin.

'I have spoken to my lord about our little...itch. He asks if you could spare me a few men, I intend to set off and find her and her friend, and silence them for good.' He made a motion with his hand, running it across his throat.

'Of course. But where could she have gone?'

'North. I believe, anyway. When I put myself in her shoes, that's where I would have gone.' He repeated the conversation he'd had with Alexander at dawn.

Balomar listened, gazing into the easterner's eyes intently. 'Very well. I will provide you with five men. Adalwin will be one of them. But first I have a question. And I will know if you do not answer truthfully.' Another

247

respectful nod from Cocconas, followed by a nervous gulp. 'Why did you bring her to me? I did not ask for a slave.'

The Thracian paused, considered his answer, and decided to tell the truth. 'I hadn't planned to. And I wasn't asked to by my lord, like I told you in Goridorgis. I went over the river with the rear guard in the raid, saw her, desired her, took her. Lost one of my lord's best men in the process of getting her out.' His voice quivered at the end, reliving the moment a Langobardi spear ripped open poor Nicoli's throat. A quiet and pious man, he had died believing his lord was the true prophet of Asclepius. *Better dead than knowing the truth. On the plus side, lord king, his death gained you a fabulous new war horse.* He didn't say it.

'Ha! You are a fool! And I suppose your lord demanded you give her over to me?' Cocconas couldn't bring himself to reply, just another nod.

'Well, we were all young once, I guess.' Balomar seemed to slip deep into thought.

Adalwin arched an eyebrow in his king's direction. *Got your own women troubles, lord king?*

'If you don't mind my asking, lord king, why did you bring her south with you? Did you not think it was a risk?' The king hit him with a fierce stare, Adalwin growled and hefted his ash-cladded spear.

The ferocity of Balomar's glare quickly wore off and he allowed himself a small chuckle. 'Ha! Same reason you took her, I suppose. She's a looker, and I like my ale served by a pretty face.' He smiled into his beard, shining gold in the sun. 'Guess I'm not as all-knowing as I think I am! Now listen,' he motioned Cocconas and Adalwin to come closer, 'I do not think she knows all our plans. She knows about the raid, I'm certain of that, she was in the hall when Bassus sent that tribune to *summon* me.' The word was spat, who dares summon a king? 'But I do not know if she knows of our next move. But if she keeps running north, she will soon find out! So find her, and quick. I trust you will have the strength to do what is needed when the time comes?' This was directed at Cocconas, who didn't shy away from the challenge.

'Of course. I let my lord down once, it will not happen again.'

'One more thing. There is a man with her, a boy really. He must be taken alive and brought back to me in one piece, understood?' Both men nodded. *Is it you who desires that? Or your bedwarmer? I know more than you think, barbarian.*

'Good. Now there's no time to waste, Adalwin, a word before you go' said Balomar, turning his back on Cocconas.

The king and his man backed away from Cocconas, who looked relieved at having being granted his lord's request. *I will not fail you again, lord.*

*

'What do you think my friend, can I trust him?' Balomar's voice a murmur, the marching troops on the road muffling their voices.

'Yes, my king, I think so. Are you sure you want me to go? I'm reluctant to miss the—'

'I know, old friend. But this is more important, there will be no next phase if she discovers our little surprise – which should be no more than a day away from here, so find her, and quick!' They clasped arms, not another word spoken as Adalwin leapt onto his horse and went off to select his men for the journey.

Balomar gave Cocconas a departing wave, mounted his own horse and re-joined the column. He decided against catching up with Aelinia, he had much to think about, and could do with some time alone with his thoughts. A rare thing for a king. *It is all in the balance.* His heart thumped in his great chest, he thought he could see its beats pounding on the inside of his mail. *The die is cast,* As Caesar once said. He remembered listening to a drunken trader as a boy, who regaled the story of the great Arminius and his war on Rome. *This is my Teutoburg. And I shall not fail.*

Chapter Seventeen

September AD 168 – North of the Danube, Germania

Licina lay scrunched in a ball in a thick picket of bush, barely daring to breathe. Their journey had been going smoothly, until an hour or so ago. Both she and Julius had survived their jaunt in the river unscathed, and had emerged on the north banks wet, exhausted and cold, but alive. They had started moving north, wanting to put some distance between themselves and the river before turning east.

They had stayed off the roads, crossing lush green fields and thick, black forests of pine. All morning they had been on the move, Julius not allowing a stop, always forcing the pace. They had been making their way through a small patch of woodland, the ground littered with rocks and twigs, when Licina had stumbled on a large rock that was dug in the dirt. She screamed as she fell, the pain in her twisted right ankle immense from the first.

Julius had scurried over, quickly trying to get her back to her feet, but the pain was too much. That's when they first heard it. The whinny of a horse, the rustle of leaves and the padding of feet moving on the forest undergrowth. 'Don't panic,' Julius had said, 'it will just be one or two local people, out and about on their business.' He was wrong.

An army passed them by. Trampling their way south through the thick forest, wave after wave of spear-clad warriors, helmets and chainmail illuminating the sun-starved forest floor. Most were on foot, no more than a hundred mounted. They were silent, intense. This was not some small raiding band, out for a spot of pillaging in their neighbour's land. This was a war host, on their way to work. And they were going south.

Licina forgot the throbbing in her twisted ankle, now curled up by her chest. She just lay in a ball and prayed harder than she had ever done to Minerva and Fortuna, *please let them pass us by.* It seemed as if they would never end, the ground shook as pockets of cavalry cantered by, and the steady trudge of marching steps like an endless beat of a blacksmith's hammer striking the anvil, beating great rods of iron into a shimmering sword.

Still she lay there; she swore the sun must be setting soon, so long had she been huddled beneath her cloak, which, thank the gods, was as brown as the dirt-filled floor. Her heart was racing, faster than her terrifying descent down Carnuntum's walls. Dark thoughts swirled round her mind, like golden leaves caught in an autumn's blustery gale. *What will happen if they find us? Who are they? Is this part of Balomar's plan? I must tell the legion! But how to get back?*

Julius was transfixed. Awe-stricken. Never in his life had he seen such a body of men.

They were an endless sea of flesh and iron; he hadn't known there were this many warriors in the whole of Germania. *Balomar.* He knew it straight away. Guilt consumed him. *I could have stopped this.* It had been months ago that Aelinia had first confessed her plans she had made with the Marcomanni king. Months. And he had

252

done nothing to stop it. He thought he understood his sister's bitterness towards Rome. After all, their life as citizens had been a hard one. But this? Surely this was too far?

He had rebuked her then, when she first shared her plans, declaring he would have nothing to do with it. He hadn't thought her grand scheme would come to fruition. A barbarian king teaming up with an eastern holy man did not sound like a winning combination. And even then, Balomar would still need to convince the other tribal leaders to stand beneath his banner, to call him lord and send their warriors to stand in his shieldwall. And the chiefs of Germania famously never got on, and would almost certainly never swear allegiance to another lord. Well, here they were, and it appeared they had.

They thought it would never end. Thousands of legs passed them by, as they lay in silence, hoping the thick bush would keep them hidden.

Eventually, the marching legs ran out. The ground stopped rumbling, Julius stopped sweating and Licina's heart returned to its normal rate.

'By Jupiter! That was close!' Julius felt as though he hadn't drawn breath in hours, and they came in quick shallow gasps now, as if he'd fought all day in the arena in armour. He clambered out of the brush, cursing as a thorn pricked him on the arm.

'My heart was going so fast I was sure they would hear it!' Licina took Julius' offered arm as she struggled to her feet. Her cloak was covered in debris from the forest floor; she shook it off, staggering as her weight went onto her right ankle. 'What are we going to do? There's an army marching on Carnuntum, we've no way of getting there before them. And my ankle is swelling up, feels like it may

253

be broken.' She sat back down, taking off her shoe to reveal a right foot twice the size of her left, black and blue in colour.

'Can you put any weight on it?' A shake of Licina's head. 'Well, there's no point going south, as you say, we'll never make it before that lot. We should keep going north, join onto the amber road...and I don't really know after that.' He stretched his back, aching after so long hunched down. Running a hand over his face, he grimaced at the sharp edges of a growing beard, his hand coming away brown, and he tried to remember the last time he'd had a decent wash. 'We should try and find a stream on the way, a quick wash and somewhere to soak your ankle. Should do us both some good. I'll see if I can find a large branch, something you can use as a crutch.'

Licina watched him walk off into the woodland. He picked up a discarded spear and tested its weight as he walked. *I hope he knows how to use that. I have a horrible feeling he may have to.*

*

Albinus was having a hard time keeping a straight face. He'd never dare to consider himself an expert horseman, but he was doing better than his fearful friend.

'Hah! Come on, Fullo, we're meant to be going north, not west!' They were over the river now, following in the tracks of Balomar and his retinue. The pace was slow, thanks mainly to Fullo and his complete inability to control the small mare he was riding.

'Why don't you piss off! You know I hate these stupid things. Worthless animals. Why couldn't we have just walked?' The mare could sense his fear, smell it. She tossed her head to the side and snorted as he tried to get her walking the right way. The action made him whimper

254

in fear. 'I mean, what's the point in them? They stink and all they do is eat and shit!'

'You've more in common with them than you realise, brother! And the point in them is that we will cover more ground with them than without them. Well, if you get your act together we will! We only have 'til sundown, so we have to move fast.' The rest of the day was all Taurus had allowed them. Albinus could see in his centurion's eyes that he didn't expect the two men to find anything, but he'd let them go anyway. *My father's shade is doing me a favour, I suppose.*

He carried on riding, oblivious to the curses coming from Fullo. *Where would I go if I were Licina?* He tried to put himself in her mind. Would she have stuck to the road? No, she would have known she was being pursued. *Through the fields and woods, then try to stay out of sight.* He had realised it was fruitless, trying to find the merchant. He would be on the same road as Balomar and his warriors, he would never get ahead of them, not on their own land. So he had decided to look for Licina herself. He knew it was desperate, and had done his best to ignore Fullo as he'd urged caution.

'Fullo, how far north do you think we should go? I think Licina would have gone east, but not sure how far north she would have gone first.' He waited five heartbeats but got no reply. He turned his horse – also a mare but a lot more comfortable with her rider – and laughed aloud at the sight of his friend, lying flat on the back of his horse, hugging her neck.

'If you tell anyone about this, I swear to all the gods—'

He slipped and fell from the mare's back; she'd twisted her neck to get a better look at what her rider was doing. He hit the floor with an almighty whack. His chainmail clanked as it struck the ground, the iron links digging into his back. The pain was sharp, like he was being pricked with a hundred barbed arrowheads.

Albinus sighed as he turned his horse round to go help his friend. *Would have been better off on my own.* 'You okay, brother?' He did his best to keep his amusement from his voice.

'More my pride that hurts than my body. Will probably have some new scars on my back, the first ones I've got there since I last rode a horse!' He stumbled to his feet, doubled over as the pain in his winded stomach was too much. 'When I get my breath back, I'm gonna go into those trees, find the biggest branch I can find and ram it up this stupid bastards ar—'

'Sorry to interrupt your rant! But we have one day to find any sign of my kidnapped wife to be. So, if you don't mind, I'd rather you did the horse up the arse another day, and tried your best to be helpful today.' The amusement was gone from his voice. His desperation clear. *We only have one day.*

Fullo looked into those ice-cold eyes; if he wasn't looking straight at Albinus he could have sworn it was Silus who had just given him a dressing down. That voice, *filled with iron.* A sad smile crept into the corners of his mouth, as he mounted back on the mare without another word.

'Why are you smiling?' His high cheekbones flushing red, Albinus was annoyed at his friend's apparent amusement to his little outburst.

'It's just that, at times you look like your old man, your eyes an' all. But that was the first time you've ever sounded like him. Reckon it won't be long before I'm calling you "sir".' He gently lashed the reins to get the mare moving, she snorted a small protest, but obeyed his touch.

'What? Don't be ridiculous! Not yet drawn my sword in anger; still not sure I'm going to be able to when the time comes.' That was something that kept him awake at night. When Fullo and the others were snoring and farting their way through the dark, he often lay on his bunk, questioning his courage. *You're an embarrassment.* He'd never quite got over that. Even after making peace and finding kinship with his father, that thought was always lurking at the back of his mind.

'Yeah, you will, you'll see. And anyway, you'll have me and the other lads by your side, we'll see you're all right.' Albinus wondered if his friend's apparent lack of concern at crossing blades with a foe was put on to help him feel better. But having witnessed first-hand what he could do with a sharp edge, he thought it probably wasn't.

'We'll see, brother. Now back to today, I say we follow the road north for another mile or so, see what we can see. Then cut off the road and head east, that's what I would have done if I was her. Thoughts?'

'Right behind you, sir. I follow where you lead.' Fullo gave a mock salute on his horse, leaning over the right side towards Albinus. Once more the mare turned sharply at the shift in weight on her back, and once more Fullo ended up eating dust off the brown carpet, his back on fire and his lungs gasping for air.

Albinus sighed. *Should have just come on my own.*

*

Two or more uneventful hours passed. Albinus was grateful that Fullo had managed to stay mounted for so long. They had passed one more mile marker on the road, and decided there probably wouldn't be many more this side of the *limes*. So rather than wasting too much time following the road, they'd cut off and headed east through a small woodland path. The shade was a relief. The sun was at its highest now, and they were both roasting in their armour. Albinus cursed himself for not having the foresight to bring spare water skins, as both his and Fullo's were almost empty. *Just comes with experience, lad.* He could imagine Bucco saying it, as he had said it a thousand times to him over the last few months. Every time he missed a step on parade, or raised his shield a fraction too late, or released his *pilum* a heartbeat too early. It seemed there was much left to learn in the art of soldiering. *The trick is staying alive long enough to learn it.* One of Bucco's more harrowing sayings.

It was quiet in the dark of the forest. So thick with pine it was hard to judge how much time had passed since they entered, as any sight of the sun was rare. Albinus's stomach was screaming at him, so he reckoned it was late in the afternoon. They hadn't stopped for a midday meal, but had chewed and sucked their way through hard tack earlier in the day.

Albinus removed his helmet from his head. The leather cap underneath was drenched in sweat, and the gentle breeze on his short crop of hair was welcoming as his mare ploughed along at a slow canter.

He was deep in thought, placing himself in his lover's mind and trying to imagine where she would have gone. He thought she would have gone back east, to the settlement. For all he knew, she believed him to still be there, or dead. There were people still there rebuilding, he knew. More veterans from around the province had flocked to the site when they learned of the attack, and had gladly offered their services to help rebuild the homes that had been lost.

It had warmed Albinus's heart, the generosity of others. Most had never served with Silus, some had never even heard of him. But the brotherhood of the legions had obliged them to go and help the families of their deceased comrades. Albinus knew it would soon be rebuilt, that by next spring new crops would have been planted and fresh barley would be growing in the fields he loved so much. But he also knew he would never return. Couldn't. *Too many ghosts.*

He was lost in these thoughts when the first sound pricked his ears. The chink of armour, the muffled curse from the warrior who knew he was about to be discovered. Then the crunching footsteps on the thick forest floor, the growl as he hefted his ash-clad spear, and the groan as he put all his strength into a mighty throw. Albinus managed to get his head round to the left as the spear whistled towards him. He just sat astride his horse, stunned and terrified as the spear arced its way towards him.

His mouth went dry and his bladder was suddenly full. He relished the chill that ran down his spine, was perplexed at his complete inability to speak or move his arms or legs. He just sat there gaping, as the spear point got closer and closer to burying itself in his head.

He'd always thought he'd think of his father, or Licina at the moment of his death. In fact, his mind was completely clear, empty and silent, like an ocean shimmering in the moonlight.

His horse saved him. The mare bolted forwards, taking him out of the path of the hurtling spear. Before he could begin to comprehend what was happening, Fullo galloped past him, drawing his sword in one fluid motion as he charged down the Germanic warrior.

The Roman pair weren't armed with a *spatha* like regular cavalry, they still carried their legionary *gladius,* a short blade more suited for the close-quartered butcher work that comes when the shieldwalls meet. The barbarian rasped out a longsword from its scabbard.

Over twice the length of the *gladius,* it looked as though the fight would be over quickly.

But Fullo fought with the strength of Mars. Leaning down from the saddle, left hand still gripping the reins, he swiped his sword from high to low as the warrior hefted his from low to high. A loud metallic clang filled the air as the blades met. The barbarian would have been forgiven for thinking Fullo would pass him by and come back round for another try.

He didn't. He slowed his mare even as the blades kissed, and using the forward momentum gained from his blade running down the longer broadsword, he ripped it back in a savage arc that ripped into the skull of the unhelmeted warrior. There it stuck so hard he had to relinquish his grip as the horse continued to canter by.

The Germanic warrior slumped to the ground. Eyes unblinking, blood trickling from his mouth and pouring from the open wound on the back of his head. He swayed on his knees for a few heartbeats before slumping head first onto the ground.

Fullo screamed in joy as he turned his mare round. The battle thrill upon him, he finally had his first taste of the bloodlust his father had often spoke to him about. *A dangerous thing it is, lad. You get a taste for it, start to think yourself invincible. Seen many a man cut down at that point of ultimate joy.* Fullo could finally appreciate his father's words.

He stopped and dismounted by the freshly made corpse. *My freshly made corpse.* He rolled the body over to look into the man's lifeless eyes. They were the purest brown, like a chestnut horse. Glazed over, the spark had gone from them. Fullo stared into those eyes a long time, and marvelled at how just moments before they were so full of hate and menace. And now, all that was gone. All the memories, the sights those eyes had seen, extinguished with one swipe of his sword. *This is who I am now. This is what I do.* He revelled in his own self glory.

Albinus still hadn't moved. His heart was still racing, his breath still came in shallow gasps. Sweat poured down face, as if he was standing in a spring downpour. *Coward.* He'd done nothing. Hadn't even moved to save his own worthless life, the horse had done that for him. *I hope my father wasn't watching that.* He cast his mind back to the winter, the anger that warmed him in the snow. His father's body burning on the pyre. He'd vowed that day to stand in the iron storm and take what was his. Vengeance. But at the first hint of combat, in a silent woodland far away from the terror of the shieldwall, he had sat on his horse and done nothing. *You're an embarrassment.* Never had those words seemed truer.

His limbs remembered they were still alive before his brain. Sudden bolts of pain in his fingers where he was gripping the reins so tight. He looked down slowly, still in a daze. Blood oozed from his blistered palms, still not healed. His knuckles were white, hands were shaking. Gently, he released his grasp of the leather reins and stared at his hands, muscles screaming now. *Not a soldier's hands.* Oh, how he wanted nothing more than to run home.

261

To Licina, to his father. To feel the warmth and comfort their presence brought him. He knew he never could.

With a start, he realised Fullo was beside him, concern plain on his face. 'You okay, brother?' He spoke gently, as if speaking to a child. Albinus tried to reply, but only managed a croak and a groan. Without warning, he leant to the right and vomited violently, sliding off the horse soon after.

Fullo leapt off his own and ran to his friend's side. 'It's okay, brother, it's okay.' He was sobbing now, lying in a puddle of his own sick. Fullo knelt, shook his water skin hoping to find some left in. It was empty.

'It's not okay, is it! We've had everything taken from us! Everything! I determined to become a soldier, to take revenge for my father's death and to find Licina. And look at me! First sign of a spear thrown in anger and what do I do? Nothing! Couldn't even bring myself to save my own life. I'm pathetic! Silus had it right. An embarrassment! That's what I've always been, what I always will be.' He curled back into a ball and continued to sob, oblivious to the gut-wrenching stench of his sick mixed with the open bowels of the dead barbarian, laying just feet away. 'I can't do this, Fullo, I'm just not made for it. I'm leaving.'

He stood slowly, took two deep breaths to slow the flood of tears, and mounted his horse.

'You're leaving? Where the fuck do you think you're gonna go? You're in Germania! There's plenty more of them where this one came from!' He pointed at the dead warrior, who took that moment to let out a slow and noisy fart. Both men jumped so high they nearly left their armour on the ground. 'Well fuck me! Habitus said that's what happened, never thought it was true!'

He turned back to his friend, hoping to see some amusement in his face. A shared joke would help ease his spirits. But all he saw was the back of his head, bobbing along as his mare made her way down the path.

'Albinus! Wait!'

'No, Fullo, I'm going. Tell Taurus I'm sorry, but maybe I'm not my father's son after all.' He didn't turn back.

*

The sun was finally beginning its descent in the west. He could feel it slipping down the back of his body. All afternoon he had ridden on in silence. It seemed even the crows were avoiding him, not wanting to waste their time following a coward, for he would slaughter them no dinner. He had lost all hope. Never would he rise from his father's mighty shadow. Never would he find his lost love and see out his days happily in her arms.

He had lived a coward, he would die a coward.

He was just coming to the end of another woodland path, the country north of the river being littered with small, thick bunches of ash and pine. He heard voices up ahead.

Smelt the smell of men and leather as the breeze brushed against his face. His heart didn't race this time. He got no cold sensation running down his spine. He accepted his fate gladly, and hoped he would do Jupiter and his father proud.

The sun's dying light was blood-red through the gaps in the trees, it seemed appropriate. He could make them out now, four, maybe five men readying themselves for an easy kill. They hefted spears, adjusted their mail, fitted their helmets. *They won't need them.*

There was more noise beyond them. It sounded like, an army? Loud roars, laughter, the clang of metal on metal.

His mare's ears pricked at the sound and smell of other horses nearby, a lot of horses by the sound of it.

Suddenly, Albinus was out of his trance, no longer wallowing in self-pity. *There's an army here!* He turned on his horse to survey the land. Looked up at the sun then to his right, south towards the Danube. He could see it, through the gaps in the trees. He concentrated, tried to picture where he was. *Somewhere between the settlement and Carnuntum.* Heart racing now, an army this close to Roman lands could only mean one thing. *War.*

He was full of fire now. Thrust back to that snow-filled day, his father's body turning to ashes atop a great pyre. The rage came back to him. Filled him the way steaming water fills a bath. *You're more like your father than you think.* Taurus's words echoing in his mind.

He didn't want to die now. Didn't want to ride into the waiting barbarians' spears. He focused his eyes on the gap in the trees, took in every detail he could see. It wasn't an army that Rome would recognise. There were no standards, no men standing to attention in neatly dressed ranks. They were a mob. One giant mob. They covered the ground as far as the eye could see. Mainly infantry, small pockets of cavalry grouped around the field.

What in the name of all the gods? He didn't have time to think, to ponder on who they were, or why they were here. A harsh tug on the reins and Albinus had his mare turned and galloping back towards the setting sun. There were shouts of alarm behind him, and he felt rather than saw three horsemen gallop after him. *They will not catch me. I will get back to Carnuntum, to my brothers.*

*

Fullo was angry. Completely perplexed and consumed with rage that Albinus could just leave the way he did. All their lives, they had been fed stories of honour and heroism in the face of danger. How there was no greater joy in life then standing with your brothers in the midst of the iron storm, for the glory of your legion and Rome.

And Albinus had just left.

Bastard. Worthless coward. Maybe Albinus had been right after all; he was an embarrassment. He was travelling west, back the way he and Albinus had travelled earlier in the day. The setting sun on his face was glorious, beautiful as it dipped down behind a far ridge, a halo of red in the deep blue sky. The breeze on his back carried him forwards, invigorated him as it crept through the gaps in his mail. He watched a squirrel scurry up a nearby tree, lightning reactions getting him away from a hungry fox. It sat atop a low branch and seemed to mock the fox, as if it was daring the predator to climb up and get it.

It was a sight that would normally have left Fullo laughing for some time, joining in the mockery of the fox. Today, he barely gave either a second glance. The smell of the forest filled his nostrils, the aroma of the pine reminding him of another life, playing at soldiers in his small fort with Albinus. *No one's playing any more.*

He tried to conjure the words he was going to spill to Taurus. He knew his centurion would be furious, and more than a little disappointed. He was a good man, and had gone a long way to look out for the two new recruits since they signed up. As had Bucco, and Habitus, Libo, Rullus, Longus and Calvus. Together they had made their *Contubernium* a real home for them both. And Albinus had just spat on them all.

He continued to his ride in stony silence. A hawk squawked overhead, he could see through the thinning trees it make its swoop down into a nearby field, eyes locked on its prey.

There was a silence once the hawk had done. Fullo began to feel uneasy. He couldn't grasp what it was, but he had a feeling he wasn't alone. He slowed and looked around. Coming out of the last patch of woodland, he could see the road in the distance. It comforted him, knowing he was nearly home. But still, this feeling, skin on the back of his neck prickling, a chill running down his spine. He stopped his horse, dismounted and rasped his sword from its scabbard. Dried blood decorated the blade, in the thrill of the earlier kill, he hadn't thought to clean it.

Kneeling close to the ground, he licked his dry lips, and for the hundredth time that day wished he'd brought a second water skin. He looked at the dusty path, it was as if it was moving. *It is!* Small granules of dirt were jumping off the surface, dancing almost. He could feel it now, a low rumble – like distant thunder – something big was moving down the road.

He looked back down, seeing nothing but the gloom of the forest in the ever-dying light. Then there was a glint, and another. The rumble got louder, hoofbeats, clearer now.

Fullo began to panic. *Stand and fight? Mount and run?* His lack of horsemanship was at the forefront of his mind. Still undecided, he looked back down the road. The first rider was clearer now, a trailing blood-red cloak, mail shirt and helmet catching the last of the sun's light. *Albinus!* He didn't slow at the sight of his friend.

'Run, Fullo! Get on your horse and run! The tribes are coming!'

'How many?'

'All of them, brother!' And with that he had gone past him in a flash. Fullo looked down the road one last time to see three riders emerging from the darkness. He didn't hang around long enough to see if there were more.

Chapter Eighteen

September AD 168 – North of the Danube, Germania

Balomar sat astride his great stallion, and marvelled in the glory of his army. Areogaesus sat beside him, the other tribal chiefs clamoured and jostled, desperate for their new lord's attention.

All around him, as far as the eye could see, the green plains of his homeland were covered with metal-covered men. It filled him with pride, so much so he felt a tear welling in the corner of his eye.

'Well, Balomar, you have delivered on your promises so far. Are you ready to lead us to victory?' said the deep booming voice of Areogaesus, king of the Quadi. Balomar despised the man. The very essence of arrogance, he had the annoying ability to always appear calm and in control, whilst nervous emotions caused a whirlwind in Balomar's belly.

'I will fulfil my promise, Areogaesus, don't you worry about that.' Irritation clear in his tone, he once again wished he possessed his fellow king's composure. *But I have a dark side, an edge, something this old fool will never have.*

That dark side was not proving enough to deal with the day-to-day hassle of keeping such a large body of men together. Over twenty thousand had flocked to his banner, an astonishing amount. But the high king was quickly discovering it wasn't bringing the men together that was the hard part, it was keeping them together.

Not even a week had passed since they had gathered in the lands of the Marcomanni. Balomar had been on his way to Carnuntum to meet Bassus, so Areogaesus had been the man responsible for gathering the tribes and settling them down into something that vaguely resembled a camp. There had been over fifty deaths in that time, as men from rival tribes took up the opportunity to settle old scores; it was almost impossible to find the culprit when a knife was plunged into a sleeping man's back in the dead of night, especially in a camp so vast.

Even if there hadn't been the tribal rivalries to deal with, food and fresh water was proving to be enough of a headache. One of the main reasons they were here in the first place was because there wasn't enough grain to go around, and now suddenly there were hundreds of bakers baking ten thousand loaves of bread a day. The Harii, the dark and mysterious tribe from the north, were doing all the hunting for the army. Their leader, Euric, quite possibly the most fearsome man Balomar had ever met – not that he had voiced that aloud – had argued passionately in the defence of his people when they had returned that morning with nothing but handfuls of thin rabbits. There was nothing in the area left to hunt, he had said, and if anyone doubted him they were welcome to go and hunt for themselves to see how they fared.

There were no volunteers.

Carts overburdened with barrels of fresh water had wheels broken, or tipped on the uneven roads, spilling the precious liquid all over the ground. He had asked the chiefs to ensure each warrior had his own water skin, but most had arrived without.

But his current frustration was the pace of the march. The head of the great column would set out at sunrise, but it seemed it was past midday when the rear guard eventually got underway, so long it was they had to wait for their turn to move. *It will be winter by the time we are at Carnuntum at this rate!*

The march had to stop well before sundown to ensure the whole army was still together. That's if they could find a field big enough for them all to sleep in. Then it was the tedious business of allocating spots for latrines, camping one tribe next to another it was friendly to, allocating food and water to each tribe, dealing with complaints from one chief or another, before finally slumping down onto the hard ground for a few hours of bad sleep.

Not for the first time, he wished his men had the discipline of their enemy. A Roman legion could march over twenty miles in a day, keeping perfect formations and ready to fight in an instant. The tribes were nowhere near their equal when it came to efficiency; he just hoped they would match them in battle.

He felt the gaze of king of the Quadi burning into the back of his head as he looked over the marching men. He thought of apologising for his bitter comment, then thought better of it. *I am the high king. The chosen one, who will lead us from under Rome's shadow.* He studied the man instead. Some fifteen years older than himself, Areogaesus had the remnants of a once fine mane of hair. What was left was straggly and shimmering grey in the sun's glory. His eyebrows possessed more hair than his head, thick and bushy, sitting atop wise old eyes that reminded Balomar of an owl. A thick, scarred nose – a constant reminder that no matter his age, this was a man well-rehearsed at spear play – sat atop a thick-lipped

270

mouth. Unlike most men in Germania, Areogaesus preferred to keep cleanshaven, and Balomar wondered if it was not such a bad idea in the sweltering summer months, when the breeze was rare and his beard itched like he'd spent the night in the lowest of brothels.

His thoughts turned to Aelinia, how she would revel in the sight of so many men, ready and baying to take their revenge on the cursed empire that ruined so many lives. She had travelled on to Goridorgis, partly to keep her safe from the fighting, and partly to give him some space to consider their future.

Turning away from his fellow king, he raised himself in his saddle to get a better look at his huge warband. *Surely even Arminius did not have so many men.* Thoughts of the long dead Chauci leader came often to him recently. The man had led three full legions into the deep dark of the Teutoburg forest and annihilated them almost to a man.

He was conscious that he had no grand plan of his own. His was simple – march on Carnuntum and then follow the amber road south into Italy, then onto Rome itself. *But first to defeat the Fourteenth. How well will they be prepared?*

He had been made aware of two Roman riders who had escaped his own mounted men. Word would soon spread to Candidus in his mighty fortress. Balomar hoped the legate of the Fourteenth would elect to meet him in the field; he knew he had neither the weapons or the supplies to maintain a lasting siege on the fortress itself. He also knew that he was marching to meet a foe with far superior weapons and armour. He had the numbers, but how much difference would that make when wave after wave of German warriors smashed into the solid shieldwall of Rome? And that would be only after the dreaded eagles

271

had darkened the sky with their vicious *pilum*. And what about their siege craft? He shuddered at the thought of hearing their *ballistae* twang and catapults crack as they rained death on his army. *Will they stand when the blood starts flowing, and men start dying?*

He looked around him. Of all the tribal warriors gathered, only the hearth warriors of each king were properly armoured and armed. Each wore a mail vest complete with arm and leg greaves. Helmets forged of solid iron, long swords four feet in length and four fingers thick at the base. These men would prove their worth when the swords clashed, but would there be enough of them to keep the other thousands in line? Pretty much all of his other warriors were farmers, each had his own ash-clad spear, but that was about it. A few carried blades or axes, but none Balomar could see had helmet or mail. He was marching against one of Rome's finest legions armed with a rabble. The thought made him chuckle. *How could Candidus possibly refuse such an offer?*

'There is one more thing you should know.' Once more, Balomar forced his mind out of his daydreams to listen to the ageing Quadi King.

'Yes, Areogaesus?'

'The Naristae. I sent a rider to their chief, Eric. But when he arrived at their lands, it was stripped of warriors. The Iazyges the same. I fear Eric and Bandanasp have abandoned us in our time of need.'

Balomar smiled a satisfied smile. *Ahh, my little secret.* 'Why are you smiling?' For the first time, Balomar saw a spark annoyance on that ever-patient face.

'Eric and Bandanasp will not be joining us. Not yet anyway. They have gone east. It occurred to me that to keep our merry band together I would need a large amount of coin.'

'And where are those two fools going to find that? There is no coin to be found in the land of the Iazyges.' His gruff tone was almost mocking.

'Ahh, but what lays east of their lands?'

'Dacia? The gold mines? Are you serious? It should have been us that tackled that!

Can we trust them to deliver?' Balomar was overjoyed to see the near panic in the old man. He was enjoying the sudden power he had over him.

'I have my reasons, my friend. Who would you say are the two tribes Rome would fear a war against most?'

'Us, of course. We rule the largest lands in southern Germania, we have the most warriors to call on. All other tribal chiefs pay homage to us as well as Rome.'

'Exactly! And that is why it must be us who strikes at their heart. The Marcomanni and the Quadi, untied for all of Rome to see. Eric and Bandanasp will provide a useful distraction, meaning the armies east of us will be unable to link up with the Pannonian legions and meet us in the field. Once they have the gold, they will scurry back through Bandanasp's lands and join us. Don't worry, my friend, I've thought it through.' *Well, Alexander has anyway.* And Balomar certainly hoped he proved as trustworthy as he seemed. It was only now it dawned on him how completely he had come to trust the eastern soothsayer, and how vulnerable he would soon be if the man had been playing him.

Not for the first time, Balomar regretted leaving Adalwin with Cocconas; it had been a rash decision made in panic. Oh, how he could have used his friend's advice and counsel in the last days, how many had it been? But he

273

couldn't have risked the girl getting back to Carnuntum and revealing his plans before he was ready. Even now he pictured her dead on a spear, and his friend making haste to return to his king's side. His good humour returned at the thought of welcoming him back and filling him in on recent events. And how his face would light up when he saw the extent of the army he had helped to gather. *Yes, my old friend will be back by my side soon.*

*

Adalwin woke slowly, his body hurting before he even opened his eyes. It was the second day on the hunt for the girl, and already he was cursing his king's name for sending him to dispose of her. They had slept on the forest floor, in the far north of the country of the Marcomanni. Four men he had brought with him and Cocconas, though the Allfather himself knew he wasn't expecting to need them. One of them, Siltric, was an experienced tracker and he had quickly picked up a trail.

All day they had followed, riding as hard as Siltric would allow. Occasionally he would call a halt, and get down onto the ground to examine footprints or broken leaves and twigs. Adalwin knew better than to question the man, for all the years he had known him he'd never seen him lose a man or beast on a hunt.

'One of them's hurt.' He was on all fours, gently probing two different sets of footprints in the ground. 'I think it's the girl. See these prints here, they're smaller than the others. The left foot goes deeper into the ground than the right, looks like she hurt herself. And see these little round holes, that's some sort of stick or something, must be using it to keep the weight off her foot.'

Adalwin dismounted to get a better look. Once more he thanked Wotan for having such a skilled man to call upon.

274

He would have never noticed the shallow footprints in the dry ground, let alone that they were different depths. He laughed aloud as he looked at the point Siltric was examining – all he saw was light brown dirt-filled ground, with dead leaves and debris scattered across the top. 'Excellent work, Siltric, that's why I asked you on our little venture! How far ahead of us are they?'

'Half a day? If that. If we push on then we could have them by nightfall.'

'Just what I want to hear! Lead the way, man.'

Vaulting back on his horse, he smiled a satisfied smile at the prospect of getting this wrapped up quickly and getting back to his king. *My place is by his side, not killing little girls.* He understood his king's desire to get this done, but it still rankled with him that Balomar had chosen to send his champion rather than one of his hearth warriors. Siltric on his own could have got the job done!

He looked round at the mounted party and eyed Cocconas bringing up the rear. He nodded to his other three men as they rode past, and greeted the easterner with a smile.

'Seems like our journey will be a short one. I reckon you will be as glad as I to get back to your master?'

'Yes. It is a pivotal time in our plans. But our masters will be pleased to have this small hiccup cleared up.'

'Does Alexander really think to become Emperor? Sorry to be so intrusive, but the question has been gnawing at me for some time.' Adalwin still didn't fully trust the soothsayer or his followers, which was probably why he had taken four men with him to find the girl. There is no defence against a knife in the dark.

'Yes! And what a great ruler he shall be. To think of all he has achieved so far, and what he could achieve with unlimited power at his disposal. The man is a marvel, a genius! The gods work through him you know.'

Adalwin tried to hide a smirk. 'Yes Glycon, so I've heard. But defeating a Roman legion is one thing, getting yourself to the purple is something else! Does he have friends in Rome? Senators perhaps?'

Cocconas slowed his horse and gripped the hilt of his curved *spatha*. 'It would appear that my master does not have the trust of your king?' Already the Thracian was plotting his escape. The three other Germani were fifteen or so paces ahead, Siltric the tracker ten in front of them. He could kill Adalwin in less than ten heartbeats, he was sure. The man must be a formidable warrior but Cocconas did not doubt his speed and skill with a blade.

'No, my friend, you have misunderstood! I am merely making conversation, just curious, is all. Let us move on to other things. Where are you from? Your Latin seems to have a greater accent even than mine.'

Eyes still narrowed but hand on sword, Cocconas gave his stallion a gentle kick to bring it back into a trot. 'Byzantium, where east meets the west.'

'I have heard of it. Occasionally traders bring stock from the east. It must be there that the great tapestries and rugs are made? Balomar has a few such grand things now.'

Cocconas couldn't hide his amused smile. It cost him a dirty look from the German, but he explained quickly. 'The world is a far bigger place than you know, friend. The luxuries you speak of come from Persia, in the far east. They have their own empire, one to rival Rome's, some say. My home is far away from their lands; it would take weeks to get there by horse.'

Adalwin couldn't think of anything to say. *Weeks?* His whole life all he had known were his king's lands and the southern borders with Rome. Come to think of it, he didn't even know where Rome was. Occasionally he would be sent across country to some tribal chief or other, but all the smaller villages looked the same. He suddenly felt very small.

'By the way, what happened to Alaric?' Cocconas hadn't seen the one-eyed old rogue since the raid in the winter; he clearly wasn't part of Balomar's retinue, or he would have seen the man since.

'Alaric? Why'd you ask?' Adalwin hadn't spared the man a thought for months.

'Curious. He was trusted to travel from tribe to tribe, sharing our gold and making promises on our behalf. And then, gone! Just like that. Curious.'

'If you say so. The man's a mercenary, loyal only to the man with the deepest pockets. Balomar trusted him enough to get what was required done, but had no further use for him. Last I saw him, he was crossing the river to join in the raid.'

'I saw him on the other side, but only briefly. Another thing, why there? Alaric was insistent on where the raid should take place.'

'Ha! Revenge my friend, revenge.' Adalwin shared the story of Alaric's downfall at the hands of Silus. 'People look upon him in awe, as if he's Wotan reborn or something. Truth is, Cocconas, the man's just a fraud. He's a washed-up old mercenary who saw his chance to get even and took it. I was told after the raid he was injured in the fighting, but it was only rumour. He'll resurface at some point; he's probably on the raid in Dacia!'

'Ahh Dacia, now that is closer to my home. Speaking of which, how do you think your friends will get on over

277

there?' It concerned Alexander, Cocconas knew, that a pivotal part of their plan was taking place without them or Balomar there to oversee. With two full tribes let loose on all the gold Dacia's mines had to offer, anything could happen.

*

Governor Calpernius Proculus stood on the battlement and basked in the evening sun. Four years he had been in Dacia now, and his time was drawing to an end. Thoughts of leaving the beautifully green and mountainous country saddened him deeply, surprisingly so. He had thought it a punishment of sorts when Marcus Aurelius had ordered him here. The gold mines in the region provided the empire with over half of its intake, and the Emperor had been informed that a large part of the mines' produce was not making it back to Rome.

It was a problem Proculus had quickly remedied. Touring the mines of Rosia Montana on one of his first days in the region, it had become clear the accountants working in the mine were about as honest as the tax collectors back in Rome – and Proculus knew how to deal with them.

One by one he had them hung in the autumn sunshine, he could still remember the screams and see the shocked and joyous looks on the miners' faces as the vicious little men were strung up and thrown deep into the biggest mine. It had made for a peaceful winter. The output of gold had risen immediately, of course there was no more being mined, but all of what was, made its way to the imperial treasury. Well, almost all, Proculus smiled to himself. *A little here and there never hurt anyone. Just got to be sensible.*

278

Sensible was a word that best described the ageing senator. All his life he had kept to the shadows, lurked in the background and let other men compete for the spotlight in the cesspit that was the senate. He had never made it as far up the *cursus honorum* as his father would have wanted, but he had done well. He expected to be given a consulship when he returned to Rome. That, combined with the gold he had been fleecing for the last four years, should be enough to see him live out his final years in luxury in some estate in northern Italy somewhere, *maybe Ravenna, I hear it's lovely there.*

Gazing out onto the sun-drenched green fields, sloping away from the wooden walls of the thirteenth legion's summer camp at Tibiscum, he had a hard time imagining it would be more beautiful than here. He was distracted from his thoughts by the sound of hobnailed boots ringing out on the battlement floor. Looking to his left he saw first spear centurion Ulpius Bacchius marching towards him. A veteran, if there ever was one. His helmet was polished so bright it was hard to look upon, such was the strength of the sun's rays bouncing off it. The red dyed horse crest at the top was combed to perfection, each hair pointing up to the gods in unison. His chainmail burnished to perfection, the shimmering iron links complete with his *phalera,* not that he'd wear his medals in battle. A blood-red cloak and matching tunic were in perfect condition, shimmering iron greaves on his arms and lower legs, he looked every inch a man of war.

'Evening, governor. I trust you are well?' His left hand lay lazily on the maple oak pommel of his *gladius*. A simple weapon, he had never bought into the fancy swords some senior officers spent their wages on.

'I am, centurion. And yourself? You are looking rather splendid this evening, I must say.' Proculus had to crane his neck to look upon the first spear's face, as usual he was struck with jealousy at what he saw. The centurion was beyond handsome, one of those men that annoyingly looked better with age. A short red and grey beard surrounded a well-rounded face. Piercing light green eyes, they sometimes reminded the governor of marble, though he had no doubt the man was stronger than that. Standing at over six feet tall he was a giant in battle, not that Proculus had ever got close enough to witness it. His torso was as muscled as the crafted metal of a bronzed *cuirass*. Compared to Proculus, short, fat and pasty, the man looked like Mars reborn.

'Thank you, governor. I am meeting a lady later, hoping my luck is in.' He winked and smiled, thoughts stirring to the beautiful Covonia, a serving girl at his local tavern; the two had been locking eyes across the smoke-filled room for months, until Bacchius had finally mustered the courage to speak to her. *Give me a barbarian shieldwall to break any day.*

He gazed over the parapet, towards a small plume of smoke in the north. A small *vici* lay on a bend in the river Tibiskos; in between the clamour of tanners, blacksmiths, brothels, jewellers and bakeries was a beautifully crafted stone building. The tavern had a giant hearth running down its centre, the place was a wonder in the cold winter months. Though he hoped the hearth wasn't roaring tonight. Standing on the north wall of the legion's fortress, the ovens were in full swing beneath him. It wasn't so much the smoke, but the heat coming off them was intense; he worried his fine tunic would be stained in sweat before even reaching the tavern.

Proculus smiled an amused smile as he saw the anxiety in the first spear's eyes. A man who could turn a battle on his own, and he's scared of meeting a lady for a drink. He was about to set off on a story of how he had first met his wife, and that he knew all too well the compounding fear of what to do and say the first time you are alone in the company of a beautiful woman. But the words never made it from his brain to his mouth.

There was a rush of air past Bacchius's face, a glint of metal sped past his eye. The arrow hit Proculus square in his left cheek. Blood erupted from the wound like lava from a volcano. Bacchius did not waste a heartbeat. He was off at once, shouting for the trumpeters on the wall to start blowing the call to arms. Dacia had been at peace all summer. They had heard of the raid in Pannonia, and the usual unrest in the borders of the Rhine, but Dacia had been as quiet as a field mouse, waiting patiently for the hunting eagle to pass by overhead.

He leapt down the final steps, grabbing a discarded shield laying against a nearby tent. The weight was welcome in his palm, a fierce-looking lion painted proudly on the front. He was roaring now, louder than the lion ever could. 'TO ARMS! TO ARMS!' His throat muscles were probably the best toned of all his bulging sinew. The arrow had come from the west, and so he ran towards the setting sun. The trumpets were in full song now, and more and more men were answering their call.

He rallied everyone he passed, ordering them to fall in line and follow him. Pounding up the stairs to the western battlement, even he felt the unwelcome tinge of fear at the sight that greeted his eyes.

Barbarians. Thousands of them. They streamed up the gentle rise, humming their *barritus* as they moved. The low humming sound had tormented legionaries for over a hundred years – it foretold death and destruction. The men in front were close, no more than sixty paces out. They were naked, and carried ladders in twos or threes. These were the berserkers, Bacchius knew. Men so devoted to their thunder god Donar they lived only to die a glorious death in battle.

There was no time to question where they came from. No time to question and punish the sentries that were supposed to be watching the western front. It was just time to fight.

There were no auxiliaries in the camp, meaning he had no archers or cavalry to call upon.

The parapet was filling with soldiers now, *pila* readied and awaiting the order to throw.

'Ready javelins!' Bacchius wasn't going to waste a second. A calm washed over him. He had never been one to be taken by the battle joy, the madness that fills a man when he is lost in the storm of iron and blood. He plied his trade with a cold and ruthless efficiency.

He waited for the barbarians to get closer, waited for the gaps in their ranks to close up as they slowed when they reached the walls. 'Now!' He judged it perfectly. Hundreds of *pila* flew through the orange twilight sky. Bacchius had time to register the first specks of fear on the bearded faces as they looked towards the gods and saw their deaths. The impact was devastating on the unarmoured berserkers. They fell almost to a man, giving him some thinking space.

'That was well done, centurion. Now what in Hades is going on here?' Legate Aurelius Rufinus pushed his way through the thronging soldiers to his first spear. A senator if there ever was one, a tall straight back, short cropped dark hair, a long and imposing nose, he was the embodiment of the ruling class.

'Can't shed much light on that, sir, was over on the western wall when the first wave of arrows took off, ran up here and got the lads to shed their javelins. And here we are.'

'I see. Well, we'll save the inquest for later. How many are there?' He squinted into the sun's dying light. A mass of warriors were ascending the hill, streaming out of a patch of thick woodland. A loose formation of archers were peppering shafts just outside of javelin range, but their arrows had trivial effect on the well-armoured legionaries behind their high walls.

'Hard to tell, sir. Looks like a few thousand at least. Orders?'

A nearby legionary looked in awe as the two senior officers discussed their predicament with casual ease.

'Get your cohort out there and halt their advance. It will give me time to sort the rest of the men out. Where's the governor?'

'Ahh. Dead, sir. I was with him on the northern battlement. He took an arrow to the face.'

'Not all bad news then!' Rufinus hated the weak-minded Proculus. *The man couldn't run a small tavern, let alone a province.* 'You have your orders, centurion, now get to it.'

With a sharp salute the first spear forced his way down the stairs until he stood in the shade of the western gate. He screamed for the first cohort to form, and waited impatiently as the double-strength centuries slowly appeared out of the throng and formed a column on the road. Gathering the other four centurions to the front, he quickly laid out his hastily formed plan.

'We form a wide line, just two deep if we have to. And then we hold! No need for heroes, no one leaves the line, we just hold them back as long as we can, the legate will relieve us when the others are sorted into their units.'

And with that they were out. As he passed the gate he saw the legion's *aquilifer,* standing as if unsure as to where he was supposed to be going. *Fighting under the eagle should stiffen the boys' resolve.* 'You there! You're with me! Fall in, soldier.' The man obeyed without hesitation, pleased to have someone to follow. 'You're new to this, right? How long have you held the post now?'

'Three months, sir. Took over from poor old Tubero after he died of plague.'

Bacchius nodded. It had been terrible for the legion's morale when their eagle-bearer had caught the plague and perished less than a week later. The eagle was a deity to the men who fought underneath it, and the thought that it could not protect its bearer let alone the other five thousand men who lived in its honour had been sobering.

'What's your name, soldier?' Bacchius sought to calm the young man's nerves.

'Cato, sir. Not had to fight holding the eagle yet, sir. Sure am missing my shield.' *Aquilifer's* fought with the eagle in one hand and their *gladius* in the other. It was up to their comrades to protect them in battle, most never lived to see retirement.

'Stand by me, son, me and the lads will make sure you're all right, won't we, brothers?' A rapturous choir of 'yes sir' filled the air, the men buoyed by their eagle's presence in the field.

They were out of the gate now, into the open field. A small road ran directly up to the gate, but either side was clear of obstruction. Bacchius ordered the men to fan out, forming a wide line that curved up at either end. He was at the centre of the curve, his double-strength century formed either side of him. He offered a brief prayer to the gods that the cemeteries had been built on the southern side of the settlement; the graves and tombstones would have made it impossible to keep his unit together.

He took in the sights and sounds of impending battle. The barbarian horde on their inexorable march towards the Roman line. Not the cohesion you would see in a disciplined legion, they scampered across the ground clutched together in twos or threes; no one seemed to be trying to push them into a shieldwall.

The familiar sounds of soldiers preparing themselves for battle rang in his ears. Nervous jokes, the screeching of swords being repeatedly dragged out of the scabbards and thrust back in – no soldier wants to find their *gladius* stuck in its sheath when a barbarian spear was trying to penetrate their shield. The snap of chinstraps being loosened and pulled tight, the smell of shit – over five hundred men squeaking out nervous farts – funny how the poets never write of that. Bacchius had time to ponder how the crows got to a battlefield so quick, their scent for blood must be greater than a legionary's for wine – and then they were on them.

No rallying speech from the first spear, his men knew the drill. With an almighty bang German iron met Roman linden – even the hungry crows had to duck for cover or risk getting stabbed with flaying edges from the splintering wood. The barbarian warriors were drawn to the Roman line like oxen to troughs of grain – and the legionaries slaughtered them like they were readying for winter.

Bacchius fought with the same cold detachment he always had, thrusting high with his shield and then low with his *gladius*, a hit in the groin always kills. They weren't advancing any more, but they were holding their own. His shield half protecting him and half over Cato to his right, he sought to build a body pile at his feet that Mars could see from the heavens.

The battle was in full swing, men grunted and squeaked and screamed and shouted themselves hoarse as they gritted their teeth, shoved with their left shoulders and probed with their swords. Bacchius killed his sixth – or was it seventh – man with a quick thrust to the throat, letting the corpse drop to his front before carefully treading over the man. A shadow flickered to his right, with the instincts only a veteran possesses, he ducked and raised his shield above his head. An almighty blow knocked him off his feet. Shocked, he lay in a daze on his back. Snapping out of his slumber in the nick of time, he looked up to see a great bearded warrior bearing a huge double-headed axe like it was a toy sword. He whirled it one-handed over his head before sending a crunching blow towards Bacchius's skull. The centurion got his shield up just in time, the axe head poked through just enough to kiss the end of his nose.

His left arm and shoulder in tatters, he mustered the energy to thrust the shield to his left and scramble to his feet. Off balance, he held out his sword to block any attack while he gathered his senses. When his eyes regained focus, he saw the giant German on his back, a great blood-filled hole where his right eye had been. 'Thank me later, sir!' Cato was covered in crimson, it was a marvel he could still see at all. On the base of the shaft that held up the eagle, a leaf-shaped javelin head stained black with blood skidded across the turf as Cato thrust his *gladius* at his next victim.

Bacchius staggered back from the line, pushing the legionary behind him to fill his space. He looked proudly at his century, their line holding true, no more than five dead on the ground. He cast a glance to the left and saw much the same there, but when he looked to his right his blood froze in his veins. The wing had caved, Germani warriors streamed through the breach, overlapping the Roman line and killing at will.

'First century, form testudo!' There wasn't time to think, just for action. His men responded in a heartbeat. The men on each wing took the flanks and joined shields. The men in the centre filed into a mini column with shields above their heads. Soon Bacchius and Cato were surrounded by comrades in the dark shell. 'Hold!'

The men on the flanks crouched down, shields against the ground, the men to the centre of them doing the same – a soldier's ankles were the easiest target when locked in the giant tortoise shell. Bacchius raised a shield slightly and stared at the approaching Germani. They had decimated the second century, which had been to their right. It looked as though a chieftain was ordering his men to leave the wall of shields and focus on the fortress. *Suits me.*

Looking left, the two centuries on that flank had mimicked his order, and were holding steady in their own testudos. 'Got a plan, sir?' The nervousness in Cato's voice was the same as before the battle.

Bacchius didn't answer immediately. He gazed intently to their rear at the fortress. Somehow the barbarians had forced the gate, and were flooding through the breach in their thousands. *Damn them to Hades!* There was no retrieving the fight now; it was over. 'We protect the eagle. We go south, to Singidunum. The sixth are there.

Make no mistake, brothers, this is no mere raiding party, there are thousands of the maggots. We will need men to come back with and avenge our fallen comrades. Now on my order, we march.' The centurion allowed himself one last glance to the north, and Covonia. It was too late to go for her, he knew. Looking down at his kit, he saw his phalera had been ripped off in the battle.

All that time polishing it. I will have my revenge on these goat-fuckers.

Chapter Nineteen

September AD 168 – Legionary Fortress of Carnuntum, Pannonia

Albinus stood hunched outside the legate's office. Sweat poured off him. It seemed hard to comprehend that the sun hadn't set since he'd ridden out with Fullo, so much seemed to have happened. Fullo was just behind him, leaning on a stone pillar, drinking deeply from a water skin.

'Remember what I said, boys. Stand to attention and look dead ahead, keep your answers to his questions short and sweet. And only state facts, if you're not sure of something, just say. He won't appreciate your guesses.' Albinus didn't think he'd ever seen Taurus look so concerned. The burly centurion had been locked in a shocked silence for a long while when Albinus had burst into his office and told him the news.

In the end, he had made his decision quickly. He'd sprinted to Felix and relayed what the young legionary had told him. Felix in turn had gone straight to the legate. And now, without having any real time to recover from the day's ordeals, Albinus was about to get his first meeting with the leader of the Fourteenth.

'What's he like?' Fullo seemed to have finally drunk his fill, and passed the now mostly empty water skin onto Albinus.

'What do you mean, what's he bloody like? He's the legate! Can't say I've shared many cups of wine with him!' Taurus sighed. 'He seems a decent enough bloke, and he's led us well enough so far, but never in such a battle as this one's gonna be.' The door opened with a start, Tribune Maximianus appearing from the shadows.

'He's ready for you.' The tribune gave the two legionaries a going over, and appeared satisfied with what he saw. 'You lads sure about all this?' They both nodded, then shared a nervous glance.

Maximianus and Taurus led them into a large and sparsely decorated office. There were no fine tapestries on the walls, no beautifully crafted Persian rugs under their feet. It was just a room of timber, much like the rest of the fortress. The legate's armour hung in the corner, a solid bronze *cuirass* resplendent in the fire's dancing light. Candidus himself was sat behind a plain wooden desk, Felix standing at his right shoulder. Maximianus was the only officer in the room to be in armour, Albinus and Fullo still in their mail from their day in the saddle.

The marched into the centre of the office, all four men offering salutes to the legate and prefect. Candidus smiled a warm smile, and ordered them all to be at ease. He was silent for a second, appraising the two young legionaries who claimed to have stumbled across a mass of German warriors hell-bent on their destruction. He first took in Fullo, a short and stocky young man. Well built, like most of the legionaries across the empire. Big dark eyes set on pale skin, his brow a knot of white lined scars.

It was the other, however, who took up most of his attention. Taller than his comrade, but thin – too thin – arms and legs long and gangly, it looked as though he was held together with string. But it was those eyes that

290

marked him out. A shimmering, pale blue, like a glistening pool of shallow water. Candidus had served with Silus for a while, and even if he hadn't been told, he would have known this young man's lineage.

'Good evening, gentlemen. It's not often two men from the rank and file are invited into this office, but I gather you both stumbled across something today that I may need to be aware of.' He arched a brow, a faintly amused expression creeping across his face. 'Tell me what happened today.' He raised a hand, inviting the two to speak.

Albinus looked towards Fullo, he felt more afraid then he had in the morning, with a giant German warrior hurling his spear towards him. Fullo gave a reassuring nod, encouraging his friend to speak.

'Sir. We were out north of the river, travelling north up the road then east across the land. It was early afternoon when we stumbled across a lone German warrior. He attacked me, launched his spear my way. My friend Fullo here dispatched of him with minimal hassle.' He turned and nodded towards his friend, who smiled as his moment of triumph was mentioned to the legate. 'I then rode further along the path, kept going east. It was late afternoon when I found myself looking at a huge German army. I couldn't even guess at their numbers, but it was vastly more than a legion. I was spotted by some of their riders; they pursued me back along the track. I caught up with Fullo here and we raced back to the fortress.' He thought to add a 'and here we are' but left it at that.

There was a moment's pause, Candidus taking in what he had heard. 'How can you be sure they were coming here?'

'Where else would they be going? The lads were talking about a merging of the tribes. We all know that doesn't happen very often, not since Arminius managed it! We need to act, sir.' Felix was answering the question for Albinus.

'Yes. It would appear you are right.' Candidus rubbed his head, the magnitude of the situation taking its hold. 'I could ask you two some more questions, but I fear it may well be irrelevant. Like why were you two out north of the river? You're not scouts, so I struggle to find a reason for you being there.' Albinus and Fullo shared a nervous glance, sweat appearing on their brows. Taurus studied his feet in hope it would cover a guilty look. 'And also young Albinus, why you decided to leave your friend and go alone? A decision I'm sure your father wouldn't have approved of. Yes, I know who you are.' Candidus registering the shock in the young man's pale eyes.

'And you are sure you saw the colours of the Marcomanni? And the Quadi?' asked the legate, still studying Albinus' face.

'Yes, sir, the more I think about it, the more I'm sure. I was raised on these borders, I know the colours of the southern tribes.' Each tribe distinguished themselves by colour, whether they wore their tribe's colour on their clothes or shield varied from tribe to tribe.

The legate massaged his brow, the weight of command appearing heavy. 'You two, wait outside. I want you to brief Maximianus shortly on the precise location of the German force. Officers remain.'

Albinus didn't need asking twice, he practically leapt from the room, feeling like he was leaving a puddle of sweat behind. 'You spoke well, brother.' Fullo patted him on the back, and noticed his friend's shaking hands.

292

*

There was silence when the door closed, just the flickering and hissing of the flames.

'Well, gentlemen, it appears we have a war on our hands. Suggestions?' The legate surveyed the room, glad for the experience within it.

'Get scouts over the river to monitor the Germani. Send for the Tenth at Vindobona and get the legion from Aquincum. Call in all the auxiliaries in Pannonia, get out there and give 'em a good licking.' Taurus was always to the point.

Despite the tension in the room, Candidus laughed. 'What would we do without you, Taurus? I want you to get the scouts out now, and get every senior centurion in the legion together tonight and explain what is happening. All the outposts are to be stripped and the men returned here, all leave is cancelled, all men on leave are to be summoned back. I want the legion on full parade out by the amphitheatre at dawn tomorrow. Get to it, centurion.' He rasped a smart salute and marched out the office into the darkening evening.

'Felix, send riders to Vindobona, Aquincum and Aquileia, that's where Governor Bassus was headed. Request all legions to march here at the double. I will leave it to the governor to write to the Emperors Aurelius and Verus. Maximianus, I will leave you to find me a battlefield. Go out with the scouts, find out where they are and the road they are treading. Ideally, we want to face them on their side of the river, but if it's advantageous to let them cross, then we will. There's no one I'd trust more to make the right decision, so go with your gut, and don't let me down.' As usual, the gruff grey-eyed tribune accepted his orders with little more than a nod.

Once alone, Candidus sank lower in his chair. The thought of thousands of Germani let loose in Pannonia scared him more than he cared to admit. He had done reasonably well so far, he comforted himself. He had fought a few battles with the tribes and had yet to be defeated. But he had never faced an enemy so big. *A united army of Germani?* He barely believed it had happened. *Mars give me strength. Why did this have to happen in my time?*

Deep down, he was no military man and he knew it. The strength and experience of men like Felix, Maximianus and Taurus had kept him on the right track, taking command in battles he should have been commanding, leading by the front and inspiring their men. He was an administrator, not a warrior. In times of peace he was the perfect man to run a legion. Kept the men paid and busy, made sure they received their coin on time. Food, water and wine were always available. Roads were repaired, new aqueducts built giving fresh water to more people – for a price. But in war? A full-scale drawn-out war against a warrior nation, he doubted he had the ability to succeed, or the stomach.

Memories of the battle against the raiding party the previous winter still kept him up at night. The piercing screams as the Roman *pila* had found their targets, the sickening stink of stale shit and black blood that rose like steam from a bubbling broth at the end of the battle. It had been all he could do to not vomit in front of his men. The cries of the wounded, the soon to be dead. Some cradling their own guts, trying desperately to shove them back in the hole the legionaries' *gladius* had carved. The squawk of the hungry crows, oh how dark it had seemed when they had hovered over the battlefield in their hundreds. He hated them, feared them even. They're not natural creatures, they live only for death, he thought, thrived off it.

For the thousandth time, he wondered what had possessed him to take this position. *Greed.* Ambition had driven him to do some pretty foolish things over the years. Betraying and backstabbing friends in the Senate had helped his rise up the *cursus honorum,* and now it seemed he was going to have to rely on one of those 'friends' to come to his aid. Decimus had treated him with indifference since Candidus had made public his affection for young boys over the warmth of his wife's bed. Divorce and public humiliation had swiftly followed. Being posted to the Tenth had been a mercy for him, getting him away from Rome and the sniggering senators.

Sighing, he reached for a half-empty bottle of falernian, sitting atop his desk. *If only I was as good a soldier as I am a politician, I could have this rebellion flattened in no time.* He thought of the great Caesar, of how much he had achieved in his life, all the enemies he had slain at home and abroad. Only for in the end to be slain himself by Marcus Brutus, a man he had revered above all others. *There is a lesson there, one I should have considered before.*

Candidus' only hope was that Decimus did not possess the same thirst for revenge as Brutus had.

He didn't even bother with a cup; the wine was gone in two gulps. He just wished he had more.

*

Albinus was bone-tired. His normally bright blue eyes were dull and almost grey, surrounded by blood-red rims. After the meeting with the legate the evening before, he had hoped to get a day's rest after spending all the

295

previous day in the saddle, a large part of that galloping for his life. Fullo, on the other hand, had awoken as fresh as the day he emerged from his mother's womb. It annoyed Albinus – more than a little. His friend's innocent chat bit right through him; it was as if yesterday had never happened.

Taurus had woken them before dawn. Tribune Maximianus had requested they join him in his reconnaissance on the barbarian army. Why, Albinus couldn't really fathom. Maximianus had said it was because he had seen them once and might be able to recognise certain things when they encountered them again. What he was supposed to recognise he didn't know; it wasn't as if there were numerous armies marching on them – that they knew of. Just one massive horde of bloodthirsty barbarians – riding out to see them again chilled Albinus to the bone.

But Fullo was chomping at the bit. His dark eyes were more alive than Albinus could ever remember seeing. He had been snoring the night before even before his head had hit the pillow, and the rest – combined with the adrenaline still coursing his veins after wetting his sword for the first time – made him the liveliest out of the trio that morning.

Maximianus and Fullo were riding ahead of Albinus, back through the woodland track they had rode the day before. Upon encountering the dead German warrior, Fullo had rejoiced when the tribune had asked him to retell the story of the man's death.

'He launched his spear at Albinus, sir. Hell of a throw it was! Whilst Albinus was busy getting out of the way I spurred my horse up the rise and met him blade for blade. He raised his sword to meet mine, after they hit I swung mine back down, split the back of his head clean open.'

Maximianus grunted, which in itself was praise enough. He was studying the ground, seeing dents in the leaves where Fullo's mare had charged, the footprints – deeper than the others, where the warrior had stopped and raised his sword. He could almost smell the man's fear, could imagine the shock he must have felt at seeing two Romans this side of the Danube.

He picked up the barbarian's sword. Its weight was alien to him. Almost four feet in length, at its base the blade was four fingers thick. The hilt was iron, the grip slick in his palm. He guessed the maple-wood grips used on the Roman short sword would not be strong enough to mount a blade this size.

'How do they fight with these?' The question was rhetorical, Albinus could see the man was more musing to himself than speaking to the two legionaries.

'Takes some strength, sir. You ever fought someone with one? My father used to marvel at how they gripped a broadsword in one hand and a shield in the other. Must be why all their warriors are so big!' Fullo was revelling in the opportunity to spend time alone with one of the legion's officers. Maximianus was famous throughout the Fourteenth, almost on a par with Silus. He was probably the most experienced tribune in the whole army, and if Fullo made a good impression with him, a promotion would almost certainly follow.

'I once fought a German with a sword even bigger than this. The fight seemed to last for ever. He was in coat of mail, a great bear pelt over the top. Huge iron helmet on his head, wrist and leg greaves. His shield was huge, bigger even than the *Scutum's* we use. He matched me stroke for stroke for an age, didn't think it was ever going to end.'

'What happened?' Even Albinus was leaning forwards now, showing more interest than Fullo.

'He tired in the end. I feinted low, he brought his shield down to meet it. Then I flicked my sword up high, slit his throat in one smooth motion. One of my best kills, I think.' It struck Albinus how completely devoid of emotion the tribune's voice was. No remorse, no pride, he wasn't boasting, just stating a fact as he saw it.

'Here.' Maximianus held the sword out for Fullo, hilt first. 'Take it. A reminder of your first kill, I'm sure it won't be your last.' Fullo took the sword, marvelled at the heavy weight. He looked down the blade, it was crisscrossed with small marks and dents, Fullo wondered if one of them was from his battle with the sword the day before.

'Thank you, sir.' There was genuine awe in his voice. 'I will look after it.'

'I know you will, lad. Now, let's get moving, we have an army to find!'

Maximianus picked up the pace for the rest of the morning. Albinus judged in his mind the distance to where he had encountered the barbarians the day before, and thought they were nearly there. 'Tribune, I believe we are not far away now. Should we maybe slow the pace, sir?'

The Tribune took in his surroundings. They were in the base of a valley, sweeping green hills running away either side. He could hear the river to the south, the rushing water the only sound, apart from the odd chorus of birdsong.

'Okay. See that woodland up ahead? We'll dismount when we get there, take it slowly from then on.'

It was dark under the trees' canopy. A cool breeze blew from east to west, welcoming on the soldier's sun-drenched faces. They walked by their horses, half

298

shielding behind them, wary of another spear thrown from deep in the brush. The silence was deafening to Albinus's ears. About now they should have been hearing the familiar sounds of an army on the march. Horses whinnying as they trotted along, metal clanking on metal as men struggled with armour in the sun's heat, shouted orders and soldiers sharing banter, mocking laughs and cursed responses. But all they heard was the rustling of the leaves.

'Albinus, where in the gods' name are they, then?' His face was a permanent scowl now, Maximianus was concerned.

'I don't know, sir. It was just at the end of this woodland I saw them. I came out of the trees dead ahead of here, and there they were.' Albinus too was fretting with worry. Only the day before a horde of barbarians had stood and breathed the same air he was breathing now, but they appeared to have gone without a trace.

'You never know, maybe they all went home!' It appeared to Albinus his friend hadn't quite grasped the gravity of the situation.

'Helpful, Fullo. The point here is, if they are no longer here, then where are they?' Albinus would have hit his friend had they not been in the company of the tribune.

'Simple, ain't it? How far away from the settlement are we? Half a mile? If I was leading them I'd have marched east from here, crossed at the ford and then marched back west on our side of the river. He would have known about us seeing his army, and would have guessed we would send more scouts this way to keep an eye on him. So cross the river before we know and march to us on our own turf.' Fullo chewed on some hardtack, took a swig from his water skin and looked questioningly into the stunned tribune's eyes.

Maximianus felt his blood go to ice as he listened to the legionaries talk. 'Crossed the river? On our own turf?' He stopped dead in his tracks, barely daring to breathe. 'Jupiter's hairy arse! The lad's right! Mount up, NOW!'

And with that he was gone, galloping back west towards Carnuntum. 'Fuck me! I was just saying that's what I'd do—'

'Mount Fullo! Gods, what if you're right? The Fourteenth will be completely unprepared! Now ride!'

*

Legate Decimus sat at his oak desk. It was midday, and he was just about to dine when a tribune had informed him of an urgent message from Carnuntum. He had been tempted to ignore the messenger and leave him to sweat in his armour whilst he enjoyed his lunch. It would of course be no victory over the weedy little Candidus, but it would make him feel good. However, something in the tribune's tone made him stop. 'What's the message, tribune?'

'War, sir. The tribes are marching on Carnuntum. Battle could commence as early as tomorrow.'

'What tribes?'

'All of them, apparently.'

The legate sat back down. 'Thank you, tribune, see the messenger in.'

A dust-ridden rider gave a tired salute as he stopped in front of the legate's desk. He noted how grandly the room was decorated, the opposite of the office of his own legate. The room was stone built, like the rest of the fortress. Beautiful artwork decorated the walls, his hobnailed sandals stood atop the grandest rug he had ever seen, surely Persian made.

300

The legate himself was as different from Candidus as could be. Tall, where Candidus was short. A thick, well-rounded torso, whereas the others was slim and unremarkable. A full head of jet-black hair against a mostly bald head. Legate Decimus stood as the messenger waited, huge fists balled up, leaning on his desk as he arched towards the rider.

'Deliver your message, soldier.' Even when trying to speak quietly, his voice boomed around the spacious room.

'Balomar and a united army of barbarians march on Carnuntum. Legate Candidus requests your aid, sir, with all haste.'

Decimus was silent for a second, taking the information in. 'When were the barbarians spotted?'

The rider looked into the legate's eyes, not strictly allowed under protocol, but given the weight of his message he didn't think he was in danger of reprimand. The eyes that stared back at him were the most alive the rider thought he had ever seen. Swirls of black set inside a deep chestnut brown, they never seemed to be still. Well-trimmed eyebrows sat beneath his great bush of hair, a broad and straight nose under those eyes. His lips were so red it appeared he was wearing lipstick, his skin pale and flawless. *Maybe it's true what they say about him.*

'Yesterday, sir. One of our lads saw 'em on their side of the water. We think they will try and force a crossing at the bridge.'

'And their numbers?'

'Maybe as many as four legions but nothing confirmed, sir.'

Decimus whistled. 'Four legions? Where else has Candidus sent riders?' Decimus knew duty bound him to march straight away. He knew it would take two to three

301

days at least to get his whole legion and supporting auxiliaries to Carnuntum; he wondered if there would still be a Fourteenth to support once he got there.

'To Aquincum and Aquileia, sir. My legate said that's where the governor was headed.'

'Yes, that makes sense. The Second and Third Italica are both within marching distance from there. But they're new, untested. Thank you, soldier, that will be all. You rode through the night to get here? Then get yourself some rest, I will send one of my lads straight back with my reply to your commander. Dismissed.'

The tribune closed the door on the relieved messenger, already picturing himself in a bath. 'Orders, sir?'

'D'you know, Marcus, it's been five years since I was posted here. Five years. You know why I was sent here?'

'I...err...heard rumours, sir. But never thought to believe them.' Tribune Marcus knew all too well why his superior had been 'offered' the opportunity to leave Rome. And the snaking line of young slave boys that followed him wherever he went was evidence enough.

'It was because of that snake Candidus. Whispered jibes in the corners of the senate house, found their way back to my wife. She then did her damn best to make sure every bugger in Rome heard about it! And here I am. Miles away from Rome, from the senate, from power!' He slammed his huge fist down onto the desk. It seemed to Marcus the whole room shook. 'And now my old friend needs my help. So what should I do, young Marcus?'

The young Tribune gulped. Just six months he had served with the Tenth. His father had jumped for joy when they had heard the news. 'Caesar's Tenth! The senate do you honour, son.' Hadn't much felt like honour at the time and it sure didn't feel like it now. 'We should march at once, sir, the auxiliaries and men on detached duty can be called in whilst we march. If we delay, then—'

'Then my old *friend* may not last the week! Ha! Sometimes the gods smile on you. We shall march, young Marcus, but not until we are at full strength, well as full strength as we can be amid this cursed plague.' Death was everywhere at Vindobona, just when you thought it was safe to step outside and breathe deep the summer air, another pus-ridden body was pulled out of a home. 'And when all hope is lost, when Candidus lays dead under Balomar's sword, who will be there to pick up the pieces and save the empire? Me! That's who! I shall be welcomed back into society with open arms, the Emperor's may even grant me a triumph!'

The legate rambled on about glory and victory, but all Marcus could keep thinking was, *four legions? Against one?*

*

The breeze was welcome at Aquileia. Governor Bassus lounged on a couch in a luxurious villa on the south side of the city. A slave stood behind him, wafting a giant fan over his sweat-glazed body. The wind coming up from the south had the taste of salt, a reminder that they were just six miles from the sea.

It had been two weeks since he had arrived, still frustrated by his peace talks with the Marcomanni king. The intertwining time had done much to calm his irritation though. Spending his days lounging in the sun, and each evening spent with a different serving girl, he had just begun to enjoy the benefits of his province being at peace with the barbarians on their border.

He had no pressing work or concerns. Dispatches had been sent to the capital requesting the agreed funds to pay

303

off the tribes be sent up to the Danube, his legion's pay was all up to date, and the deaths from the plague were falling by the week. He smiled in satisfaction at the thought of autumn and the vast harvests that Pannonia would reap in; *the bad times are behind us.*

His peace was interrupted by his chief of staff's non too polite cough. Cleandros was a slave, Greek by birth, he had been bought by Bassus' father for him when the two were both young men. Many years they had now spent living in each other's shadows, and though neither man would care to admit it, they would be reluctant to have it any other way.

'Messenger, governor. It's urgent.' The wiry old Greek, as always, came straight to the point.

'Oh curse you to Hades, how important can it be, you old wretch? Can't you see I'm resting?' *Resting from what?* There were even some lines Cleandros wouldn't cross.

'As I said, governor, it's urgent.' Bassus raised himself off the couch. He knew that tone. Flat, lifeless. He was always like this when the news was bad. Looking into the slave's eyes, his suspicions were confirmed. There was sympathy in the old, watery pale green eyes. A fixed, sad expression on the age-lined face. Boris would always read or listen to whatever messages were for Bassus, and the governor trusted him to judge what was urgent or relevant, others would wait until he was ready – or in the mood – to reply.

'Send him in then.' With a nod, the slave exited and came back quickly with a tired-looking cavalryman. 'Speak.' With a hurried gesture, he urged the messenger to deliver his message. By the time the man had finished speaking, Bassus wanted the ground to swallow him whole, and drag him down to Hades' lair.

There was silence, an awkward, nervous one. It seemed no one was willing to break it. The messenger stood to attention, his message delivered. Cleandros stared at his sandals, knowing all too well the emotions that would be pumping through his master's veins. The slave had stopped wafting his fan, and worried that if he started again the governor would notice he had stopped. Bassus himself stood stiller than the marble statue of himself in the corner of the room. Rage slowly began to take over, his face grew redder than the setting sun's rays.

'When did you leave Carnuntum?' His voice was calm, deliberately so.

'Yesterday morning, sir.' The cavalryman was uncomfortable now, and wanted nothing more than to be away from the angry governor.

'The Marcomanni I can understand, but the Quadi? I had long since hoped they had turned their spears into ploughshares.' Pacing a little, to regroup his thoughts, he carried on. 'So, the battle could already be over. The messenger to Vindobona left the same time as you?' A nod. 'Then they should be on the way already. A map, Cleandros, a map!' The slave scurried off and quickly came back with a map of the province. 'We are here, now what troops do I have between here and Carnuntum. None! I Italica at Raetia and II Italica at Regensburg, Boris, send men out to them now. I have two *alae* of cavalry here, they will have to do for now. We leave at once, march straight for Carnuntum, with luck, we will meet a victorious Fourteenth and Tenth when we arrive. Well, don't just stand there, come men, to war!'

Chapter Twenty

September AD 168 – Legionary Fortress of Carnuntum, Pannonia

Fear froze him, and they hadn't yet left the comfort of their home. They had returned late the previous day, but early enough to ride past the fortress and scout out the enemy. Their army was huge, almost all the men in all Germania, or so Albinus had thought. And now here he was, in the dim light before the dawn, trying and failing to shrug his mail shirt over his tunic.

The thing weighed more than a large hound, but it felt heavier today. He was rushing in his panic, and his hair kept catching on the metal links. Exasperated, he threw it to the floor and slumped down on his bunk. 'Come, little brother, let me help you with that.' Bucco was already dressed in his finest. His segmented armour shone in the blue shade that was the pre-dawn. Habitus had laced the back as they talked and joked as if they were off for a morning's sentry duty, and not on the way to fight the largest army to threaten Rome's borders in a hundred years.

'It doesn't fit me, Bucco. Too tight at the neck and too wide at the hips. Plus it's shorter than my tunic, I swear people can see my balls when I walk!'

Bucco fought to hide a smile. 'You wanna get a new loincloth, brother!' Calvus never missed an opportunity to give someone a dig.

'Don't worry about that, Albinus, I can't see your balls when you step out of the bath, so I doubt the girls are gonna be able to spot them as you march by!' Laughter erupted in the small barrack room at Libo's joke; he didn't make many, but they were well received when he did.

'Think how poor old Libo feels. That *vitis* he has between his legs must chafe something terrible in that old loincloth, it's no wonder he gives it a good rub every night when he thinks we're all asleep!' Rullus was never far from the banter. He too was ready and impatient to go fetch his standard from the shrine room in the *principia*, where it was stored along with the other cohorts' standards and their blessed eagle.

Albinus knew the jokes and camaraderie of his brothers in the *contubernium* were in part the core of their day-to-day life, and part to help quash his growing nerves. They were soldiers of the first century, first cohort, and would therefore be the first into the fray. Even Fullo was quiet, giving his *gladius* one last go over with the edge of a whetstone; it didn't need it, but it gave him something to do.

Albinus reluctantly rose to his feet and raised his arms, allowing Bucco to shrug the mail over his head. He laughed to himself, 'like dressing a child, eh.'

'I remember dressing you as a child. You had run away from your mother, covered in mud you were, we were going to a wedding – Bucco tried to stop himself but couldn't, talk of weddings wouldn't help improve the young man's mood. 'Sorry, son. We'll find her, all of us, together. Just one small battle to get out the way first.' A chorus of 'aye' greeted Bucco's words, Albinus didn't know how he would ever repay the kindness these men had shown him in the last months. Without them, he knew he would have failed at the first hurdle.

'Right then, you maggots! Ready for a scrap?' Taurus barged his way into the small barrack room, fixing each man with a fearsome expression. 'YES SIR!' the men replied in unison. 'Good lads. Now listen up, I need you boys on top form today, could be a long slog, you need to set the example for the rest of the century.'

'Don't we always, sir?' Longus seemed offended that the eight men would do anything but.

'In battle yes, out of it…less said the better.' Grins at their centurion's joke. 'Look after yourselves today, as much as you lot can be a right pain in the arse, you're good lads. My century would be weaker without you.'

Libo took that moment to reach down to his bunk and grasp his sword belt, giving Taurus an unwelcome sight. 'Jupiter's hairy arse, Libo! How many times I gotta tell you to get a new loincloth! The bloody Germani gonna see them swinging in the wind!' The eight men seemed to find that funnier than it was, Rullus filled in the centurion as he stood looking perplexed. 'Ha! Well Maybe we can have a tumble in the training yard one day, Libo, but I gotta warn you, you'll need to have a right hard on if you're gonna get the better of this beauty.' Taurus' vine stick licked out, three feet of smooth wood with a rounded top, it struck the nearest bunk with a crash.

The veterans all winced, knowing first-hand the damage the centurion could do with one flick of his wrist – the bruises took weeks to fade. 'The trumpets will sound anytime now, so be ready.' With a curt nod he was off, barging into the barrack room next door, presumably to give a similar speech.

'He's a good man.' Simple, but with meaning from Calvus. Each man nodded, knowing there was no finer centurion in the whole army, let alone the Fourteenth.

'Aye, he is. Takes someone with real iron to take after Silus, but he's done us proud so far. Let's make sure we do good by him today, eh.' Rullus fixed Albinus a look as he spoke, the younger nodded in acknowledgement at the praise of his father. 'Come on then, brothers, let's get this done.'

The eight men emerged into the rising sun's light. The trumpets sounded as they made their way to the east gate, aiming for the amphitheatre where they would form into a marching column.

Albinus shrugged his shield onto his back – impossible to march whilst carrying the heavy linden board, particularly with the leather cover fastened over the top. Fullo hadn't bothered bringing his, insisting they would be home in time for supper, but Albinus didn't want to take any chances.

It seemed surreal to Albinus that people were getting on with their day-to-day lives, whilst he and Fullo were probably marching to their deaths. The bakers were already open, the heat from the ovens hot on his face, the glorious smell of freshly baked bread getting their bellies rumbling as they passed. The local tavern was only just closing, the last drunkards being sent on their way by a tired and grumpy innkeeper. Albinus eyed a local drunk nearly fall into the blacksmith's anvil; the man was furious, his kit clearly just placed outside whilst his forge heated. The tanner next-door laughed as he dumped a barrel of fish oil outside his workshop, a vital ingredient for turning animal hides to leather.

The *ludus* seemed to be open for business. Slaves with horses and cart were making their way out for provisions, and the cheers and grunts from gladiators in training could be heard from within. Just past the *ludus* was the amphitheatre itself. Of course, no match for the grand Colosseum in Rome, it still seated up to fourteen thousand people. The early sun's rays shimmered off the timber tops, soon they would be stretching down to scorch the sanded floor. Fullo was in love with the gladiatorial shows regularly put on inside the giant dome, but Albinus found them to be a waste of human and animal lives.

'They got some Christians and lions in there tonight. Let's hope we make it back in time.' Albinus recoiled from the heavy nudge Bucco gave him as he spoke, clasping hands with Fullo at the same time. Wrinkling his nose, Albinus bit back a reply at the thought of watching lions rip some poor Christians apart. Christianity had fast become the most hated religion across the whole empire, their priests were fanatic, preaching loudly on every street corner, they put doubt to the fact that only Emperors were immortal, with claims that the son of the one true god had risen from the dead just three days after he had been crucified.

'I fucking hate Christians.' Habitus hawked and spat. 'One god? How can there only be one fucking god? And what's all this heaven bollocks? I'd rather go to Donar's hall with all these barbarian scum we're about to meet. At least I'd get a good scrap every day!'

'Do not worry, Habitus, I think you'd end up in hell anyway, my friend! You know it all started in your shitty country, don't you?' Calvus had spoken in secret to men

310

from the second cohort, who had been praying to the one god and his son in secret for months. He was secretly taken with the new cult, but wasn't yet ready to share his beliefs with his mess mates.

'S'pose it's all my fault then, is it? What about all those boy-loving priests in the swamp you come from? All cuddled up on their little island of Mona, weren't they? Hiding behind their big fucking masks! Your shitty gods didn't do 'em many favours when the legions turned them over!'

Calvus rolled his eyes. *Jesus help me.* 'Well, they're hardly my gods, considering we stopped worshipping them about a hundred years before I was born! And where were your gods when you lot got turned over? Or Libo's when the legions took his land? Think about it, old timer, if we all got one thing in common, it's that at some time or other our ancestors were done over by soldiers wearing the same uniform as us!'

Albinus joined in with the chorus of 'ayes', thankful to have something other than his impending death to think about. 'And those uniforms are gonna do over some more barbarians today!' Optio Abas marched up to the small group, now standing and waiting for the rest of their cohort to form up on the large field outside of the amphitheatre.

'You think everyone's a bloody barbarian! Greeks, all the same!' Only Libo would have got away with an insult to an officer, his sheer size and brutality would make even the hardest bitten of centurions think twice before raising their vine sticks in his direction.

'Because you are! There is only one superior race, and it is us Greeks. You should read some Homer sometime, Libo, it would blow your mind.' Always calm, the optio

311

barely ever raised his voice, but when he spoke, people seemed to listen intently.

'Who in Hades' arse is Homer? Superior race? If you're so superior, then why was Greece one of the first places to feel Rome's wrath? And why the fuck are you wearing that uniform?' Spittle flew from Taurus' mouth as he berated his second-in-command. Abas' smile was a rueful one, *should have known the bloodhound would sniff me out at the wrong moment.*

'I think we all know who the brains behind this cursed empire is these days? Who does the thinking? Freedman, Greeks, that's who. Who stitches back together these fine men after we've sent them charging into a nest of barbarian spears? Greeks, that's who.' His eyes were a mixture of amusement and challenge as he faced his centurion off. Lost for words, Taurus bit like an ill-trained hound.

'Any more of your lip and I'll see to it that you're promoted! Understand?'

'You wouldn't dare!' Despite their many arguments, Abas could not imagine a life in the army without his superior, a man he loved more than he could ever admit. Twice he had turned down promotion to the role of centurion, choosing instead to remain his friend's right-hand man.

The trumpets sounded, interrupting their argument. Legate Candidus came into view, mounted on a fine white stallion. Behind him were the legion's tribunes, also mounted.

Behind them on foot was the legion's *aquilifer* and cohort's standard bearers. Centurions' voices could be heard as they quickly ushered their men into formation, and a deathly silence endured as the legate rode the length of the column and inspected his men.

Albinus stood shivering; the fear had full hold of him now. His father dying, Licina's capture, becoming a soldier, it had all never felt more real than it did at that moment. A shivering hand wiped a small tear from the corner of his left eye. His brain was fuzzy, unable to think straight, he swayed like a drunk as the tingling between his ears took control of his body.

Fullo raised a hand and pressed firmly on his friend's shoulder; they shared a look that spoke louder than a thousand words. *I will be with you, brother.*

The legate rode past, resplendent in a shimmering bronze helmet and *cuirass* to match, his blood-red cloak seemed to glow in the sun's rays, and the white horsehair on his helmet's crest seemed whiter than the purest snow. He dismounted when he reached the first cohort, and to Albinus' and Fullo's surprise, acknowledged both men with a nod.

'Morning, first spear. Your men seem in fine spirit this morning.'

'Sir! Always raring to go, sir. We won't let you down.'

'Good man! You will hold the left wing today, Taurus, Maximianus shall hold the right and I will hold the centre myself. I know the first normally has the right, but Maximianus is worried about being flanked by the river, so it's your job to make sure your wing holds. And as for me, too long I have sat back and watched you and the tribune steal all the glory, I'm going after some for myself today.'

Taurus stood in shock. It wasn't custom for legates to fight alongside their men, only in times of desperate need. He wondered if that was the real reason the legate had

313

decided to blood his sword, *things really that bad?* 'Of course, sir. We'll play our part.'

'Good to hear, centurion. When the trumpet sounds the advance, you have the honour of leading us out.' With a nod he was off, Albinus thought how less impressive he looked walking than when he was mounted. The advance from the trumpets thrust him from his thoughts and without delay they were off. Albinus fixed the bridge a long hard stare as he trudged by, gazing out into the wilderness beyond. *Where are you, my love?*

*

Licina winced at the sound of hoofbeats. The ground rumbled as the horses stopped a spear's length from her face. She recoiled from the smell of sweat and leather as the riders dismounted. It took Julius' strong arm round her back to stop her squealing when a horse put its head to the ground and let out a loud whinny, seemingly at her.

The pain in her ankle was intense, any movement at all sent shards of pain screeching up her leg as though she was treading on freshly forged iron nails. Julius' breath was hot on the back of her neck, and despite the immediate peril the two were in, she was sure she could feel his erection against the small of her back. *That's the least of my problems.*

Doing her best to keep her breathing shallow, she watched the riders' booted feet and listened as the farm owner came out of his home to greet the newcomers. One man, she presumed to be their leader, got straight to the point with the land owner. 'I'm looking for two people, a boy and a girl. They're Roman, seen anything?' His tone was gruff, distant, accusing.

'My lord Adalwin. Been many summer since I last saw you in these parts. A boy and a girl, you say? Roman? Not

314

seen anyone like that, lord.' The man was old, clear from his weak, earthy voice. Licina watched as his knees bent when he finished speaking, as if he'd given a bow. Her shaking grew stronger at the sound of Adalwin's name; from the little time she had spent in Balomar's fortress, the man had not appeared to be friendly, or forgiving. 'Are you sure, old man? They would have passed here not half a day ago. Have you not been out tending your land on this fine summer's morning? There will be a reckoning if we find you to have lied.' His was a voice she would have known anywhere. She let out a whimper as her blood ran to ice. Sharp tingles ran through her whole body, she could barely feel Julius pressing himself further into her, his arms now constricting rather than embracing her body.

Adalwin translated the thinly veiled threat, but the old man insisted he had seen no one. 'Well, maybe I'll just go search your home. You here alone? Or anyone that could keep me company whilst I look?'

Adalwin didn't translate the last part. 'Easy, Cocconas, let's not scare the old man off. He may yet be some use.' *Cocconas*. In all the time she had spent with the bearded and groomed easterner, she had never known his name. She thought it didn't suit him.

'I'll give you one last chance, greybeard. Then I will let my wolves loose on your livestock. Have you seen two Romans running north?' The aggression was clear in the gravel, Adalwin was running out of patience.

'I'm sorry, lord, but I've seen nothing.' Again a twitch of the knees, another short bow.

Licina tore her haze from the men's feet and looked left, startled to see a man on his knees. He was fingering the loose dirt on the ground, sniffing it almost, as if he could smell the two hideaways, almost within touching distance.

315

'Search the barn, lord Adalwin.' His wolf like stare, she thought he was looking right at her, seeing through the cracks in the ageing timber.

'You sure?' said Adalwin, squinting up at the old building. It had started to decay on one side, the western wall now stood higher than the eastern.

'As sure as I can be. We've muddled the tracks with our own and the horses. But they were here, and that seems the logical place to hide.'

A quick order to his men, and the gates to the old barn were thrown open. Sweat poured down Licina's head, the taste salty in her chattering mouth. She tried to calm her breathing as she lay, her chest shuddering with every in breath.

She could hear her heart beating, racing as the thud of footsteps grew closer. There was a silence that seemed to stretch out so long she almost wanted to jump up and scream to her pursuers, just to end the gnawing tension in her belly. Julius lay rigid behind her, his breath coming in short gasps, Licina worried it was so loud they would hear.

Adalwin stalked slowly into the seemingly lifeless barn. It was damp and dark, like a miserable winter's night. He paused in front of a stack of rotten hay bales, and listened.

Nothing. 'You're not gonna keep much livestock fed and warm with this worm-ridden hay, old man.' The old farmer nodded. 'I should have built the barn on stilts. Unfortunately, the Allfather got his ravens to withhold such foresight.' He touched his thumb to his head and spat on the ground, to ward off the misfortune that could come from speaking ill of the all-seeing Wotan.

'Careful when insulting the gods, old man, you may be meeting them sooner then you wish.' Contempt in

Adalwin's voice, any self-respecting farmer knew to keep his hay and grain off the ground.

'Aye. Well, I shall be in Donar's hall soon, feasting and fighting with my fallen brothers.'

'You need to die with a blade in your hand for that greybeard.'

'Goes to bed with me every night, lord.'

Adalwin grunted, eyes still drawn to the damp hay. 'Siltric, anything?'

The tracker was down in his knees once more, eyes peeling the ground for signs of life. 'It's been swept, lord. Any tracks there may have been are gone.' Adalwin spun to the greybeard farmer, who stared resolutely back, unfazed by the power and imposing presence of the man. 'Care to explain?' said Adalwin, his voice quiet, but the tone menacing.

'So I swept my barn out? What business is that of yours?'

'It's my business when you've swept it out to hide the tracks of two runaways, now you better tell me who's been here, old man, or you won't see another winter!' Spittle flew as Adalwin raged. His place was with his king, not on some jaunt across country looking for two people he cared not for.

'I swept my barn lord, cos it needed sweeping. I ain't seen no runaways, and I don't care about no runaways. Now go to Hel.'

Adalwin's men drew their swords, ready to put an end to the greybeard's time in this world. Adalwin and Cocconas shared a look, then the German burst into laughter. 'Sorry, old man, I can see I am wasting your time. Wasting my own time even. We will leave you be. Come, let's move on.'

317

Licina watched through the cracks as the party remounted and made their way down the same path they had ridden up. Her breathing calmed and the shaking stopped, but she dare not speak. For a long time she and Julius lay like that, their slowing breaths the only sound.

'Have they gone?' His voice was a whisper, warm on the back of her neck.

'Yes, they went back down the path we came up. By all the gods, that was close!' She rolled over, gazing into Julius' eyes, and wishing it were Albinus staring back at her.

'We should stay here for the night, let them put some distance between us. Get back on the road first thing.' Julius shuffled back as he spoke, Licina could not help but notice a small wet patch on his tunic where the bulge of his manhood had been moments before.

'Yes, but maybe spread out a bit? No need to be quite so…close.'

Julius could feel his cheeks burning as he looked down and saw what she had been staring at. 'As you wish. How's your ankle?'

'I'd say bad by the way she limped in 'ere.' Julius froze and Licina screamed. The old man just chuckled. 'Comfortable, are we?'

The pair shuffled back until their backs were against the wall. Covered in damp hay, they left the small enclave they had been hiding in, Julius rushed to his feet and grasped his spear in both hands. 'Ha! No need to be so scared, if I was gonna hurt you I'd have just given you away to the whoresons who were looking for you.' Licina took stock of the old farmer, seeing him for the first time. Well into the winter of his life, lank grey hair falling round his cheeks, his red scalp creeping through the thinning

318

strands. Eyes so dark they looked as though they belonged in Hel itself, a crooked nose, split lips and a mouth with no teeth.

'You knew we were here?' She didn't even realise she was speaking.

'I watched you hobble in. Was about to come in and send you on your way when that lot turned up.' A motion with his thumb at the door. 'Figured you needed a hand, thought I'd give you one.'

'Why?'

'I gotta son, a good lad, if not a little lost. Now he don't trust that Adalwin. And if my lad don't trust him, then I don't either. Simple.' Licina winced at the man's stink, he was moving ever closer, and smelled as though he hadn't bathed in years. The grime that clung to his skin confirmed that.

'Well…err…thank you for your help. We should probably be on our way.' Julius moved in front of Licina as he spoke, his hand taking hers.

'Now what's the rush! You don't wanna go tearing out there where you can be caught. Those wolves will sniff you out like a couple o' hares. You even know where you are?' The two shook their heads. 'Ha! You're lucky I speak your tongue. Most don't up here. Where you headed?'

'What do you know of the north?' Julius squeezed her hand in an effort to keep her silent, but she had to ask.

'Bit broad that. Big place. Anywhere specific you wanna go?'

'I've heard tales of a frozen sea, of a land where the sun never shines. A world of ice, constantly carpeted in thick snow. I want to go there.'

319

'Aye. I know where you're headed. You need to go through the land of the Jutes, take passage on a ship north. The land of the ice giants, that's what they call it up there. Donar's lair, where he fights with his great hammer to keep the giants at bay. You can hear him when a storm's up, the rumble as his hammer flies, the spark of light as he smashes through ice. 'Tis a hard land, or so they say. You sure that's where you wanna go?'

There was awe in his voice, reverence. He spoke as though that land was the most holy place in all the world, and maybe it was.

'That's where I want to go. I always dreamed of travel as a child, a place to reinvent myself, and start again. But then I fell in love, with a man so great and pure he made me forget all me demons. But then you lot showed up, and now my love is lost and I am all alone. I will not go quietly into the cold embrace of my mind from which he awoke me. I want to go north.' Tears burnt her cheeks as she spoke, her voice quivered with passion and her eyes promised murder. This was a lady who would not be moved from her path.

'Well, north it is. You'll be needing a guide, someone who knows the land, keep you off the beaten track. Might be you'll even make it without being caught! 'Tis a long road you wish to travel, that ankle gonna hold?'

'I will manage.'

'Good. Just so 'appens I got a guide for you 'ere, he was just about to go north 'isself. Al, get out here. Al!' The greybeard turned and shouted towards the small farmhouse. There was a pause, Licina and Julius sharing a concerned look.

A heartbeat later a man emerged from the house, walking gingerly down the small steps into the dirt-ridden path. He wore a hat, black in colour, the sides drooping low over his face and ears. An eye patch covered his right eye, the other shrouded in the hat's shade. A broken nose, split lips and toothless mouth, just like the greybeard. His right arm was in a sling, covered by a long dark cloak. His mail coat gleamed, made brighter against his dark beard. He carried a sheathed sword in his left hand, the blade as long as his legs, a black pommel poking out of the top.

Julius let out a whimper, and backed further into the hay, wanting it to swallow him up. 'Julius, what is it?' Licina couldn't grasp it.

'Well, well, well. What 'ave we got 'ere then?' The man spoke through a wretched grin that promised nothing but blood and terror.

Chapter Twenty-One

September AD 168 – East of Carnuntum, Pannonia

Balomar breathed in the scent of summer. The smell of grass, the pollen from the plants, blown gently into his face from the breeze off the river. His vast horde spread out around him, distinct coloured trousers and shields marking out where each tribe held their place in the line. The Fourteenth stood arrayed for battle in front of him. *So tiny. One meagre legion.* He never thought he'd look upon a legion and think that, but with the manpower at his disposal, it was impossible to think of anything other than certain victory.

He felt exhilarated, a bloodthirsty smile fixed on his face, one he would not be rid of if he wanted. Finally, he was ready to give battle; the tribal disputes, the struggle for food and water, the agonising of where to camp – it was all behind him, at least for today.

His men were ready, their blood up, same as his. A great sacrifice had been given to Donar the night before, twelve willing souls sent to his great hall. The auspicious verdict from the priests had served to boost the tribes' morale, unify them even. A quiet word in the high priest's ear had seen to that. He could see it in the whites of the men's eyes, in their eagerness to close with the Roman line, today they would give a great slaughter. Longswords and axes glimmered in the shining sun, there was not a cloud in the sky as he arced his head up and breathed deep. He spied two ravens circling the battlefield, and could almost feel the Allfather at his side, willing him on to victory.

He looked right to share the moment with Adalwin; the empty space dampened his spirits. *Where in Donar's name are you?* It was a moment his faithful captain would have relished, another great victory the two would have shared. His grin returned as he thought of the boasting he would do when the man finally returned. *It will be as if I won the day on my own.*

There were no more than a hundred paces separating the two forces now. A small cobbled road with large, flat, green flanks was the battlefield; it was perfect. His one fear had been facing a barrage of heavy artillery, but as he scanned the enemy, it seemed they had marched without it. *The arrogance. I will damn them all to Hel.*

He focused his gaze and rage on the colour party in their centre; his tribe would have the honour of facing them. It seemed their legate had decided to fight alongside his men.

Honourable, but foolish. I will slay him with my own hand.

Dismounting his fine black stallion and throwing the reins at the nearest warrior, he pushed his way to the front rank. Rasping his sword from his scabbard, he thrust it the gods. 'Today we rid ourselves of our oppressors. Too long have we suffered under the yoke of Roman rule. Lived off the scraps they toss us in disdain. These men would take our lands if they could, spill their seed in our wives' bellies. Eat the crops we work so hard to grow. Well, today the rulers become the ruled! We will crush them like the parasites they are! We will grind their bones to dust! The Allfather watches us, brothers! Are you with me?!'

With a roar so loud the mighty Donar could have heard from his distant frozen plain as he battled to rid the snow-ridden wasteland of the cursed ice giants – the Germani broke into a run. An inexorable tide of metal and wood, they cheered and snarled as the ground shook under the weight of their charge. *Victory shall be mine.*

*

Albinus couldn't stop his limbs from shaking. His teeth chattered like he had bathed in an ice-covered lake in the depths of winter. Sweat streamed down him, soaking his tunic and making it cling to him. His leather cap that was meant to keep his helmet in place was so slippery with sweat he could feel it sliding over his lank hair. His eyes were red-rimmed and stinging; so much salt-filled water was seeping down his forehead, it was all he could do to keep them open.

His mouth was as dry as the desert, his bladder full to bulging. Taurus had just ordered his men to piss now while they could, but to Albinus' embarrassment, he found he couldn't.

The field already stank of piss and shit, as men around him followed their centurion's orders and splashed the heels of the men in front or squatted down to relieve their bowels – much to the disgust of the men around them. A young recruit behind Habitus threw up down the veteran's back; it took both Libo and Longus to stop the old Syrian running the poor man through.

Albinus' armour felt heavier than it had ever before, his feet already in ruins, he could feel the blisters rubbing on his heels against the worn-in leather of his boots. He was ashamed to see how much his shield was shaking in his left hand. It quivered up and down, like a tent flap caught in the wind. *Courage. Courage.*

He willed himself to be brave. For his father's honour he prayed to Mars and Mithras to grant him courage, to see him face his fears like a man. *You're an embarrassment. How did I end up with a son like you?* The words came back to haunt him. But how he wished he was back at that settlement, merely facing his father, rather than a horde of German iron.

He adjusted his sweaty palm on the grip of his *pilum,* trying to imagine himself actually using the thing for real. Panic rose in his throat as he recalled the incident in the forest, where only Fullo's quick reactions had saved him from certain death. *Coward. You didn't even move. Why should it be different today?* He couldn't stop the vomit if he tried. It flew from his mouth, covering the back of his shield and his arm. He was dizzy – staggered, vision blurred, ears full of the beating of his own heart. He could feel himself slipping away, as if he had been lifted from that blood-fuelled place. There were arms around him, gentle, warm and welcoming. And then he heard her voice, shrouded, as if it were covered in mist. *Stay strong, my love. You must be brave. For me, be brave. I will see you again.* And then her lips were on his, warm and embracing, like a roaring hearth on a winter's night. Her breath filled him, her touch awoke him. He snapped open his eyes as if awoken from the deepest slumber.

'There he is! Bad time to have a nap, lad!' Bucco's strong hands brought him to his feet. He shook the dizziness from his eyes, and suddenly there was Fullo, and Calvus, and Rullus, their hands on him, holding him up. Someone shoved his sick-covered shield into his hand, his *pilum* into the other. And then he was back in the line, and the tribes were not a hundred paces off, the ground shook as they began their charge.

325

'You okay, brother? You can go back if you want? No one's gonna make you stand in the front line.' Fullo's face was creased with concern, but not for the charging barbarians, just for his friend.

'I saw her, Fullo. *Felt* her. She is alive, I know it.' Awe-filled conviction in his voice.

'Then you must stay strong. We will find her, together. But first we must survive today.' Eighty paces the gap, and Taurus barraged his way next to Albinus in the line.

'You okay, son?' His voice was low.

'Fine, sir. Not sure what came over me,' Albinus said, rather unconvincingly.

'Good. Now get that fucking javelin ready. FIRST COHORT, READY JAVELINS!' No more than fifty paces off now, the ground shook. Crows began to circle overhead – they would be feasting by sunset.

Albinus raised his *pilum* above his right shoulder, lead-weighted iron point aiming for the crows. His arm shook in anticipation, and he struggled to maintain his grip in his sweat-filled palm. Raising his head, he winced in pain as his neck guard dug into the gap between his shoulder blades. *Curse this damned helmet.* Focusing on the charging barbarians, he picked out a target. A slim man with a wide blade, naked from the waist up, a heavily tattooed body atop dark blue trousers. A menacing snarl fixed a scarred face, dark eyes seemingly pouring into his own. Albinus tried to visualise the throw, judge the angle where the javelin would fall onto the man's chest. *As if I'm gonna hit him. Just give the damned order so I can throw the bloody thing.*

'LOOSE!' Iron darkened the sky as the javelins fell upon the charging Germani like a summer storm. Albinus' throw was good, his target going over with a javelin sticking from is chest. *I did it! Bless you, Fortuna, I hit him! Wait…was it even mine?*

'Ready second javelins!' No time to worry whether it was his kill or not, Albinus readied his second *pilum*. 'LOOSE!' Again, the iron storm raged down on the helpless barbarians. Albinus didn't even aim this time, but the enemy were so close it was impossible to miss. The heavy javelins cut the air with a whistle as they crashed down and tore through armour, flesh, gristle and bone. Blood splatters misted the air; the red day had begun.

With a rasp Albinus drew his *gladius* from his sheath. If he'd had time to think he would have noticed his palms were no longer wet with fear, his body no longer shook, the need to piss was gone. He would not have recognised the vicious snarl on his face, eyes burning with the hunger for blood.

The mocking voice in his head silenced, no man would call him a coward again. He changed his stance, left leg forward, shield braced in front, hunched down and ready. Silus would have been proud.

He fixed his eyes over the rim of his shield, could feel his brothers around him, hear Bucco screaming as he urged the Germani to come and meet his blade. He felt nothing but pride, and just had time to wonder why he had let fear grip him his whole life…then the shieldwalls hit like thunder in the night.

BANG.

By the gods, what a noise. The Roman line got pushed back, five – ten paces. Albinus held his own, leaning into his shield and letting his nailed boots do their job, he stood firm.

He felt hands on his back, his comrades pushing back against the tribal tide of wood and iron.

327

It was a shoving match now, a test of strength. The months of training paid off for Albinus. Once a figure so slight, his hardened arms and legs ensured he gave as good as he got. The warrior facing him was as young as he; ale-filled breath warm on his face, he lowered his head as the young barbarian spat at him over their shields. It cost him his life. Ducking down, Albinus raised his right hand and thrust with all his might, his *gladius* licking in and out, straight into the open mouth of the young German.

Next was a greybeard, as wise as he was toothless. He came on slow, steady, a thick spear propped atop a small round shield. Albinus hunched back down behind his shield, recoiled from the clang that was the spear rebounding off its boss. *Patience.* He stood unmoving, not wanting to be the first to risk a lunge, leave an opening. Sweat filled his eyes, squinting his only option now. The adrenaline of the first rush was wearing off; already his shield was heavy, sword hanging lower in his palm.

Albinus blinked – and blinked again. His eyes closed for longer on the second one. 'Look out, brother!' Fullo's warning saved him, he snapped open his eyes and there was the spear point, dancing inches from his face. Wrenching his head back, he thrust up his shield and knocked the spear towards the sun. The greybeard staggered, shield hanging wide to his left.

Albinus seized his chance, sword scything the blood-drenched air as it flew into the old man's guts. It went in with no resistance, flesh sucking it further in – too far. Albinus screamed in pain as his sword jarred against the ageing spine, a loud snap as something broke – sword or spine, no way of knowing.

He released his grip on the sword; Albinus dropped his shield and staggered back.

Left arm supporting the right, something had gone in his shoulder. Taurus, on Albinus' right, reacted quickly to stop the line from breaking. Two short blasts of his whistle, the Roman front rank turned side on, fresh troops poured through the gap and slammed the German line, pushing them back.

Albinus retreated through the ranks. His shoulder was on fire, right arm hanging limp.

'Albinus! Are you okay?' Bucco was there in a flash, gently helping him to sit on the ground.

'Not sure what's happened. My shoulder...I can't move my arm.'

'Fullo! Get a medic here now!' Off Fullo went, deeper into the ranks.

'I saw you fight, lad, you did well. Silus would have shed a tear in pride to see you standing there with your brothers.' Bucco unclipped Albinus's cloak as he spoke, and went to help him shrug off his mail.

'Stop! Ahh, it hurts!' Tears fell now, he was shaking, bone-weary. How long had he been fighting? Hours? Mere heartbeats? He'd no idea.

'Over here, quick!' Fullo appeared with a young doctor, leather apron already soaked in crimson – there would be much more of that before the day was out.

'What happened?' Albinus quickly explained about his sword thrust, the blade getting wedged in the greybeard's spine. The doctor nodded, murmuring to himself. 'Get his mail off. Sounds like your shoulder is dislocated, it will need resetting.'

Bucco and Fullo ignored Albinus' protests as they ripped the mail from him. The doctor didn't wait, grabbing Albinus by the arm he heaved with all his might, and they heard a snap as the arm was forced back into the joint.

329

'Jupiter's fucking balls, that hurt!' Albinus jumped up, as if the movement would rid him of the pain. But already it was better, a tingling down the arm as the feeling and strength came back. 'Thank you, doctor.'

'My pleasure. It will happen again at some point, I'm sure, once these things happen once they tend to repeat.' With a nod he was off, plenty of wounded pouring back from the front that needed attention.

'I must get back to the line. Stay here if you need to.' Bucco was off, charging back through the ranks, desperate to re-join the fray.

'Fullo, help me get my mail back on.'

'You're not going back in there?'

'Course I bloody am! The battle still rages, I must do my part.' He struggled with the iron-linked shirt, the weight a burden at the best of times.

'Do you not think you already have? You've fought, taken a wound. No shame in sitting out the rest of it.' He moved to help his friend anyway, knowing full well his words would be ignored.

'Would our fathers have sat it out? Let their comrades fight in their place? I cannot.'

'You're no coward, brother. Don't think you have something to prove.'

'I don't. I just want to do my bit.' Mail and helmet back on, he clipped his cloak round his shoulders and flexed his arms. 'Better already! Let's go.'

With that he was off, not looking back to see if Fullo followed. Eyes fixed up, he headed straight for the banner of the first cohort like a moth chasing a flame. In no time he was there, pushing through the rear ranks, picking up a discarded sword and shield as he went.

The noise was incredible. He stood behind Habitus in the second rank now, bunched in, shoulder to shoulder with Fullo and a nameless legionary. It was unnerving, he thought, standing and watching whilst other men fought. *Come on! Let me at 'em!*

Habitus fought like a street cat in front of him. Breaking from the sanctuary of the shieldwall, he spun and twirled as his blade licked out to claim life after life. One in the groin, next one to the neck, then a gut-opening slash in the midriff. With a shout from Abas, he quickly backed up and re-joined the line. 'Get ready, brothers, switching ranks soon,' said the optio, working up his rage to stand in the front rank himself.

Here we go. I can do this. I will stay alive for you, my love. I will come for you. And there was the whistle, two short blasts, clearly heard over the cacophony of battle. Habitus turned to the right, shield protecting his body as he turned, and with a snarl Albinus leapt into the fray.

The first kill was easy, a nameless raider, eyes still locked on the retreating Habitus – Albinus took him in the throat with his first thrust. Got his shield down quick, eyes darting ready. The next one took longer: the man was built like an ox. For what seemed an age they duelled and danced, feinting and retreating, each waiting for the other to make a mistake. Neither did. In the end, it was Fullo that landed the first blow; a sharp stab at the German's elbow as his spear darted for a non-existent opening on Albinus' right. With a squeal the spear clattered to the floor, quickly submerging in the ever-softer terrain – becoming a hazard it was so splattered in piss, shit and blood. The barbarian reared his head to the gods as he recoiled in pain. He never saw Albinus swoop in and take him high in the chest.

331

Am I making you proud, father? Are you ashamed of me now? He wanted to roar it to Elysium, wanted the old man to see him in all his gore-stained glory. He risked a glance left along the line: Fullo was still at his shoulder, fighting in silence, but with ruthless efficiency. Further down was Abas, and next to him Taurus, the first spear had probably been there since the first clash of blades – and he would stay there until the last. To his right was Calvus, shouting and growling in his mother tongue – his short axe dripping wet in the sun. Longus the other side, then Libo, and Rullus with the standard. *My brothers.* A whoosh past his ear, the glint of a spear point, close as a lover's breath. *Fuck! Concentrate.* A small man, yellow trousers, stolen Roman *scutum*, advanced at a crouch.

For twenty years Sisbert had fought for his king. Twenty years. Areogaesus had been good to him. Silver, women, spear fame, he'd taken everything the old man offered. But never had he been more reluctant to fight them now. He was proud to be of the Quadi, proud to serve in one of the largest and most formidable tribes in all of Germania. So large, and so formidable, the cursed romans even recognised Areogaesus as a king – the only chieftain to be given that honour, and offered him tribute and promises of friendship.

And then Balomar had come along. *May Wotan curse the fool.* The Marcomanni had got bigger and stronger with every year, more and more tribes submitting until there were none left between him and the Quadi. Life had become tougher then. Roman tribute stopped, and then so did the raiding. Caught between the eagles and Marcomanni iron, Areogaesus had banned his men from raiding into their territories, claiming they could not afford a war with either foe. *Man's gotta eat.*

Then to top it all off, the arrogant cur Balomar sent that snake Alaric to his king's hall, asking the king of the Quadi to fight Balomar's war. *What a load of bullshit!* Everyone in the land knew Alaric could not be trusted, he changed allegiance with the wind, but it seemed he too had been won round to Balomar's cause. And now not a year later, here he was, fighting for the 'high king'. *Fucking bullshit! Hear me, Allfather, don't let me die for this whoreson.*

Sisbert was angry. The march here had been a disaster, twice he had narrowly avoided been knifed in the dark by some fool from a rival tribe, and once he had managed to get his revenge the next starless night – cold iron finding the base of the man's spine while he pissed. There had been no food, no water, no order of march, *no fucking plan!* They had marched blindly into battle, Balomar had boldly claimed the gods were on their side, as they only produced one legion to face them. *As if ol' one eye arranged that!*

So here he was, one hand gripping a pillaged Roman shield, the other his blood-wet spear. He faced a boy, taller than he, but all arms and legs. The boy was distracted, eyes darting left and right. *I'll have some o' that!* Spear licked out, a fraction too far to the right. *Getting sloppy in me old age.* Startled, the boy's head snapped back to the front, the most dazzling blue eyes Sisbert had ever seen. *Wotan's arse! He's a pretty one.* It seemed every day he was asked why he remained unmarried; he always claimed service to his king came before love and that there was no point in taking a bride when he could be dead on a spear by the end of the next summer. He'd never picked up the courage to tell his comrades the real reason. *Who'd follow a boy lover into the spear din?* Best no one knew.

333

He was torn now, off balance. *Don't think me a fool, great Donar, but he's a looker.*

The pretty boy sensed the old man's hesitation. He pushed with his shield, his weight on his left foot. A loud clang as the two shield bosses met. Sisbert staggered back, disconcerted by the wiry strength in the young man. A sword point followed the shield, but Sisbert managed to deflect it with his spear, forcing the Roman's arm wide. Catlike reactions, combined with years of experience, Sisbert snaked the spear point up, a lightning lunge, meant to take his opponent in the base of the skull. Instead it skidded along the side of the young man's face, tearing off his helmet, revealing an untidy mop of hair, the colour of wet sand.

The youngster staggered back out of spear range, dropping his sword and clutching his bloodied face with his hand. Sisbert moved in for the kill, spear point aimed at that pretty face. *Shame. Ahh well.* Thud! A gurgle and a gasp. Stunned, he looked down to see a small wooden shaft protruding from his throat. He couldn't breathe, felt weak suddenly. A metallic taste in his mouth, black blood pouring from his lips. *Knew we should never 'ave come 'ere.*

Wotan, father, take me to your hall.

Albinus staggered, his right cheek burned, helmet gone. He dropped his sword, grabbed his face, horrified to feel his teeth exposed through the ripped skin. *Coward! You're not dead yet! Get your bloody sword and fight!* His father's words ran true in his ears. He crouched, hands probing, grateful to feel the clammy Maplewood grip. Standing, eyes wide, desperate to sight his foe. 'You're welcome! Now get out my way, you're bleedin' everywhere!' Still unsure of what was going on, he looked

334

down to see his attacker flat on his back with an arrow in his throat. Habitus barged him out the way. 'Fullo! Get Albinus out of here!'

Fullo backed away warily, turning once they were past the dense ranks of waiting legionaries to see his friend. 'By Jupiter! What happened?'

'Ha! Well, you were standing right next to me! Nice to know you got my back!' There was blood everywhere, Albinus' right cheek torn to shreds, crimson-stained teeth braced in pain. His mail shirt looked as though it had been dunked in red dye, thick lumps of blood matter caught on the small links.

'Well fuck! I was fighting myself! So, this is what it's like to be a soldier, eh?' The two stopped talking and took in the carnage around them. At the rear of the Roman line, men lay strewn out on the blood-soaked ground. All kinds of injuries were on show: men with holes in their torsos, some with limbs hacked off, one man laying hunched over, desperately trying to squeeze his guts back into his open belly. It was harrowing.

Albinus forgot the throbbing pain in his face. He surveyed the front line of the battle, and felt immense pride at seeing the left flank more than holding their own. He could spot Taurus' red crested helmet, still standing strong in the front line, unmoving, like a rock facing the seas crashing waves. *So, this is it. I have felt the battle frenzy, the bloodlust. I have stood with my brothers and survived. Just.* The pain in his cheek was returning as he thought of it. He winced – which only made it worse. 'Suppose I should get stitched up?' he said. It hurt when they laughed together.

'Aye, brother. Think we've had our fill for today. Come, let's find a doctor.'

They had just started moving back, away from the screech of iron and the screaming of men. Albinus had his head in the clouds, observing the circling crows and giving thanks to Fortuna, when he heard the battle change. Felt it. Spinning, his gaze fell to his front and right, the centre of the Roman line. It had crumbled.

The barbarians were streaming through the breach, hacking down retreating Romans as easily as they would reap their harvest. Panic engulfed him. Swamped him – the way the rushing tide swamps a desolate beach. His fear froze him. Rooted. *No! Not this! Not again!*

Move! Coward.

Fullo was pulling him back, yelling in his ear. But Albinus couldn't hear. He turned his head slowly, away from the incoming tide of German iron, and looked at his friend.

Dazed.

'Come, brother! Move!' But Albinus just stood there, his mind lost in a fog.

The ground shook, rumbled. And there was the cavalry. Charging into the melee, curved *spathas* spitting blood as they rasped them down into flesh and bone.

The shape of the battle had changed now, the left flank cut off from the right. The Romans were retreating, shields still locked together. In moments Albinus found himself back at the centre of the first cohort, surrounded by frightened legionaries, eyes darting with panic glances to the rear.

'FORM SQUARE! FORM SQUARE NOW! ON ME! ON ME!' And there was Taurus, blood-splattered, bone-tired, but still orchestrating his men with speed and purpose.

'Albinus? That you? Jupiter's arse, lad, but that's a pretty one!' He patted Albinus on the shoulder as he marched past, berating a soldier for not getting into line quick enough. 'Right, ladies, here's what we're gonna do! Keep the square intact, and keep marching backwards. We're only half a day from the fortress, stick together, stay with your brothers, and we'll be back in time for supper! Understood?' A shout of 'Yes, sir!' filled the air. Even to Albinus' untrained eye the situation appeared desperate. But Taurus was calm as ever, growling as he forced his way into the front line of the square, leaving Abas to dictate their speed from the centre.

Albinus staggered, faltered as his dogged steps took him forever backwards. He suddenly remembered his water skin hanging at his back, and gratefully drank deep, losing half of it through the gaping hole in his cheek. *Mars, give me strength. Mithras, are you there? You always stood by my father, look out for me now. Give me strength. Must be strong. Courage.*

Fullo was gone, into the right flank of the square, his sword strokes keeping the flanking barbarians at bay. There was no order in the square now, no centuries or cohorts fought together, men fought next to strangers – united in their desperate struggle.

Abas stood next to Albinus, calling the pace like he was captain of a galley, ordering the strokes of his sea-wary oarsmen. 'Albinus, can you fight?' Startled, he turned to his optio.

'I think so, sir. Where do you want me?' *Courage.*

'At the rear. These goat-fuckers will try and cut us off! Hold that line for me, keep the men moving. Ares be with you, brother.' With that he was gone, an endless bundle of

337

energy, shouting and encouraging as men fought for their lives.

Hold the line? Me? Surely there was someone better placed? Where are all the centurions? He raced back to the rear line, starting to buckle under the pressure of the rampant Germani, swamping their wall of shields, spears darting in and out, searching for the weak link.

He stood in the second rank and looked for an officer, but there wasn't one. *Could they all be dead?* The men around him were scared. He could smell it, amongst the stink of leather and sweat. Before he knew what he was doing, before he let the same fear that built within him overwhelm him completely – he began to shout. 'Come on, boys! Push! Push forwards! Keep moving and we'll live, you'll see! That's it, push, step, push, step!'

The legionaries were stunned at first, and who could blame them. Veteran killers, loyal servants to their eagle for more summers than they cared to remember, being encouraged by this gangly youth and his cracking voice. But when they turned to look, their courage rose and they pushed on command. The young man behind them looked like no green recruit. He was helmetless, a mop of sweat-drenched hair atop his head. His eyes were ice, cold iron almost glowing against a face covered in splattered blood. Half his cheek was missing on his right side, you could see him grinding his teeth through the mess of torn flesh and matted blood. If this man was still fighting, then so would they.

On they pushed, for what felt like hours. Albinus stood behind the front line, calling the steps. More and more barbarians were shifting round the retreating square onto the rear line, determined to prevent them leaving the battlefield. On and on they went, along the straight road

338

that led back to Carnuntum, and sanctuary behind the fortress's high walls.

With the help of Fortuna, the square stayed intact. Albinus could hear Taurus the whole time, holding back the flooding tide of Germani to his rear. Abas was still in the centre, prowling like a caged lion. The small band of reserves he'd kept with him had long since been thrown into the fray.

Albinus could feel his voice box fading, his cheek was on fire, his legs like anvils, he could no longer raise his shield arm past his shoulder, but still he kept going. Dogged step after dogged step. Until he could see it. 'Up ahead, in the distance! Home! We're nearly there, boys! Keep pushing!' The walls could be seen, the finest wooden walls there ever were. And there were the east gates, resplendent with twin watchtowers. And they were opening, men were marching out. 'Relief force coming! Come on, keep pushing! Push! Step!' His voice had gone now, just a rusty squeak remained. But he didn't care, and neither did the men around him. They were there, home.

It wasn't long before the Germani realised they were about to be caught between two Roman shieldwalls. They scurried off to either side, tails between their legs as they gave the cheering flanks of the square a wide birth. And then they were gone.

The quiet was eerie. Disconcerting, after so many hours of screams and the clash of iron. In the background they could hear hoofbeats, muffled, as the survivors of the cavalry continued to screen the retreat as best they could.

Albinus slowed, half collapsed on the floor, but a stranger helped him to his feet, thrust a water skin in his hands. 'Gratitude, sir, we'd have been goners if it weren't for you.'

An ageing man, white speckled in his beard. 'I'm no officer, just a recruit.' It was all Albinus could rasp out, breathless, a mouth full of blood.

'Just a recruit? I think you're more than just that, lad!' And there was Taurus, still brimming with energy, as if the battle had lasted heartbeats instead of most of the day. He was an epiphany of gore, it covered him, consumed him. His armour redder than his cloak, but Albinus would have put good coin on none of it being his own. 'Abas tells me you led these men back, kept the line intact. That true?'

'It is, sir. He picked us up when we were beaten, about to be overrun. Without him we would have floundered,' said the greybeard, rasping a salute as he spoke.

'Then you have my gratitude, young Albinus. And my respect. I'll make sure the legate hears of it, if he still lives, that is.'

They were near the fortress now, passing the great amphitheatre where they had begun that red day. People still sat outside their homes and taverns in the outlaying *vici*, despite the rampant barbarian horde coming their way. Taurus ordered men to go to them, tell them to get within Carnuntum's walls.

'Albinus! Albinus!' Bucco was running, tears streamed down his blood-drenched face. His old segmented armour was bent on all sides, sword dents clear in the long thin lines where the blade had kissed the metal. 'Thank Mithras, you're alive! I've been looking everywhere for you!' His embrace was stifling, the smell awful, but Albinus couldn't remember being so comforted and relieved. 'Bucco! Are you okay? Where are the others?

Fullo?' Panic quickly gripped him. He hadn't seen his friend since the beginning of the retreat.

'Fine, fine! They are at the back, Calvus took a wound to the leg, and Libo's left arm is a bit of a mess, but they will live. Jupiter's fucking balls, what happened to your face?!'

'He was daydreaming! And he still ain't thanked me for saving his skin!' Old Habitus wore a wicked grin. One arm was round the limping Calvus, the other clutching his small bow.

'And I'm told you're now a hero! Well, I'll tell you what I do know, you're buying my drinks for the next month, little brother!'

Little brother was a line he'd heard a lot. But it was only given from the veterans to the recruits when they had proved themselves worthy. Albinus smiled at the recognition the old Syrian was awarding him. 'Gladly, big brother! As long as we're still getting paid!'

'Albinus! Brother! How are you?' And there was Fullo, as blood-splattered as the rest, but otherwise unharmed. 'Look at your face! You need a doctor!'

He laughed, even though it hurt. 'I know! I can feel the wind whistling through the hole!' They both laughed, the exhilaration of having fought and survived ran through them, even if they had been defeated.

'Can it wait a few hours, Albinus? I want to see if the amphitheatre's still gonna open tonight. Nothing better than watching some Christians get eaten by lions to cheer you up after a beating! You never know, they might even have some of them Camel-Leopards they had in there a few months back. Size of 'em! Fucking necks longer than Libo's cock!' Bucco smirked as he spoke, Calvus groaned in dismay. The rest laughed. They were all there now, the eight of their *contubernium*, alive. Albinus had never felt such a deep connection with the others. He knew they had suffered a serious defeat, and that there were many more

341

battles to come, but with soldiers like these around him, he knew he wouldn't let his eagle, or his father, down. *I just need to find my love. Where are you?*

Chapter Twenty-Two

September AD 168 – The Amber Road, Pannonia

The summer's sun was still strong, the flowers in full blossom, almost welcoming, as the German army marched ever south through the green lands of Pannonia.

Alexander was in a grand mood. He sat atop a small bay filly, and chuckled as she thrust her head left and right, licking and nibbling the horses around her. She reminded him in many ways of his own daughter when she was little, excitable, filled with the joys of life and the sights and smells around her.

He could scarcely believe how well his plans were going, and how superbly Balomar was playing his part. *It will be a shame when he has to die.* The Fourteenth legion had been destroyed, less than two cohorts surviving the slaughter. Their legate had been cut down by the Marcomanni king's own hand, and the centre of the Roman formation had crumbled soon after. What followed had been harrowing, even to a veteran raider's eye.

Watching from atop the walls of the great fortress in Carnuntum, he saw with glee two measly squares of Roman soldiers stagger back within the great gates. The cavalry had followed shortly after, having done all they could with their limited numbers to keep the German horde at bay.

When the gates were closed, and the locking bars in place, the Germani had run riot. The city of Carnuntum

343

itself had its own walls made of stone, but they were short, standing not much higher than a man in his prime. It had been short work for the raiders to throw themselves over, the raping and pillaging that followed lasted well into the night.

He had forced himself to look sombre, hurt and angry as he walked amongst the remnants of the defeated legion. Glycon in hand, he blessed those that approached him, forgave them their sins and handed out potions to the wounded to send them off into a never-ending dreamless sleep; all for a price, of course.

It had been simple to sneak out the following morning. The gates had been opened as Tribune Maximianus had led men out to survey the damage in the city, and rescue what citizens they could. Alexander had simply mounted a horse and rode out as if he was going to join them, before slipping out onto the road that ran south to catch up with the German army.

The week that followed had been joyous to his wicked mind. He had watched on as the raiders destroyed every farm, village and town in their path. Thousands of women and children were marched in the midst of the vast horde, chained together with long iron rope, they would make a fortune in the slave markets back in the north.

Scarbantia, Savaria, Poetovio and Noviodunum had fallen one by one. The towns were poorly walled, defended by small pockets of auxiliaries that hadn't used their spears in anger for many years, it had been all too easy for Balomar and his pack of ravaging wolves.

News had reached them that Eric and Bandanasp had secured the gold from the Dacian gold mines and were now striking through Moesia into the heart of Greece. *My dream is almost complete. Rome on her knees, desperate for fresh leadership, a strong arm to guide her. I will give her that.*

His thoughts began to drift to the beautiful purple cloak he had in a chest somewhere in the baggage column. All morning it had taken to get the measurements just right, not too tight, not too loose. Not too short, or long. It was perfect. *I will look magnificent.*

He chuckled again, gaining nervous looks from the warriors around him, who were always on edge around the mysterious old man and his venomous snake god. One of his men had brought him a message, from Emperor Marcus Aurelius no less. He had revealed he was marching north with an army, two fresh legions recently raised from the men of Italy. Many years it had been since an Emperor had forced the men from their homeland to fight under the eagles, *such are the times.* He had asked for advice; how could he appease the gods and end the suffering of his people? Alexander's laugh had been a rasping breath as he replied: Throw two lions into the river Danube, give them to the gods. They must be alive and intact. Surely no Emperor has ever made such a strong offering to the gods? They will revere you, and so will your people when you swipe these raiders from your lands.

Ha! He could picture it now. Two mighty lions, set free from their chains as some poor men fought to get them into the river's current. *Can lions swim? I hope so!* He took great joy from picturing the furious beasts, leaping from the water and tearing their keepers apart. *Even the philosophic Aurelius will see he is doomed then. And when he writes me again, to say it has been a catastrophic failure, I will send him and Verrus some wine. A nice bottle of falernian to apologise for my misreading of the signs.* Alexander stroked the neck of his Glycon, the snake

345

wrapped round his right arm. It responded to the touch, baring its fangs as it swivelled to see its master. *Yes, a nice bottle of wine, with a bit of extra flavour.*

*

Aquileia was a fortress. Imperious and unmoving. Trying to capture it had been like the wind trying to move a mountain.

His men had fallen upon its walls like waves hitting rock, but the rock will never submit to the tide. In their thousands they had charged, tribe after tribe in their patchwork collection of coloured trousers, wooden ladders in hand, and in their thousands, they had fallen; never to rise again.

Balomar watched on as another attack faltered. The Roman heavy artillery was taking its toll, this time the tribes didn't even reach the walls, the twang of the *ballistae* spaced out along the city's north wall filled the air. Dart after dart found its target, some even sending up to three or four men to their end.

He could feel the sun's heat fading as it basked him. October was upon them and summer was slowly rolling into autumn. The first hints of orange could be seen on the leaves, the wind becoming stronger. He had hoped to capture a major city by now. Somewhere to rest behind secure walls, ready to march south on Italy in the spring. Instead his men were camped out in the open, Aquileia refusing to open its gates to him.

Aurelius and Verrus were marching north to meet him with two fresh legions, the Tenth blocked his path north at Vindobona, the remnants of the Fourteenth still licked their wounds at Carnuntum. He had never felt more alone.

Casting his gaze north, he longed to see Adalwin riding south to greet him. What he wouldn't give for the man's council, just his presence to use as a sounding board. The tribal chiefs were growing restless, declaring they either head for home or take a city. How would they feed their men through the bitter winter months? He knew each man had crops growing at home, but no one was there to reap in the harvest.

He had been expecting to find food in abundance, abandoned farm holds with barns brimming with grain, but it seemed the plague had not released its grip on this land yet. Famine still ruled. Already some of his own men had fallen ill of the sickening disease. It seemed to follow his army like a swarm of whores. Bodies covered in pus-filled lumps, they seemed to have a pulse of their own. Men slowly lost their minds as the fever took them, mumbling incoherently in their half-conscious state.

The stench was the worst, foul and unforgiving; even in the late summer's breeze the high king of the Germani pinched his nose as he thought he caught a whiff of the ghastly smell. *Just my mind playing tricks,* he assured himself.

He could feel the glare of the chieftains on his back as he turned away from the failed assault, the third one of the day. A decision would have to be made. Head on south and meet the Emperors in the field? The legions would be fresh, well fed and eager to defend their homeland under their rulers' watchful eye. The raiders on the other hand would be tired, footsore and hungry. He had no doubt his force would vastly outnumber anything the Romans could put in the field, but he doubted numbers would be enough.

A man called Hannibal had done it once. He remembered the story well. Had made it further south than Rome itself, but had been defeated in the end.

347

'Balomar, we must talk.' Areogaesus stepped forward from the crowd of chiefs. He spoke quietly, but assertively. 'How long can we keep this up? Aquileia will not open her gates to us, and we do not have the artillery to take the city. The time has come to move on, before we have an army chasing us.' Balomar could sense the other chiefs nodding and agreeing with the Quadi king. It angered him. Areogaesus had spoken just loudly enough to be heard by the others. Balomar had been told of whispered conversations around fires at night, led by his fellow king into the ears of the lesser chiefs. *Does he wish to challenge me? Declare himself high king of the tribes, lead them to glory? Ha! He will find no glory here, not while I still draw breath.*

Fuelled by anger, frustrated at his inability to take the great city before him, he unsheathed his great sword in one fluid motion and with a double-handed swing from left to right, took the head clean off the king of the Quadi.

Silence. Just the thud of the head hitting the floor, the body slumping heartbeats after, the blood dripping off Balomar's blade. No one shouted out, or even whimpered. There was no great gasp, no shouts of fury, just silence.

They stood in a sea of men and metal, but if you closed your eyes and let your ears explore for you, you would have thought yourself alone on a ship in the middle of the deep blue. The chieftains huddled together, the fear pouring off them, Balomar could almost smell it.

'I know what this turd has been doing. What you have all been doing! Whispered nothings into the fire's glow, secret plans swapped in the flames' shadows. Well it stops now! I am the high king here, the only king here! I brought you into this cursed empire, and have I not brought you glory? A legion destroyed, countless slaves ready to toil your fields, warm your beds or fill your halls with silver! And this is how you treat me? Like a fool?' He spat as he screamed, white spots of spittle falling like rain.

'You all swore, to Donar and the Allfather himself, to follow me into battle. And now, at the first sign of trouble you would have us running for home? Roman iron digging into our backs as we go? Well? Speak then! Let me hear your grand plans!'

The wind was the only voice, whistling through the long grass. The warriors had formed a circle round their leaders now, they stood, shocked as they stared at the headless body of the king of the Quadi.

A man pushed through the throng, his green cloak shading his face from the sun. 'Ahh, Alexander, glad you could join us. We were just getting to the bottom of a little rebellion my dear friend here thought he would lead.' Balomar pointed at Areogaesus' head, which still maintained an unnervingly calm expression. 'It seems some of these fearless leaders want to scuttle off home, tail between their legs like the whipped hounds they are. I thought I would make their decision somewhat easier.'

He stood and watched as the Greek slowly lowered his hood, the snake as always wrapped around his right arm. 'Maybe there should be a vote,' he said. 'Votes go to me, anonymously. You either vote to carry on south, or vote to go home. Thoughts?' His words were quickly translated and greeted with smiles and nods.

'Alexander, a word with you in private.' The high king moved off, pushing through the throngs of Quadi warriors who came to kneel at their king's side. One ceremoniously picked up the man's head and held it to his chest as he wept.

The two moved away from the crowds. Balomar studied the eastern priest as he summoned the right words. 'You seek to undermine me, priest? Here I am, alone in command of thousands of men, and you give them the opportunity to brazenly defy my orders?!' He was furious, could feel the fear oozing from the priest as he snarled at him.

'Undermine you? No. Gain the chieftains respect for you? Yes. Your campaign is over for the year, we both know it. Don't argue! You have two legions marching north to meet you, at least one more waiting by the Danube. You can't fight them all, Balomar! Our plan has worked better than I could have imagined. Rome is terrified, defeated. But to linger here only gives them the opportunity to gain their revenge. Aurelius is no fighter, but Verrus is. Remember he is only back from victory in the east not yet a year ago. The man's a fighter. A more skilled general than Candidus was. Retreat back into your lands, and I guarantee you will have your tribute come spring. Plus the gold you have acquired from Dacia. You have rattled their cage, Balomar, you may find you don't like what you see if you prize it open.' Balomar hated that whisper of a voice. It had given him nightmares on more than one occasion, not that he would admit it. He was consumed by doubt, unable to make a decision.

'And what do you gain from me running back to my fortress? I seem to recall this all being your idea. And yet here you stand, with no Roman aware that you masterminded their defeat. If I retreat now, you could go scurrying off to your Emperors, tell them my weaknesses and give them the advantage if it comes to war in spring. I do not trust you, Alexander. I agreed to this enterprise as a last option. To make Rome listen! You were the one hell-

350

bent on destroying them! And now, when we stand at the gateway to Italy itself, you would see me turn away and leave it untouched?'

'I never wanted the empire destroyed. I plan to rule it, remember! I just need the people, the senate to doubt the men that rule them. My friends in Rome have been doing a marvellous job at getting them to see things from my point of view. I just need a chance Balomar. And remember the agreement, when I am Emperor, Rome's borders and coffers will be open to you and your people.' His voice was almost human as he spoke, such was the passion behind it.

'Okay, priest. I will heed your advice, just this once more. The chieftains will vote to go home, and I will lead the tribes back across the river. Do you think you will be in position by spring? It will be a long winter for my people; food on our side of the river will be scarce. It will take more than gold and silver to keep them onside next year.' That was his greatest worry, food. He knew from Aelinia's many letters that the barns surrounding Goridorgis were less than half full, that the crops had not grown and flourished as they should, the experienced hands all being south with the army. His thoughts darkened as they strayed to his bedwarmer, another winter of avoiding marital probes and hints awaited.

'By spring I think I will be in position. Our Emperors are soon to have a small problem with a couple of lions, and I have a lovely bottle of wine to gift them to help ease their pains.' He grinned as he spoke. Balomar thought it was something sent straight from Hel, a thing of pure evil.

*

Albinus shivered as the early morning breeze swept under his tunic. He stood at the banks of the river Danube, next

351

to the great bridge that stretched out into Germania. He wrapped his cloak tighter around him, and for maybe the first time, wished he was wearing his armour, just for the extra warmth.

It was the Ides of November and autumn was fully upon them, the red day that had effectively ended the Fourteenth as a fighting force seemed a long time ago. He had learned much of what happened that day in the weeks that had followed. Balomar himself had led the charge with his tribe in the centre, slaying legate Candidus and breaking through the Roman line. With each wing cut from each other, the Germani had poured through and caused havoc.

Tribune Maximianus had been commanding the right, and had quickly given the same orders that Taurus had on the left. The two squares had held together and made it back to the fortress, but the losses had been horrific. Over four thousand of his father's beloved Fourteenth had perished. Less than two cohorts' worth of men remained, plus the remnants of the cavalry still led by Vindex. At least Maximianus had saved the eagle.

The weeks that followed had been amongst the hardest of Albinus' life. Even after losing his mother he could not remember ever being so miserable. The screams from the innocent people in Carnuntum had been unbearable. It seemed to go on all night, but he must have succumbed to sleep at some point.

He had awoken the next day to find he could barely move. His arms and legs felt as though they were on fire, his feet in bits, and his freshly stitched cheek hurt so much he couldn't bring himself to try and eat. It was a week before he even attempted to rise from his bed, another week before he stopped allowing Fullo to grind his food to mush before he ate.

Fullo had been back out the following day, into Carnuntum to rescue what they could with any other men able to stand. He never spoke about what he saw, but Albinus had since seen enough of the charred ruins of the city for himself to understand that the sight must have rolled his bowels and brought hot tears to his eyes. Fullo had seen the same thing done to their home, after all.

The Tenth legion had arrived a week too late to support the Fourteenth. Habitus and Longus had been on guard duty outside the *praetorium*, they said you could have heard Maximianus' raised voice from the heavens as he regaled their legate for his lack of speed.

He was in charge for now, Maximianus, and it was he who had ordered the legion to stand to on the banks of the river. They had heard from the Emperors, who were chasing Balomar and his host back across Pannonia as they fled to their homeland. The Germani had crossed near Aquincum, not wanting to risk meeting the Tenth on their travels, and that is where the Emperors' message had come from.

'I still don't get how chucking two fucking lions into the river is gonna make everything better!' Calvus had limped down to the river without the use of a crutch. The wound in his calf had been deep but was healing well.

'It's that fucking Paphlagonian, Alexander! He reckons he has spoken to the gods and this is what they demand! Fucking easterners.' Libo sniffed. 'Right bunch of—'

'Paphlagonian? Fuck me, that's a big word, Libo! Abas been teaching you some Greek history?' Habitus piped up from further down the line.

'Piss off, old man.' Libo shrugged off the rebuke.

Before the conversation could go any further, the trumpets blasted out and the men stood to attention.

353

Tribune Maximianus strode to the front, his back to the small floating islands of green that clung above the surface in the gushing waters.

'Men of the Fourteenth. We are here today to make an offering to the gods on behalf of Emperor Marcus Aurelius. Alexander of Abonoteichos is a man known to us all. He spent time here recently, and is a man known to be close the gods. He has declared that they demand an offering, and once delivered they will lift us from the curse of this damned plague, rid us of these wolves from the north.' The men cheered, though Albinus noted it was muted. It seemed him and his friends were not the only ones that doubted the validity of what they were to undertake.

'So today we give to the gods two kings of the wild. We give them to Jupiter, god of the mighty sun, to Juno, his beloved wife and goddess of hearth and home. To Mars, god of war, the heroic sun of the father of the gods...' On and on he went, so long Albinus feared he would mention every god there ever was, Roman or not.

'...and now I give you, our lions!' Maximianus thrust his hands up to the great bridge, where a dozen men were wrestling with the chains of two great male lions, who were thrashing and clawing in their desperation to be free from their captors.

'I have a feeling this will not end well,' said Fullo. It hurt to smile, but Albinus did anyway.

'For us or the lions?' he asked.

'I'm not sure, brother,' Fullo replied, 'but we're about to find out.'

With a clang and a roar, the lions were freed. One managed to rip the face of one of the men, who fell off the bridge to his watery grave without a sound. The others quickly hefted long spears and pushed and pronged until the lions were teetering on the edge. One man, who must have been the leader, gave a signal and they all drove their spear tips forward together, forcing the mighty beasts off the side. One roared in defiance, the other seemed to yelp in fear. It took less than two heartbeats for them to hit the water with a mighty crash.

There was no cheering, no celebrating amongst the gathered soldiers. They stood sombre, uncertain about what they had just witnessed. Even Maximianus, who had tried to put a brave face on it at the start, stood grinding his teeth as the two beautiful beasts failed to emerge from the deep green shine of the river.

'Well, that's that the— oh fuck!' Longus thrust out a finger, pointing to one of the floating islands off to the left, down current from them. Atop it, limping and bloodied, was one of the lions. 'It survived! Fortuna's tits, it fucking lived!'

There was cheering now, men shouted and pointed in glee. Albinus spied coin changing hands as some legionaries had bet on the outcome. He was laughing at a red-faced Fullo who was handing over four *as* to Rullus when there was an explosion in the water to their front. The other lion shook his gleaming red mane as it emerged from the river. It swam with purpose, straight towards the waiting legionaries.

'Jupiter's balls, its coming right for us!' Habitus started the panic. Rubbing his greying beard, he seemed in no rush to run. Others were. Centurions were rendered powerless as men streamed away, heading for the safety of the fortress gates, though they stood nearly half a mile away. 'Spears! Spears! All men armed to the front! Stand ready!' No chance of Taurus running. He stood as though he'd have stayed on his own if he had to.

Some men turned back and followed him to the riverbed, but only those that were armed. Albinus looked desperately around, finding a discarded *pilum* on the ground, dropped by a runner in his haste. Scooping it up, he ran to his centurion's side. 'Albinus, good lad! Why don't you show him your best side, might be enough to scare him off!' Albinus smiled. He didn't think there was anything in the world that could ruffle his centurion.

The lion was nearing the riverbank now, biting and slashing its way through the reeds and tall grass that lined it. Albinus could see the river's dirt on its back, dark lines streaking down its otherwise golden fur. And then it was on them. It charged into a man to the right of Albinus, spiralling him through the air. With lightning reactions, it swung left and bit the arm of the next man, tearing it from its socket. And then the spears found their mark. Taurus struck first, his spear digging into the animal's belly so hard it yelped to the sky in pain. Albinus was next; he felt his tip hit bone as he struck the top of its left hind leg. Pain ripped through his right shoulder, so much he let go his spear and fell to the floor.

Next thing he knew Fullo was at his side, Bucco at the other. 'You should be resting that shoulder, lad, not fighting lions with it! That was bravely done, though.' They helped him to his feet. The pain throbbed again as Fullo pulled him by his right arm. 'Sorry, brother! Has it come out again? You need a doctor?'

'I'm fine, its fine. Just let go! Ahh, that's better. It's just sore, is all. Thought it would have healed better by now.' He didn't know whether to laugh or cry. His whole childhood had been spent detesting soldiering for all that it stood for. Convinced he would spend his life a peaceful man, growing crops in the summer and enjoying a hearth's warmth in the winter. And here he was, panicking he would not be able to fight any more because of a ruptured shoulder. *It's a funny thing, life.* He stopped dead in his tracks, fighting to hold back the tears. A long-forgotten memory of he and Licina, the children they were, splashing and playing on the banks of the very river he stood by now, not a day's ride to the east. An otter had emerged from the river, shuffling its way up the bank until it was close enough to smell them. Closer it had come; Licina had filled her palm with bread, offering it to the otter. Closer and closer it had crept, until it was close enough to see and smell the offering for itself. Looking from the bread to her eyes, it seemed to them both that the otter offered them a smile of gratitude, before jumping back into the water and swimming off with the current. *'Funny thing, isn't it, life? The different types, the things you see.'*

She had been so full of wonder and joy to see the small creature approach. The tears flowed like the river's current; his heart felt as if it had stopped beating.

'Albinus?' He barely felt Fullo's touch on his arm this time.

'It's nothing. Just a memory.'

'Her?'

He nodded, swallowed. 'Yes. They're always her. Gods' brother, I must get her back.'

'I know, brother. But where would we start? How do we even know she's still alive?'

'I know it, brother. I can *feel* it. The gods will provide the answer.'

Fullo nodded, eyes downcast. He wanted to help his friend, wanted to find the girl who had been a sister to him, more than anything in the world. But it was fruitless, as far as he saw, hopeless. The empire was such a big place, let alone the world outside it. How many lands were there that didn't call Rome master? It could be a lifetime's work. After all he and Albinus had been through, he didn't trust the gods to bring them the answer they craved.

But when they got back to Carnuntum, they did.

Chapter Twenty-Three

November AD 168 – The northern shores of Germania

Licina winced as the gusting wind covered her in salt spray. She stood upon a thin strip of beach, a hint of yellow against a backdrop of dull grey sea and the dark, rain-filled clouds. She couldn't decide if she was pleased or disappointed to find the sea wasn't frozen. It was endless, or so it seemed. The waves rolled towards her, attacking her, as Neptune encouraged his troops as he waged his war on the land. He was winning, for a time. It seemed with every new rushing wave, the land retreated further and further into itself, having no answer for the engulfing white-topped predator.

'I was always told the sea was blue? Why is it not?' She'd only said it for something to say. She had been quiet towards Julius for three days now, the tension between them visible, to the delight of the mocking Alaric.

'I do not know. I saw it once before, on the western shores of Gaul. I seem to remember it being bluer then. It was mid-summer though, maybe the sun's light makes it so.' He reached out a hand as he spoke, tried to take hers in his. She recoiled from his touch, guilt weighing her down as she did. *What have I done?*

The loneliness, exhaustion, the pain of her ankle – it had all become too much four nights ago. She wept as they camped under the autumn stars. Wept for her parents, for

Vitulus and Turda, but most of all for him. *Where are you, my love? Why have you not come for me?* She had known it was stupid. *How could he come when he has no idea where I am? Or if I even still live!* Shame consumed her. She envisioned her love roaming the wild lands, leaving no stone unturned as he scoured for her. She dreamt of him, regularly waking with her thighs sapping wet, a warm feeling in-between.

That night Julius had found her weeping by the fire's glow. Alaric had gone out to hunt for dinner. The two had been alone, a rarity in the last weeks of their long march north. Licina was convinced they had been walking in circles, though one patch of woodland looked much like the rest. Though they had seen no sign of their pursuers, Alaric had been true to his word on that. The journey had been tough on her ankle, which was swollen and black and blue, but she had bared her teeth through the pain as she limped with purpose to keep pace with the men.

'Licina, what it is? Julius had said as he dropped down next to her. It had just made her feel worse. His love and desire for her was so clear he may as well have worn it on a wax tablet round his neck – or tattooed it to his face, as was the habit of the local menfolk.

Her sobs had got worse as she snuggled into his shoulder and let out the woes and fears that were threatening to consume her. He hadn't said a word, just sat and listened as he stroked her back. And when at last she had finished, 'Don't worry, Licina. I am here for you, I always will be.'

She had melted at that. *He deserves so much more. For all he has sacrificed for me.* She had given herself to him then. Pulled all the right faces and made all the right noises as he entered her. His excitement was visible, audible, and thankfully got the better of him before he could get in his stride. He shuddered as he spent himself inside her, teeth digging at her neck.

Alaric had reappeared soon after, perhaps too soon. A triumphant gleam in his eye, half smile on his face. He had seen, Licina was sure, but she didn't care.

He had been strangely quiet, the one-eyed German. Julius hadn't spoken a word to him, and she hadn't been able to get the Roman to speak in his presence. She knew their history, of course, of how the barbarian had captured Julius and his treacherous sister from their inn room in Gaul. How Julius had been wounded from his fights in the arena, how he had been made to watch as Alaric's men raped Aelinia. It had been this man and his followers that had set Aelinia on a path against the empire she had called home. This man who had turned her into the conniving, two-faced rapist she was today. Licina tightened her thigh muscles just thinking about that night in Carnuntum; she was still not over the horror of it.

She turned away from the savage waters to observe Alaric, who was talking with a local ship owner to secure her and Julius passage through the salt spray to the mystical lands beyond. She didn't feel threatened by the man; she even felt some pity for him, to have to live like this now and remember the man he used to be. It pleased her in a way, that her father, Vitulus and Silus had not lived long enough to have to live with their own dwindling mortality. It would have infuriated the old soldiers, to watch their once formidable bodies wilt away in front of their eyes.

'What you lookin' at, lass?' It frightened her, how much she had slipped back into her old self these last months. Here she was, staring at Alaric, lost in her own mind. He had finished his deal with the ship's captain, and walked over to confront her before she could snap herself from her trance and avert her eyes.

'I was thinking that I pity you.' She decided to front it out, not give him the satisfaction.

'Pity me? What you chattin' 'bout?' he scoffed.

'You were once a fearsome warrior. My father told me stories about you. The oath breaker, battle turner, king killer, ring giver. You've had many names over the years.'

'Ha! That I have! Y'know what one is my favourite?'

'And now, now you're nothing. A shadow of the man you were, a whisper. How far the mighty fall.' She turned her back to him, both ashamed and exhilarated to have stood up to him. The man her father had fought against for years, the man who had caged Julius and made him a slave, turned Aelinia against her homeland and set her off on a path of destruction.

'Nothing, am I? You wanna know how I got this wound, girl?' He motioned to his strapped-up shoulder. 'Well, I'm gonna tell ya. I arranged for a little raiding party to skip across the river last winter. Didn't wanna go far, just had me one clear target.' Licina felt her heart stop, knees go weak and she shook as she sobbed. Breathing was difficult, it came in gasps – shallow, like the waves rolling close to her feet.

'You...you...'

'Yes, me. We watched from the riverbank as you and your friends drank yourselves senseless through the night. Then with the first glimmer of daylight, we forded those icy waters and made us a merry slaughter. You think I don't know who you are, girl? You were supposed to marry his son, weren't you?' His voice was quiet, but menacing, full of gravel. His toothless smile pure evil, his one eye alive with the joy of regaling the slaughter.

'Whose...son?' A pointless question, when both already knew the answer. She felt dizzy, her eyes were blurred, maybe that was just the tears.

'Silus. That arrogant fucking son of a bitch. The man who took my eye, reduced me from the most feared warlord in all Germania to a wandering old man. I had to reinvent myself, be patient. But I did it. I won back the trust of the chiefs and kings, grovelling at their feet like I was some fucking slave. I pandered to them, told them what they wanted to hear. See, I've always had a way with men, especially men of power, know how their minds work, see. So, when I tell 'em I've got the ear of ol' one eye, that he saved me from certain death, they looked at me different. In awe. I like that. So, I put on the hat, wrapped myself in a black cloak, and I went along with it, see. And when the time was right, I put my plan in action.

'So, there we were, thousands of us, slaughtering your little farmstead. I knew the eagles would come, that Silus wouldn't face us without sending someone to them. But that was okay, I weren't planning on sticking around 'til they turned up. Silus, o' course, met us as we crossed. Couldn't have had more than a hundred men, but by fucking Donar, they fought well. I hung back, clever see, no point catching a spear in the first wave. When their shieldwall was broken, pockets of greybeard eagles fighting for their lives, that's when I stepped in.'

Licina sunk to the floor. She could almost picture it, though she had been inside when it happened. The snow cascading down, the howling wind, and how it carried the piercing screams. iron met iron with a clang, blood flew through the air and mingled with snow, which was red before it hit the floor. Fullo at the doorway, yelling in defiance, wielding his sword like he was Mars himself.

Turda with her knife, pleading with Licina to run. *But to where?*

Cocconas gripping her in his arms, dragging her through the throng. Men clawing at her with their hands, their blood-soaked hands. Breath on her neck, her cheeks. Ale-sodden and rotten. She could see it all, *feel* it, like it was happening all over again.

Her heart raced, she squatted on the floor, unable to breathe, to think. She tried to move, but her legs were like stone, unmoving. Alaric cackled a laugh at her pain; he wasn't done with her yet.

'I stepped through the snow, and saw ol' Vitulus cut down. Took about ten of 'em. Surrounded him they did, stabbed him from all angles. He was dead before he hit the floor, if that's any comfort. And then I found him. He'd been hit by a charging horse, I thought he was dead, and you know, that frightened me! I was scared that after all my work, all the planning I'd put in, some other fucker would get to kill him.

'But, he got up! Staggering, blood-soaked, life draining in front of my very eyes. I made a mistake then, let him grab up a spear. Underestimated him, never should have done that. I arced me sword up – this very blade, and I sent it crashing down into his skull. Split like a fucking melon! Only thing is, didn't see his spear lick up, didn't see it 'til it was sticking out me shoulder. Hurt like Hel, I can tell ya! Passed out, I did, thought I was on the way to the Allfather's hall, could almost taste his mead.

'But then I woke. Beautiful it was. Everyone was gone, just me and him it was, laying on a bed of snow. I knew ol' one eye loved me then. I could see the flames, your pretty little homes burning to the ground. Could hear the screams of your women and children. As tempting as it

364

was to join in the raid, get me a woman of me own, I knew the eagles would be along at some point, so off I scampered, left old Silus to the crows.' His laugh was straight out of Hel itself.

'I know who you are, lass. I know Cocconas took ya, and I know who his master is. I know the lot of it! You know what happened to your husband to be? That brat? I met him once, he ever tell you? I had this piece of shit locked in a cage.' He pointed at a gaping Julius.

'How's your sister, by the way? Ha! Funny old world, ain't it! D'you reckon he made it? Albinus, that was his name, right?'

Her tears were so many she thought they might drown her. 'Why are you doing this? Telling me this?'

'Why the Hel not! You're getting on this ship, and you ain't ever coming back! You wanna know where he is before you go?'

'Albinus?' A whisper on the breeze, it was all Licina could manage.

'Yeah, him. He's a soldier now, you believe that?! That fucking wimp! He signed up to the Fourteenth after the raid. He would have been in Carnuntum when you were. Think on that! You staying in the same fortress as him! Haha! Cracks me up. He wrote you a letter, I'll let you 'ave it when you board the ship. He looked for you, you know.'

'Oh Albinus, you're alive.' She smiled as she spoke, tears still streaming.

'Was alive. Yes.'

'Was?'

'Well, he was in the Fourteenth, weren't he. Oh, that's right! You won't have heard. Balomar crossed the river with all the tribes, destroyed the Fourteenth somewhere in Pannonia, was marching on Italy itself, last I heard.'

'Des...destroyed? Albinus?'

'Some survived, or so they say. But anyway, he wrote you a letter, paid a bunch of merchants to look for you whilst they were north of the river, asked them to give it to you should any find you. Trouble is, I paid them all as well. Sent one back with a reply, telling him you were nice and safe, right here in the north. Now all I gotta do is wait. Wait for him to come racing up to me, puppy eyes all shining as he comes to find his love. But I'm afraid, all he's gonna find is the sharp edge of my blade. If he still lives, that is. For what it's worth, I hope he does.'

It was all too much. The memories of the raid, of Albinus. His touch on her skin, the feel of his lips on hers. It burned through her. This man had taken everything from her, her joy and happiness. She'd be damned if she was going to go quietly.

With a scream, she jumped and charged him. His one good arm reacted too slowly to stop her clawing at his face, kicking his legs. And then Julius was there, arms like windmills as he landed blow after blow, raining punches on Alaric's face and body.

And then there were hands on her. Grasping her thrashing body, dragging her towards the sea. She regained control of her mind as she was thrown onto the ship. Watched in horror as Julius was beaten in front of her face. The captain barked orders in a foreign tongue, sounded more like he was clearing his throat than speaking actual words. And Alaric was there, one arm holding him up at the side of the ship.

'Here's your letter, little girl, I hope it brings you misery, knowing you will never again see the face of the man that

366

wrote it. I want you to know I won't let him die quick, it will be slow, agonising. Just like the rest of your miserable fucking life!' He launched the rolled parchment at her, blood splatters on the outside. It hit the deck at her feet. And then he was gone, and the ship was moving out to sea. *What have I done? Maybe everyone was right after all, Minerva truly has taken my wits.*

She took the parchment in shaking hands. There was a seal on the outside, broken, but she could make out the Capricorn stamp on the dried wax, the symbol of the Fourteenth. Her wet dress slid on the deck as the ship rolled the oncoming waves. Julius whimpered next to her, bloodied face down on the deck. She barely noticed. Unrolling the papyrus with all haste, she gasped with both joy and despair to see the familiar handwriting of her love.

Licina,

I pray to all the gods this finds you. Ten of these I have written, ten letters to ten different merchants, ten chances of finding you.

I run through that night and day in my mind every waking hour, and then I dream of it as I sleep. Why did you have to wake up? Why didn't you wake me too? Sometimes I get angry at you, though I know it to be foolish. Why didn't you just stay with me? If you had, maybe we would still be together. Gods! Please forgive me, for I do not want you to think I blame you.

We have been taken from each other, and I despair each day that I have lost you. You are the light that ends my darkest days. I long to see your face again, to touch you. The spring that should have been the happiest of my life has been the most miserable. I wept all day on the day that was to be our wedding day. Some of the lads in my mess tried to cheer me up, but it didn't work. By Jupiter! I should have mentioned! I joined the army – no really! I enlisted in the Fourteenth, first century, first cohort, just like my father. (Though not as a centurion of course) Bucco found me that dark day, I was searching the fleeing people for you, praying to find you in the throng. I didn't. Bucco whisked me away, off to Carnuntum to rally the Fourteenth to march to our aid, of course they came too late.

I'm sorry to say Vitulus died, my father too. I found their bodies on the battlefield the day after, I won't speak of the horrors I saw on that snow-ridden field. Fullo, though, lived, a nasty bump on his head, but he recovered well. He enlisted with me, and we have of course remained inseparable, perhaps even closer now then we were. We share a goal, a mutual hatred. We have vowed to bring down whoever was behind that cowardly raid, and to find you in the process.

There is a rumour going around that the Marcomanni king Balomar is the one behind it. Governor Bassus sent our senior tribune to his fortress to demand he attends a peace meeting here in Carnuntum. Pah! A pox on peace, I say. Let him come with all his armies, the Fourteenth will meet him on the field and crush him where he stands.

I met an interesting man today, Alexander of Abonoteichos. A soothsayer, he discovered a new god – Glycon it is called. The god has taken the form of a snake, and is constantly entangled on his right arm. Me and a few of the lads, Fullo included, believe it to be a farce. But word round the barracks is he has the ear of Emperor Marcus Aurelius himself, so there must be some credibility to his tale. Anyway, I paid a denarius for him to read my future, he said I would crush my demons and live a prosperous life. When I asked of you, he seemed a bit curt, dismissive. I decided I did not like the man, or his followers, and I have a suspicious feeling one of them is following me. An easterner, oil slick beard and tied back hair, I seem to find him wherever I go. Must be a coincidence, I suppose.

But I digress. I merely write this letter in the hope it finds you well. I want to tell you that I love you, that I think of you with every heartbeat, and that I will find you. I will. There is no army, no mountain, no ocean, that could keep me from you. Please stay safe, I know you are alive, I can feel it. And I know we will be together again. That dream we had, when we were planning our wedding on our sleepy little farm, gods, doesn't that seem a long time ago now! That dream of sitting on a sun-drenched porch, cup of wine in hand as we watch our children roll around and play, we will have that, with Ceres as my witness, I make you this promise.

But for now, just live! Stay alive and well, and write back to me if you are able. If not then give a message to the man that finds you, I have picked good men I believe, honest and trustworthy. They will bring back to me any message you want. Just tell me where you are, and I will be there as fast as a horse can carry me!

But until that joyous day, know that I love you, and that I remain, and always will, yours.

Albinus.

The wind tore through her. Hit her, like a slap to the face. She didn't feel it. Julius was vomiting, from the beating he had taken or due to the rolling motion of the ship, she didn't know, or care.

She rose to her feet, slowly, in a daze. She was at the front of the ship, the prow. The sea was endless, the dark grey expanding as far as the eye could see. There were no birds in the sky, she'd heard once they rarely strayed so far from land. The sky itself was full of cloud, thick and black with the promise of rain. She wrapped her cloak tightly round her shoulders, and bit back the tears that threatened to overcome her.

His letter had broken her heart in more ways than she thought it would. His confidence in facing Balomar's army, meeting Alexander, the confirmation of the deaths of Silus and Vitulus, she didn't think she had ever felt lower, even after the death of her parents.

She cackled a bitter laugh. *I escaped from Carnuntum, and he was there the whole time.* Sometimes the gods are cruel.

Minerva, are you there? Maybe you cannot hear this far north, maybe your presence is not welcome here. But if you are, then listen. I don't know what I have done wrong, what I did to turn you away from me. But please be with me now. I have made mistakes, I admit. I have been weak when I should have been strong, have shied away from you when I should have sought your counsel. But I am seeking it now. Help me find a way home, to my Albinus. Deliver me into his arms, and I will devote my life to you. My first daughter will be named in your honour, I will build you the greatest temple you have ever seen. Just get me to him, before it's too late. I beg you.

Thunder cracked in the sky, lightning exploded from the black clouds. There was a commotion behind her, the ship's captain arguing with a member of his crew. Although she could not understand the language, the reason for the shouting was obvious. The captain was pointing north, out into the endless grey. The other pointing back to where they had departed, his other hand pointing to the thunder.

Licina held her breath. *Has my prayer been answered?*
Has Minerva delivered this storm to save me from myself,
and take me back towards my love? Or is this Donar's way
of spiting me? I have angered the thunder god by praying
to another in his world. Has he sent this storm to punish
me? To send me to a watery grave?

The argument continued. Licina held her breath,
resisting the temptation to try and intervene. To her
dismay, the captain won in the end, and the ship continued
its journey north, the rowers moving with greater urgency.

She turned her back to the men, and sobbed into the
wind. *Oh, what a fool I have been.* She hung her head over
the ship's prow, hands clinging to the strange beast carved
onto the front. There was an explosion in the water to her
left, so close the spray soaked her to her bones. A monster
leapt from the depths, twice as long as the ship she stood
on, its colour a darker shade of grey than the sea. Its eye
was tiny. She imagined there was another the same on the
other side of its great head, though she could not see. With
its mouth open it looked as if it were smiling as it plunged
face-first back into the water. The body seemed to follow
it for an age, a great spout of spray rupturing from the top
of it somewhere. What she assumed to be a tail crashed
through the waves, and then it was gone.

'Gods! What was that?' She was speaking to no one in
particular. She hadn't heard the captain approach behind
her.

'Ha! That little girl, is why we call this the whale road.
Go and sit by the mast, try and get your friend over there
with you, we're in for a choppy ride!' Shocked that he
spoke such good Latin, she rushed over to Julius and
dragged him to the middle of the small ship. Hugging him
close, she thought of everything she was leaving behind, of

371

how she was going to get back to Albinus, and what she might find when the ship eventually docked at its destination.

Epilogue

December AD 168 – Legionary Fortress of Carnuntum, Pannonia

Winter gripped the land. The snowstorm had raged so long it seemed impossible to recall a time it had not. Mist streamed over the frozen Danube, rose up from the ice like a serpent, snaking its way towards the land.

Small pot holes could be seen off the banks of the once-green islands, frozen in place by the winter's icy grip. Brave legionaries had risked their lives on the crossing, praying to Fortuna the black sheet wouldn't crack. Using their *pila* to force a hole, they suffered the bitter winds in search of fresh fish, easiest way to make a few *as* when the merchants were busy restocking for spring.

Albinus braved the cold on one such mist-ridden morning. He cursed as he struggled to harness a reluctant horse. His fingers blue, he fumbled with the straps, watched in dismay as the horse whinnied and shifted and the whole thing slid down onto the hard ground with a crash. 'Fortuna's tits! Give me some luck today, you wicked old bitch!' His cheek burned when he spoke. Months since the battle and still the wound hadn't fully healed. A surgeon had removed the stumps of his ruined teeth, stitched him and given him a large pot of balm to rub on the wound three times a day. The pain though, was still intense. At least it stopped him thinking about the agony in his shoulder.

He didn't hear the pad of feet behind him. 'Bit cold for a ride this morning, lad. You might wanna invest in some of those trousers the Germani are so keen on.' Taurus stood in the doorway to the stables, unarmed, wrapped in a gloriously red cloak, he leaned on the door with a half-smile planted on his face.

'Morning, sir! I thought I would just go for a short ride, sir, clear my head. I'm off duty today, sir.' Startled, he snapped a salute as he spoke, harness crashing back to the ground.

'Really? Seems to be a pretty big bag of supplies you got there. You taking anyone with you?'

A pause. 'No, sir. Can never be too careful though, right?' Albinus cast a weak smile. The feeling in his gut told him he was rumbled.

'Oh, I agree. No one wants to get lost in the depths of winter. And where might you be going on your little ride?'

'East, or south. West maybe. Not north.' He was stuttering, eyes on his feet as he spoke. His hands twitched.

'Oh really. It's just that I had a little visit last night from an old mate of mine. A merchant, used to march under the eagle like you and me, though. He told me a story, said he was so moved by the whole thing he had to tell someone. Shall I tell you?'

Albinus nodded, eyes glum. He knew the story.

'He said that last winter some recruit took him a load o' his first month's wages, asked him to keep an eye out for a young lady with striking red hair, long sweeping legs and emerald green eyes. He said the young'un had told him she was Roman, and that he believed she had been taken slave among the tribes. He also gave the merchant a letter, no wax tablet mind, just a rolled-up bit of parchment, sealed with the legion's symbol.'

Albinus gulped. Sweat trickled down his forehead, despite the cold.

'Now, this mate o' mine, being the honourable old chap he is, said he would of course keep an eye out, and would be happy to deliver the letter to said redhead if he came across her. And more than happy to bring a reply. You enjoying the story so far, pup?'

'...Yes, sir.'

'Good. Now then, this merchant didn't hold out much hope of finding the girl. After all, Germania is huge, the tribes endless. Now as summer turned to autumn he was up in Rugnum, a small fortress in the lands of the Suevi, right up by the frozen sea. On his way to do a bit of amber trading; don't pay tax on what you buy and sell outside the *limes* see? Now anyway, there he was, passing through, doing a bit of business here and there, when all of a sudden, he sees her. Fire-red hair, emerald eyes, legs long enough to wrap around a tree trunk. She was a beauty, or so he said. So he approaches her, asks her name. Can you guess what it was?'

'...Licina...' A whisper on the wind.

'Right! So he gives her the letter, she rushes out a reply, and he scampers straight back here, to the dumb young legionary who paid him in the first place.' The centurion's eyes burned into Albinus, he dared not meet them, in case they set him a-flame.

'Sir, if I can explain—'

'Explain?! I don't think there's much to explain lad, do you? You get a whiff of half-truths from some old con artist who would sell your soul if it thought it worth his while, and off you go! Deserting the army and riding off to almost certain death! What was your plan exactly?'

'Plan?'

'Yeah! How were you going to get from here to the north of fucking Germania unseen, and get Licina home again? And what were you gonna say to me when you returned? Sorry I deserted for a whole season, but hey I'm back now so let's forget about it!'

'I wasn't going to come back—'

'Weren't fucking coming back? You want to be flogged to death by your own mess mates? That's what we do to deserters, lad! Twenty-six years you signed up for, and twenty-six years you'll serve, less you meet the sharp end of a barbarian spear!'

'But...Licina...'

'Needs rescuing. No doubt. But how do you know she's really there? Got any proof?'

'Well...her letter...'

'Recognise the handwriting, do you? Any secret little pet names in there she called you by?'

'Well...no, but—'

'You've been lied to, boy! Wake up! How was old Corvus ever gonna find her in all those forests and valleys!' Taurus cackled, head arced back as he laughed at the ceiling. 'Oh, someone has her all right, and they want you to go racing up there like a dog on heat. But I promise you, lad, all it will end in is a nasty death for you. Her too, probably. Make no mistake, someone's got in in for you, lad. I don't know who, or why, but they want you dead.'

Tears welled in Albinus' eyes. 'But Corvus, he's ex-army, trustworthy.'

'Ha! That old piece of shit is about as trustworthy as a smiling senator. He was kicked out the Fourteenth, stealing supplies and selling them on, he was lucky he weren't crucified! Ha! Bet he wishes he has been now!'

'What did you do?' said Albinus, not entirely sure he wanted to know the answer to the question.

'You let me worry about that, son. You just worry about you.'

Albinus fought to control his emotions, fists bunched at his sides. 'What do I do?' His words were desperate, pleading. 'I must get her back. I can't go on without her.'

'Oh, you gotta go up there, no doubt about it.'

'But you said—'

'But if I was you, I wouldn't go alone, and certainly not dressed as a legionary. I reckon you're gonna need to recruit a few rogues, men who know how to look after themselves in a tumble. Happily, I think I know just the right bunch of lads. Abas!'

The bald optio glided into the barn, a wide grin fixed on his ageless face. He swung back the stable doors to reveal a huddle of men, bunched together against the morning's cold. 'Here they are, all ready and raring to go!'

And there they all were indeed. Bucco grinned like a madman, hands wrapped round a large hunting spear. Libo scowled at the cold, seemingly already regretting his decision to tag along. Habitus flexed his small bow, the string hidden away beneath his cloak to keep it from the elements. Calvus twiddled the shaft of his axe, the blade rotating in the dull light of the winter sun. Rullus and Longus stood side by side; the standard bearer's big bushy beard floated on the wind. And then there was Fullo, walking towards him. They embraced in the warriors' way, both fighting back the tears. 'We'll find her, brother, together.'

About the Author

Adam has for many years held a passion for the ancient world. As a teenager he picked up *Gates of Rome* by Conn Iggulden, and has been obsessed with all things Rome ever since. After ten years of immersing himself in stories of the Roman world, he decided to have a go at writing one for himself. *The Centurion's Son* is Adam's first novel, and the first in a trilogy set against the backdrop of the Marcomannic war. He lives in Kent, with his wife and three sons.

Made in United States
Troutdale, OR
11/24/2023

14861977R00229